Key Keeper's Daughter

Brian K. Kerley

Map – Northern Continent

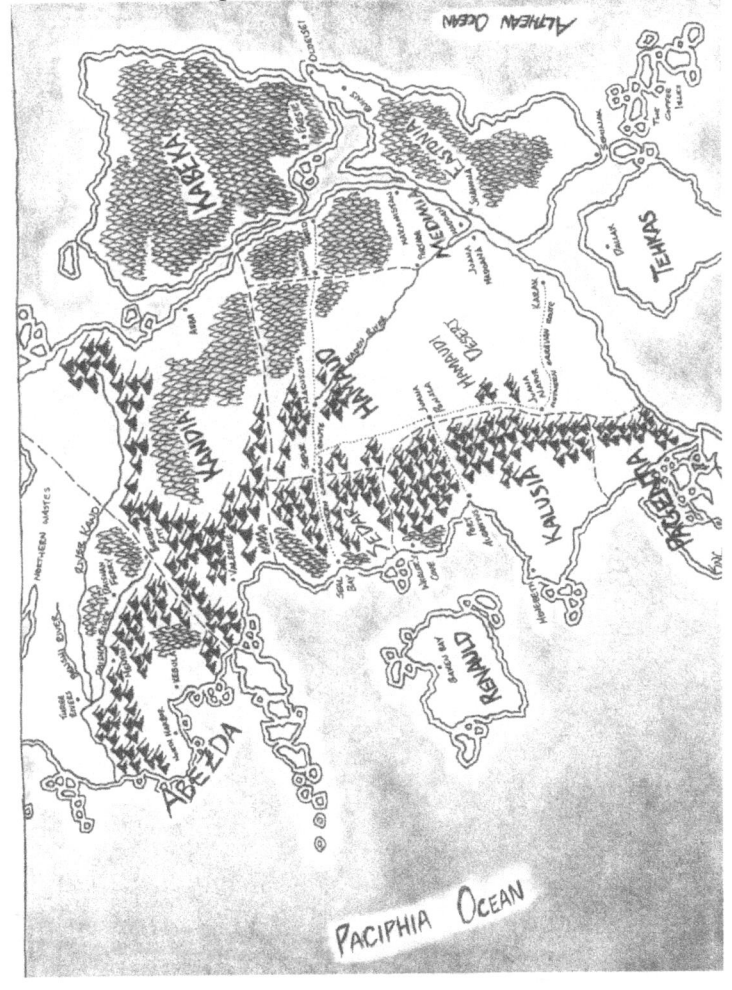

Map – Southern Continent

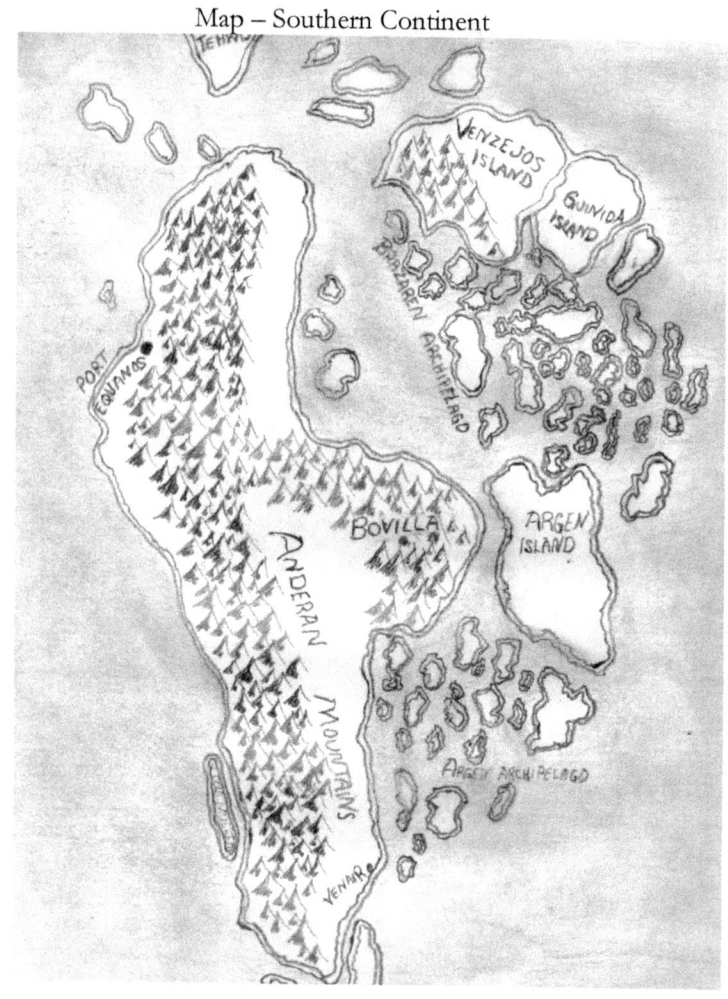

CONTENTS

ACKNOWLEDGMENTS

This project had a lot of delays and a lot of changes. For those of you that have waited so long since *The Octagon Key*, I'm sorry and thank you again for your patience and encouragement.

Thanks to my editor, Emmy Hammond.

Thanks to my artist Kristen Puckett.

Thank you Stefan Coleman for the first and better of the two maps.

Thank you, Barb.

PROLOGUE

The Kalusian city of Port Augustus nestled comfortably at the base of the foothills between the rugged Western Range and the Ocean Paciphia. Her natural harbor was formed by two curving spits that reached into the sea, like skinny arms too short to embrace the great belly of the deep water bay. Strong tides defended the passage from even the heartiest oarsmen, which limited ships to incoming floods and outgoing ebbs. Only at slack tide could two-way traffic pass through the formidable channel, and even then it took either favorable winds or strong arms. The waterfront sprouted a forest of masts with jutting yardarms like stiff winter trees with branches festooned in furled sailcloth.

Ships from all over the known world sailed into the massive port. Carracks from the Coffee Isles competed with the caravels of Tehkas, bringing spices and sugar cane to the western markets. Galleons loaded with exotic wood from far off Eastonia often topped their holds with grains and fine cloth from Medimia as well as strange furs from the vast forests of Kabeka. The highest quality steel came from nearby Pagentia in shallow drafted galiots and misticos. Even vessels from the pirate haven of Renauld Island could be seen tied to the docks or moored in the bay, so long as no warrants were issued for that ship's involvement in acts of piracy against a ship of the Western Alliance Kingdoms—Abezda, Sedar, and Kalusia. Piracy against Kandia was encouraged.

Once in a great while an old trireme from the southern reaches would wallow in with winter produce. It would be converted to carry cargo, but often as not live freight outweighed the tonnage of produce hauled from equatorial regions. On those rare occasions, the preceding effluvium of the slave ship would announce the arrival of its dread cargo. Most citizens of Port Augustus found slavery repulsive nor would the stench tainted fruits and vegetables sell to any but the poorest and most frugal buyers. However, the slave market was still lucrative. Most of the unfortunate wretches were purchased by the sultans of Hamaud. Slaves rarely lived more than a few years in the Hamaudi desert salt mines causing a high turnover in the 'forced labor' workforce.

The female slave market spread far beyond buyers of Hamaud. Girls and young women generally lived longer and in better conditions if bought for the brothels or for household servants in a wealthy estate. In the Alliance kingdoms, slaves had leave to buy their freedom through indentured service though they were less fortunate elsewhere in the world.

The great trade city had no defensive wall, but Port Augustus had never come under direct attack in remembered history. The nearby seas were patrolled by the

Kalusian royal navy, most of which would soon be deployed north for the defense of Sedar's Seal Bay for the impending invasion of the Kandian Armada.

Port Augustus crowded all of the sloping lands near the bay with docks, warehouses, inns, restaurants, and taverns. Other businesses, as well as residences of diverse classes, cluttered the adjacent foothills to the east. Farms and a large number of vineyards sprawled into the rolling countryside to the south. The higher ground on the north side of the city was sparsely dotted with the estates of the wealthiest aristocrats and nobles of Port Augustus. One of the largest estates sat gracefully upon the highest hill in the district. That one was the Murdoch estate.

The Murdochs' house faced the city to the south. They had a large dining hall for parties, but most of the time Lord Travin and Lady Akala Murdoch used the space for exercising their sword skills. Travin and Akala preferred dining with the household—a practice considered taboo among most of the aristocracy. The smaller common table was on the west side adjacent to the kitchen. One could sit here and enjoy the view out large glass doors and windows, across the lawn and hedge, over the ocean bluffs, and to the sea beyond. Lower on the hill, near the bluffs, a row of large eucalyptus trees was planted to minimize strong seaward winds. Another table was just outside these windows, on the west lawn, for enjoying meals out of doors when the weather was pleasant.

Above the common dining room, the west side lanai could be accessed from either the second floor or by the outside steps where it joined the rising ground, which was terraced for the garden. Akala's garden was a place of beauty as well as a source of a bountiful harvest. It was her pride and joy, tended by her own hand since her retirement from a more strenuous lifestyle. There she grew citrus, vegetables, herbs, and flowers that her husband brought her from distant lands.

The east side balcony sported a view of the compound and training grounds of the Murdoch Free Companies. The banner of the white ship over crossed swords on a field of black flew over the barracks. Beyond was the archery range, which butted against brown grass-covered rolling foothills that rose into the forested mountains. Red and golden leaves blended to dark green with elevation. Above the timberline white termination dust powdered the distant peaks.

Hidden from view in those hills was where the Murdochs manufactured guns, cannons, and black powder copied from the samples taken at the battle of Valekrie. It was there that they built the first successful prototype airship, the *Elbienus Raptor*.

Traven and Akala Murdoch came by their wealth from the greatest treasure find of the century back when they had had only one ship and a loyal crew of adventuring privateers. Twenty years earlier they had sailed into Port Augustus with tattered sails hanging from scorched yardarms and a blackened mast, riding low in the water with a bad starboard list, and a hold full of gold and jewels. Amid that hull full of wealth they also brought back an energy converter. At first, they had no idea what it was, just a strange item in sealed packaging that in time revealed itself to be profitable technology.

The couple and their first mate, Imar Amirson, bought lands and patents of nobility and kept quiet as to their source of wealth. What few crewmembers had survived that adventure either faded into obscure retirement or became honest traders of respectable wealth. However, it could be noted that those well off working men now dressed considerably nicer, carried well-crafted weapons, and increased their waistlines from fine dining, not to mention the improved quality of their beverages.

The co-captains, Travin and Akala, knew how to fight and knew how to sail, so they invested in mercenaries and shipping. It was a sensible investment; when soldiers were deployed, the ships would transport them, and when warriors were home in training, their vessels sailed the seas as merchant marines. Travin ran the ships, Akala handled the books and the business, and Imar was weapons master. He was in charge of the soldiers and their training until his father called him home to lead the Abezdan border patrol in defending his frontier hometown against Kandian raiders. Imar took his wife Anisha Murdoch and his young daughter Aideen to the northern frontier until the events of the octagon key brought Anisha and Aideen back to Port Augustus and Imar on a quest to find the ruins of Oldeisie.

CHAPTER 1

The sun beat pleasantly upon the Murdoch estate. Carriages came up the lane and deposited their young, finely dressed occupants into the courtyard, then moved off to allow the next carriage in line to do the same. Children of all ages ran up the hedge-lined walkway, followed by their teenage nannies, towards the front door of the great mansion. The children were redirected by a waiting servant to a wide, gaily festooned lawn on the west side of the house. Tables were joined together to accommodate the children of Port Augustus' high society. A smaller table sat slightly lower on the lawn for the nannies of the privileged children. On a lanai overlooking the celebration sat a few of the mothers who had chosen to take the time to attend. Since it was a child's affair, adult attendance was low. The birthday girl was Aideen Amirson, granddaughter of Traven and Akala Murdoch. It was her eleventh birthday.

Akala was in the kitchen sitting on a stool working

the crank handle of an ice cream maker. "I think it needs more salt, and a bit more ice," she said to Ninole. With her free hand, Akala pushed a strand of her silver-streaked light brown hair behind an ear and rubbed her lower back.

"Half a minute, milady," replied the middle-aged cook as she removed another cake from the oven, setting it to cool upon a marble slab next to other cakes already stacked in triple layers.

"I thought we were long past such formalities, Ninole," Akala said with an exasperated sigh. "You've been here longer than anyone, even Dorfin."

"Aye milady," responded the cook. She took a scoop of rock salt from a canvas bag on the floor and slowly poured it into the outer ring of the ice cream maker as Akala continued cranking. "But today's one o' those days it might not hurt t' keep up appearances." She went to the evaporator, opened the freezer side, and removed a canister of crushed ice. "By the way, I think the heat exchanger's got a bad bearing. It squeaks when it's makin' ice." Ninole raked several ice chips into the bucket. "I remember when Lord Townsend had a man flogged for improperly addressing a lord, and the poor wretch didn't even work for 'im."

At the mention of Townsend's name Akala's face went flat. "If anyone causes trouble for you, they'll deal with me," she asserted.

"Yes Milady," Ninole agreed. "I doubt it not. You aren't like other folks born to wealth and privilege. See that's the difference. One o' them's insulted, an' they'd have the culprit in the stocks, but not you. You'd be teachin' 'em manners by the strokes o' that sword o' yours, even if'n they was a lord."

"Oh come now," Akala responded with a sheepish grin. "I think you've been reading too many romance novels."

Ninole returned the canister to the evaporator, and then wiped her hands on her apron while looking boldly at her boss. "We've all heard you practicin' with Lord Travin. You can't hide the sound of clashin' steel behind a closed door." Her gaze narrowed on a point below her employer's chin.

Akala reached up one handed and fastened the top buttons of her blouse, self-consciously aware that one of her scars was giving away some history. She pointedly focused on making ice cream. When Ninole harrumphed and returned to frosting cakes, Akala used her teeth to pull a creeping cuff over another scar.

Ninole looked over her shoulder as if she were about to say something more when the door burst open. The housekeeper entered with a small piece of paper in one hand. "The demanding little brats all want something different. I can't believe the magistrate's daughter actually wanted . . ." She stopped when she saw her employer on a stool working a crank on a bucket. Her hand went to her mouth as if the vacuum from her inhaled gasp had sucked it there. The woman's eyes widened and she tried to speak, but her apparent apoplexy only allowed her to emit squeaks and stammering. Akala's grin and Ninole's squirrel eyes betrayed their amusement. The excitable housekeeper clamped her teeth long enough to take a couple deep breaths and then proceeded in a rush.

"Milady," she gasped. "You shouldn't be seen doing menial tasks. The Lady Lillian of house de la Mere is here asking for you. If she were to walk in, t'would be scandalous."

Akala groaned.

"Give 'er a break, Elsie," said Ninole. "Lady Akala just wants t' do somethin' for her granddaughter before she goes sailin' to the Southlands after her husband in that new flyin' ship of hers. Lady Lillian ain't goin' t' sashay in here an catch no one, specially if'n you take the ol' girl a snifter o' brandy."

"Ninole is right," added Akala. "Lillian does like her brandy. Give her a glass of the good stuff from the Rochelle vineyard—that'll make her happy."

"Yes, milady," said Elsie as she went to a counter and set to putting glasses of lemonade on a silver platter along with a large snifter of brandy. "I'm sorry ma'am, about getting worked up about you working. We all here never been treated better nowhere else, and when you jump in and lend a hand it makes us feel . . . well, like . . ."

"Like family," Ninole finished.

"Yes," agreed Elsie. "Like family. Meaning no disrespect, but we're all loyal as family, and we just don't want you to slip up. It could give credence to the rumors."

After all these years, the thought sobered Akala, as she softly queried, "Rumors?" She and Travin had tried very hard to act the part of high society, attending parties, appearing at social functions, and attending the king's court when a council was called. King Gerald often hired the Murdoch's elite mercenaries and mariners. Time had taught him, and other kings, that Akala's advice and judgment was every bit as sound as her husband's. Royal respect had buried their past, or so she had thought. The most difficult part was acting aloof to all but the loftiest when in public. Once or twice she or Travin may have commented on the weather to a servant or inquired about

9

their thoughts on economics or politics, but it was usually overlooked, even if considered unusual. Akala asked again, "What rumors?" She was barely aware of the rapidly increasing viscosity of the ice cream.

Elsie's eye twitched slightly. "I thought you knew all about those tall tales of how you and Lord Travin sailed the seas as pirates before coming here and buying your titles with the spoils of a hundred ships."

Only partly true, Akala thought. Looking beyond Elsie, she watched one of Ninole's eyebrows raise pointedly.

"They're mostly stories that mothers and nannies use to scare children to obedience," continued the housekeeper. "Like, 'You'd better be good or Akala, the pirate queen will put you in her crow's nest and never let you down.' Or, 'If you're bad the Murdochs will make you a pirate and the king's navy will hound you to the burning lands.' It's all just nonsense, milady, but some folks really believe all that tavern talk."

Akala forced a smile. "I see."

"The nobles and the well-off trader families will cause trouble if you don't act like them."

"You mean worthless but wealthy?" Akala asked sarcastically.

"Elsie's right," Ninole agreed. "Ya can't let none of them 'better-than-thou' types catch ya bein' common, even if'n ya are rich."

Akala decided to change the subject. "What was it you were saying about the magistrate's daughter?" she asked.

"Oh yes," replied the housekeeper. "Young Lady Amanda ordered me, not asked I might add, but demanded I bring her a glass of red wine."

"I don't think so," Akala said dryly as she stood and pulled the stirring mechanism out of the ice cream maker. "Little miss priss can have a lemonade like the other children." She fingered a dollop off the dasher and stuck it in her mouth. "Mmm, that's good. Come help me clean the frame."

Ninole abandoned the cake she was frosting and joined Akala and Elsie at cleaning the ice cream maker with their fingers. It was most unladylike—Akala smiled.

The party was a success. Akala organized games for the children and even included the nannies. The few mothers that attended looked on from the upstairs lanai while a maid kept their glasses filled. Akala never understood motherhood, or rather the lack of it, among the upper crust. When they had first taken up a land-based life of luxury, Akala had hired a nanny for Anisha, more for appearances than need. Akala had tried to keep the bond that they had as a family at sea, but Travin was often gone aboard the *Avenger* while her time was consumed with running the business from home. Young Anisha enjoyed the newfound wealth but became emotionally distant from her family, and puberty only amplified it. When Akala looked at the ladies on her lanai, she realized how much her daughter fit in with the society she had been raised in. It was Akala who didn't fit.

Aideen looked to the lanai as often as her grandmother did. Akala knew the girl wanted to see her mother there, but it was not to be. The day sped past filled with the glee of children's laughter, finally coming to a graceful end before the sun sat a hand's breadth above the sea. Tired nannies ushered their chattering sugar filled charges into the waiting carriages. Lady Lillian de la Mere slurred her thanks to Akala as she swayed precariously down the walkway supported by two other ladies only slightly less intoxicated. Their stumbling steps were so completely out of sync with each other that Akala was surprised no one fell. However, it did take the driver fifteen full minutes to assist the ladies into the carriage.

In her bedroom, Akala hung her afternoon party dress in the closet and tied her ponytail high on the back of her head. She was now dressed in loose grey cotton pantaloons tucked into high boots with daggers protruding from each side. Her white linen shirt was contrasted by her tight black leather vest. She looked out the window at the few high cirrus clouds painted crimson by the evening sun. A full third of the scarlet orb had set below the ocean's horizon. "Red sky at night, sailor's delight," she muttered, relieved that her departure would probably be free of turbulence and, hopefully, unnoticed. She pulled on a skirt to hide her men's clothes in case she was seen traveling to the airfield. She had no logical reason for secrecy or a night departure, but her intuition told her to be cautious. Tucking a pistol in her bag and another in her belt, she wrapped her rapier in her cloak and left the room.

Dorfin had been waiting in the hall as stoic as ever. He took her bag and walked with her to the stairs, his fastidious brown ponytail motionless on his back. The only grey he had was at his temples. "We have orders for more airships, as well as rifles and cannon. The navy cleaned us out of all our big guns."

"Our ships have been fitted and our soldiers are armed?"

Dorfin nodded. "Yes, but the king's army needs more rifles."

Akala smiled. "Good. We can charge more for our rifle brigades until we get caught up on backorders."

"Not bad," agreed Dorfin. "But we still can't keep up with the demand. I'm afraid we'll have to contract out the extra work. We can still carve a bit off the top for the patent now that our engineers replaced the flash pans with percussion caps."

"I trust you to take care of business better than me," Akala replied. "You usually do anyway even when I'm here. As long as we hold the patent on the energy converter powering the airships we don't have any legal concerns, but just to be on the safe side, only sell engines that run on solar or wood. Let's keep the engines that use rapid organic decomposition power for only our airships and sea vessels."

"I was planning to talk to you about that before you left. It will be only a matter of time before the Kandians capture one of our ships. On that . . .," Dorfin paused. "I am concerned with spies and sabotage what with this war and all, even should the fighting remain up north. Have you thought about my proposal to build more manufacturing plants?"

"Yes, and I agree. I like your idea of building one in Pagentia." She looked up at his clean shaven face as they started down the curving stairway. "Dorfin, you are much more than a steward or even an associate. You are a business partner." She paused briefly, waiting for a reaction. Neither expecting nor receiving one, she continued, "I drew up the papers and filed them with the Ministry of Records the day before yesterday. I'm sure Travin would approve. We'd certainly spoken of it often enough." She was disappointed that Dorfin's usual demeanor did not crack at this revelation, but the twinkle in his eyes satisfied her. "We will, of course, have to purchase a patent of nobility for legal and social purposes. That is if you don't have one already. I remember Ivan mentioning your pursuit of higher education being rare among the high born. I've been meaning to ask you about that, but we've been busy what with Townsend's treachery and Anisha's duplicity. Then there was Baker's murder and finding another spy to watch both Townsend and my daughter; well, we've all had a lot to haul in, so to speak."

Dorfin was silent as they came off the stairs and crossed to an office adjacent to the modest foyer. He closed the door behind them while Akala took a seat at the desk and began signing papers from a thick stack. Taking a chair, he massaged one hand with the other and said, "You've never asked me of my life before coming here. As I've come to know you and Travin these past five years I've learned that you take people for what they are, not what they were. I appreciate that. I'm also thankful for your trust in making me a partner. You really didn't have to; my compensation is greater than any other steward or manager I know."

Akala had never seen the man fidget before. "It's a common rule among buccaneers not to ask too many questions beyond what ships one has worked and their experience. So Dorfin, you needn't share your past if you don't want to."

"It's okay." Dorfin paused a moment, and then as if nodding to himself he began. "I left Medimia when I was but twenty. I was my father's second son. My uncle was the king without an heir. Many called him a tyrant." He cleared his throat and added, "The situation was ripe for rebellion. There were many injustices I didn't agree with back then, so being an incautious idealist I joined a group that advocated overthrowing the throne and replacing it with a congressional republic."

Akala was stunned. She was sure it showed, but she bit the inside of her cheeks and remained silent.

"I thought I was clever," Dorfin continued. "I was sure I had given my watchers the slip one evening when I went to a meeting of the New Median Republic. A half hour after the meeting commenced we were raided by the royal guard and arrested. I was imprisoned along with everyone else, only I was not tortured for information like my comrades. The other rebel cells were found out and captured or at least broken up. Some got away, most were imprisoned or sold into slavery, but the guillotine stayed bloody for days."

Akala had never seen Dorfin display emotion, and he showed none now. Only his closest friends could spot amusement in his eyes, and no twinkle glittered in them now.

"On my fourth night in the dungeon my father and my older brother came to my cell." Dorfin's eyes glazed with a distant look for a moment. "I can still remember the chemical hum and the blue tint cast from the heat lamps they carried. My brother signaled me to silence. I thought they had either gained my release or, at least, were moving me to another more comfortable cell. Instead, they took me by a circuitous route to a well-provisioned horse outside the gates. My brother told me that my uncle was planning to make an example of me by not showing leniency to traitors—especially those of his own family."

Akala's eyes widened.

"I was to be executed the next day."

"No," Akala gasped, her whisper hoarse, "your own uncle?"

"I was speechless when my father stuck a stout pouch of coins in my hand, warning me never to return."

"Dorfin, I am so sorry. Where did you go?"

"I went west across the great Hamaudi desert. I paid for passage in a caravan bound for Seal Bay." Dorfin's eyes twinkled briefly when he said, "Looking back, I'm sure the caravan master cheated me. My coins seemed to slide through my fingers like the desert sands. When I reached Seal Bay I soon learned that I had no skills to live on when my money ran out, so I spent the rest of my dwindling funds on tuition at the university at Sedar. After that, I took jobs as a scribe, bookkeeper, and even went to sea for a while as a ship's purser. Anyway, it's been twenty-five years since I left Medimia. And if I keep talking you'll never get out of here. Coulig will be here soon to take you to the *Elbienus Raptor*, and you still have to say your goodbyes to your daughter and granddaughter."

"But, what about . . ."

"Please, Akala, another time," Dorfin urged, foregoing his usual formality. "For now, I will consider my options. I'm not ready to share my history with anyone else or any more than what I've told you and none of that while we live under the rule of a monarchy. If I must file for a patent I will, but I'd like to hold off on that as long as possible. If I do, it might be wise for me to use an assumed name."

"Okay," Akala agreed, stifling her curiosity. "What of our new spy?"

"Bill is his name. He works for us as an expediter. He's more reliable than Baker, and being land based he isn't gone on cruise most of the time like our former spy. Townsend propositioned him to spy on us two days after Baker turned up floating in the harbor. Bill came to me right away, so I hired him, or rather rehired him as a double agent. He still arranges tools and provisions for our ships, and I give him some harmless information to give to Townsend. I doubled his pay."

"Good. What is Townsend up to?"

"Bill's not sure, but something is brewing. Townsend has been hiring sell-swords in Juana Pohala. In fact, he brought a dozen here from the desert just a few days ago. Not only that, Khaled has disappeared. He's been gone for three days now."

"I don't like that. Hamaudi assassins are dangerous enough when you know where they are."

"I suspect he is connected with the murder of Townsend's wife at Chateau Aleman. Besides Lady Lenora, the whole household was slain, which doesn't make sense for an assassin. They generally take out only one target without anyone the wiser, but Khaled has fits of rage unlike others of his order."

"That would be out of character for Townsend as well. Hamaudi assassins charge plenty for being on retainer, and their rates only climb for collections and extortion. When they actually kill, their fee quadruples." Akala scrunched her brows and continued, "But Townsend is so cheap he can squeeze the nuts off a buffalo silver piece. He owns most of the piers and nearly all the brothels and nightclubs in Port Augustus. He cheats us on merchandise every chance he gets when he can't get away with outright theft of our cargo over his docks. I could see him contracting the murder of his wife; the inheritance would be substantial and a Hamaudi assassin could pull it off in broad daylight in the middle of a crowd, but why would the cheap bastard pay to kill the household staff?"

"Perhaps Townsend didn't authorize it. From what Bill says, the assassin is psychotic. Khaled thinks he is serving the nameless god by cleansing the world of sinners and sending the faithful to a better place, presumably heaven. He believes his sword is guided by the hand of god."

"Wonderful, a fanatic," exclaimed Akala. "I hear these nameless god followers are all like that, but an obsessive Hamaudi assassin?"

"Not all; I've met a few of that following that were decent people, but they are the quiet ones. As religions go, it is an admirable faith, perhaps the only true faith. The basis of their religion theorizes that the different gods are really just one god—the same one. The confusion is eliminated by removal of the name."

"I find it all confusing." Akala looked at Dorfin, wondering where the man's spiritual leanings lay. They had never discussed religion before. She usually avoided the subject, opting to keep her mind open but remaining non-committal. "I've only met the outspoken followers of the nameless god and most of those were troublemakers." Akala decided to change the subject. "Is my daughter still seeing Townsend?"

"I'm afraid so. She was there all day. In fact, she was still there when Bill reported an hour ago." Dorfin tapped his fingers uncharacteristically on his knee and said, "You know, Aideen has the sixth sight. She could probably tell us what Townsend and her mother are up to."

"No. I thought of that already, but I would rather

she not see her mother in the middle of one of her adult escapades." Akala's face twisted up and she shuddered. "Just the thought of Anisha and old Townsend makes me want to vomit. I prefer that Aideen not be subjected to that."

"I'm sorry. I hadn't thought of it quite like that, but I see what you mean."

Akala's expression was sad. "You know, she was such a good little girl when we lived aboard the *Avenger*. It wasn't until we came here and lavished her in luxury that she became spoiled and greedy. If I could only do it over . . ."

"You can't undo what's done."

"I know, but Anisha should've been here for her daughter's birthday. Instead, it was me organizing the games for the children and entertaining pompous parents. Poor Aideen has hardly been here for two months; half those kids she barely remembers from when she was little, and the other half are strangers. She's lucky to have Missy for a nanny because her mother is not really mother material, but then that is the way of Port Augustus high society. Again, the fault is mine."

"You can't blame yourself for the way of the world."

"You know, Aideen had a chance growing up on the Abezdan frontier in Border City, even with the wealth, but here, and surrounded by society's high and mighty," Akala shook her head. "These next years are impressionable years. I really don't want to see my granddaughter grow up to be the selfish, spoiled little brat her mother became."

"It was good of you to postpone your journey for

the girl's birthday." Dorfin took a breath, and said, "You know it's been nine months since Traven took the *Avenger* south to buy produce. You should steel yourself for the possibility . . ."

"No," she cut him off. "He's not dead. Something's happened to him, but he's still alive. I feel it in my bones. I should have left months ago, but this whole deal with the octagon key, and then one thing after another piling up as if an avalanche deposited the events in our unready laps. Being around my daughter is too much stress. I have to go find my husband and save my sanity. I just worry about Aideen."

The sound of boots caused Akala to look out the window. Coulig's stocky features swaggered up the hedge-lined walkway, followed by Jax and Brin's younger and leaner frames.

"My escort is here," Akala said a moment before the knocker knocked three solid raps.

Dorfin stood and slid some books aside on a shelf to reveal a small safe to which he applied the combination, opened it, and removed two leather bags. His muscles tensed as he hoisted the bags and placed them in Akala's duffle with a muffled jingle. "I wish you could take Aideen with you. That girl has seen two battles in as many months—that can't be easy, and her mother isn't much comfort. I've heard you go to her when she cries out in her sleep."

Akala sighed, shaking her head with closed eyes. "Believe me, I thought about it, but it's too dangerous where I'm going."

"I know, but the girl does have remarkable skill with a sword, I've seen you two at practice. She could probably best a common foot soldier twice her size. She takes after you and her father."

"Thank all the gods for that, but there are other dangers down south I'd rather not expose her to. That and I'm getting too old to be raising my grandchildren." Akala gave Dorfin a quick hug. "Take care, Dorfin." She took up her cloak-wrapped rapier and went to the door.

Dorfin slung her bag over a shoulder with a grunt and followed her out to the foyer. A maid had admitted the mercenary captain and his two lieutenants. Aideen and Missy were also in the foyer waiting to say their goodbyes. The girl ran to her grandmother and slammed into her as Akala squatted to one knee. The impact nearly knocked the wind out of both of them.

In a voice loud enough for only Akala to hear, Aideen said, "Oh Grandma, I wish I could go with you. I really don't want to stay here."

A tear ran down Akala's cheek to the corner of her mouth. The brine entered and spread the taste of salt across her tongue. A second tear followed, and then a third. Akala felt the damp dew of the child's tears on her shoulder.

CHAPTER 2

Aideen stared at the ceiling. She had slept some, but whenever she indulged in sugar, which wasn't often, she didn't sleep well. Raiding the freezer for another bowl of ice cream had probably been a mistake. It would have been a lot harder if not for the noisy bearing in the evaporator. Sneaking around at night was tough, but there were other ways to prowl the halls.

On their journey through the Kandian wilderness, Dalla had helped her develop her talent. The first thing the girl learned to do was a sensory sweep. Aideen could locate a mouse and tell if it were scared, happy or hungry. People were easier to find. Dalla had urged her to practice often, so she did, and her talent grew. Aideen could also mind-speak, but unfortunately, both mind-speakers had to have their minds open and focused on the other person at the same time for it to work, and only Ivan and Dalla could mind-speak with her. It had something to with the old wizard and his daughter being GEBs. Enhanced is what

Ivan called it. *That's it*, she thought. She would call Dalla with her mind.

Aideen lay flat on her bed. As her mind slowed to the point where she felt ready, she dozed off. She was roused by her own snore. Then a soft scuff followed by a faint click caught her attention. Reaching out to Dalla was forgotten.

Night sounds were not unusual, but the huge house seemed a little spookier with her grandmother gone. The girl strained her ears, but the silence wore on until she lost count of heartbeats. She chided herself for imagining noises. It was probably just the cat or somebody in the privy. Her mother habitually wandered in during the wee hours of the morning, and she was not known for courtesy to a sleeping household, especially if she had been drinking.

That reminded her; it saddened the girl that her mother had missed her party. She understood her father's absence, he was on a quest, but it would have been nice of her mother to show up. She didn't dwell on this long before a feeling of dread came over her.

Goosebumps prickled the back of her neck. A shiver waved across her back. *There's no reason to be scared*, she thought. Aideen paced her breathing. She wondered if she was having a premonition.

She remembered Dalla's warning, "What you perceive and what you think you perceive can feel the same."

The girl calmed. She thought about lighting a lamp. Aideen looked to the window and appraised the yellow glow from a yard lamp. The light was comforting, but her uneasiness persisted, making sleep impossible. On her bedside table was a heat lamp. She twisted the flint striker; the chemical fizz took only a second before a light blue glow cast a faint tint across the room. *Much better*, she thought, opting to conserve fuel by keeping the setting on low.

Aideen climbed out of bed and took down her sword from the rack. Gripping the wooden sheath in her left hand made her feel more confident. The polished black wood glistened in the dim blue and gold light. It was a small two handed katana her father had given her when she had reached the honored level of *Pro Conscientia* at age eight. It was the level most students of the sword did not attain until their late teens, and then only if exceptionally skilled. She was a child, but not defenseless; even should her moves only allow distraction to effect an escape.

Aideen went to the window and looked down into the courtyard. It was quiet—no movement. Heat lamps glowed amber but she saw no sentry. He was probably just making his rounds. "Don't be silly," she murmured to herself. "You're much too old to be scared of noises in the night." Aideen went back to bed, prudently laying her sword on the covers next to her. Even without night noises, she knew there were dangers in the world. She had seen what men and women could do to one another in a shield wall.

Stuffing a pillow under her knees, Aideen began some calming exercises as a prelude to meditation. She decided to do a sensory sweep. The girl expanded her awareness around the area. Once focused, she could detect anything living by sensing the emotions of what she encountered. Her empathic feelers first found her teenage nanny. Missy's snoring was like the purring of a pussycat— a rather large asthmatic cat. Missy's snore, accentuated by her wheeze, purred with a low whistle.

Aideen got up, padded barefoot across the hall, pausing for the unavoidable squeak when she stepped into the hall and shuffled into her nanny's room. Missy's rainbow-like aura glowed faintly on the edge of the girl's vision. She pulled back the blanket, rolled the older girl onto her side, and replaced the covers. The maneuver relieved Missy's labored breathing. Maybe Aideen would be a healer like Dalla. The floor protested the return to her room with another squeak. After a minute in bed, her meditative calm resumed and she was soon reaching out her empathic tendrils.

Dorfin's room was down the hall; he too was asleep. She felt the steady rhythm of his breathing through her mind. Her eye gave an involuntary twitch to mimic his rapid eye movement. Dorfin dwelt in the world of dreams. She wondered what he dreamt, her earlier fears forgotten.

Aideen narrowed her perception into a concentrated beam, gathering her will to penetrate Dorfin's private thoughts. Her father told her it was not polite to read minds, but he never turned down information when he could get it either. She couldn't always do it, nor was it actually reading thoughts. It was more of an awareness of moods, like knowing when someone was lying or planning something that caused guilt or pleasure. Aideen could tell when somebody was up to something.

Dorfin's mind was like a sphere woven into a latticework of layers upon layers of lines, winding in and out, over and around, with light bursting out from between the bands. This was his consciousness the way she saw it from within herself. His mind was within that sphere. Aideen floated forward, but rebounded, and then it was all gone. It all went dark. She almost had the sight, like Dalla's, but failed. She wasn't ready. Patience wasn't her strong point.

Aideen knit her brows from where she lay on her bed. Beads of sweat dotted her forehead. Her senses detected Dorfin's sweet pleasure of sleep, but nothing more. She bore forward towards the steward's dreamscape but again bounced away in blackness.

The girl pressed on, just sensory sweeping, and not trying to raid people's privacy. Her awareness diffused and reformed in her grandmother's room, which was, of course, empty but for a mouse raiding her cracker stash. The little creature's elation over scoring such a treasure was mixed with greed and joy as it stuffed its stomach. The rodent's position was marked and its emotion was grand satisfaction. Not to be discouraged by failure at reading the dreams of her friends, Aideen decided to attempt reading the mouse. It happened so fast and so easy and with unexpected results.

Aideen's breath caught, and then she breathed deep, but at the same time it was also rapid—the rodent's—and slow—and hers. She lay with closed eyes upon her bed, but her vision cleared and she sat, squatting on her haunches, beside a hanging sheet and a gargantuan bedframe overhead. Grasped in her front claws was a huge piece of cracker. She chewed vigorously, working the heavenly salted prize into her bulging cheeks. She took another bite. Odors flooded her nostrils: fabric, hair, human, and mouse. A pair of slippers towered over her, and not far away stood the biggest dust ball she had ever seen. Her little mouse heart pattered faster when she detected another smell—cat. She opened her eyes on her bedroom ceiling and the mouse's perspective vanished—it was like being along for the ride. Dalla had never told her about seeing through an animal's eyes. Totally unprepared, the event left her tingling all over.

Mustering her courage, Aideen sent her awareness back into her grandmother's bedroom, but this time, all was dark, she could feel no living presence. The mouse was gone. Disappointed, she moved on. Her mother was in her room. *Home early tonight*, Aideen thought sarcastically. As her mother's mood filled her awareness, a tense feeling of apprehension knotted her shoulders.

Aideen tried entering her mother's mind, as she had done with the mouse, but her objective shot away in the dark as if she had stepped on a greased ball. She tried to work out the differences. Missy was asleep, but when physically next to her Aideen saw her aura. Dorfin being in another room she sensed his mood, saw his consciousness, but could not enter or see his colors, and once she bounced off his barrier all went dark and stayed that way. Each time she reached for her mother's mind it slipped farther out of reach as well. Yet there was the mouse…and she had hardly tried for that. She still wasn't sure how she did it.

Aideen then concentrated on mood colors, but again nothing. At least, she had empathy. So far, this talent was only possible for her when she could completely clear her mind in meditation, and focus on empathic energies. When she first accomplished this technique, a few meters was all that her maximum range could engulf, but that range grew each time she practiced. Her sensory sphere could now span dozens of meters.

When Anisha finally calmed down a little Aideen moved on. Next, the girl found Ninole downstairs in the privy, but a dog barking, followed by a yelp somewhere outside, distracted her and she found herself looking at the ceiling from her bed. A half a minute of deep breathing was all it took to regain her astral flight. Aideen could hear the cook making her water; the tinkle of urine into the aqua duct and the flow of the water that took the household waste away from the estate made a soft whoosh through the pipes. It sounded clearly in her mind's ear as if she were right there in the water closet with the cook. She did not hear the sound directly, but rather felt what Ninole heard through her brief touch with the cook's consciousness.

All was well in the house. Dalla's advice to practice was paying off, her talent was getting stronger. The healer had said she had never heard of a natural-born person capable of directional empathy or mind-speech. Aideen stretched her awareness out further. Ninole finished her relief and returned to bed.

The girl moved her awareness to the courtyard. She detected a faint feeling of fear shrouded in a haze of darkness. It came from the shrubs along the walkway. The energy was so weak it took her a minute to recognize the sentry. She could not remember his name, but something soured her senses. The sentry was in a very deep and dreamless sleep—this was wrong. A thousand pins and needles prickled her spine in a wave. The guard was not asleep, he was unconscious.

Aideen felt her scan slip as the goose bumps returned. She calmed herself, regained control, and scanned the area again. The guard and...a dog, so weak she wondered if it was dying. She needed to go wake Dorfin, but in the back of her mind indecision argued with good sense. If she could use her talent to find out who knocked out the guard, and why, it would make her look more useful and more grown up. She was, after all, eleven years old now and it was high time to take some adult responsibility. The sensible voice rebuked her for selfish foolishness. The stubborn voice told her there was no harm in waiting a minute or two before sounding the alarm.

Like slow trickling liquid poured perfectly upon a flat surface, her awareness spread in an ever-widening circle. Aideen sent her senses outward. Across the yard, she came upon a hare. The animal's brownish dark orange fear glowed dully in the girl's mind. That was strange; it, like the mouse, allowed her to see aural colors without being physically next to the subject. The hare's heart hammered as it stood tensely poised against the stone wall of the house watching a movement to one side of the front door. She had just asked herself how she knew that when a bombardment of perceptions washed over her in a wave.

Sights, sounds, smells, tastes, and even the rough surface of the cool ground under her pads came to her at once as Aideen realized she was the hare. No, that was not quite right, she could see and feel all that the animal did, but she had no control over the creature—along for the ride. The taste of grass mingled with the stringent smell of medicine coming from two, no three, directions. The first was the unconscious guard; the effluvium of the drug wafted off of him and came to the hare's twitching nostrils. Beyond the guard near the lane was one of the watchdogs laying on its side unmoving. It had a dart protruding from its neck. The medicine on the dog smelled different.

Both odors, mixed with the smells of man and steel, came from just ahead beyond the front door. Aideen saw, through the eyes of the hare, a dark shape of a man in the shadows sliding a wire under the closed window. When she slid her senses to where the hare saw a human, Aideen detected nothing but the faintest of a blue haze. It was like an aural color, but it seemed enhanced as if it were partially artificial.

From the hare's long furry ears Aideen heard the latch snick, and she watched the dark shape flow into the house through the opened window. She stretched her awareness ahead to the room where the hare saw a man shape enter, and all went dark. A pang of loss pervaded her soul when the animal's senses left her bereft of all but her own feelings. She opened her eyes and again saw the ceiling of her bedroom. She had to tell Dorfin, but the lure of her talent drew her into one more look.

Aideen knew someone was in the office next to the foyer, she saw the figure climb through the window, but she could detect nothing. Perhaps the intruder moved quickly. She spread her awareness and found only those friends and family she had encountered before. She felt her way back to the office her grandparents and Dorfin used for keeping the accounts, but she felt no presence there. Moving her mind to the foyer, she found that empty as well. Aideen swept her consciousness up the staircase and stopped. On the stairs there was something—she could not quite put her finger on what. It was like something was there, but wasn't. She focused on the nothingness for nearly a full minute—and then it moved! Like a lightly shimmering sphere exuding a tranquil translucence of blue. It was barely perceptible.

She should not be able to see aural color through her empathic senses, but then there was the hare and now this. However, this was not a true aura, at least not totally, and she didn't really see it. She could feel the presence, albeit faintly, and she felt the blue. Could it be that she felt the hare's dark orange aura of fear? Was her mind forming colors out of her empathic perception?

Aideen couldn't see the stairs, but she could sense the presence where the stairs should be, and it was moving diagonally up. Slowly, step by very slow step, it crept up the stairs. It was on the curve, near the top, but there was no detectable mood, no emotion whatsoever. She felt nothing and saw only a hint of blue.

Aideen recalled Dalla forming various colors of glowing globes in her hands. "And this shade of blue is shielding," said the healer. "Beware should you encounter someone enveloped in this hue. They will have the talent to hide from you, sneak past your defenses." The girl zoomed across time back to the present, but she did not lose her hold on her spectral surveillance. It was like a blind one feeling the floor to know how far away the thief was.

An intruder was shielding! Her mind spun. *Why?* she wondered. *Unless they knew someone here had extra sensory perception?* Aideen knew of no other empaths besides Dalla, herself, Ivan and Sumas, but she herself was the only talented one who had not come out of cryosleep. *Who would expect an empath?* All the genetically enhanced were far away. There were only a few people in Port Augustus that knew of her talent. She probed at the nothingness as she ruled out the names, *Mother, Missy, Dorfin* . . . No, she trusted all of them.

The intruder got to the top of the stairs. Aideen could feel, if barely, the faint blue hue in her meditative state, but she could not detect emotion or identify the person. There was the slightest creak, started and stopped as quickly as begun, hardly enough noise to twitch a mouse's ear, but Aideen caught it.

The nearly invisible sphere ceased its motion. The girl imagined the person suspended on one foot, the other hovering over the offending step, and lifting ever so gently to continue in silence, up to the next higher stair. But of course, her mind's eye saw nothing of the sort, it was just her mind making guesses. Aideen pushed away her imagination and concentrated. She considered herself lucky to have caught a trace of the shielding shell. It was no more than dullness, a mockery of emotion, like when one thinks real hard about something funny in order to smile for a portrait, only the shield was devoid of feeling almost like the opposite of sensitivity, yet it was attached to the same current.

In that static moment when, from what was the start of a noise to the beginning of the following silence, she felt it. In that fraction of a second, while she blanketed the faint blue shield with emotional receptors more sensitive than a safecracker's sanded fingertips, she caught the briefest of emotional vibrations. Only a small bit oozed through, like the passing of an odor through a cheesecloth curtain, but it was enough, more than enough. Had she not tried so hard by exposing her empathic senses to detect the hidden, then perhaps the recognition when it came would not have been like raw nerves pressed upon hot steel. The intensity of determination and suppressed anger ran over her empathic waves like synaptic surfs crashing upon her body where it lay on her bed.

Nausea ran up Aideen's body from toenails to scalp with an electric chill permeating her in revulsion. Her eyes snapped open, her body felt like little finger size demons were poking her with little spears. She rolled to lean over her bedside wastebasket. A low growl pushed through clenched teeth as she willed herself not to spew. Aideen knew that vibration, that empathic wave. It was like when a dog knows his master is home by the sound of his horse's hooves or by the carriage's wheels. Just like, no matter what mood they were in, Aideen could tell Dorfin from Missy, or her mother from a stranger. She knew who was on the stairs even though she had met him only once on the outskirts of Valekrie.

Her body convulsed, abdominal muscles rigid as reverse peristalsis lurched violently through her slight frame. It was Khaled. Bile filled the back of her throat as she forced her tongue up, and tightened her jaws till they ached. It was the assassin she shot in Kandia. *So this is what fear feels like.* She didn't remember it making her sick, but then she had never been alone when danger this great was so near, nor had she ever exposed herself the way she just did.

Her neck hairs stood on end, and she held her body locked until near muscle failure. When at last the symptoms retreated, her body relaxed, but only for a moment. Aideen knew she had to run, but feared she would throw up if she moved too soon. She had a yell tipped on her tongue ready to voice aloud when she bit it back.

The assassin was too close—it was too dangerous. If someone came to her aid Khaled would kill them. Sweat beaded her forehead and neck while time ticked away, and the assassin was coming. He was coming for her. She knew this fact as plain as breath. There was no one else here that he wanted. Khaled came for her. If she could get away maybe everyone else would be okay.

Aideen got up, and swallowed; the bitter tang made her cringe. She spit into the waste basket, wiped her mouth with the back of her hand, and then scrambled to arrange her pillows as if she were still under the covers. She grabbed her sword, looked around desperately, and ran to the window. It was too high to jump, and there was nothing on the wall with which to climb down. Aideen opened the window; the soft sliding of the pane's wooden frame caused goose bumps on her neck to roll down her arms. Had he heard it? Did it matter? Could the assassin know for sure she was here? The fresh night air cleansed her nostrils. She was barely aware of the cricket chorus clashing with the silence of the house.

The killer was almost to her door—she had to hide. Aideen ran on bare feet to her closet, and abandoned hiding there because her legs would show above the cluttered mess of the closet floor, even if she hid behind the hanging garments—and it was the first place anyone would look. Her heart hammered like running hooves. The latch on the door slid soundlessly till it terminated with a click. Part of her mind realized that the floor outside the door didn't creak. Another part of her mind said it was a ghost while another told her it wasn't real, just her imagination. Fear made her frantic and then she realized she had a white knuckled grip on the wooden scabbard of her sword.

Aideen bared her blade—the steel whisked free and reflected the dim blue lamplight from her bedside and the amber hue from the window. Fighting with swords in practice or play was one thing, but this was real or would get that way very quickly. She stifled a scream. As good as she was with her katana, the girl knew she could not stand against a bigger and stronger foe for more than a few short defensive moves. She would rather flee. Dropping to her belly, she slid under the bed. The spine of the horizontal blade was just scant inches from the top of her head. She held her breath as the door opened. The fingers of her free hand splayed like a spider, anchored her to the floor.

The Hamaudi assassin entered and went to the side of the bed. Soft black leather boots was all she could see. The smell of grass and leather damp with dew was overpowered by the severe medicine-like odor that followed the sound of liquid sloshed in a bottle. One foot came under the edge of the bed. The girl heard the covers thrown back. Pillows flew to the floor behind his feet. Aideen felt the heat and saw the red aura of anger ooze out of the black on the edge of her vision. She remembered that glow and the hatred he had glared at her when she pierced his shoulders with a pair of arrows two months before. It was a good bet he was still angry about that. Silently she wished she had her bow now. She would stick him again, but from across the room.

Maybe he won't look under the bed, she thought.

Everyone looks under the bed. *Please don't look under the bed.* Aideen wished with all her willing might. *Please don't look under the bed!*

A small slip of hope slid over her when she saw his feet walk to the window. *Now,* she thought, *now is the time to run,* but she couldn't. Fear froze her. In an instant of decision to cut and run, her muscles tensed to move, but it was too late. Khaled came back to the closet side of the bed between her and the door.

The assassin opened the closet, pushed some hanging garments along the rod, and toed her shoes and dirty laundry to one side. He then returned to the bed. Aideen needed to breathe. Her thudding heart throbbed in her ears and she feared the assassin could hear it too. *Please don't look under the bed.* He knelt down. *He's going to look under the bed.* His left hand, while gripping a stinking rag of medicine, braced against the floor. The loose ends of his black kufiya head wrap touched the floor, spooling as his head lowered to look. When the left side of his dark face appeared she struck.

Her blade darted out like a striking snake. Had her position been better, and the assassin not so fast, Aideen's narrow blade would have entered his brain, but as she lunged he dodged. Her sword tip caught his eye and grated along the outside of the ocular orbit. The blade sliced the side of his face nearest the floor, cutting below the temple and removing the top of his ear. She felt only the slightest resistance as razor steel exposed bone and parted flesh like a hot knife through warm butter. She saw the ear tip on the floor as she backed away.

Khaled leaped to his feet as Aideen scooted out the other side of the bed. To his credit, only a low grunt of pain barked from his throat. Aideen backed up to the window with her katana raised at a defensive angle. The assassin blocked the door, growling in a mixture of anger and agony.

Khaled's hands were empty of weapons but for the drug dosed rag, which he instinctively pressed to his eye. He pulled it away as if it stung him and threw the rag to the floor. The tall man swooned, and caught himself with a sliding half-step.

His glare was gruesome, but her sight tunneled first to the deflated ball of the sliced eye, and then to the clean cut that ran from there, exposing bone, to where it stopped after removing the top of his ear. Free flowing blood gushed down into his short black beard and onto his shoulder. Towards the nose, aqueous humor from the ruined orb diluted the blood to a shiny pink, and then it was quickly covered with the palm of his left hand.

Aideen could have sworn that black flames of hatred burned from his good eye. Wrath radiated from him like an open furnace. She knew this was the best time to run past him to the door—while he was distracted with pain and dizzy from the drug. She tensed, and even took a step forward, but then hesitated. Every sympathetic nerve in her body screamed at her to run, but to fly would take her closer to her nemesis. Fear would not let her flee.

The assassin drew one of his scimitars, spun a vertical circle once and stepped towards the girl to strike her down. She took a reflexive step back and moved her sword to block the slash that didn't come. Khaled's sword ceased its downward arc. His arm seemed to shake, to struggle with itself, as if in stasis between kill and abort. With a frustrated hiss, he aborted the blow and slammed his sword back in its sheath.

Aideen flashed a glance behind her, seriously considering the seven-meter drop. She figured it would probably break her legs. The girl had waited too long, now she had to fight—it was hopeless. Or was it? The assassin was wounded, swayed as if he were drunk, and had had little time to adapt to his loss of depth perception from one eye. His good eye watered and probably blurred his vision. She fervently hoped the medicine on that rag went into his wound—if only it had been strong enough to knock him out. Aideen might have a chance to fight her way around the wounded, drug drunk assassin if she could just get to the door and run.

Khaled's breath was ragged. His good eye squinted as if he had difficulty focusing. He turned his head and rubbed his teary eye with his shoulder, right arm high, momentarily blocking his vision. Aideen jerked for a slash and stopped as the moment passed. She wanted to kick herself for not striking him sooner and running for the door. Another opportunity slipped by.

"I should kill you, you little bitch," he rasped. "But I am sworn to bring you in whole and unharmed." He spit on the rug. "I would have drugged you, but the rag is soiled." Then angrily added, "With my blood!"

Aideen flinched, but kept her eyes on her enemy, and her guard up. She regretted her hesitations. Twice now she might have fled. She could not just give up—she was too scared to surrender, but fighting past a Hamaudi assassin terrified her. If only she could flee. A voice from without gave her both hope and fear for her friends.

"Now we do it the hard way. I'll apologize to my employer if I break too many bones bringing you in. Or perhaps I will pass up my payment." Khaled slowly began to draw one of his black batons. "I should kill you."

Aideen attacked before the club cleared the sheath. The assassin's draw accelerated. He hardly noticed the bite of her sword on his right arm as he bounced back and blocked her blade away. She used the motion of his parry to follow through with a circling slash to his blind side. He parried again, without taking his left hand from his wound. Khaled's club met her steel, as he squat and blocked with an angled parry. Her katana glanced off the baton, passing harmlessly over his head. The razor edge shaved off a third of the wood's width and half its length. The painted slice of wood flew off arcing like a leaping salmon in the dim light.

Aideen stepped back, then sprang off the ball of her trailing foot. She charged, screaming a battle cry, in a desperate hope to get past her enemy. Her right-hand slash would have cleaved his damaged baton and perhaps his neck, but he stepped in and blocked before full momentum from her blade could sever either. The wood struck her hilt guard, and he shoved her sword to the side. He released the stick and backhanded her face. The blow stunned the girl but she kept her feet. Her eyes watered and she tasted blood on her lips as froth flowed from her nose. The assassin grabbed her wrist and twisted hard. Aideen shrieked, and her sword fell to the rug with a muffled thud.

Khaled's lip curled in a malicious sneer. The girl struggled with both hands until she remembered how to break a wrist hold the way her father had taught her. With a twist of the wrist and a bend of the elbow, Aideen broke free and punched a right jab up against the hand covering his wounded eye. The assassin howled. The girl kicked him hard in the crotch and ran for the door. She had no sooner yanked the door open when she was whirled around to face the bleeding assassin. The last thing she saw was a bloody Hamaudi fist coming at her face, and then darkness.

CHAPTER 3

Anisha looked at her sleeping daughter with a mixture of suppressed emotions. The girl wore a simple white smock and lay upon a narrow bed in a sparsely furnished room. Dark purple bruising covered the right side of her face, swelling closed all but the slit of her eye, and adhesive putty splinted her broken nose. A healer tied off the second suture in the child's lip, and then wiped her hands on a towel.

"She was not to be hurt," Anisha said softly. Keeping her feelings distant and proprietary usually came easy but at the moment a drop of moisture welled in the corner of her eye.

"What was that, my lady?"

Anisha regarded the healer's seamless face; it contrasted with the woman's premature grey, yet complimented her hazel eyes—appraising eyes. Whether the healer was estimating Anisha's health from a professional interest or judging her social status by her dress, she was not sure. The woman's indeterminate age was baffling. Her voice sounded young, but it had an air of experience. Anisha had not meant to be careless by showing compassion and revealing her connection with her child. She covered her comment by cooling her tone. "What's your name?"

"Folks call me Etta, my lady," replied the healer.

Aideen stirred. Anisha glanced at the door. Her daughter was motionless again. "Will she wake?"

"I doubt it. I gave her something for pain an hour ago."

The girl moaned softly. Anisha decided to be bold. "I'd rather she didn't see me."

Etta leveled a look at Anisha a moment and then nodded. She stowed her suture kit in a black satchel and removed a vial of clear, amber-tinted liquid. Using an eyedropper, she counted three drops into the girl's mouth. "There, that'll keep her sleeping awhile. It'll dull the pain as well." She returned the items to her bag, and added, "I wouldn't worry if she woke. It's doubtful she'd remember anything."

"These clothes," Anisha indicated the pile at the foot of the bed. "They seem awfully bloody."

"Aye, indeed they are," replied Etta as she placed a dab of salve on a piece of cloth the size of a thumbnail, and stuck it to the girl's wounded lip. "The girl had a bloody nose for sure, but all that didn't come from her." The healer pulled the ribbon binding back her silver hair, shook it loose and said, "Now if you'll excuse me." She moved to the door.

Anisha hid her relief. Earlier when she had seen all that blood in Aideen's room she had feared the worst. By the time everyone had streamed out into the hall, Aideen and her kidnappers were gone. It had not been very easy sitting through the magistrate's questions while maintaining a properly distraught appearance. It wasn't all an act. The sight of all that blood had filled her with concern for her daughter. She thought her performance was exemplary, but as the minutes turned to hours her concern only climbed. It had been difficult getting Dorfin to cancel the order to send a company of soldiers to Townsend's estate to look for Aideen. Had it not been for the magistrate agreeing with her discretion, Dorfin would not have relented. An incident had to be avoided.

The healer was nearly out the door when Anisha caught her arm. "Etta, wait." She forced the urgency out of her voice at the healer's surprised look and removed her hand. "Whose blood is it? Can you tell me what happened?" Forcing the next word out was like pulling a molar. "Please?"

Etta looked at Anisha, then at Aideen, and back again. "Your daughter?" inquired the healer.

Anisha nodded. *There, the cat was out. It would be okay*, thought Anisha. What few who knew of her and Townsend's plans kept their silence out of loyalty to their purse or from fear of his pet assassin.

Etta leaned out the door and looked down the hall in each direction, stepped back into the room, and closed the door. "She has your black hair. It's kind of hard to compare the eyes with all that swelling." The healer smiled. "I can't say for sure what happened, but I'd guess she gave far better than she got." She hunched slightly forward in a conspiratorial manner and said, "You know that desert devil Lord Townsend has working for him?"

"Yes."

"Not the soldiers fresh in from Juana Pohala. The black robed bastard with the perpetual scowl."

Anisha caught herself before she rolled her eyes. With feigned exuberance, she answered, "Yes, yes, I know the one. Khaled is his name. May his nads wither to dust. He gives me the creeps."

"That's him. What woman doesn't find him vile? One of the gardeners put on some trousers to trim back the raspberry vines, so as to save her legs from the thorns, and he whipped her for wearing a man's clothes. When she told him that stupid laws like that were stricken a century ago, he hit her and told her that women are not to speak until spoken to."

"She should have taken it to Lord Townsend."

"She did, but his lordship only laughed."

Anisha's brows lowered. Her opinion of Townsend was diminishing daily. She needed him to execute her plans, but the day would come when his usefulness would expire. "What happened this morning?"

"The lord swore me to secrecy, but since the girl is your daughter I don't think my silence extends to you. But to be on the safe side, I'd appreciate it if you didn't tell anyone that I told you anything."

"Of course," Anisha agreed. Her patience was strained to breaking, but she didn't snap at Etta even though she certainly wanted to. "Now what happened?"

"In the wee hours, before the first cock crowed, I was summoned."

"Yes, that's when he took her. It was early this morning."

"I didn't even know about the girl until about four hours ago."

"What? You mean she lay here all day without treatment?"

"Pretty much, yes," replied Etta. "When I was finally told about the child I cleaned her up and checked her for a head injury. With no coon's eyes or bruising behind the ears, I sat here and watched her for a few hours to be sure she didn't have a concussion. Poor dear was in a lot of pain, but the meds can do worse damage if there's a brain injury. I finally gave her some extract of opium. She hadn't been asleep long when you came in. The periorbital hematoma looks worse than . . ." she stopped, straightened, and shook her head. "Sorry, what I meant to say is that black eye she's got looks a lot worse than it really is. The swelling should be considerably less by tomorrow."

"What about early this morning?" Anisha knew that Khaled had abducted her daughter as planned, but the assassin was extremely skilled, and she doubted Aideen could've cut that much blood from a trained killer. Even as skilled as she was with a sword, she was just a little girl. Anisha assumed Khaled must've taken an accomplice with him, and that that's whose blood was all over her night clothes. "You said you were summoned," she prompted.

"I was," replied Etta. "It's not unusual to be called at strange hours to treat illness or injury, but this was something I haven't seen since the border battles up north." The healer chuckled. "The black robed one was carved up pretty good. His eye and the tip of his ear were gone. I had to debride the socket and pack it with a poultice. His face took thirty stitches and his arm fifty."

"Wait a minute. You mean Khaled was injured? Not another?"

"There was no one else, and that devil wasn't talking either. When I was done patching him up I was brought to the girl. That's when I put it together. That Khaled went to steal a kitten and found a lion unwilling to go peacefully."

Anisha was stunned. She had seen Khaled hold three expert swordsmen at bay. Had it not been for Aideen's arrows the assassin would have bested her husband, and Imar was no slouch with a sword. She looked at her daughter. The girl was a mess. Aideen had paid for her defiance, but was the assassin done with her?

Etta interrupted her thoughts. "I don't know what's going on here, and I don't want to know. It's none of my business, but that girl will need looking after so long as that one-eyed desert devil is around. Now if you'll excuse me, I have to go." The healer opened the door and then stopped. She withdrew the vial of pain medicine from her bag and handed it to Anisha. "Here, she will want a few drops of this when she wakes."

Anisha took the vial and went to Aideen. When the door latched shut behind her she absently put it in a pocket. What had she done? Well, it was too late to turn back now. She would have the octagon key, and if this was what it took to get it, so be it. Anisha was not one to let motherhood stand in the way of ambition. She left her daughter to sleep and strode down the hall to have a word with his lordship.

She found Lord Townsend in his office at his desk. Khaled sat across from him, his face and upper right arm wrapped in bandages. Anisha suppressed a grin at the assassin's humility. His attempt to look emotionless was futile. Khaled glared at her with his good eye as she entered. Anisha couldn't help but feel a little pride in her daughter for rearranging the assassin's face.

Anisha interrupted his lordship as she entered the room, but the words were coldly addressed to Khaled. "You were supposed to drug her and bring her unharmed. You had no right—"

"You failed to inform me," Khaled cut in, his voice hoarse as he spoke through gritted teeth, "that the girl was armed. What kind of parent teaches a girl child to fight?"

"That was my husband's doing, and as far as you're concerned none of your business," she snapped. "Never the less, you should have been more prepared, since it was my daughter who shot you last summer."

"A lucky shot," rasped the assassin. "The key keeper would be dead if not for the girl's bow."

"Yeah, and by the looks of you, she keeps her sword sharp too."

Khaled leaped to his feet, but he grimaced in pain and froze at Townsend's bark.

"Enough," shouted Townsend.

Khaled eased himself back into his chair with a grunt.

Anisha turned on Townsend. "You need to get my daughter out of the city. Dorfin suspects you. He has already sent out several platoons of cavalry to search the roads as well as a number of carrier pigeons. It was all I could do to stop him from sending a platoon over to search your house. The magistrate said he would personally investigate."

"Yes," Townsend replied. "The magistrate has been here and gone." He smiled at Anisha's frown.

"He didn't search the grounds? Dorfin implicated you as a prime suspect what with the business war between our families."

Townsend's voice was like silk. "Oh, didn't you know? The magistrate has been in my pocket for years." Then his face soured as if he had eaten something disagreeable. "I daresay his purse was substantially heavier when he left."

"You should count yourself lucky my mother isn't here. She would have already stormed your estate and questioned you by sword-point."

Townsend's face flushed. "I have already considered that," he snapped. "Why do you think I waited until your mother left before we kidnaped your daughter? She is too impulsive, too rash, but she is away now. Dorfin, on the other hand, is patient. While he contemplates attacking my gates and risking an incident, we will sneak out of the city."

"Don't be a fool. Dorfin has spies. He will know who kidnapped Aideen soon enough. If you don't move now it will be too late."

Townsend leaned back in his chair "I am having the child moved to a safe house outside the city within the hour. Khaled and I will catch up tonight. We will be well away before the light of another dawn wakes the city of Port Augustus. Once I am gone I will have the ransom letter delivered to you." He sat up and pierced her with an intense stare. "Let me remind you that this little plot was your idea, but it is not foolproof, and Dorfin is no fool. I would be surprised if his spies aren't watching you as well. It would behoove you to exercise extreme caution."

Anisha began looking around the room for peepholes. Her eyes fell on the spot where the assassin's sword penetrated the threadbare tapestry and wallboard behind. Khaled had claimed that he had smelled the spy hiding within the walls. Sure enough, the seaman-turned-spy had accessed the space between the walls from the cellar. Baker's body had been disposed of, but Anisha thought she could still smell his blood souring the air. "Baker was one of your spies, but he betrayed you. What of your new man?"

"Bill?" Townsend raised his brows. "He seems confident enough. He's yet to give me anything useful, but time will tell."

Talk of spies was making her nervous, so she changed the subject. "What's in the letter?"

"Are you sure you'd rather not be surprised?" he asked.

"I'd rather be prepared."

"Very well," Townsend acquiesced nonchalantly. "It states my demands without implication to either of us. If Imar follows the instructions he will go to Juana Pohala to trade the octagon key for your daughter. As you know, the desert lands east of the mountains are out of the king's jurisdiction."

"Be careful what you say around Aideen, she can talk telepathically to Dalla, though she can't always do it, or so she says."

"I'm hopeful she will guide her father to Juana Pohala in that respect. Can she speak to her father directly in this manner?"

"Not that I know of," Anisha replied. "Only Dalla can talk to her through their minds. That healer is different."

"You don't really believe she is from the long lost past, do you?"

"I'm not sure," replied Anisha thoughtfully. "Her hair is true blonde and I've never seen anyone with skin as white as hers, nor is she albino."

"So she's odd and telepathic."

"I also saw her cremate two bodies in a couple of minutes. She did it without flame or smoke."

Khaled sat forward and looked at her, but Townsend simply said, "We had best use caution."

"I better go home and look upset. I will leave for Juana Pohala as soon as I get the ransom note. Be sure the instructions tell me to come with minimal guard."

Townsend nodded his agreement and said, "Dorfin will want you well-guarded. Try to keep the numbers small. Also, I think it would be best if you waited a day, so we can get a good start ahead of you. My men will overpower your escort and take their place once you are on your way. You will eventually meet up with your husband. Once you do, stay with Imar until I have the key."

"Until we have the key," she corrected. "After that my husband should be dead and I'll want to stay close to my interests."

"Our interests, my lady," he amended. "I sent some of my agents to Juana Pohala to hire additional mercenaries and guides to take us across the desert and on to the ruins. We will have to take the Southern Caravan Route out of Juana Napur; the northern route is filling with soldiers. I hear that King Drayden's Kandian infantry is digging in on the plains of Northern Hamaud."

"Why not cross the desert at Juana Pohala?"

"Ha, ha, ha, ha, ha," the assassin's laugh sounded like sandpaper on rough bark.

Anisha and Townsend faced him.

"You foolish woman," spat Khaled. "You should stay home and busy yourself with needlepoint or whatever it is that worthless rich women do."

Anisha began a retort. "Why you insolent, one-way . . ."

"That patch of desert," Khaled cut her off. "Those infernal sands between Juana Pohala and the Kaden River have killed hundreds of men. Do you hear me, woman? I said, men! That desert has destroyed hearty desert born men, even those true to the one faith and trained by my guild." The assassin's eye glazed as he spoke. "First is the thirst. You will drink all your water and then want for more. Your clothes will burn you as if you were in an oven. Fools peel off that lifesaving protection and then their skin blisters and bubbles until they pass out because they are too weak to die screaming. Your shoes harden and melt to your feet, and then there are the beasts." Khaled's fanatical gaze changed to a haunted look. "You are stupid. I will say no more."

Silence filled the room, but for the breathing of the occupants.

49

A gastric growl rumbled from Townsend's stomach. "Okay then," he began. "That was informative. Thank you, Khaled. As I said, we'll take the southern caravan route. We will take the fortress and once the king of Eastonia abdicates his throne to me," he coughed, "I mean to us," he corrected, "we will wait for Drayden to come deliver his crown since he is on his way there with a rather large and slow moving army. We will then return across the continent, conquering all who defy us."

"Drayden will not just hand over his crown."

Townsend smiled like a snake. Anisha almost expected a little, forked-tongue to dart out and back in. "Oh, I think he'll come around after a little demonstration—perhaps a bomb blasting half his army to ash," he mused.

Anisha's eyes sparkled ambitiously and she joined him with fanatical fervor. "Yes, a demonstration. The healer spoke of such weapons. She called them nukes." She shook herself out of her insane reverie. "That foolish woman would destroy such power." Before Townsend could say more, she changed the subject. "I want Aideen off the drugs as soon as possible. She'll need it for pain, but I don't want her getting addicted. As you said, she can commune with the healer and thus guide Imar with the proper information where you want him to go, but she can't do it doped up."

"Of course," Townsend nodded.

"I want her treated well, like royalty, so keep your dogs under control." Anisha turned a fearless gaze on Khaled. "If Aideen is mistreated in any way I will hire six Hamaudi assassins to exact my revenge." She tipped her head at Khaled. "I will start with the dismemberment of that one."

Khaled rose again. Townsend signaled him to stand down. He remained on his feet, but his eyes rolled to the expanding red spot on his arm-bandage.

"Oh," said Anisha sweetly. "It looks like you pulled some stitches."

The assassin's nostrils flared, but he remained quiet.

Back to business, Anisha continued, "My daughter is a lady of houses Amirson and Murdoch. She is not to be touched."

"The girl is genteel and shall be treated as such," assured Townsend in a placating tone. "I will see that she is cared for as befits her station."

"Good," Anisha answered, and then grudgingly added, "And, thank you. With a little luck, I will see you in about a week."

CHAPTER 4

Dalla stared through trees, dirt, and rock. She saw little within her vision. Old soldiers called it 'the stare.' In her mind, she tried to disseminate intangible shadows shouting inarticulate warnings at her. The trail widened. She started as if roused and looked around as if seeing the terrain for the first time. Imar was turned in his saddle looking at her curiously. Her horse picked its way down the hill, around a small patch of manzanita to where Imar sat his horse waiting for her beside a dead-standing lodgepole pine.

He nudged his horse to walk when she pulled up beside him. "What is it?"

"What is what? You've asked me that ten times already today."

"And you keep telling me nothing," Imar sighed. "You've been like this all day. Vidar told me not to think anything of it, and Hager said it's a woman thing, perfectly normal for the gender, but I'm concerned."

Dalla looked back up the hill to where Aksel and Egil were coaxing the packhorses around a switchback that sprouted some tempting sweet grass. She turned back to Imar and said, "I don't know what it is."

"When I've seen you like this before you were sensing danger, like the time Aksel and Egil barely escaped Bamsen's soldiers. You're having a premonition, aren't you?"

"I don't know," Dalla answered, irritably. "I've been trying to contact Ivan and Aideen, but so far, nothing."

"I thought you needed quiet meditation for mind-speech."

"I do, but your daughter is different," Dalla answered exasperatedly. They crossed a small stream and then proceeded down a gentler slope. "Aideen is the only non-genetically enhanced telepath I know. The first time she did it she was walking along daydreaming. I thought I would try to reach her as we rode."

Imar looked unconvinced. "So you've been telepathically talking to no one all day?" His sarcasm was obvious.

"Look," said Dalla, with more vehemence than she'd intended. "I don't know what's forming at the back of my mind, but I really don't need to be nagged right now. It's no different than how you've described your lost memories. It's like grabbing shadows."

A vein stood out on Imar's forehead, his jaw muscles tightened, and his voice grew louder. "I wasn't aware that you had a head injury. When you get ready to be civil, let me know. I'm going ahead to find a campsite." Imar shook his reins and trotted ahead.

"Good," Dalla said with knit brows to his retreating back. "You do that."

An hour later Dalla dismounted in a fairly flat clearing that overlooked the tan sands of the desert of Hamaud. Far below and dozens of kilometers out from the base of the mountains stood the trade city of Juana Napur. It stood at the junction of two major roads, the west end of the Southern Caravan Route, and the southern end of the road running north, skirting the mountains to Juana Pohala and on to the border town of Sepur on the Northern Caravan Route.

Hager was building a stone fire pit ring while Vidar and Imar dragged a large sitting log out of the sparse brush. "Nice campsite," she said.

"Not bad," agreed Hager. "Imar found us a good one."

Dalla tied her horse to a picket line someone had strung as Aksel and Egil rode in with the packhorses. They were still at high elevation, but the forest was getting more arid the closer they got to the desert. She gathered a few twigs and joined Hager at the fire pit just as Imar and Vidar positioned the log. "It's a beautiful evening," she said. "Our days will soon become unbearably hot."

Vidar sat on the log. "I'd guess we have another day of pleasant temperatures."

"I'll gather some firewood," Imar said quietly as he walked to the woods.

"We should drag another sitting log into camp," Vidar suggested to Imar's back, but Imar ignored him. Vidar lifted one brow. "What's got his goat?"

Hager's eyes went to Dalla and back to Vidar. "Let him be. I'll give you a hand."

Dalla knelt and placed the kindling in a tepee stack. She focused her mind on the small pile with her hand stretched palm downward over the top. A tendril of smoke began to snake upward from the center of the twigs when all of a sudden the pile burst apart in flames. Hager flinched, and Vidar fell over backwards.

"Whoops," exclaimed Dalla. "I'm sorry. I've been a little distracted today."

"Ah, we've noticed," said Vidar. He got up and went up the hill to a two-meter log that was two-thirds of a meter across.

Hager pulled on a pair of gloves from his belt, picked up the burning twigs and piled them in the fire pit. "You don't need to apologize, just try not to burn down the tent." The little flames grew and crackled. "I'm getting spoiled with you starting fires the easy way." He set a few dry sticks on the fire and grinned. "I'm not even sure where I put my flint." Hager stood up and looked to where Imar was snapping dead branches off a downed tree. "You two have a spat?"

Dalla sighed. "It was stupid, really. I think the strain of his amnesia is getting to him."

Vidar was grunting exaggeratingly with the log. "What happened to that help, Hager?"

"In a minute," replied the surely veteran. He turned to where Aksel and Egil were unpacking the horses.

"Hey, would one of you guys go give Vidar a hand?"

The young men spoke to each other briefly, and after losing at rock-paper-scissors, Egil went to aid Vidar. Imar came to the campfire and dumped an armload of firewood, then returned to the woods for more without saying a word.

Hager squatted by the fire. "What about his marriage to Anisha? That seems to be causing quite a strain on both of you." He added a stick to the flames.

"Oh, Hager," Dalla was close to tears. "They have no marriage but for the paper making it legal and Anisha won't give him a divorce. She gives him grief, but no fidelity or support, yet he is miserable with guilt if he so much as holds my hand. Gods forgive him should he think about giving me a kiss."

"I think I know what you both need," said Hager dryly. He smiled, and then continued soberly, "If Imar could get his memory back it might help him find himself. He's not even sure who he is. If he were to…" he paused, searching for words. "No," he said. "*When* he regains his memory, his forgotten inner self, not just the person his friends told him about, he can then work out how to deal with love. Maybe he can find a way out of his marriage."

Dalla rocked gently where she knelt. It helped her get control of her emotions. "Anisha set him free to pursue another relationship so long as he's discreet. She admits to having frequent adulterous rendezvous of her own. If she won't give him a divorce is he just going to live like a celibate monk? He's being ridiculous, and the frustration is making us both rather cranky. Why can't he just give in to his passions? His marriage is nothing but paper anyway."

"Imar has always been honorable," Hager said gently. Then he added, "Almost to the point of nauseating perfection. Just because his wife cheats on him and treats him badly..." Hager cracked a sideways grin. "Actually, Anisha treats everyone badly." He straightened his back, popping a couple vertebrae, and said, "What I mean is that Imar won't bend his morals, even for someone who stabs him in the back like Anisha. Legality has little to do with it. Imar gave his oath. It doesn't matter if Anisha broke her vows. Until she frees him from marriage by divorce or death, Imar probably won't break his word. At least, that's the way he was before his knock on the head, but I think his honor is too deeply engrained in him for amnesia to block it out."

After a tiresome meal of carrot and potato stew, taken from their merchandise stores, the sun sank behind the western peaks. They watched the lengthening shadows on the desert below while Dalla performed a sensory sweep of the area. She found nothing bigger than a marmot for several kilometers. "There's no one near," Dalla reported. "It's up to you, but I think we can all sleep peacefully tonight."

"We haven't seen a soul on these trails since entering the mountains," Vidar added. "You chose this route well, Dalla. It has been slower going, but we haven't had to dodge patrols either."

Imar sat idly poking at the coals with a stick. "Okay," he said. "We'll skip posting a watch tonight." His tone was sullen.

Dalla excused herself and went in the tent to meditate. She tried to connect with her father. He should have left Sedar by now. She hoped he was en route to meet them in Juana Napur. Ivan did not respond—again.

It had been two weeks since they had joined in mind-speech. Dalla was emotionally drained. She went to sleep early and slept like the dead. Hours into the night she woke up.

Dalla guessed it to be the third hour past midnight. It surprised her that she had slept through everyone else bedding down. She deduced that her stress must have exhausted her. That nagging feeling in the back of her mind returned, only this time, Aideen came to the forefront of her thoughts. She decided to try contacting the girl. Amazed that no one was snoring, she listened to the rhythmic breathing of the others and then stood, pulling a wool blanket around her shoulders. Her enhanced vision allowed her to easily find the lantern in the dark tent.

She took the lamp and stepped out into the moonless night, finding her way to one of the logs by the fire pit. Only a few dull red coals covered in cooling ash remained. The sparse forest of lodgepole pines surrounding their high rocky campsite stood quiet, like dark pillars supporting a night sky shot with a million brilliant stars. She looked to the east and saw the lights of Juana Napur shining brightly on the dark desert below.

With an effortless twinge of pyrokinetic thought, a small flame was born within the womb of the lantern's globe. Placing a saddle blanket on the ground, Dalla assumed the lotus position and set the lantern on the log. The feeble glow created shadows where none before had existed, but it was a comfort and would help focus her mind.

Taking a small strip of leather lace from a pocket, she pulled her blonde tresses behind her head and tied them into a golden ponytail. She looked at the flame, emptying her mind while concentrating on the slow steady rhythm of her breathing and the beating of her slowing heart. With breath, balance, and focus she melded mind, body, and spirit into her meditation.

She sat in the quiet realm of mind resting meditation for twenty minutes. Then she heard Aideen's voice speaking faintly in her mind.

Dalla ... Dalla ... Please be there. I need you. The child's strength grew with each word.

Aideen? Dalla thought. The girl's fear struck the empath with chilling force. *What's the matter?*

I have been taken.

What do you mean taken? Who took you, and taken where?

I ... don't know. Khaled came and took me ... away ... somewhere, but now they're taking me somewhere else.

They? Dalla thought. *They who? What happened?*

I hid under my bed, but he found me. I was so scared. I am still scared. He hates me. I cut his eye out with my sword and that made him real mad. He hit me. That's all I remember till now. I don't know..., her thoughts stammered. *I don't know how long I've been out.*

Dalla hated to see people hurt. That was one reason she became a doctor and in this world a healer. She had devoted her life to caring for the sick and injured, however, she could not help rewarding herself with a small grin thinking of the assassin getting his comeuppance. It especially amused her that, knowing the Hamaudi assassin's view of women, Khaled's recompense came from an eleven-year-old girl's sword. *Aideen, where are you now?*

59

I don't know. I am on a horse, my hands are tied and I'm blindfolded. Wait. We are going uphill and it is getting steeper. There are several horses and I can hear three different voices of men.

That could mean you are going north or east. The terrain south of Port Augustus is flat and if anything, slopes downward. Just keep paying attention to every detail. Try not to let them catch you using mind-speech. We will come for you.

Okay. Just hurry. Oh Dalla, it hurts so bad; my eye, my nose and my . . . oh Dalla, my whole face really hurts.

Dalla reversed her empathy into their link and coaxed dopamines to the girl's pituitary gland. It was better to be closer, and best to touch, but she could still feel the girl's pain ease slightly.

That helped, thank you, thought Aideen. *They gave me pain medicine earlier, but my mind was too foggy for mind-speech.*

It's okay, Aideen. Dalla assured her. *Ask them for some more. You will feel better tomorrow. Try to reach me then or the next day. Keep your ears open. Maybe you can learn where they are taking you.* Sensing that the girl's distress was considerably diminished she added, *Be brave, Aideen. It may take a while, so be brave. Goodbye for now.*

For now goodbye, Aideen answered in the ritual style that she had heard Dalla use with Ivan.

Dalla ended the link. Since she was still in the realm of astral thought projection, she focused on her father, but Ivan was unresponsive. She could sense traces of jumbled thoughts from him, but nothing coherent. It soon became obvious to her that her father was drinking, and quite probably drunk. She sighed with some exasperation as she roused herself from her meditative state. Ivan was too far away to be of any help, but she still would have liked his counsel. She would contact him later, and hopefully he would be sober.

The healer reentered the tent, hung the lantern on the center pole, and knelt by Imar. She knew to always be cautious when waking warriors, whether by touching the foot of an outstretched leg or softly calling to the sleeper, it was best to keep some distance. Dalla had seen soldiers prodded with a stick come out of sleep swinging, but Imar could wake to Dalla's voice easily. The healer feared no attack when she roused him.

"Imar," she said softly, placing her hand gently above his elbow. "Wake up."

Imar's eyes opened. He was on his side looking at her. In two heartbeats his look questioned, *What?*

Dalla heard it as clearly in her thoughts as if he were using mind-speech. Momentarily taken aback, she recovered and replied with her mind. *Can you hear my thoughts? It's Aideen, she's been kidnapped.*

Imar furrowed his brow, rose to his elbow. "What?"

Hager and Vidar roused. Dalla made a mental note of Imar's thought projection and proceeded to the business at hand. "Aideen's been kidnapped."

That got their attention. The men were on their feet with hands on weapons, ready to go instantly, and then in the next moments sought details.

"You contacted Aideen," Imar said, still struggling with sleep inertia.

"Perhaps you should start from the beginning," offered Vidar.

61

Hager nudged Aksel's leg with his foot and then shook Egil awake in the same fashion. "Wake up guys," he said. "The captain's daughter has been kidnapped."

Aksel ran out, dagger in hand, and then returned for his boots. "We have to go back," he said, grabbing his saddlebags and sword.

"We have to sit down and hear the details," said Hager. "It's better to think first."

Egil rubbed the sleep from his eyes. "How do we know about Aideen?"

"Dalla," said Hager for an explanation.

Egil mouthed an 'Oh.'

Hager sat down on his bedding and began slowly pulling his boots on.

"Besides," Vidar said to Aksel, "if you went charging up the trail you'd probably break your neck. It's dark with no moon."

Dalla went to Aksel and touched his arm. His tawny hair stuck out in wild disarray. The boy instantly calmed as she spoke. "We could all use some coffee. Could I get you and Egil to stir up the fire and brew us a pot?

"Sure," he replied. To Egil, whose dark hair was just as wild, he said, "I'll get the fire if you get the coffee."

Egil finished putting on his boots and followed Aksel out of the tent muttering. The fire pit was close enough to the tent for the boys to hear Dalla recounting the mind-speech conversation that she had had with Aideen. When she shared the part about the girl putting out the assassin's eye, a whoop came from outside the tent.

"Good for her," shouted Egil.

"Yeah," added Aksel. "Too bad she didn't stick him someplace more vital."

"Back in Kandia," Imar began, "I told Aideen that I was glad she had only wounded Khaled. I'd hoped she never killed anyone. Now I can't help but wish that her arrows would have pierced his heart." His voice grew tense with the last sentence.

"It wouldn't have mattered," rumbled Hager. "The assassin is a hired tool. Whoever sanctioned this would have just hired someone else."

"You're right, of course," agreed Imar, but his tone betrayed barely restrained rage.

When Dalla told them of the girl's injuries the jubilation of the child maiming Khaled turned instantly to anger. Oaths were sworn, hands went to hilts, and swords were rattled in their scabbards. The healer was certain the assassin's ears were burning. She did not anger as easily as Imar, but the thought of anyone hurting a child made her blood boil. Dalla could see Imar's facial muscles tighten. Her empathy felt the heat of his kindling anger.

Dalla had tended Imar's head injury a few months before and was satisfied with the healing except for his amnesia. In addition to his memory loss, she had seen Imar occasionally display sudden fits of emotion, which was common with a brain injury to the hippocampus, but since those episodes were usually before a fight she could not be sure if it wasn't just the battle rush, which is similar to the berserker's rage. As an empath, the healer saw and felt Imar's emotional turmoil. His dark wavy hair was tied back exposing a reddening to his olive cheeks.

"Dalla and I will leave for Port Augustus at first

light. I want the rest of you to go on to Juana Napur." Imar looked as if he was having trouble concentrating.

Dalla took his hand. He looked at her and they merged as their gazes locked. The healer entered his mind, spreading cool calmness to the raging fire burning inside him. Their earlier attitudes towards one another were shoved aside. The anger in Imar was focused on Khaled. Some of it burned at the unknown entity that was responsible for the kidnapping, but it was Khaled who had hurt his little girl. Dalla saw a flash image of the assassin cut in many places, and then another of him writhing in flames. The healer stilled those thoughts and brought the flames of Imar's anger down to simmering coals. She slid out of his mind, broke the gaze, and felt the tension in his hand relax. She looked back up at his brown eyes.

Imar took a breath. "Thank you," he said. "That helped."

"Let's sit down and plan what to do," said Vidar. He then removed a map from the top of the gear pile in the corner and spread the chart on rumpled blankets between them where they sat cross-legged in a circle. He studied the map intently, tracing roads and trails with a finger.

Aksel and Egil entered the tent. Egil passed out cups while Aksel poured the coffee.

"You know," said Hager. "Khaled's involvement points to the octagon key as the ransom. If he wasn't in this, I would guess they were just after money." He scratched his beard. "I wish we knew who he was working for. What I would like to know is how the kidnappers plan to give you a ransom note?"

"They must know of mine and Aideen's link,"

replied Dalla. "No one knows where we are. They will expect Aideen to lead us to her."

"So," Imar added, "someone learned of my daughter's abilities in Port Augustus, perhaps from a servant speaking to the wrong person or one of Aideen's friends could have been overheard talking about it."

"Anisha is quite the socialite," Vidar opined. "She may have been overheard praising the child's abilities."

Hager harrumphed. "Anisha doesn't praise anyone." He sipped his coffee. "There's no sense going back. It will take too long." He looked at Imar. "You may want to consider hiding the key. Then you can ride openly on good roads."

"What if I need the key to bargain for Aideen?" Imar looked at the map.

"You can't give up the key," said Dalla.

"I may have to," Imar retorted hotly. His tone leveled, but it was low and laden with deadly conviction. "I will get Aideen back first. Once she is safe, we can get the key back, but I intend to have some words with Khaled."

Everyone knew that Imar's 'words' would be said with steel.

"Whoever took Aideen," said Dalla, "will know where we are going. They won't know if we're using the Northern Caravan Route or the Southern, but with war and winter coming up north, they have probably guessed we are going east via Juana Napur. Aideen said she was in the mountains. They are going east, I'm sure of it. The road out of Port Augustus goes to Juana Pohala. We should try to intercept them there."

"I agree," said Vidar. "Your best bet would be to stay with us until Juana Napur, and then go north to Juana Pohala. But Captain," he added seriously, "we should stay together. Dalla will eventually be able to tell Ivan where to meet us, and you don't know what forces or how many you may be up against. You may need our help."

"Vidar is right," said Hager. "With Khaled involved, you need every sword you can get, though personally, I'd rather just shoot the bastard from a distance."

"We are nearly out of Kalusia." Vidar made a sweeping gesture over the map. "Hamaud is lawless and controlled by tribal war chiefs that guard their wells with passion. West coast kings send patrols into the borderlands all the time. As long as they pay their tolls for using the wells there is no problem. I would not be surprised if there were patrols from Kalusia dedicated to searching for you and your key. It would be wise to exercise caution."

Imar faced Dalla and said, "You need to be open and vigilant to Aideen's telepathy."

Dalla was going to remind him that that was exactly what she had been doing but decided not to bring it up now that they were getting along again. "We still need to watch for misinformation. They may have her lead us into a trap to kill us all and take the key."

Imar nodded. "Okay, we'll go down to Juana Napur, and sell this pack train of potatoes and carrots so we can travel faster. We could use a break, but until we hear different I only want to spend one night in Juana Napur before we push on to Juana Pohala.

"Oh good," exclaimed Aksel. "I hope I never see another carrot for as long as I live."

Vidar chuckled, and Hager said, "I agree with the lad. I'm ready for a fat juicy steak."

Dalla added, "And I'm ready for a hot bath.

CHAPTER 5

Aideen wanted to contact Dalla again but decided to wait. The drug they gave her had worn off, but her mouth was dry and her tongue felt thick. The blindfold made her eye hurt all the more and the pain all over her face was beginning to throb. Her wrists itched, but the bonds holding her to the saddle prevented her from scratching. "Water," she croaked, trying unsuccessfully not to sound pleading. "I am very thirsty. May I please have some water?"

"Shut up," someone snapped in a harsh tone.

It was Khaled. Aideen recalled his voice. At first it seemed like it had just happened, maybe the day before, but moments of recent memory lapses made her guess her captivity had been longer. There were times of pain filled lucidity that alternated with dreamless fog-filled lethargy. She forced her thoughts over that time, and thought she remembered hearing her mother's voice, but she shrugged it off as another incomplete dream or pain induced vision.

Aideen bent forward, hands straining against her fetters so that she could touch her nose, and felt the hardened clay pasted to it. She sniffed, thankful her sinuses were clear, touching off only a small twinge of pain. The blindfold was putting uncomfortable pressure on her swollen eye. She ran her fingers over the stitches on her upper lip; it was numb and it tingled. She was going to ask for some pain medicine as Dalla had suggested in mind-speech, but decided against it so that she could think clearly, and possibly glean some information. She straightened in her saddle. Her tongue came off the roof of her mouth with a small smack.

"Water," repeated the girl. "Please…"

A wave of black animosity rode in on her empathic waves. Nausea struck her, and she clenched but willed the feeling down, refusing to heave. It was the same dark empathy that she had encountered in the assassin before, and it made her sick. She wondered if that feeling identified the assassin or evil in general.

Aideen heard trotting hooves clop up beside her and felt the force of dark hatred exude from his presence. She did not need her vision to tell her it was Khaled. The smell of dried blood and fresh wounds assailed the girl's olfactory senses. Her air passages opened wide as fear driven adrenalin coursed through her veins. She gasped as her hair was roughly seized and her head tilted painfully back. Fear dulled the pain of his grasp. She did not even hear the stopper pulled from the canteen before water flooded her mouth, causing her to gag. The grip on her head was released. She bent forward to the right side of her mount opposite from her nemesis and retched, water streaming from her nostrils. Pain flared in her sutured lip and returned to her nose.

"Enough," cracked an imperious command. It was followed by galloping hooves and creaking harnesses.

Aideen heard more than one horse advance. She knew that voice, but the name that went with it eluded her. She had not heard it since she was a little girl. Recovering from retching and wiping her mouth on her sleeve, she then straightened in her saddle. Tears soaked her blindfold. She assessed that Khaled had just been collared and chained with the arrival of the man wielding that commanding word. She sniffed once and wracked her brain to recall that voice. Horses reined in on each side of her, one forcing its way between her and Khaled.

"What do you think you're doing?" the commanding voice continued angrily. "You lay hands on the girl like that again, I'll have you whipped." His scolding settled, but he went on with pompous authority. "You overstep your place, assassin. I think it would be best if you stay away from the child. Go back down the road a ways and make sure we're not followed."

Aideen felt the force of indignant anger, like the rush of heat without the temperature rising, but she heard no reply. Instead, she heard his horse wheel and race away in a full run. The evil aura diminished, taking her nausea with the retreating hooves as they faded in the distance. She immediately felt relief. It was easier to breathe.

"Remove her blindfold," said Lord Pompous.

Aideen felt calloused fingers brush against her neck as the cloth covering her eyes was gently untied. She squinted against the torchlight, which at first seemed very bright. There was a pair of horsemen ahead and another to her right and left. She looked behind her and saw two more soldiers wearing leather armor. One of the soldiers behind her was a woman, and she thought that one of the warriors riding point was a woman as well. Outside of the guard to her left was the seventh man. He was older and dressed like a lord—he was obviously the leader that had spoken—his fur trimmed cloak looked well-made and his jeweled cap could feed a family for a year. With Khaled, that made eight, total.

Aideen could smell the naphtha soaked cloth earlier, but now occasional wisps of the acrid smoke stung her eyes. Beyond the torch-lit nimbus of their procession, all was black. It was like the dark tree limbs and roadside brush entered their firelight oval and slid by into the black void behind them as they clopped along in their own orange torch-lit world. The trees parted momentarily for the girl to gaze up at the stars. Above, in the dark depths of the distant void, the Milkmaid's Swath spilled across the sky in all her glittering glory without contest from the absent moon. The moment passed, and the sky's dark beauty was again swallowed by overhanging branches of golden leaves. The girl knew her stars well enough to know that they were, at least for now, traveling east.

With a gesture from the leader, the rider to Aideen's left moved ahead.

When his lordship pulled up beside her recognition ran upon her. "You're Lord Townsend," she blurted.

The grey haired lord smiled, appraising her a moment, then said, "My Lady Aideen, please pardon any distress Khaled may have caused you. You can't really blame him for his anger; after all, you did blind one of his eyes, not to mention a couple of severe wounds requiring, at least, thirty stitches each."

Aideen smiled in spite of herself. She tucked her chin to hide the fact and realized she had on a purple cloak trimmed in red fox as well as a well-made dress of light blue Medimian cloth. Her memory flashed back to her encounter with the assassin when she scooted from under her bed and saw a strip of flesh on the floor. "How's his ear?" she asked smugly.

The grin was not lost on Townsend. He raised an eyebrow. His patronizing smile turned to a pursed-lipped look of reproof. "It is a long road to Juana Pohala young lady. I suggest you try not to antagonize him."

"Yes my lord," she answered, trying her best to sound contrite.

Townsend nodded and rode to the front. Aideen's mind reeled. They were going to Juana Pohala. She tried to contact Dalla again but was unsuccessful. She would do it later when they stopped for the night.

Aideen slept fitfully, her head rolling with the rocking rhythm of her pony's gait. When the animal stopped she sat there with chin on chest, settling in for a good doze. She was barely aware of the strong hands that carefully took her from the saddle and placed her on a fleece covered cot. Woolen blankets were draped over her. She heard soft steps followed by the scraping of a flint. Opening her eyes, she saw one of the soldiers with his back to her. He was bent and blowing on a brazier. She heard crackling as flames caught in the kindling and cast orange and yellow flickers of light all around the tent, but for her half, which was shielded by the warrior's silhouette. The man took from a canvas bag what looked like black chunks of charcoal and placed them on the fire. Smoke columned up through a hole in the tent roof.

The soldier turned and she closed her eyes to slits

that barely allowed her to see. He moved to her side. There was enough light in the tent for Aideen to see the lines on the man's brown face. She opened her eyes only slightly more and the man was looking right at her. He could see that she was awake, but he said nothing. Crow's-feet crowded closely at the corners of his eyes. She estimated the old soldier to be about fifty, but he still looked fit for his age. The man had a faraway look as he stood there. She wondered if he was aware of her gaze. He shook his head slightly, as if at some private thought, and then at a noise from without he wiped his face into an emotionless mask and left the tent.

Aideen did not want to wake up. She was in that stage of waking where indistinguishable dreams blended with reality. Then suddenly she found herself floundering in fear. Her neck and arms bristled in goose bumps and nausea clenched her stomach, but she recognized it as a sign of the assassin's presence. Her eyes snapped open. The dying coals lacked strength enough to cast a shadow in the dark tent, but a darker form loomed before her. She went cold within her warm bed, expecting him to strike. Her body went rigid, but he just stood there motionless.

Four or five terror-filled seconds felt like forever to Aideen until the tent flap snapped up. The girl jumped, both startled and relieved to see a man in leather armor bristling with weapons. Behind him, dawn's early light gave the forest a greyish blue tint. The arm holding the flap deftly tied it up with one hand while the other hand held a steaming bowl of spiced oatmeal. The aroma instantly roused Aideen's roaring appetite despite the assassin's presence. Strangely, tell-tale nausea passed as rapidly as its onset. The man at the door was one of her captors, but his presence greatly assuaged her fear. Khaled said nothing while he faced this interruption with stoic interest, but

Aideen could feel his cold energy sizing up his comrade as if the man were an adversary.

As the man walked into the tent, his free hand moved to rest upon the hilt of a large knife sheathed at an angle in his belt. It was a habit Aideen had seen in every soldier she had ever met. "I'll see to the girl," said the soldier. "She'll be ready to go shortly." His brusque voice had a don't-mess-with-me tone to it, nor did his actions betray any indication of intimidation from the assassin. Khaled whirled to the tent door, his loose robes swirling, the air trailing him with the smell of old blood and sweat. The warrior's eyes tracked Khaled's departure. Aideen watched the exchange in wide-eyed curiosity, but now that the assassin was gone she was glad to see the man's face soften as he cracked a small smile. She sat up on the edge of the cot.

Aideen took the proffered bowl from the warrior and nearly burnt her tongue with the first bite. "Ho-ot," she said with an open mouth, sucking in cool air to slow the singeing. The next few bites were prudently blown on before devouring.

The man took a knee next to her. "I'm afraid you'll have to hurry, my lady. We'll be breaking camp in a few minutes." The roughness was gone, replaced with a deep but gentle tone.

"Please don't call me that, my name is Aideen."

"Okay, but only out of earshot of lord high-and-mighty and his pet snake."

Aideen giggled a quick smile but did not stop inhaling her breakfast. She liked this middle-aged warrior. Grey strands of experience streaked his dark brown hair. Above each shaved side of his head, he wore scalp braids woven tight like two flattened fingers that joined into a single weave on the back of his head. The braid's end was secured with a brown leather lace. The ornate hilt guard of a hand-and-a-half Pagentian saber rode above his right shoulder. A small buckler on his left hip partially covered one of the matching long knives worn on each side, and a six-pack of throwing knives were sheathed horizontally like ribs in his boiled leather vest. He was not tall, but in Aideen's opinion, he was a stout man of medium height. His leathery skin was the color of creamed coffee, and his face had a fierceness that brooked no foolishness. He was muscular and his attitude reflected strength and confidence. She felt as if she had an ally amid her enemies. "You're the one that removed my blindfold last night." She didn't remember all the knives, but she had been very tired. "And you carried me in here," she paused, "thank you."

"You will want to wear those today," he said, ignoring her and glancing at the folded leather trews and riding boots laid out beside her sleeping cot. "A dress is not practical for long journeys on a horse, but his lordship insists, so wear it over the pants."

He stood up to go as she scraped the bottom of her bowl. He took the utensils from her and went to the doorway.

"Wait," she said before he stepped into the grey morning. "Don't go yet." She stood, faced away from him, and pulled on her pants under the dress she had slept in. "What's your name?"

"Hazim," he answered.

"A desert name," she stated.

"I am Hamaudi," he said. "Though I'm told there

is a Kalusian in the woodpile. Does it matter?"

"No," she replied. Aideen worded her next question carefully as she finished pulling on her boots. "How far is your sword sold?"

"To Juana Pohala, where I collect the balance of my pay," he said with just as much care. "We were hired to escort his lordship, a simple job without expected conflict. Lord Townsend is expecting us to sign another contract to cross the desert. He plans to make the crossing with thirty or forty additional swords." Hazim's eyes grew flinty. "Nothing was said about taking children prisoner," he added flatly. "I am sorry for your situation."

Aideen had grown up around mercenaries. Free companies were a family business on both sides of her family. Her father had a company of mercenaries contracted to patrol Abezda's border and protect the locals from Kandian raiders, and then her grandparents on her mother's side had, at least, a battalion of hired soldiers working for them. They were contracted out wherever there was a need and enough money to pay for their services, so long as the cause didn't conflict with what her grandparents thought was ethically just. She knew the loyalty of a sell-sword lasted only as long as the contracted terms of service. Pulling her thick dark hair back and tying it into a fluffy ponytail she asked, "Will you re-up?"

Hazim leaned outside the tent and looked for prying ears, and then back at Aideen. "Perhaps," he said slowly, "unless I find a better-paying employer."

"What if . . .?"

"Shush," he cut her off and raised a finger to his lips. "Guard your tongue, lest you lose it and me my life. I have taken coin, and that's that. Now come, your horse is ready."

Aideen had expected to ride the same sure-footed pony again, but instead Hazim led her to a brown and white paint.

"Lord Townsend's orders," he said as he tied her hands comfortably to the pommel.

The girl saw her tent collapse amid the other flattened shelters as she rode out of camp. Lord Townsend took the lead. Aideen was flanked by Hazim and a scarred female fighter named Hana. Aideen assumed the others would catch up when they finished folding the tents. She did not see Khaled following down the back trail, but she knew he was there out of sight. The sickness in her stomach that always indicated the assassin's presence was becoming a controllable signal rather than an actual illness, more like a knot in the belly than real nausea.

The party kept a steady pace for two hours before stopping to rest the horses. Aideen tried to spark a conversation with Hazim and Hana, but she got only short clipped answers until a frown and headshake from Townsend insisted she cease her chatter and satisfy herself with silence. She couldn't help but feel a little betrayed by Hazim whom she thought was a friend. *Maybe he is being dutifully distant so as not to arouse suspicion, or perhaps he is just another jailor in this prison journey. Mercs are a hard lot,* she thought. She forced herself not to put much hope of escape in that sector.

When Townsend rode ahead out of earshot Aideen turned her attention on Hana. "Khaled seems to avoid you. Anything that keeps him away from me is a relief. I hope you'll stay close."

Hana looked back briefly, sniffed and said

nothing. Behind them, only two mercs were in view about thirty meters back. Hazim was riding four furlongs in front of her and Hana. Aideen looked up the road to where Townsend rode beside the mercenary they called Akil. They were about two hundred meters ahead and turning onto a switchback where the road began to incline steeply.

Satisfied, Hana said, "Lord Townsend ordered us to watch you." She inclined her head towards Hazim, "We are to prevent you from doing anything stupid, like running off, or crying for help should we meet travelers."

Aideen let out a sigh. "Oh, good…"

"We are soldiers," Hana snapped, forcing her volume low, "not babysitters."

Taken aback by Hana's vehemence, but glad she was getting the woman to talk, Aideen changed the subject back to the assassin. "Why does he avoid you?" Aideen persisted. "Khaled, I mean."

"The Order of Hamaudi Assassins does not accept women," Hana replied. "Their religion shuns us."

"What gods do they worship?"

"There is only one god, and that one is nameless."

Warning bells rang in Aideen's head. If Hana was a nameless god worshiper, it would behoove her to tread cautiously. "So Hamaudi assassins worship the nameless god?" asked the girl. *No surprise there*, she thought. She had seen nameless god worshipers up north in Border City. They would eat the spotted mushrooms and then yell crazy things in the streets until they got locked up.

"They are forced, from a very young age, to learn their own version, but the Hamaudi Assassin's sect has warped the true teachings of the prophet."

Aideen felt like she might be delving too deep, but her curiosity got the better of her. "In what way?" she asked. "And who is the prophet?"

Hana looked at her. The woman's hawkish stare made Aideen think of a falcon preparing to rip into a rodent. "You ask a lot of questions," said the warrior.

"How am I supposed to learn anything if I don't?" asked the girl. Hana's gaze remained unchanged, so Aideen plunged on, "Khaled did this to me." She circled her bruised face with a forefinger. "Last summer Khaled attacked and stole something from my father. We were on the outskirts of Valekrie." Aideen could see she had Hana's interest. "Until then I thought my dad was the best weapons master in the world, but he was only able to defend himself, his one claymore against the assassin's twin scimitars."

She could see the woman's eyes shift to look off at nothing as if she were trying to picture the scene. "I nocked an arrow, drew and waited for a clear shot," Aideen continued. "My father was tiring and so was my arm. I started to shake. I no sooner let off the draw to rest when the assassin kicked his feet from under him. I drew again as Khaled raised his swords, and I loosed. My arrow struck him in the shoulder. I reached for another shaft while the first was still in flight. I pierced his other shoulder and then he ran off, but I will never forget that look of hatred he stared at me." The girl's voice became a harsh whisper. "The heat—I could feel the heat, as if from a furnace." Hana was now looking at her in fascination. Aideen's voice returned. "He means to kill me, and I don't want to die. The more I know about him, the better my chances."

The woman's face became an emotionless mask as her green eyes studied the girl. Then as if coming to some decision she said, "Okay, what would you know?"

"Tell me everything you know about the assassins of Hamaud."

"There isn't much to tell," said Hana. "Much of what goes on at Kashan Castle is ..."

"Kashan Castle?" asked Aideen.

"Yes, it is the headquarters of the assassins. They take boys and train them to master seven skills. Many of them are orphans, but they buy slaves and choose boys from the lot to become assassins. They take debt children as well." Hana noticed the girl's blank look and explained. "When a man has debts he cannot pay, he can offer his child to the Order of Assassins, and they will pay his debt."

"Wait a minute." Aideen scrunched her brows in thought. "You said they take children, but earlier you told me the Order doesn't accept women. Do you mean they take girls but not women?"

Hana took a breath and blew it out through expanded cheeks. Aideen looked around. Lord Townsend and Akil were above them, and rounding another switchback. Hazim was entering the first turn above them. They were still out of hearing distance as long as they kept their voices low.

"It is complicated," said Hana. "Basically, everyone they take in is either a slave or becomes a bondservant to the Order of Assassins. The boys are tested. If they prove to be sharp of wit and have fast reflexes then they are trained in the arts of murder. Boys that fail the testing are either killed for practice or castrated so they don't make babies. The girls, if they are fit, become breeding stock. Any of the slaves, no matter what their age, may be chosen for murder practice, including babies born with the slightest defect."

"That's…" Aideen thought she was going to be sick. "That's horrible." Her horse trailed Hana's as they rounded the first corner of the steep hill, then she urged her mount alongside the warrior when the road straightened.

"Inside the Order," Hana continued, "girls and women are nothing but chattel; they have no rights, not even to the afterlife. Their horses and camels get better treatment. The assassins hold all in contempt who are not fit men and worshipers of the nameless god. The only good thing about them is they give a lot of money to the temples of the nameless one, even if they have twisted the message."

Aideen was silent. Hana's last words felt like an invitation to a religious discussion that the girl would rather avoid. She was curious about the seven skills but decided to postpone that line of questioning for now as well. Dipping her head towards Hazim's back, Aideen said, "Have you noticed how everyone gives Khaled a wide berth but Hazim? Oh, they scowl at each other like they'd love nothing more than to stick their knives in one another, but Hazim acts like he has no fear of the assassin."

"Yes," Hana answered slowly. "I have noticed." She scrutinized the middle-aged warrior as he passed by them on the next higher switchback. "Perhaps it is because he is older and more confident. I have practiced the sword with Hazim—he is very good."

"Maybe," Aideen responded, unconvinced. The

girl appraised the female mercenary for the first time. Hanna was as tall as Hazim, but leanly muscled with olive skin and an aquiline nose that was slightly crooked as if it may have been broken at one time. Aideen touched the clay splint on her own nose wondering if it would be crooked as well. Hana's light brown hair was shoulder length with blonde highlights. She kept it tied back in a warrior fashion braid with two loose strands hanging on each side of her face. A scar on her left cheek marred an otherwise beautiful face. She too favored the back scabbarded hand-and-a-half Pagentian saber. The inner side of each of her studded forearm bracers also carried short daggers with two more protruding from her tall boot tops.

"If it wasn't for your names," Aideen said, "I probably wouldn't know that you are all from Hamaud, although desert people usually stand out. It's probably the clothing. Khaled looks like he's from the desert because of his burnous, but the rest of you look like most any other merc dressed as you are in leather armor." Aideen preferred wearing similar warrior's garb, especially on the road, but she had to content herself with what she was given.

Hana looked at her with one brow raised, and asked, "Where are you going with this?"

Aideen hadn't had much opportunity to chat with anyone for a while, so since she had the chance now she was making up for lost time. "Well," she said. "I didn't see it at first, but if you put a black burnous on Hazim he would look like an older version of Khaled. I wonder if they are related."

Hana looked at Hazim's back again. This time, her eyes narrowed. "That, I did not notice."

When they came to the top of the steep hill Townsend was waiting for them to catch up. Akil was not there, and Aideen assumed he was scouting ahead. The sun was just cracking its first beams from atop the eastern peaks causing steam to rise from the dew coated ground. There were more evergreens at this elevation and the few deciduous trees had lost a goodly number of leaves. The other two mercenaries left behind to break camp caught up with them and continued ahead to have the camp ready when his lordship arrived.

Aideen's stomach knotted. She was not surprised to see Khaled bringing up the rear. As the assassin reached the hilltop Aideen noticed her sword stuck in his belt. "Hey," she said. "That's my sword."

As the assassin neared his lordship, Townsend asked, "Is that true?"

"It is," said Khaled in his scratchy voice. "It is my trophy now."

"Nonsense," replied Townsend. "Trophies are won in battle, not in scraps with little girls."

A few of the sell-swords snickered but hushed when the assassin swept a one-eyed gaze at them.

"Give it to me," Townsend ordered. When Khaled hesitated a full three seconds, his lordship's face reddened. "Now," he barked. The assassin relinquished the sword. Then Townsend said, "Go on ahead and join Akil. Warn us of patrols."

Khaled rode down a short diagonal descent and then up a forested rise where the road cut the side of the next hill rather than going over the top. He was soon lost to view, but his horse's hooves could still be heard when Aideen heard someone mutter, "Akil is going to love that."

There were more snickers, but Townsend ignored them. He tucked the katana in his own belt and to Aideen said, "You can have your sword back when this business is done."

Aideen was provided with a cloak that was too big for her. The air was getting cooler with elevation, so she was grateful for the warmth. However, she was instructed to keep the hood up. With her hands tied she lacked the freedom to adjust it, so it eventually fell forward obscuring most of her view. They occasionally encountered other travelers going in either direction, but each time she was instructed to be silent before they overtook the other party.

Around midday they passed a half dozen Medimian traders leading a pack train of mules, bound for Port Augustus. The men and women of the party nodded politely as they passed them, but Aideen was sure at least one of them noticed her bonds.

After two such incidences, Townsend reined in beside her and said, "I will free your hands if you give me your word you won't try to escape."

Aideen pretended to consider alternatives. The girl spoke up when she could see his lordship's patience slipping. "Oh-kay," she drawled. "I promise not to ride away."

Townsend nodded to Hana before riding back to the front.

"You push your luck, girl," Hana said as she

leaned from her horse and untied Aideen's hands. "I don't know why you've been kidnapped . . ."

"It's because I'm . . ." Aideen interrupted, but Hana cut her off.

"Rich?" Hana spat. "Or the daughter of some rich family?" she queried with contempt. "That's obvious. You are a spoiled little rich kid that thinks she knows everything. Let me tell you something. You being from a wealthy family has nothing to do with it." Hana looked ahead to be sure Townsend was out of earshot.

"But . . ."

"Shut up and listen," hissed Hana. "Bruises like yours are usually worn by those who run their mouth, so take heed. If you interrupt me again I'll backhand the other side of your face."

Aideen flushed. She looked back and saw Hazim and two other soldiers behind him stoically taking it all in. She turned back to Hana with a retort on her lips but the warrior's menacing look stopped her, so she prudently remained silent.

"Lord Townsend is filthy rich," Hana continued. "He has no need to ransom you for money. He wouldn't risk losing his head for something he has an abundance of already. He has a different purpose in mind. I don't know what, and I don't want to know, but the moment he decides you aren't worth the trouble, that assassin will cut your head off and laugh while he does it."

With her hands now free, Aideen pulled her hood back slightly to see better and looked ahead beyond Townsend and the guard beside him. She did not see Khaled, but the pit in her stomach told her he was there just out of sight. She could almost feel the heat of the assassin's hatred coming from around the next corner of the road.

"You got lucky when you marked him, but at the same time, you sealed your doom." Hana's voice lost some of its vehemence. "You can bet asses to camels that when Townsend is done with you, he'll give you to Khaled. Nothing but death can stop a Hamaudi assassin."

The hairs on Aideen's neck bristled. Even though she saw Khaled go farther up the road, she looked behind her and scanned the woods to each side. She had to clamp her teeth tight to hold back the tears.

One of the men behind Hazim spoke softly, but loud enough for Aideen to hear. "I was told this was a simple guard-some-rich-ass-lord job. Nobody said nothin' about kidnapping a girl."

Hazim twisted in his saddle and said, "Mind your words, Jamal. Khaled has uncanny hearing."

The woman fighter next to Jamal said, "Had I known an assassin was part of this I would not have taken the job. Those people scare my bowels empty."

"I'm with Maha," agreed Jamal. "Khaled isn't right in the head. Hamaudi assassins are supposed to be emotionless, but this one storms around like he's looking for heads to lop off."

"Yeah," said Maha. "And I just heard the girl is related to the Murdochs. I was hoping to sign on with that outfit after this job. Murdoch mercs train hard and they're well equipped—elite. If they haven't sent a company of hired killers up this road, they will."

"Enough talk," said Hazim. "Just to ease your mind, we'll have a few reinforcements joining us tonight or tomorrow."

Silence followed Maha's words. Aideen was not reassured. A rescue would be nice, but to be a hostage caught in a battle had its dangers, and then there was Khaled.

She ate her lunch of smoked fish and cheese while the horses drank from a stream. She was still chewing her last bite when they left the creek at a canter. Supper in the saddle was hard tack and water. As the sun painted the bottoms of the scattered clouds scarlet, Aideen started to nod. An hour later the exhausted girl fell asleep in the saddle, head lolling to the rhythm of cautious equine steps.

CHAPTER 6

Seal Bay was Sedar's capital and a major seaport. It was here that the Northern Caravan Route began at the sea and meandered through the mountains of Sedar, across the plains of Northern Hamaud to fertile Medimia, fur-rich Kabeka, and exotic Eastonia. Seal Bay was now a hub of activity as soldiers and sailors, ships and wagons, armorers, engineers, and mercenaries flocked to the city like filings to a magnet. Some came for duty, but most came for the profit they smelled when the impending doom of war settled on the city. A large number of the population had packed up and fled because they feared the essential byproducts of war: rape, pillage, death, and destruction.

News spread like flames through dry grass when King Drayden of Kandia had requested King Bertil of Sedar to grant him permission to bring his armada of warships to his beautiful city of world trade so that he could move armies and supply wagons across Sedar for his campaign in the East. It was a taunt, and everyone knew it, but the Kandian king made it look like he was truly trying to be polite. Drayden's ambassador had delivered the request to Bertil at the council of the western alliance. The ambassador also brought the grisly gift of Jarl Bamsen's salted head in a basket; this inauspicious gift was given to King Thorson of Abezda, who was attending the council. Bertil's reply to Drayden was an adamant denial. Thorson added a message of thanks to Drayden for ridding him of his traitorous cousin.

Michael Ivanovich, more commonly known as Ivan, sat in bored patience as King Bertil of Sedar droned on with his daily rereading of the treaty, as he had for the past few weeks. Mock snores mingled with real ones by the time the rotund king got to the third page. "As agreed by the allied nations of Abezda, Kalusia, and Sedar, hereby forming the Alliance of the Western Kingdoms, should any act or threat of war be imposed upon any of the aforementioned countries by any power, foreign or domestic, the members of this union shall act in concert against …"

"Oh, please spare us," a voice from the assembly called out.

"We've all got it memorized by now," added another voice.

Bertil scanned the crowd, but could not identify the suspicious parties. He put the treaty down and addressed the council. "I'd like to thank the ambassadors from Pagentia for attending."

A delegation of swarthy men and women looking more like tradesmen than nobles stood from a side table, bowed briefly, and sat. Applause echoed in the hall.

Bertil continued, "We would also like to welcome

the magistrate of Renauld Island."

A big, black-bearded man in a full double-breasted red coat, blue scarf, and bright blue pantaloons was sitting with his colorful attendants. He stood, and with a flourish, removed his three-cornered hat and bowed to a mixture of applause and boos. The big man's eyes sparkled with joy. His smiled flashed a gold tooth which matched the ring hanging from his left ear. "We delegates of the haven of … ahem … freebooters, humbly accept yer welcome." He and his party sat and his smile grew with the mutters.

Ivan knew the man, and he was glad his pirate friend took the incriminating remarks as high praise.

"Order," said Bertil. "Order, please." When the voices quieted he continued. "We invited tribal chiefs from Hamaud, but they were unable to attend."

A voice called from somewhere near Ivan. "That's because they're too busy fighting each other to take time out for a war."

The king rubbed his short trimmed bearded chin and looked at the wizard as if he had made the comment.

Bertil cleared his throat and said, "King Drayden claims his campaign is to conquer Kabeka."

"We all know better," said King Gerald of Kalusia. "Kabeka isn't even a nation. It has no government or cities, only small communities."

A thin man wearing the rank of a general of Sedar rose and said, "King Gerald is correct. No one is fooled. Kabeka is a wild land, an unclaimed territory thickly forested and fat with game. Entrepreneurs from Medimia and Eastonia harvest timber and furs from the Kabekan frontier, but there is nothing there to plunder. Drayden's target is Eastonia. He plans to seize the impenetrable crypt of the ancient world near the ruins of Oldeisie. He wants the rumored power."

"Thank you, General Pavel," replied Bertil. He turned and addressed the assembly as a whole. "My brother kings, neighboring ambassadors, and magistrate let us stop this threat here and now. Help me defend my city."

Ivan cleared his throat and got noisily to his feet. His chair scraped across the black and white marble tiles and then fell with a crash from the weight of his heavy oilcloth cloak, which had been hung over the back of the chair. A puddle of rainwater pooled beneath the dripping cloak. Everyone in the hall went silent and turned toward the muttering wizard as he stooped to set aright chair and cloak. His head throbbed when he bent over and he swooned with vertigo as he straightened, silently cursing himself for his previous night's overindulgence. His mood was as sour as the stale wine he could smell on his own breath.

King Bertil raised one dark brow and asked, "You have something to say, Ivan?"

"Oh sit down and drink your coffee, Bertil," snapped the wizard a bit more harshly than he had intended. Ivan ignored the gasps from the courtiers on the sidelines. He continued in a softer tone, "You are saying the same thing over and over, day after day and I agree with you, but the repetition is tiresome." Applause accentuated the wizard's words. The portly monarch blinked twice and sat.

Ivan glared at the dignitaries seated at the high council table. "King Gerald and King Thorson have been hesitant to commit the necessary troops because they are wasting resources chasing after the octagon key." He paused for dramatic effect. "It is a waste of time," he articulated. "The key has slipped back into hiding. It's time to cease such nonsense and deal with the war at hand. Thorson, at least, has his navy and privateers dedicated to patrolling the North Sea, from where the armada will come. And, we can thank Captain Baden and his freebooters from Renauld for harassing Kandian ships." Ivan gave a nod to the magistrate and then sat.

King Thorson stood and ran his thumb and forefinger down each side of the silver streak that parted the center of his long black beard. "My navy is stretched thin and outgunned with its feeble blockade against King Drayden's massive armada. Even with the help of the pirates, the best we can hope to do is harry them with hit and run tactics. The units I sent after Imar Amirson were small and unsuccessful. They were never a sizable enough resource to affect the defense of our sister kingdom of Sedar." The thin northern king sat down.

Captain Baden stood and said, "Please, pirate is such a harsh word. Arg. We are but humble privateers." His face parted with a magnanimous smile as he took his seat.

Gerald stifled a yawn and stretched his lean frame. "We need to find the octagon key, Ivan. Our three kingdoms can't stand against the massive numbers of Kandia. We must seek an advantage, but I see your point. We are indeed out of time. I am beginning to think that our best bet now is to secure the fortress before Drayden gets there. That is his ultimate goal."

"It won't do him any good without the key," Ivan lied. At least, he thought he was lying; he wasn't sure now that the secret of gunpowder was out. Enough explosives will solve nearly any problem. "You should be sending troops to slow him down, if not stop him. As for the key,"

Ivan paused to glare dramatically at the three kings, "it is not for any of you to just take. How long do you think this alliance would last if one of you had it?"

The monarchs glanced uncomfortably at one another and their generals shifted in their seats.

"Precisely," exclaimed the wizard. "Whoever has the key will find their friends become enemies looking to take it. Imar Amirson has had to evade patrols that you have all sent after him. The key is his by right. The octagon key was put into the care of his family for good reason. Leave it alone and deal with this threat before you are overrun. You need to stop Drayden from seizing the fortress." Ivan left out the part about giving Imar time to get to Oldeisie first. "The Kandians must be stopped here. Once Drayden overruns and occupies Sedar and Northern Hamaud he will roll through Medimia and take Eastonia. The Eastonian ruins of Oldeisie were once called the District of Columbia. It was an old world seat of power, now buried by time and continental shifting. There are great secrets there that no one of this age is ready for. If Drayden takes it he will still need the key to enter the control center. However, in time and with the help of my old colleague Sumas, he may find a way in. If that happens, you can kiss your kingdoms goodbye. Whoever holds that underground fortress could, quite probably, rule or destroy the world. I don't mean just this continent, but all the other unexplored lands on this planet as well."

"We need to stop him from taking my city," chimed in Bertil.

Thorson stood again, still fingering his beard. "Ivan is right. Imar seems to have disappeared, and it is doubtful that he is still on the coast, so Gerald's ships could be put to better use. The technology for cannons and muskets has helped us even the odds and the range and accuracy or the new rifles is even better. Our smiths are working around the clock and they have been successful in building working units. We have been supplying soldiers in the field with rifles as fast as they can be produced."

"Thank all the gods," exclaimed Bertil. He refilled his coffee cup from a decanter. "I knew I could count on you, Thorson. How about you, Gerald? We could really use your ships and your army."

Ivan sat down and watched the young, clean shaven king with his light brown hair tied at the nape of his neck. He could see the clicking gears behind Gerald's serious face.

After a few eternal moments, Gerald spoke. "I still want the key. I will keep some men reserved to search for it, but I will send my ships and troops to your aid." He turned to the swarthy middle-aged man to his right whose muscular frame gave him the appearance of a walking tree trunk. "General Jakez, what would you advise for dealing with the Kandian forces marching into the upper plains of Hamaud?"

The military man stood and went to a wall map of the western continent. He pointed to Northern Hamaud and said, "Intelligence reports contingents of Kandian cavalry on the Northern Caravan Route. They are larger and more organized than previously estimated, yet to date, the trade caravans have not been molested." Jakez turned and faced the assembly. "I suspect that the vanguard of Drayden's infantry is still in the mountains of the Kandian wilderness. With winter approaching, the army will have to hunker down in plains. The main threat and three-quarters of the Kandian force will come by sea."

The muttering grew to a roar. One of the Sedaran

sea captains stood to speak, but Jakez signaled him to wait. The captain nodded, and then in a voice accustomed to bellowing orders he shouted, "Quiet people, quiet. The general is not finished. Let him speak." The crowd calmed, but the muttering continued. He stared down the section still talking. When they ceased their chatter the captain sat.

"Thank you, Captain Greldik," said Jakez before addressing the assembly. "Our situation is grim, my lords. Even with the combined might of the alliance, we can only hold out for a while before Seal Bay falls. Nearly all of Kandia has joined the army, making their forces too great." Jakez paused and pointed at Seal Bay on the map. "Drayden needs the port and the Northern Caravan Route to move the bulk of his army and supplies. The troops coming into Hamaud have rough terrain to cover and their supplies will run low if Drayden doesn't take Seal Bay soon. We have already sent cavalry units to welcome them, but if they march west we could be caught between the hammer and the anvil." Jakez turned to a balding man and said, "Captain Sherman, please tell us about our new muskets."

Sherman stood and said, "Not muskets, sir, but rifled bores for greater range and accuracy. Furthermore, thanks to the new percussion cap rifles coming up from Port Augustus, we have a distinct advantage over the enemy. The new rifles are faster to reload and work well in the rain. One of our rifle platoons took an entire enemy company because their obsolete flash pans failed during a downpour. Unfortunately," he added, "it is only a matter of time before some of these new rifles are captured and copied."

"Thank you, Captain," said Jakez. He struck the wall map with a pointer and said, "We have garrisons at Sepur, Nacuscus, and Hashid with mobile forces patrolling the caravan route. Infantry battalions are being deployed as we speak." With the pointer, he began describing enemy and friendly troop locations as well as implemented combat strategies. The other generals, admirals, and captains added to the discussion.

The business of war was finally underway. Ivan sighed with relief knowing he could leave this political mess to go meet with Imar and Dalla in Juana Napur as they had planned. Without bothering to excuse himself, the wizard snuck out.

Outside, Ivan scowled at the morning fog. He descended the wide stone steps and hailed a carriage as he passed the twin stone sea lions standing vigil on either side of the capital's entrance. He paid the driver in advance with some softly spoken instructions before climbing in.

After several streets, the wizard noticed the same horseman that had dogged his steps since coming to Seal Bay. Upon turning into an alley the driver snapped the reins, and the horses bolted down the passage at a break-neck speed. The carriage rounded a corner on outside wheels and then another before suddenly pulling up short on a narrow street of live-in shops. Ivan jumped out before the coach came to a complete stop. The wizard ran into a bookstore as the driver wheeled into the next alley. Through a parted curtain, Ivan watched the horseman race past.

A voice sounded from behind him. "Some things never change. Who did you piss off this time?"

CHAPTER 7

The wizard wheeled around with a grin and strode to the tall grey haired man leaning on a crutch. "Quinlan old friend, it is good to see you." The two men embraced and patted each other's backs. Ivan stepped back and eyed the bookseller's stump where it was amputated below the left knee. "Where's your prosthetic leg?"

"Hah," Quinlan grunted. "The old one got termites, and the straps on the new one make me itch. When it gets a little colder, I'll fasten it over my long under-hose." He raised an eyebrow. "You didn't answer me. Who are you hiding from?"

Ivan glanced briefly at the door and then back at his friend. "I was just shaking a tail. Being followed annoys me, and to top it off I have a headache as well. Who knows, it could be any one of the kings, but I think King Gerald is having me watched." Ivan could see thoughts racing behind Quinlan's hazel eyes, the questions growing exponentially. "Have you got any tea good for a headache?"

The bookseller smiled. "It depends on how drowsy you want to get. I have skullcap and willow bark or poppy tea, which would you like?"

"Skullcap and willow will be fine, thanks. I need to keep my wits."

"Come on back." Quinlan turned and led Ivan to the back of the store where he had a small living quarters attached to the rear of the building. He talked as his crutch thumped on the wooden floor. "We will hear if someone comes in, but it is doubtful anyone will. People are thinking more about fighting or fleeing than about books right now. Besides, I've had most of my good stock hauled out of the city."

Ivan looked around at the sparse shelves. A dozen here and a few there, some books were lying flat for lack of an adjacent support. "Last time I was here, your shelves were packed."

They came to a small table with jars of dried herbs and ground coffee. Ivan sat while Quinlan gathered cups. Taking a steaming kettle from the stove, the bookseller set the pot on the table's ceramic placemat. "I have no intention of handing over my inventory to invaders who would use my books to feed their cook fires." He sat down with a plop across from the wizard. "Help yourself," he said, indicating his selection of teas while preparing coffee for himself in a one-cup dripper.

"You have a few left, maybe the Kandians will read them," Ivan said, as he poured steaming water into his cup over a tea strainer bulging with willow bark and skullcap herb.

"Ha," snorted Quinlan. "The illiterate bastards are

welcome to them. They can read, burn, or wipe their butts with the pages for all I care."

"Have you any honey?"

Quinlan slid an earthen honey jar over to the wizard. "All that's left are a few romance novels about werebeasts and oversexed bloodsuckers. I have already hauled all the good literature out to my homestead in the mountains."

"I take it you're leaving?"

"It seems the sensible thing to do. The first part of a rout is usually complete chaos. Once things settle down I'll come back. If my store hasn't been burned to the ground, I'll chase out any vermin residing here and sell books and coffee to the enemy. I may even learn a few things to pass on to our side."

"Try to remember that they are people too, not much different from anyone else. They have the same needs and concerns as anyone else."

"I know, I know," replied Quinlan, reaching for his wooden leg where it leaned against the corner. He pulled up his bobbed trouser leg and began buckling the prosthetic's leather straps to his stump. "In truth, I intend to spread the seeds of democracy. The people are tired of being under the control of one man's inherited government."

"I have lived under the rule of a democratic republic. They wasted more time and money fighting each other and destroying each other's work. That government was just as controlling as any monarchy I have seen in this world. The only difference is that the elected ruler is on their best behavior at first, but when reelected to the last term, there is no incentive for restraint."

"You're the one that got me started on reform. What are you saying now, that we would be no better off with representation?"

"No, of course not," replied the wizard. "You just have to take steps to prevent your new government from growing into an unstoppable monster or you'll have the same oppression and tyranny that you are subject to with absolutist kings. People will argue. This is especially true of politicians. If they can profit from their arguing they will bleed the treasury dry, wasting time with yammering and oppressive law making. They will keep making laws to justify their own existence and tell you it is for the good of the people. Every law passed is another freedom lost. Political pockets get fat, the people get relieved of their coin, and the nation gets burdened with the chains of government policy."

Ivan made a face as if he had bit into a piece of rotten meat. "Policy," he spat. "From the highest official down to the lowest bureaucrat, they will break out that word to excuse their laziness and incompetence. They'll wave it in your face like a flag of freedom to distract you from their lack of sensible thinking." Ivan realized he was getting wound up. He took him a few seconds to settle down before he continued, "It is important to change all seats in government constantly, right down to the very last bean counter. One public servant allowed to remain beyond a few years will see opportunity and soon claim experience is a reason to advance his or her own position into a career. It is like letting the meat sit out too long— one germ will grow into many and then the meat rots. Next thing you know your supper is crawling with maggots and surrounded by rats, the harbingers of disease. Politicians are no different."

"You know, old friend, we could use someone like you to lead our reformation."

Ivan held up his hands and shook his head. "Oh no, not me, I hate politics and I hate politicians even more. Why would I want to become something I despise?"

"That is precisely why you are perfect for the job."

"Forget it."

The front door to the bookstore opened and closed. Quinlan called out, "Half a moment."

"I am meeting a friend here," said the wizard. "I meant to tell you, but I got sidetracked. Sorry about that."

The bookseller pulled a boot onto his artificial foot and stood up. "No worries," he grinned. "I'm just as guilty. Who are we expecting?"

"My traveling companion; his name is Hawkins." Ivan got up and followed Quinlan out into the bookstore. He didn't fail to notice that his friend walked with a normal gait without any sign of a limp.

A tall man clean-shaven man with short brown hair and trim physique was reading from a selection he had taken down from a wall shelf. He turned when he heard the two men approach. "It seems like nearly every book I pick up anymore is about werewolves."

"You'd be surprised at how many feature horny vampires," replied the bookseller.

"Quinlan, this is Hawkins, first mate on the *Bedford Lee*," Ivan introduced.

Hawkins returned the book to the shelf and stepped forward to clasp hands with the bookseller. The older man took him in a firm forearm grasp commonly used by men-of-war.

The sailor's surprise was not lost on the bookseller. "I did not always sell books for my bread," said Quinlan with a smile. "I used to command a battalion of infantry. After a Kandian arrow cost me my leg, I retired into a business where I could enjoy the smell of book paper and listen to intelligent conversations. It sure beats the insults preceding a battle and the screams that follow. I also find bookstore odor preferable to battlefield stench."

"Many of the king's officers, as well as mercenary captains, seek Quinlan's advice," piped in Ivan. "He has also written books on tactics and strategies." The wizard turned to the old soldier and said, "We could use your help and your counsel now. I need to send a bird with a coded message to Juana Napur, preferably to the Mozar Abibi. We need to get there fast. And ..." Ivan paused and took a breath.

Quinlan shot one eyebrow up. "You might as well spit it out. You already said that you need my help. That rarely ever entails only a few words. Come on, out with it."

Ivan nodded, his expression serious. "We are being watched by the spies of at least one king, maybe more. We need to get out of the city without any of them knowing that we left."

Quinlan's eyes widened. Then his brows lowered, a grin spread across his face, and he began to laugh. Ivan's seriousness melted away and also turned to laughter.

The young man seemed baffled by all this unexpected humor. "What is so funny?"

Ivan and Quinlan laughed harder.

Hawkins looked concerned, almost angry. "What have I gotten myself into?"

Quinlan slapped the seaman on his back. "It'll be fun, you'll love it."

CHAPTER 8

The grey morning was again graced with rain. The precipitation was so light it could almost be called mist, but for the swirling gusts that would slap a body with wetness as if sprayed with a dock hose. The air was cooler and wetter than the previous day. Quinlan hunkered in woolens against the damp chill and rubbed an arthritic knee as he pulled the wagon to a stop at the East Gate. A young soldier stood in the doorway wrapped in an oilskin cloak. He shivered in tiny bursts. In place of a helm, the guard wore a grey woolen watch cap that dripped onto his matching scarf. The sentry glared ruefully at the sky before stepping away from his shelter. His boots splashed in a puddle as he approached the wagon with a face that matched Quinlan's for misery.

"Morning, Stephanos," Quinlan greeted gloomily. He noticed the absence of smoke from the stove pipe. "You should build a fire. You'll catch a cold in this weather if you're not careful."

As if to endorse Quinlan's warning the guard sneezed. "The last shift didn't refill the stack," explained Stephanos. "They were full of lame excuses when we relieved them. I sent Fisk for some firewood."

"Good," replied the old veteran. "A wet duty day will pass faster with a warm fire and a bit of food." Quinlan handed the guard a cloth wrapped bundle that smelled of fresh bread. "I stopped by the bakery for road snacks and thought of you and Fisk standing in the rain."

The young man's eyes lit up. "Thanks, Quinlan," he said, taking the offering and tucking it under his cloak out of the weather. "Is this your last load? It looks almost too big for your team."

"It's more bulk than weight, an easy pull for two horses, and yes, this is my last load. I'll be back when the fighting is done."

"I don't blame you. I've sent my wife and children to my sister's place in the mountains." The guard walked around the wagon inspecting the boxes and bags that the tarp did not cover on the sides. "What's with the extra mounts tied to the tailgate?"

"I bought 'em before the market freeze on livestock. The army has all the horses for the war now, except of course black market mounts, and who can afford that? I have the receipts if you want to see them." Quinlan realized he was holding his breath when Stephanos began opening some boxes. He forced his breathing back to normal and tried to sound cooperative. "Shall I untie the tarp?"

"What's in the big trunks?"

"Books," Quinlan huffed with a small laugh to sound casual.

"No need to untie the load and get your books wet," said Stephanos as he strode to where Quinlan was perched upon the driver's seat. He offered his hand and the two men gripped forearms. "Good journey Quinlan and thanks again for the bread. Have you any advice before you go?"

"Stay alive. You'll do no one any good if you're dead."

The two men looked each other in the eye briefly, and then released grips. Quinlan shook the reins and clucked the horses into a walk.

East Road was also known as the Northern Caravan Route and there was a sizable amount of traffic on it going both to and from the city. It increased as the day progressed.

The rain stopped around midmorning, and small patches of blue sky peeked through the clouds from time to time. The road was in good condition, allowing Quinlan to make good time until he caught up with a battalion of infantry marching east. In order to pass, he would have to wait until some solid ground presented itself beside the road. The old soldier slowed the wagon to a crawl, opting to keep his distance from the army in case the commander decided to appropriate his horses and wagon, papers or not.

Near noon, Quinlan turned off East Road and followed a less used track that was commonly known as Porcupine Path. It was more than a path, and the team kept a steady pace despite the gentle incline as it wound through tall pines and firs. The forest was not dense, and the evergreens were offset with occasional patches of yellowing birches and aspens. Their leaves shimmered in the barely perceptible breeze wafting in from the west.

Another two hours had passed when the old veteran, once sure of solitude, pulled up on the reins and set the brake where the horses could reach a small rivulet that ran across the trail.

Quinlan untied the tarp and pulled his effects off of the two large trunks. He had no sooner lifted the lid when a layer of neatly stacked books rose at an angle and spilled from a thin board to reveal a grumpy wizard scrambling, stiff and cramped, out of the trunk. Ivan wasted no time stepping past his friend and nearly leaping off the back of the wagon. He barely made it to the roadside in time to pee. His relief was accented by a large exhale. Half a minute later Hawkins scrambled faster, if not as cramped, from his trunk and stood beside the wizard, in a similar pose.

"I thought my bladder would burst," complained the wizard. "Couldn't you have found us a place to get out a little sooner?"

Before Quinlan could reply, Hawkins added with more respect, "The air hole helped tremendously, but it was a rather long time to be locked in a trunk. If I had known we would be half a day in a box, I would not have drunk so much coffee this morning."

"The old trickster knew exactly what he was about when he kept our coffee mugs filled at breakfast. Recall his grin when he crammed us in those chests."

"Man up," replied the bookseller with a wry grin. "You're alive, free, and not followed. You two sound like a couple of old women."

Ivan's face was a storm cloud, but to their credit neither he nor Hawkins responded; instead, they turned their attention back to watering the weeds.

Quinlan retied the load and did a final walk around the wagon. "It is not much farther to my house," he said, climbing into the driver's seat. "One of you will have to ride in back unless you want to saddle your mounts."

"I think I'll walk a bit and stretch out the kinks," replied Hawkins.

"Me too," added Ivan, rubbing his lower back with both hands. "Besides, I think I'd like to save the horses. They'll have a hard enough going tomorrow." He looked down the trail, turned back and said, "Our rooms at the inn are paid to the end of the week, but whoever had me followed has probably reported that I did not return yesterday. It's a good bet they are looking for me, despite the personal things we left behind for appearances."

Quinlan nodded, climbed in the driver's seat and started the horses into a walk. It was not long before Hawkins climbed up beside the old veteran. Ivan arranged the baggage into a comfortable seat that soon found him snoring in reclined repose. The sun was resting in the western treetops when the bookseller turned down a barely used track and soon after that another, and then finally up a trail to the left.

Hawkins raised one eyebrow. "Where do all these trails go? They look fairly new."

"They go nowhere. My grandsons made them to confuse strangers." Quinlan chuckled lightly and added, "It gives the bored little brats something to do." His face became serious and the muscles below his eyes tensed. "Before my wife passed away we built this place up here for retirement. When I lost my leg the army gave me the boot; no jest intended. When Kianne took ill our pension went to physicians, and her medicines were exorbitant. I was forced to deal in the black market." Quinlan waved at some gnats and pretended to wipe one from his eye. He took a breath, let it out and said, "Money, medical problems, and the stress of selling smuggled goods was too much for my poor Kianne." The old soldier just stared ahead at the road for a few minutes. "After she passed I jumped into the jug for a while. I lost my house and I was too disreputable at the time to move in with my daughter's family. What money I made fencing stolen goods I spent on drinking and gambling. At the time, Ivan was frequenting the waterfront taverns in Seal Bay. We became drinking buddies. I don't know what he saw in me, but he got me to back off on the booze."

"You're joking, right?" Hawkins said with a sarcastic laugh. "I've spent some time at sea with Ivan, and at the inn in town. I have yet to see him turn down anything with alcohol. One time we were pursued by Kandian warships and had to jettison our cargo, but Ivan wouldn't let the wine or grog be cast overboard."

"He probably spared your captain a mutiny."

Hawkins looked indignant. "The crew of the *Bedford Lee* are disciplined seamen. They would never mutiny."

Quinlan quirked a one-sided grin and ignoring the seaman's remark, he continued, "Once I got the drinking under control, Ivan introduced me to some his pirates friends. Before this, I was dealing with middlemen. They made all the profit while I took all the risks. I started making some real money once I began dealing directly with the pirates."

Hawkins, trying unsuccessfully not to sound judgmental, inquired, "I take it these pirates were not privateers authorized with letters of marque."

The old soldier harrumphed. "Of course not, but they limited their prizes to Kandian vessels, for the most part. Anyway, I began collecting books and before you know it I bought a house. I was tired of renting rooms in noisy inns. Besides, being so close to the ale tap was doing me no good. I needed a quiet place to write as well as a home for my books."

"It's a little more out of view for illegal activities as well."

"Yes, but my neighbors' muttered suspicions got back to me. I needed a front for my illegal activities, so I remodeled my house and made it into a bookstore. In time, my legitimate income equaled my nefarious activities, so I got out of the fencing business, for the most part. When word of the invasion came my son-in-law was ordered to sea. Before he shipped out he asked me to take my daughter and grandsons to the homestead. I was planning to anyway, but I'm glad he asked first." Quinlan chuckled. "I used to think him a moron, but I guess he has more wit than I gave him credit for."

The trail got very steep, then leveled out on a fairly flat topped hill sporting a large clearing with a log house in the center. Just before they left the tree line a young old boy of about twelve years, camouflaged with green and black face paint, spruce twigs, and leafed willow wands, charged out of hiding with a wooden sword brandished high. His battle cry startled the horses, and Hawkins nearly jumped out of his skin. The seaman leaped to his feet then fell back on the wizard who had been feigning sleep.

Quinlan swore as he pulled hard on the reins. As soon as the team stopped and was under control, he got off the wagon and began a mock sword fight with his crutch clashing against the boy's wooden sword. Sword practice ended with grandpa tickling the boy to tears and the kid begging quarter between howls of laughter.

Ivan and Hawkins slid off the wagon and met a woman that stood three steps from the open door of the house. She was medium height, had light reddish brown hair, olive skin and angular green eyes like her father's.

"Hi Ivan," she greeted. "Who is your friend?"

"Hello," said the seaman. "I'm Hawkins."

She shook his hand. "I am Helga and that ridiculous boy rolling in the dirt is Jimmer."

An older boy of fourteen years wearing similar camouflage as Jimmer stepped out of the woods with a bow in hand and a quiver of arrows across his back. He had a rabbit and two grouse tied to his belt. The black and green streaks painted diagonally across his face made his scowl fierce. "You all make too much noise," he grumbled.

Helga took a breath and let it out as the boy stomped toward them. "Aris, Ivan is here, and this is Mister Hawkins."

The boy threw the game down at his mother's feet without stopping as he stormed into the house saying over his shoulder, "I killed them, you can clean them."

Helga's eyes widened and her face flushed red. She opened her mouth to retort, but before she could speak her father shouldered past her into the house and slammed the door behind him. Quinlan's shouting was accented by sounds of overturned furniture followed by a series of thumping. One could easily assume that Quinlan's hand was being vigorously applied to Aris' butt. There was a half-minute of silence, and then some harsh speech from the older man. The door opened and the boy stepped outside. Quinlan was just inside the door tightening the straps on his wooden leg.

Aris rubbed one side of his butt; his face paint was smeared on both cheeks. "Please forgive my rudeness; I've had a hard day."

"Ha," said Quinlan sarcastically, "a hard day hunting and fishing? When other boys are hard at work and drilling for war? Oh please, spare us your excuses and finish your apologies."

Aris went to Hawkins and shook his hand. "I'm pleased to meet you, Mister Hawkins." And to Ivan, he said, "It is good to see you again, sir."

With an impassive face, Ivan nodded. Hawkins thought that the wizard would've beaten the little brat's butt if Quinlan hadn't been as swift to chastise his grandson.

The boy picked up the cony and birds and to his mother said, "Forgive me, Mom. I'll clean these. Will you cook them for us?"

"Of course, I will, my dear," she said, hugging her son.

Aris' face darkened with the affectionate display, but his expression softened when he saw his grandfather's darker scowl searing into him. He broke free and fled around the house to tend to his chores.

Frost coated the morning white before the three mounted travelers departed. Ivan was already having second thoughts about taking a teenager with him. *I should have my head examined*, he thought. Quinlan and Helga stood before the house while Jimmer remained in bed snug in slumber.

The boys had said their goodbyes the night before after Quinlan spent considerable time convincing Ivan to take Aris with him, "to learn some things, or get turned into a toad in the process." Ivan let that implied lie stand uncorrected. If the boy thought the wizard could turn him into a toad then perhaps the sullen youth would behave better for him than he did his mother and grandfather. Besides, who was he to call the boy's grandfather a liar?

Still, Ivan felt like he had been outmaneuvered by his old friend. He sat his horse and looked at the sour-faced boy where he waited on his own mount next to Hawkins. Helga had already hugged and kissed her son several times. Aris was impatient with her, acting like he was in a hurry to go while at the same time being gloomy about leaving.

Ivan leaned over in his saddle and spoke quietly to Aris. "Keep in mind boy, I won't tolerate any disrespect. I don't take grief from men or kings, so I'm not about to take it from you."

"I understand," said Aris.

"You damn well better," said Quinlan. "You will do as Ivan says or …"

"I got it," Aris interrupted impatiently, but the scowls from Ivan and his grandfather encouraged the boy to repeat his words in a more respectful tone.

"I'd be careful if I were you," Hawkins advised softly. "Ivan can be pretty grumpy, especially in the morning. I once saw him turn one of my crewmen into a seagull."

Ivan restrained his grin at the bald-faced lie, but Aris' eyes widened.

"Aris knows the mountain trails," said Quinlan. "He can guide you down to the flatland. You'll know your way after that. It is autumn here, but the desert will still be blazing hot. Good journey, old friend." He reached up and gripped the wizard's forearm.

Ivan noticed how relaxed Quinlan had become. "Thank you for your help," Ivan said aloud. Then in a softer tone that only Quinlan could hear he said, "I *will* get even with you for this."

Quinlan laughed. "I'm sure you will. Take care."

"You too," said Ivan. He turned his horse and the three of them rode down the trail with Aris in the lead.

CHAPTER 9

The *Elbienus Raptor* bounced in the chop of the convective turbulence. Occasional gusts of wind buffeted the craft as it climbed towards the smooth clear air above the clouds. Huge cotton candy-like puff balls of clouds floated all around in every direction, slowly building in size and altitude. As the ship passed the cloud bottoms and maneuvered between the nebulous masses, the air became more stable and smooth. The air was cooler and had a clean quality to it found nowhere near land or on the sea.

Upon reaching the blue endless sky, the ship leveled and dancing across the cloud tops, using only wind for propulsion. Captain Beros bled off some gas, expanding from the increase in altitude, and trimmed the pitch to compensate for the increased lift.

A smaller crew could operate the airship as compared to his seafaring brig the *Coastal Raider*, but the *Elbienus Raptor* required more manipulation of controls from the pilot than that of a seagoing helmsman. Beros glanced at the big oblong gas bag cradled atop the short masts and then barked an order to furl the sails. The sails had been doing a good job running them before the northwest wind, but once he engaged the propeller they'd only act as drag to slow them down. At 2,500 meters above the coastline, he estimated that the winds aloft were pushing them forty kilometers per hour. He hoped to triple that.

The air blew the young captain's wavy red hair forward around his face. Beros swiveled the pilot chair around and looked abaft. With his hair forced out behind his head, he tied it back into a ponytail using a leather ribbon he took from his pocket. He watched the neutral propeller turn idly in the wind, and at the same time took in the beauty of the blue sky as they skimmed across a sea of scattered clouds. Turning back to his controls, he checked his instruments. Heat flow in the solar tubes was good. Pressure tank readings were low but adequate. The temperature gauge for the energy converter was just rising into the green when Beros engaged the drive to the propeller. The thrust following the whir of the spinning prop caused a few exclamations around the deck as unprepared crewmen reached for rails or ratlines to prevent tumbling across the deck. Crewmen in the rigging cast good-natured guffaws at their fellows below. The ship climbed a hundred meters before the captain pushed forward on the yoke and readjusted the pitch to adapt to the increased speed and consequential lift.

Beros stuck a finger under the black patch covering his left orbit and scratched before resuming his hold on the pilot box handrail. He turned to the very tall, dark skinned and colorfully attired man leaning on the starboard rail. "What do you think Gavin; will we ever be able to fly without a lift bag?"

Gavin's long braid swung aft, now that the relative

wind had changed under the power of the propeller. The tall man moved to the pilot station, grabbed a handrail and answered in his deep rhythmic voice, "I think a time will come when we won't need sails or a big bag of hot air hanging over our heads to fly."

"Gas," Beros corrected. "The energy converter creates gas for lift and fuel for the engine. But you are right if we could get more power to the propeller, thrust alone would keep us aloft."

"While we are at it, let us ask for engines that don't break down."

"You know, I think the engine is the key. If we could lighten the ship and build a compact energy converter and a smaller drive motor that could provide enough thrust to overwhelm the weight we'd have it."

Gavin nodded. "Bigger airfoils would help," he said. "Streamlined body and bigger wings would give us more lift, like a bird's."

"Perhaps," replied Beros. He opened a valve, closed another, and fine-tuned adjustments on two other control knobs. "We are now just storing sun power and running on organic decomposition from last night's garbage. Now if we built a smaller ship with lighter wood …"

"This hull is about as thin as we dare, and the *Elbienus Raptor* is so sleek and streamlined I can almost leap from amidship to the quarterdeck. The forecastle is so low the cook has to stoop to prepare our meals."

"Yeah, I heard some complaints about how cramped it is in the fo'c'sle. No, I was thinking of a much smaller ship; one that could haul no more than four people and gear."

"We should draw up some plans," said Gavin. "The Murdochs would probably fund our idea."

The hatch opened from the forward face of the quarterdeck and a middle-aged emerged. The two men looked to where their employer stepped out on the main deck. She stood in the ship's waist and took in the beauty of the horizon as she inhaled the fresh air with obvious pleasure. Beros appraised her fit figure. He was not attracted to her; his likes were for much younger women. It was a liking that all too frequently got him in trouble, but he admired her for her hard earned accomplishments. He knew of no other woman of wealth who would take up arms and personally see to the rescue of her husband.

Akala's hair was tied high on the back of her head. She wore loose, comfortable looking black cotton pants tucked into knee-high black suede boots with daggers sticking out the tops of each. To ward off the cooler air of higher altitude, she wore a thick cotton purple pullover.

"Ahoy there, my lady," Gavin greeted.

Akala turned and waved with a smile, then came up the larboard steps and over to the pilot station. She grabbed the portside handrail on the pilot's console. "Good morning, gentlemen."

"It's good to see you up topside," replied Beros.

"It's smooth now. You know how much I hate turbulence."

"It was a bit choppy down in the heat," Gavin agreed.

"How long before we come to Port Equanos?" Akala inquired.

"If this wind holds, we should arrive near sunset," answered Beros. "We passed landfall before sunrise, and we're about halfway to the city. I'd guess about 450 clicks to go. How do you want to set down, by water or land?"

"The locals are friendly to traders, but the sight of an airship will certainly stir up a lot of curiosity. We're the ones asking questions, and I'd prefer to keep a low profile. None of our other ships have turned up any information on Travin. It's as if his ship went down without news or a trace."

"Perhaps we should set down somewhere outside of town," suggested Gavin. "We could spread out and ask questions in different quarters. We can blend in as common seamen if they don't know about the airship. I could take Jon with me; the little thief was quite useful at Valekrie."

"That's a good idea, I like it," agreed Akala.

"I'd like to go with you to the shipping agent," said Beros.

"Is there anyone else that knows how to fly the ship?" Akala inquired.

"Watkins is capable. I'll be leaving him in charge."

"Okay then, I'll have Coulig, Jax, and Brin check the local jails. That should cover our bases. I hope we get some information in Port Equanos. The Anderan continent is 7,000 kilometers long. That's a lot of country to cover."

"Yeah, and it's only 700 clicks at the widest point," added Beros. "It is basically a mountain range sticking out of the ocean."

Akala looked at him. "You've been down this way before?"

Beros nodded, but Gavin answered, "Remember when the *Sea Spray* was taken by pirates, and the crew sold to Argenian slavers?"

"Oh yes," she said. "So you guys were on that mission. Excellent, you'll know the seas and some of the ports."

"The *Coastal Raider* came here with the *Avenger*," continued Gavin. "Travin bought the crew their freedom, at least, those that survived, but we had good information, so we knew where to find them. The archipelagos east of Anderan Range are vast."

"We never recovered the ship," added Beros. "There are millions of islands in the archipelagos. If nothing turns up in Port Equanos, we'd do well to start with the bigger islands first. That's where the largest plantations are. That's if he has been thrown into slavery."

"I don't know what else it could be down here," Akala replied thoughtfully. "Slavery is considered distasteful in the more civilized and more populous places, but many of the colonists think of it as a necessary evil. They claim that shipping costs to the populated North prevents them from competitive prices if they have to pay wages. The plantations are structured around slavery."

"I wouldn't rule out Bovilla," said Gavin. "It's near Argen. That area is full of mines which are also worked by slave labor. It could take a while to cover that much territory."

"Whatever it takes," Akala stated flatly. "We'll comb every island if we have to."

Beros knew better than to suggest the possibility that Captain Travin might be dead.

CHAPTER 10

The *Elbienus Raptor* landed five kilometers north of Port Equanos shortly after sunset. Akala waited while Captain Beros set the ship to float against taut lines. The airship was secured to the trees circling a clearing barely large enough to fit the craft. The shallow keel rested three meters above the ground. A watch was set and the power converter was left on in case a rapid departure might be needed. Rope ladders were hauled up once the away teams had departed on foot to the city.

Jax and Brin stood by Coulig as Akala addressed them. "Go to any possible slaveholding areas first. Then check the jails, and find out if they have a prison here."

Coulig nodded curtly and asked, "What's our rally time?"

Akala turned to Beros. "You've been here before. What time should we rally back here?"

"Because of the heat," said Beros, "business is done mornings and evenings. Anyone caught out after midnight is suspect, and probably up to no good."

"Okay then," said Akala. "We all meet here no later than midnight. If you're late, go due west to the beach. That'll be rally point two. Anyone late and not there by two in the morning gets left till tomorrow night—same rally points, same times."

Akala noticed that Gavin and Jon carried only knives on their belts. "No swords?" she asked.

"Lady," said Jon, "we're going to visit taverns. Swords might be frowned upon, and we don't want to appear too intimidating. We hope to charm information from the locals with friendliness and our generosity at the bar."

Akala was about to protest when Gavin patted his loose linen shirt and said, "We have pistols, my lady."

She nodded her approval, rested one hand on her own pistol and the other on her rapier, and said, "Okay, let's go."

They headed out together. The three groups split up when they reached the town's edge. In one of Travin's letters, he had given Akala directions to Egan's Shipping Agency & Consulting, owned by Jade Egan. Akala and Beros followed the waterfront boardwalk after leaving Gavin and Jon at the first pub they came to. They found Egan's office on a back street from the marina.

Upon entering, they found a portly man of middle years perusing a stack of papers and taking notes. There was a nearly naked and oiled slave girl on each side of the sweating man slowly working a feathered fan. It had been some years since Akala had been to sea, but she had prepared herself for diverse customs. However, seeing girls barely into puberty exploited in this fashion automatically put her on the defensive.

Beros had traveled the world more recently, and his tastes ran only slightly higher, but Akala noticed him scowling in distaste at the shackle each girl wore on the ankle. They weren't chained, but the skin around the metal was heavily calloused. Beros spoke first, "Mister Egan?"

"I'll be with you in a moment," said the man brusquely without looking up. He had thinning black hair and a bulbous nose splotched with broken capillaries. His linen tunic clung to his bulk with patches of odorous sweat. He wore a large gold nugget ring that stood out ostentatiously when he stopped once to sharpen his quill pen before dipping it again in the inkwell. Black ink-stained the thumb and two fingers of his right hand. Yellow heat lamps shined overhead, giving him a jaundiced pallor.

Akala ground her teeth but waited impatiently. After two more eternal minutes, he finally put the stack aside, tossed the stub of his feather pen in a wastebasket and said, "I'm Egan. What can I do for you?" He appraised their attire. "If you're looking for work on a ship, see my clerk next door. I only deal with ship owners and captains."

"I'm captain of the…"

"I'm part owner of Murdoch Shipping and Free Companies," Akala said before Beros let out a ship name. She wasn't sure why, but she didn't want either the *Coastal Raider* or the *Elbienus Raptor* mentioned by name.

Egan looked at her in surprise. His right eyelid began to twitch. "This is about the *Avenger*?"

"Yes," she answered. "I am Akala Murdoch. I'm looking for my husband."

Egan looked her up and down without meeting her eyes. "You're wasting your time here. I don't know where he is. I advised Captain Travin to go south for seal oil and skins, but he was adamant about obtaining produce. I told your other captains this already. I sent numerous birds as well." He licked his lips as his eyes roamed her body again.

Akala felt her skin crawl. She wished she would have worn something over the loose sleeveless top that she had chosen for the heat and this gods-awful humidity if only to deprive Egan of his lascivious stares. "You still have not told me where he went."

"He may have fallen prey to pirates," said Egan. "There's no navy to speak of in these waters. Half the ships down here have taken a bark or two between working honest loads."

"We know," said Akala. "One of our ships, the *Raven's Glory*, had to dump her load in order to outrun slavers."

"Slavers," exclaimed Egan, his eyes fixed on her shoulder. "I've heard of slavers taking ships, it does happen, but they rarely attack battle ready merchant marines. They usually raid primitive and poorly armed villages in the archipelago."

"Do you deal in slaves?" Beros asked.

"Of course not," Egan replied indignantly. He noticed the pistols in their belts and stared curiously at them. "Slavery is frowned on in Port Equanos though there are other ports that are less scrupulous." He shifted his gaze to Akala's neck. "Captain Travin spoke of doing business, but he never retained my services. I gave him the name of a plantation on Venzejos and told him if he procured a load there he could send me my commission, but I don't know if that is where he went." Egan's eyes occasionally darted to Akala's breasts, but he never looked her nor Beros in the eye. "The *Avenger* departed on a moonless night. No one could discern for sure which way they went."

"That's a load of crap," exclaimed Beros. "No experienced seaman in his right mind would try to navigate this channel in the dark."

"I didn't see it myself," replied the agent nervously. "I'm just relaying the reports from the harbor."

"It's your job to arrange cargo," said Beros. "He chose your agency to expedite a load of fruits and vegetables. To which plantation on Venzejos did you send him?"

"I didn't send him anywhere," Egan said exasperatedly. "I only suggested he go there, but you might try Vasquez. As I said, Travin didn't retain me."

"You lie!" Akala's voice grew louder. "Travin's last letter said he paid you thirty Kalusian gold sovereigns as a deposit on a shipload of produce." She drew her rapier and put the point to his throat, causing the slave girls to drop their fans and run shrieking out the back door. "You've been lying to us all along. It's time to come clean. What have you done with my husband?"

Beros sighed. "I knew your patience wouldn't last much longer," he said to Akala. His cutlass whisked from its scabbard and he drew one of his pistols from his belt, cocking it with an audible click. "I think we might want to get going. Those shrieking girls will bring backup."

"Now," said Akala in a low deadly tone. Her sword point caused a trickle of blood to run down a fold of fat in Egan's neck. "Where's my husband and his crew?"

Egan squirmed, scooting his chair back against the wall. He looked from side to side, licking his lips, still avoiding her eyes. "I told you, I don't know."

"Look at me," shouted Akala sharply.

Egan's eyes snapped to Akala's fiery glare for the first time. The sound of trickling liquid tinkled beneath his chair. A moment later the acrid smell of urine assailed their nostrils.

"Lady," Beros grinned with scrunched brows, "you made him piss his pants."

Akala was not amused. She growled at the agent through gritted teeth. "I'm going to start cutting off pieces if you don't start talking."

Egan stammered, trying to become one with the wall. "I told you everything I know."

"Where on Venzejos is Vasquez? Is it a port?" She got no reply because the back door burst open, and two men stormed in brandishing short swords.

Beros shot the one in front, felling him back against the other man. The boom of the pistol startled them. Two more men pushed past their tangled fellows and came in swinging blades. Akala parried and slashed one across the face. He jumped back and stumbled over the desk, colliding with Egan and causing them both to crash to the floor. Yells down the hall meant more were coming. She lunged with a thrust, smoothly running the next man through before dancing back into a defensive stance. Akala's sword reflected crimson in the yellow light and her eyes lit with adrenaline as if she hungered for another opponent. The man stood still a moment and then crumpled to the floor.

Beros opened the front door as he slashed the next attacker back. "C'mon Lady, let's get out of here."

Akala made one last defensive slash before running past Beros out into the night before Egan's men could regroup. Together they ran north up the street as four more brutes boiled out of the shipping agent's office. Egan's shouts to "Get them!" rang into the night as Akala and Beros tried to outdistance their pursuers. They turned right down one street and left down another, but Akala was getting winded. She had not had to run like this in many years, not since her and Travin had been buccaneers. Age and living the easy life for the past decade as an aristocrat were taking its toll on her now. She began to slow, so Beros matched her pace, but Egan's thugs were catching up.

"Stop," cried Beros. "Draw your weapon and shoot." He halted and drew his remaining pistol.

Together they took aim, and when the men were within five to six meters, they fired—boom, boom, one after the other. Akala's bullet took a man in the chest—he hit the ground, face down with a thud. Beros' ball smashed another man in the ribcage on the right—he fell and rolled gasping. The other two men stopped in their tracks, obviously wary of these weapons that spouted fire and death.

Akala was gasping from her run and wishing she would have brought another pistol. She flipped the spent gun in her left hand, aware of the barrel's warmth as she gripped it like a club. Beros did the same. They each stepped a pace apart and waited.

A lone street lamp lit the men's unshaven faces. Both adversaries were a good head higher than Beros, and, at least, twenty kilos heavier. Their sleeveless tunics were dirty and patched. Akala's breath began to come easier until she caught a whiff of their unwashed bodies from only four meters away. The mixture of body odor and urine was so strong Akala wondered how they could stand their own stench.

One of the men said to his partner, "Those...things...whatever they are, must be good for only one shot."

The second man nodded, and replied, "A one-eyed man and a woman ain't much threat now. We should get a good price for him even with the patch, but she's a bit on the old side."

"Naw," said the first man. "She looks pretty fit. I bet she still has it where it counts."

Akala fumed, but she contained it, working out possible moves in her head. She heard Beros take a sliding step, so she whispered only loud enough for him to hear without taking her eyes off the enemy. "Wait for it. They're just baiting us."

"Tell ya what," said the second man to the first. "We'll try her out first, and adjust our starting price with the slave master accordingly." Then to Beros and Akala he said, "Drop your weapons and we won't kill you." When neither of them responded, he added, "How 'bout it. Better a live slave than dead in the street." Both men's faces split into yellowed, gap-toothed grins.

"I'm afraid you two will be the dead ones here shortly," Beros said in a low tone.

"I'd like to question one of them first," Akala said conversationally. "You can kill them after I feed them their own testicles."

That was too much for them. The two men roared and charged with swords held two-handed, high overhead.

Akala's mind raced as time slowed. It was the move of amateurs to attack like that without armor—it left the vitals wide open. *Fools*, she thought, as she stepped forward and bent her knee with a ballerina's grace. She thrust her slender blade before her. The tip entered two fingers below the man's sternum and slid upwards through his heart as he ran onto her steel up to the basket hilt. The flat blade exited out his back between spine and scapula. It happened so fast he didn't have a chance to bring his heavy sword down. The man stopped and looked bewildered as his blade fell from slack fingers—it clattered on the cobblestone paving behind him. He looked at her, bloody spittle forming in the corners of his mouth; his hands came down and pressed against the wound around her slender blade. Akala gave the blade a quarter turn twist, causing the man's eyes to flick wider before they glazed. The brute fell over sideways like a falling tree, sliding off her sword, as she straightened her stance.

Akala looked over at the body at Beros' feet. The bloody neck was hacked halfway through, spouting arterial blood rapidly, but the pulsations lost strength with each pump. "So much for getting answers out of this lot," she said regretfully. She bent over her victim and wiped off her blade on his shirt.

"That one's still alive," replied Beros, pointing with his bloody cutlass.

Akala went to the man that Beros had shot and knelt by him. The scarlet froth at the man's mouth and the bubbling sound coming from the hole in his thorax made it obvious that he had a sucking chest wound. Akala estimated the man's lifespan in seconds. "Where is the *Avenger*?" she asked the dying man urgently. "Where is Travin Murdoch?"

The man squeezed his eyes shut and pulled his lips back, exposing bloody teeth. He whispered something inaudible. Akala leaned over him and turned her head to better hear his words. "What did you say?"

One word and one word only escaped his lips. She could barely hear him when he rasped, "Dragon." He shuddered once and went still.

CHAPTER 11

Beros' silhouette worked through the thick foliage to find a way back to the airship. Akala stayed close behind him so that she would not walk into unseen spider webs. She hated even the smallest arachnids, and the tropical spiders she had seen so far were the size of small dogs. Beros stopped with a raised fist, and they both held their breath to listen for pursuit. They heard none. Akala let out her breath and said in a whisper, "I don't know how you can find your way in this jungle. Why don't you use the path we cut earlier?"

"I would if I could find it," answered Beros. "It's darker now. That trail we made could be a meter to our left or right for all I know." Beros began leading her deeper into the trees. "Come, it can't be much further."

There was no way to be quiet pushing plants aside and stepping on twigs. They were soon able to make out the blue glow of heat lamps off to their left. Beros adjusted his course to move in that direction with Akala occasionally stepping on his heels. The audible snick of a rifle being cocked caused them both to freeze. "Who goes there?" The soft challenge came from the direction of the blue glow.

"Two for a flight," Beros answered with the password.

"Come ahead, Captain," replied the sentry.

Akala stepped into the dimly lit clearing with relief and made her way to the rope ladder that dropped over the side of the ship. Ascending, she asked, "Have the others returned?"

"Not yet, Lady," replied the crewman holding a rifle at the rail. He extended his arm, and she took it.

"Do you know the time?" Akala swung a leg over the rail and climbed on deck. She made way for Beros, who was right behind her.

The crewman called to the watch on the quarterdeck, "Watkins, what time is it?"

"A quarter past the ninth hour," replied Watkins.

Beros addressed the crewman at the rail, "Ziggy, arm the watch with rifles and blades. Ready the ship for liftoff, but do it quietly. We leave as soon as the away teams return."

"Aye Captain," Ziggy saluted. "Are we expecting trouble?"

"Maybe," answered Beros. "Lady Akala shot one of Egan's men. I lost track of how many she stabbed with that skinny sword."

Ziggy's eyes widened and Akala's face flushed.

"Lively now man, let's be ready," said Beros.

"Aye, aye, Captain," Ziggy repeated. He scrambled off to arm the watch.

Beros went to the pilot station and relieved Watkins at the controls. Akala was pacing amidships by the rail. It impressed her to see the watch armed, rifles charged, and at their stations in less than three minutes.

Ziggy returned to Akala's side at the rail and asked, "Did you really slay the agent's men? I thought you wore that sword to look tough."

"I only stabbed two," Akala replied. "Captain Beros took down more. He was right to carry two pistols."

"How'd the guns do in a fight?"

"The man I shot dropped like a sack of rocks. The one your captain shot inside Egan's office liked to deafen me and the smoke was thick."

They started at the sound of bantering voices intermingled with swearing. Akala could easily make out Gavin's deep voice.

Ziggy pointed his rifle into the woods and called, "Who goes there?"

"Go shove off and let us up," Jon's voice shot back with a slur.

The two men stepped into the clearing as Gavin replied, "Two to fly, or some crap or the other like that." His foot hooked on a vine and he fell on his face.

Jon turned away from Gavin and freed himself for

a pee.

"Lady Akala is at the rail, you oaf," Ziggy called down.

"Oops," said Jon. He turned his back to the ship and urinated on a tree.

"Asshole," Gavin said to Jon as he got to his feet. He struggled his way up the rope ladder and rolled onto the deck. "Hi Akala," he said cheerfully from his supine position, omitting his usual formality.

Akala could sense they were struggling with trying to maintain a level of sobriety. She understood the difficulty with getting drinking people to talk to strangers if they didn't indulge in shared libations. Information on everything was passed around in the taverns and few other places with as much vigor. Jobs for dockworkers to deckhands, merchants to sea captains, it was learned about, picked up, had, given, bribed or shared, at the pub.

She also understood the risks that Jon and Gavin were taking as well. The nightlife of any seafaring community had its dangers, but the risk of escaping a dangerous confrontation grew with intoxication. Besides the thieves and slavers, undermanned vessels would sometimes employ press gangs. Their favorite target: intoxicated seamen. More than a few seafarers have awakened the worse for wear on a strange ship and found themselves working with a strange crew.

"You guys look like you had a busy night," Akala said as Jon climbed aboard. "Did you learn anything?"

Jon gave Gavin an arm up. The big man stumbled, but Jon steadied him and kept him from falling. He blinked and replied with a slur, "Some, but not mush." He blinked again slowly as if concentrating, and then slowly repeated with more clarity, "Some, but not much. Excuse me, but their beer tasted like pig piss, so we switched to rum, wish...which was quite excellent."

"Perhaps we should wait until Coulig gets back to share your report," Akala said patiently. "Why don't you two go get some sleep? I'll have someone rouse you when they return."

"Aye, Lady," replied Jon. He helped Gavin towards the gangway that led down to the crew deck. Gavin started to sing out of tune as he swayed.

When Coulig, Jax, and Brin failed to arrive by midnight, Beros maneuvered the ship over the treetops to the second rally point on the beach. Though the night was dark there were plenty of city lights for local navigation.

This time, Akala asked Beros not to anchor, so he landed directly on the strand and stayed at the controls. At an hour and a half past midnight the last away party stepped silently out of the trees but stayed in the shadows.

"Ahoy the ship," a voice called out with moderated volume.

Akala and Ziggy were amidships. Ziggy had a rifle trained on the trees. "Who goes there?"

"Three for a flight," replied the voice.

"About damn time," said Ziggy. "C'mon, another half hour we would've left ya."

One figure ran to the ship. As soon as he began climbing aboard the next man came, and so on. In less than two minutes they were up and away. They went north for an hour, following the coastline, flying forty meters above the sea.

Akala stood by Beros at the pilot station. "How can you see when it's this dark?"

"I can't," replied Beros. "That's why I'm flying so slow. You see that white strand of beach there just off the starboard bow?" He pointed.

Akala peered ahead to the right. Out of the darkness, she could see the faint outline of a narrow spit sticking out into the sea. "Yes, barely," she said. "We're passing it now."

Beros turned over a sandglass timer and turned the tiller five points to port. "I saw an island on our way down. We should come on it before the glass runs out."

Akala remembered the island. When they had passed it she had noticed that it was wooded, which meant it had water. "Good choice," she said.

As predicted, the sand was only two-thirds drained when a topman perched in the rigging called, "Island ho."

"Where away?" asked Beros.

"Ten points to larboard," answered the topman, pointing with a white-sleeved arm.

Beros swung the bow to the island. "Prepare to heave to."

The island was small and uninhabited. Beros flew back and forth until they found a clearing in which to land that would keep the *Elbienus Raptor* unseen from the sea. Once the ship was secure and sentries set, Akala decided to wait till morning to debrief the away teams. She was sure Gavin and Jon would be difficult to wake anyway, and she was sure they had not slept off enough of their drink to provide intelligent or coherent information. Alas. Another drawback to this form of intelligence gathering—those guys will pay for it later.

Dawn came much too early. By orders of Captain Beros, except for the usual watch, all away teams were to sleep-in. Beros wanted the crew rested and fed before debriefing. Akala was anxious, but she did not argue. Travin had been on the forefront of her thoughts until the dim dawn light came through her stateroom porthole. She only got about three hours of sleep.

Akala figured that she was the last to get up with the least amount of sleep. When she came out on the main deck she was slapped in the face with unbelievable humidity. The heat was far greater than she had expected, but it was bearable, if barely. There was no wind. Vines hung from huge trees, and the ground foliage towered above the ship's rails. Visibility into the jungle was no more than a few meters. Birds sang and flew from branch to branch. Lone leaves fell every minute or so, making light clicking noises as they glanced off limbs on their downward spiral to the ground. Small animals of undetermined identity scurried and skittered in the undergrowth.

Gavin was at the bow seeing off a team of five men and two women who were deployed to haul water. He came aft and stopped when he saw her wide eyes. He seemed a little unsteady and he still smelled like a distillery. Concern filled his face. "What is it?"

"What is that?" Akala breathed, pointing to a spot in the trees a few meters above the starboard outrigger.

Gavin leaned forward and peered at it. "Oh that," he said, straightening with a laugh. "I think it's just a large variety of banana spider."

"What?" exclaimed Akala. "Do they grow hundred kilo bananas down here?"

As they watched, some dark species of bird, half the size of a pigeon, flew into the web. It struggled, effectively snared. In the space of a few heartbeats, the five-kilo spider stung the bird repeatedly and wrapped it in a webbed coffin. Akala left the deck and went below with expeditious efficiency. Gavin joined her moments later in the officer's mess. She had no appetite, but she forced herself to eat some fruit and yogurt. The previous night's away teams breakfasted together while they debriefed.

Beros sat at the head of the table and told of his adventure with their employer. None of these men had sailed with Akala in her younger adventuring days, so they were quite astonished to hear of her skill and fierce prowess in the fight. Beros embellished the tale somewhat, as is expected, but his crew knew he told the truth about the basics of the battle.

The crew no longer thought of her basket hilt rapier as just-for-show. From here on she would have to give her all to maintain their respect. Oh, how she missed her garden. Once word got out to the rest of the crew they would all look on her with admiration. Well, there were certainly worse outcomes.

Akala blushed, but she turned to Gavin and Jon. "What did you two learn," she asked, "anything good?"

The tall quartermaster straightened and gripped the table with closed eyes. His breakfast sat before him untouched. Sweat beaded his forehead and he looked as pale as his brown skin would allow. He opened his eyes, unclenched his jaws, and started to speak, but his away team partner saved him.

"We visited four different seaside taverns, my Lady," replied Jon.

Relief mingled with misery on Gavin's face as he slouched back in his chair and massaged his temples.

Jon was normally an energetic young man, but today he spoke slower and softer than normal, and his eyes squinted as if the light from the orange heat lamps was too bright for him. His sandy hair was still wet from washing and his bloodshot eyes were puffy as if he had had too much sleep. Even so, the diminutive man spoke with forced enthusiasm. "The news is mixed with sailors' superstitions."

"He's right, my Lady." Gavin's deep voice rumbled its assent. He started to add more, but stopped and pressed his lips tightly together instead.

Jon took the cue and continued. "Many a drunken tale tells of dragons carrying off whole ships to an island in the archipelago where they feed sailors to their spawn. Some say it is no island but a place on the Bovillan Peninsula."

"Dragons," hissed Beros. "One of the men I shot spoke of a dragon."

Akala looked at them. "Dragon…" she paused thoughtfully. "That's what Egan's thug said before he died or it's what we thought he said. He may have been referring to Argen Island. The names sound alike. Argen is separated from the Bovillan Peninsula by a narrow channel. It could be a dialectal error. That's probably why there are wild tales of dragons. There are no dragons, only

Argens, and Argenian slavers. I bet he is on Argen or in the vicinity." Her eyes burned with interest. "Go on Jon," she said. "What else did you hear?"

"Well, besides the increasing number of missing ships," continued Jon with increasing momentum, "there have been vessels frequently arriving in Port Equanos that have been refitted and wearing fresh paint—they sell quickly. One of the brokers is Egan's Shipping & Consulting."

Beros slammed a fist on the table and said, "That son of a bitch."

The muscles around Akala's eyes tightened. "We still have no proof." She turned to Jon and said, "Continue."

Jon nodded. "There have also been a few slave ships spotted in the area, their stench is unmistakable, but none come to Port Equanos. Slaver crews avoid this city. There are too many here that carry the scars of the whip and shackle. It is said that slave traders sometimes come here in a clean sloop disguised as merchant marines to arrange the sale of their live cargo, but every now and then one is recognized by a former slave and either killed outright or tied to a pier at low tide."

Akala began to have a sick sinking feeling in the pit of her stomach. "From whence do they come?"

"No one knows for sure," said Gavin.

"No one admits knowing," Jon corrected. "By the routes of the missing ships, I would say north is our best bet, and perhaps east around the cape to the archipelago."

"I understand going north if that is where ships have been disappearing," Beros said slowly, "but why the

Brian K Kerley

archipelago?"

"That's easy," Jon answered quickly. "There are mines in the islands. Most of them have gold, and the bigger ones are farmed. Few kingdoms mean fewer laws and any lawless region or unjust kingdom will use slave labor. The only time it doesn't is when there is a high population of former slaves. Those kinds of men will fight slavery with brutal passion when they see it. Many a drunken sailor with scars on his wrists and neck said they would never take a berth on a ship bound for the Eastern Islands. The fear of being taken as a slave again is too much of a nightmare for them." Jon paused. "That's all I can think of unless Gavin has anything to add."

"No," the big man responded miserably. "I think you about covered it."

Akala turned to the stocky mercenary captain. "What did you learn, Coulig?"

Coulig's brown hair was neatly braided and his goatee freshly trimmed. During Jon's discourse, the veteran had been engaged in a hearty attack on his second plate of scrambled eggs and potatoes. He scooped the last three bites into his mouth, applied a cursory chewing, and gulped down the mass. With a last longing look at the sausages still on his plate, he said, "We found a few jails. The jailers weren't real talkative at first."

Akala could not help but recall the poor fare aboard ships. Her and Travin ate well aboard their ship and consequently had sailors at every port wanting to sign on. This tradition continued on in their fleet. Coulig's armor was beginning to look snug on him.

"Yes," said Brin. The young man with the short dark hair looked alert but in need of a shave. "But once we bribed them, you'd of thought them our best buddies."

"The jails are mainly drunk tanks for sailors that get too rowdy," continued Coulig. "If a tavern or inn owner needs to lock someone up till they sober up they can pay for a locked cell for only one night. The fee is about half the price of a seedy inn. A stone and steel bar cell, some straw, a blanket, and a bucket to pee in are better than a berth on some ships. It only lacks bad food, hard work, and low pay. Sailors a long time between ships sometimes rent a cell to save money."

"It was a dead end," said the lean man called Jax. He too had a three or four days stubble, but his light brown hair was barely long enough to tie back in a rabbit tail. "We asked each jailor about slave pens, and they usually became irate. At one jail the keeper reached for a club, but thought better of it since we were all armed with short swords." Jax grinned. "A few asked about our pistols. We didn't tell them anything, but I'm betting word is out by now." He looked at Akala and Beros. "Anyway, it's like Jon and Gavin said, slavery is despised by all but a few locals who keep their clandestine operations secret.

Akala's brows furrowed. "What do you mean?"

"There are no slave pens," Coulig resumed. "But they have a small prison. It was built and abandoned by the Kalusian navy when it got too expensive to maintain a garrison and a prison. The people we talked to said it hasn't been used for years. We learned different."

"Where is this prison?" asked Beros.

"It's about three clicks south of town," answered Coulig. "It sits against a high bluff and has a dock deep enough for longboats. We went there to investigate and found signs of recent use."

"What sort of signs?" asked Gavin. He was starting to pick at his cold breakfast.

"We found a dirty pot that had old gruel in it," replied Brin.

"That could have been there awhile," Gavin responded.

"I don't think so," said Brin. "There was no mold and it was full of ants. This place is so humid my tunics are getting musty in my duffel. Not only that," he paused with a disgusted look on his face, "there were rats. There were so many rats that I bet if we went back the pot would be clean."

"It was a pretty modern prison as prisons go," said Jax. "It's Kalusian built with an aqua duct sewer system. Somebody went to a lot of trouble to open the valves to make it fully operational, but there's more." He turned to Coulig and said, "Show 'em what you found in the guard's lockers, Captain."

Coulig was still chewing the last of his sausage when he stood up. He removed a long stag handled knife in a tooled leather sheath from under his tunic and passed it to Akala.

Akala gasped as she took the blade. "That's Travin's," she said. "I gave it to him for his fiftieth birthday." She pulled the fighting knife from the sheath, exposing a single edged blade twenty-five centimeters long. On the ricasso, just above the hilt guard on each side of the bladesmith's mark were the initials: T-M.

A tear from one eye tracked down Akala's face. Another began to form in her other eye. She put the knife and sheath down and dabbed at her eyes with her napkin. When she brought her hands down, her grief was replaced by a look of angry determination. She stood, and everyone at the table also stood. Akala carefully put the knifepoint in the sheath and then slammed it home.

In a low deadly tone, Akala said, "I'd like to go back to Port Equanos. I have a few more questions for Mister Egan."

CHAPTER 12

Egan put his papers aside. He had made the foreman fidget long enough. Looking at a spot on the wall beyond the man's shoulder, he said, "Mister Snakenose…"

"It's Snakehead, sir," corrected the foreman.

"Snakenose, Snakehead, whatever," replied Egan. "I trust you have come to tell me you have seized their ship?"

"Ah, no, sir," said Snakehead. He pulled off his headscarf and began wringing it in his hands. "I sent two sloops to block the channel last night just like you ordered, Mister Egan, but they aren't in the bay. In fact, they're nowhere to be found."

Egan slid his notebook over and began scribbling nonsense in order to look busy. Without looking up, he said, "They have to be somewhere, Mister Snakehead. They were dressed like sailors, and I have no doubt that they are indeed who they claim to be. The only way they could have gotten here is by ship." Eagan scratched at the velvet patch covering the wound Akala's sword had given him the night before. "I expect results, Mister Snakehead. Do you hear me? Results! They jeopardize my enterprise, and by doing so, they jeopardize your...ah...livelihood," he said, emphasizing the last word so pleasantly that there was no mistaking the implied threat.

"Y-yes sir, of c-course sir," stammered the foreman. With an obvious effort, he stilled the quaking in his voice. "But sir, they couldn't have slipped out before we blocked the channel. Just to be sure, before dawn this morning, I sent out two fast sloops, one north, and the other south. Both ships sent back birds, just arrived this hour, with no news of ships other than your own slave galley, the *Screaming Banshee*. She was spotted up north, bound for the horn on a slow tack."

"So," said Egan. "If they aren't up or down the coast, and they aren't in the harbor, where are they?" Egan shifted his gaze to the man's collar. "Let me remind you that your promotion last night came when the previous foreman failed to personally oversee the pursuit of Akala Murdoch and Captain Beros."

"But, sir..."

Egan waved him to silence. "I know, he was injured, but a facial laceration is hardly enough to hinder his duties." Egan's attempt to appear stern made his pudgy face look comical. "He failed me, Mister Snakehead. He should have gone after them."

"Excuse me sir, but if I could speak with Foreman Wiggins he might be able to share some useful information."

"Good idea," Egan nodded. "I had him clapped in irons and hauled down to the old prison. Before you leave to interrogate him, I want you to seize his family and take them with you. We would hate for his enslavement to be lonely." Egan smiled coldly.

Snakehead struggled to cover his shocked expression. "Yes, sir."

"Finding Akala Murdoch is your first priority. I also want extra men on guard around my home and office in case she returns." The portly shipping agent resumed his perusal of the papers before him and said, "I suggest you find them if you don't want to find yourself working the mines." Without looking up, he made a dismissive wave and added, "That will be all."

Snakehead wasted no time exiting. As he went out, a confident woman of middle years entered carrying a sheaf of papers. "What do you plan to do about employee death benefits?"

"What do you mean?" asked Egan.

"Slave deaths are common business losses, and thankfully not common knowledge locally. Some of the residents around here would string you up if they knew you had slaves." She looked at the girls fanning her employer. She tipped her head towards them. "You can get away with a few indentured servants, but if word gets out about the mines, you'll be lynched." She shook her head. "No, the losses last night were employee losses, and they have families. If you don't pay the grieving families something they may not be inclined to keep secrets."

"Hmm," said Egan. "I see what you mean." He stroked his second chin thoughtfully. "Their deaths were most unfortunate, but look on the bright side. Today is the end of the pay period." His smile was genuine as he considered the reduced payroll. Akala Murdoch and Captain Beros had at least caused some positive results with their disruption. Egan's joy at not having to pay wages to dead employees dispelled any fleeting grief he may have had. There was a bright side to everything.

The woman leveled her dark brows, and said, "By rights, custom demands that you pay the dead men's wages to their aggrieved families."

Egan frowned. "You can really be a pain sometimes. You do know that, don't you?" His face slowly eased as another idea came to him. "Let us offer to provide funerals for all the deceased at our expense."

"I'm impressed," said the woman. She looked truly surprised. "You would do that?"

Egan nodded sagely. "Of course; they were hard working men in our service."

"Most, if not all, were men of the sea."

"Yes," he agreed. "I don't think the families will mind if we consolidate the services to simultaneous burials at sea from one ship."

"What's the catch?" the woman asked, suspicion creeping into her tone and demeanor.

"No catch, Talia," answered Egan, his smile returning. "Once the funeral is finished the ship can continue on to Bovilla or Argen Island."

"You're going to enslave them?" Talia had difficulty making it sound like a question. "How will you explain the absence of the families?"

"We'll pass the word that we have provided a retirement home in the east for the widows and schools for the children at no cost to the families."

"Well," said Talia, "your partner will be pleased with not having to pay slave raiding costs."

Egan's smile vanished. "Everything has a cost, my dear. Del Pero will still be responsible for his half of the usual flesh value fee."

Talia assumed a stoic expression. "I might have known."

"It's just wise money management."

Talia dumped the stack of papers she had been cradling on Egan's desk. When he made no acknowledgment of the paperwork, she said, "You might want to take the time to read the top dispatch. It came in this morning by bird from Kalusia." The caustic edge in her tone could not be missed.

Egan grabbed the top sheet. "What does it say?" he asked while reading the message.

"It's from the Murdoch's chief steward in Port Augustus," she said. "Their granddaughter has been kidnapped. The ransom is not for money. Apparently, the kidnappers are after some item, perhaps an heirloom. That part was unclear. But if you're going to read it, why're you asking me?"

"Yes," Egan replied without looking up. "It looks as if the child's mother is traveling to Juana Pohala for the exchange, without the ransom item, in hopes of negotiating for the girl's release." He stared at the paper and drummed his fingers on the wooden desktop. "If only I knew of this yesterday. I could have sent Akala packing, back up north. This foolish quest to find her lost husband can cause some serious problems. Now we don't even know where she is."

"What will you do?"

He thought a moment and then without looking up said, "Send this information to Del Pero. Perhaps he can use it to some advantage. His last letter indicated a reluctance of cooperation from Captain Murdoch."

CHAPTER 13

Imar led his horse down a steep and narrow game trail. Since leaving their camp at first light they had had to go single file, occasionally dismounting to navigate the rocky declivitous terrain. Descending the high mountains was arduous work, much of it trackless. With each step, the air grew warmer, not only from the decline in elevation but from the sun's warmth as it rose out of the vast desert before them. The evergreens became sparse, yet the brush was thick in places, making the going slow at times. It was late morning when they came to the foothills.

Imar stopped next to a knee-high boulder of rusty red iron ore to rest. Placing a foot on the rock, he massaged his calves. Spending the last hour walking downhill was straining muscles he didn't know he had. He looked out over the plain and saw fewer dust clouds going to and from the city than he had seen earlier that morning from a higher elevation.

"There's less traffic now," Imar called up the hill

behind him. "Is that because of the heat?"

Hager was a short way behind, leading his horse around a thicket of thorny shrubs. "That'd be my guess."

Dalla was next in line behind Hager. "We should pick up the pace or set camp before it gets too hot to travel."

"I think I'd rather push on," replied Imar. With barely a tug on the reins, his horse followed him down the hill.

When they came to a dry arroyo near noon Imar called a halt so they could change clothes. "None of us are accustomed to this heat. It will take a while to adapt."

"We'll have to be careful of sunburn," said Dalla from the other side of her horse, using the animal as a privacy barrier to change her attire.

When she was finished changing Dalla came around her mount wearing an airy light blue top. A soothing breeze shifted the gauzy material, revealing the hint of a black athletic bra underneath. Imar had seen her use the modest top as a swimming garment when bathing in mountain streams. She rolled up her practical leather pants and put them in a saddlebag along with her riding boots. In place of her snug black trousers, she now wore a pair of light beige and very comfortable looking cotton pants with the legs rolled up to just below her knees.

Imar suddenly noticed the silence. The men had not only stopped talking, they had stopped moving as well. His eyes remained on her. Dalla could wear anything and make it look good, but Imar had not seen this outfit before, so he took his time appreciating her beauty.

"Where did you get the sandals?" he asked. After months on the trail hiding and evading pursuit, they had had little time to shop for more than basic necessities and trade goods.

"Remember Elsie?"

Imar scrunched his brows, "The farmer's wife?"

"Yes," replied Dalla. "She knew I would need some different clothes once we crossed the mountains."

"She's twice your size," exclaimed Imar incredulously.

Dalla smiled, causing Imar's heart to skip a beat. "She wasn't always, ah, large. She had lots of stuff that didn't fit her anymore."

Imar nodded and the men resumed motion. "Is that wise?" Imar asked. "I mean your skin is so fair. Won't you burn in this sun?"

"I need to break into a tan gradually," replied the healer. "The same goes for the rest of you."

"I don't burn," said Egil. "I only get darker."

"You'll burn in this heat," Dalla countered. "The desert of Hamaud is like no place I've ever seen. In the old world this location on a day like this would be about twenty-five Celsius, but right now it must be at least thirty-seven degrees, and it'll get hotter as the day progresses—a lot hotter. The temperature will climb even more as we travel deeper into the desert."

Imar was sobered by Dalla's words, but his curiosity made him ask, "What was this place called in your world?"

Dalla looked around, scrutinizing the area, and said, "Much has changed. Some mountains crumbled whereas others thrust higher or broke off to fall into the ocean to either sink or become islands." She turned around once more and looked at Imar. "My best guess would put us in what was once called New Mexico."

Imar sounded the strange syllables over his tongue while Dalla kept talking.

"We will all have to cover our exposed skin before long," added the healer. "When we get to Juana Napur, it would behoove us to purchase burnouses."

"What is a burnous?" Egil inquired.

Vidar spoke up, "Do you remember that black robed assassin that attacked Imar up in Kandia?"

The young man nodded.

"He was wearing a burnous." Vidar tied his bandana and pulled a strand of brown hair from the knot. "It's the common garb of the desert. It allows air to flow underneath while protecting the body from the intense desert sun."

"It seems like it would be hot," piped in Aksel.

"Your skin will fry if left bare," replied Vidar. He swung into his saddle. "C'mon, we're burning daylight."

They had not traveled an hour when Imar began feeling his skin tighten from the sun's rays. A rivulet crossed their path. It was lined with small scrubby looking trees. The horses went straight to the water and began voraciously drinking while the group dismounted. A chorus of canteen corks popped from jugs. Exhaled exclamations about the heat were followed by the sound of several people chugging water.

Hager pulled off his vest, tossed it on his horse's rump, and then pulled a long-sleeved shirt out of a saddle bag and donned it. He went to one of the pack horses, pulled an old shirt from his things and cut a large piece out of the back with his knife. With this, he tied the bandanna on his head so that it shaded his ears and neck. When he turned around, everyone was watching him. He looked at them briefly then went about filling canteens.

"Well," said Dalla, "I think Hager shows good sense. We had better do the same."

Imar gave in and pulled on a long sleeve tunic. The heat made the garment feel oppressive, but he noticed that the skin on his shoulders was sensitive to the rubbing of the cloth. He wondered if he had sunburned.

By mid-day, they had left the foothills. No trees remained, only a few stunted growths of yellow or red flowering cactus. Imar could see Juana Napur in the distance; heat waves made the image blur and waver. Each step that his horse took brought him closer the unchanging horizon seemed to make the city just sit there as if their mounts were walking in place, trudging along wearily under the harsh sun. Minutes stretched to hours, making him doubt that they were even nearing their destination where shade and cool water awaited.

"It doesn't look like we're getting any closer," complained Aksel. "When will we get there?"

Vidar answered him in a dry raspy voice. "We'll get there when we get there. Save your breath and drink some more water." He took his own advice with a long pull from his water jug.

Aksel drank, as he was advised, but continued

complaining about the heat, the sun, the dryness, and the temperature of his water. Imar was sure the youth had repeated, "Are we there yet?" a dozen times.

The others also seemed too miserable to silence the young soldier, so Imar just tuned him out. He took several swallows from his warm canteen. The heat was making him dizzy and he absently noticed he was sweating profusely.

He slumped in his saddle, breathed the hot air, and disconnected himself from the increasing heat. He dug deep into his past before he had woken up in a hole with no memory. It was like chipping away at a gray wall with no substance. If he were to swing a pick at a wall of like colored granite he would, at least, meet some resistance and be rewarded with a chip of rock for his effort. The wall blocking his past yielded nothing as if his pick of inquiry swung freely through a cloud of mist. When he tried to penetrate that barrier he saw absolutely nothing, except when he thought about his daughter, Aideen, or his friend, Hager. At times when he looked at either of them or thought about them, he would see undefinable images floating almost out of view in the mist. These visions were becoming more frequent and slightly, but only very slightly, more definable. Now he was seeing shadows when he thought of his mother.

Imar thought about his wife, Anisha. He had apparently married her out of duty for getting her with child. Anisha even said as much, that she had played on his honor by trapping him with her pregnancy because he was a natural leader as well as very rich. *But, why Anisha?* he thought. He could not think of anyone with whom he was more incompatible. *Was I that much different? I must've been incredibly drunk*, he thought, *to fall for a trap like that*. Every question that came to his mind only brought more questions. *Her parents are wealthy. Why would she need more wealth?*

Imar's wealth came when adventuring at sea with Travin and Akala. A vast treasure turned the hard working privateers into wealthy aristocrats with purchased patents of nobility. He could not remember any of it, at least, nothing beyond a few months ago when he regained consciousness from a head injury sustained in battle. That's when he met Dalla and thereafter learned of the octagon key. It seemed like he had been running and hiding ever since if only to keep it from the wrong hands.

He looked at his own hands, wondering is his were any better than those who would kill him for the key. It seemed a shame to destroy all that knowledge. Dalla even wanted to extract data from the bunker before destroying it. She would eliminate the weapons, but the sword can save as well as kill. It depended on the will of the wielder.

Imar looked over to where Dalla rode beside him. She turned and met his eyes with a smile, and as usual, his heart melted. She was beautiful, but the heat was getting to her. *Poor thing,* he thought, *she's wilting. She may be from this great technological past, genetically enhanced and all that, but she is still human.* From the moment he had awakened in her cabin after she had healed him with a mind meld, he had fallen in love with her, but they were honor bound to be miserable because he was married. Or were they? It seemed to him that some people saw marriage as a legal obstacle in a situation like his. Many of his friends advised him to just follow his heart. Even Dalla was starting to see him as a prude.

Memory loss confused Imar. An oath given is not lifted lightly. Considering that he had stayed with Anisha for eleven years, he must have had the same principles before his amnesia. It wasn't easy to go back on a promise even when it was dissolved with a legally binding contract, which it was not. Anisha had laughed in his face when he had asked her for a divorce. She told him her ambition to rule would be stymied since high society frowned on divorce. She told him that he could bed the healer for all she cared and admitted to her own numerous extramarital escapades, but divorce was out of the question.

This was too much for Imar. He had taken vows of fidelity when he married. Just because his wife didn't keep her promises was no reason for him to belittle himself by becoming an oath breaker. If he ignored their contract, he would be no better than Anisha, yet when he looked at Dalla he felt his resolve begin to slip.

Imar struggled with this dilemma. He had only kissed Dalla once, shortly after she had healed him, and what a kiss it was. Butterflies spun in his chest with the memory of that first, sweet, long and lingering kiss. Sometimes when he thought of it, he wished he would have just grabbed her then, laid her down on his bed and made love to her right then and there at the Daishon Ferry Inn—only they had had to escape Sigurd and his men. The timing was certainly inappropriate for sex, but at least, he was able to vent his frustration that night with a quick little battle.

Why shouldn't I seek Dalla's embrace? Imar thought. *Why shouldn't we love each other the way two people in love should?* He began to picture himself with Dalla, the two of them alone, unrestrained from the conflicts that complicated their lives. Imar realized he was still looking at her and she was blushing. His musing expression of deep thought changed to a questioning look.

"Were you reading my thoughts?" he asked.

"It was kind of hard not to," replied Dalla.

It was Imar's turn to blush. He straightened in his saddle and began counting from one hundred backwards to suppress his amorous thoughts.

The sun rested on the western peaks when they came to Juana Napur. Unlike other cities whose outskirts were normally dotted with farms and homesteads, the barren desert ended where the city began. Nor was there a wall defending its inhabitants. The desert city of Juana Napur was built in the typical defensive manner of circular streets intersecting with straight-lined thoroughfares jutting from the center like the spokes of a wheel. The city sat at the junction of the western Hamaud highway and the Southern Caravan Route. The northern and southern caravan routes were used alternately by seasons—the northern route was open in the summer and closed in the winter by snow while the southern route was rarely traveled in the summer due to the extreme heat. The autumn heat was so debilitating, Imar wondered how anyone could live here in any season.

The rectangular tan and red adobe buildings at the edge of town were low and squat with narrow walkways and alleys between them. Imar could see that the buildings grew taller towards the city center. A few of the houses sported yards with low fences made of coarse brick, but most of the dwellings seemed to be packed close together. In front of some of the places hung signs, indicating home based businesses.

There were only a few people out and about in the stifling heat. Shortly after entering the city they came to what appeared to be a small tavern. The vented shutters were closed, as was the lath door. Adjacent to the empty hitching rail sat a large watering trough. A small person, probably a child, swathed in a dark yellow burnous with only their eyes uncovered, approached from the side of the building. A yoke with a bucket of water at each end was straddled across small shoulders. The horses lapped up the water as it was poured into the trough.

"Don't let Duco cheat you for drinking his water before you pay," said a boy's voice from under the yellow cloth.

"Who's Duco?" inquired Imar, but the boy was already scuttling away with his buckets.

They gathered in the shade of the porch when the door opened revealing a short round-faced man of middle years with a shaved head. The hood of his amber burnous was thrown back. "May cool water quench your thirst," greeted the man with a smile. "We do not open until sunset." He glanced briefly at the drinking horses. A frown passed over his face for half an instant to be replaced with the smile again. "Ah, but you are from the West, are you not?" He continued without giving them a chance to reply. His eyes lit up with glee and he began rubbing his hands together. "Come in, come in," he said, opening the door wide, bowing and backing into the cooler interior. "I am Duco, good sirs, and gracious lady. I will open early just for you. Come in, come in."

"Thank you," replied Imar. He gave Vidar a look, then flicked his eyes at the horses and back again before turning back to the tavern owner.

The boy returned, burdened with more water for the trough.

"Aziz," Duco called loudly to the boy. "Get these horses under shade."

"Sun will set in half an hour," replied the boy.

"Do as I say," snapped the tavern owner.

Imar, Dalla, and Hager followed the host inside. Vidar remained and halted Aksel and Egil. "Help the boy with the horses," he said aloud. In a quieter voice, Imar heard him add, "One of you shall stay with the horses at all times once they are tended. Take turns if you must, but do not leave our cargo unguarded."

When Imar entered the dark interior he immediately felt the restoring coolness of the tavern. Vidar soon joined them at a round wooden table near the wall. Duco was placing a clay pitcher of water and pewter mugs on the table when Vidar asked him about the water and stabling. "What do we owe you so far? I mean for the horses."

Duco straightened, smiling, and rubbing his hands together said, "Two silver pieces per horse for water and shade, or perhaps you have gold?

Four stunned faces looked at him.

After a few seconds, his face took on an injured look. "What? Water is very expensive in the desert. There are only a few wells in Juana Napur and those are controlled by the potentate. There is also the expense of hauling the water."

Vidar's face went flat. "I was expecting a sum tallied in coppers." Then his face softened, a smile slowly working its way onto it. "Would you be interested in a trade? We have packs of carrots and seed potatoes. Much of it is still fit for the table."

The tavern owner, still smiling, raised his brows and replied, "I would be most interested."

"How do two silvers and a bushel of carrots sound to you for watering all of our horses?"

It was Duco's turn to look stunned. Vidar laughed, drank down his water and sprang to his feet. "Come," said Vidar. "Let us go inspect our goods and perhaps we can make a deal. Would you be interested in some packhorses? I would be open to a good offer." Vidar was in sales mode, and his voice rattled on non-stop as the two men went down a hall, followed by Hager. Imar heard them exit a back door. Alone in the tavern, Imar took Dalla's hand. They were silent, sipping their water, enjoying being alone together. It was a rare occurrence, and not to last. The back door sounded again followed by Egil's heavy tread stomping along the hall and up to the table where he plopped into a chair. He drank down a full mug of water in one draft, refilled it, and drank it down again. The young man did not notice Dalla's hand slipping from Imar's.

"What news, Egil?" Imar inquired.

"I think Duco is going to buy the whole lot, packhorses too, everything but our riding horses. Good riddance too, if you ask me. I for one am tired of potatoes and carrots. I want meat."

"I think we can all use a good meal," agreed Imar.

"I've got to get back out there, Captain, and relieve Aksel. I just came in to cool off and get some water." Egil took several more swigs, rose noisily and thumped down the hall and out the door.

Barely a moment had passed when Imar and Dalla witnessed a repeat performance. This time, Aksel stomped in, pounded water, and expressed his desire for a change in diet. In less than a minute, they were alone again.

The echo of the shutting door had hardly ceased when Imar turned in his chair and kissed Dalla's unresisting lips. It was a soft and gentle kiss, long and caressing, that slowly built in passion, becoming less soft, less gentle, growing with intensity and immediacy. It was one of those kisses, that had they been truly alone, they may have found themselves expressing their love in a more profound manner. It was not to be, though, nor would the kiss continue much longer. They were both aware of the frustration of bottling up the restrained love that Imar's unhappy marriage had placed on them—it was constantly in the back of their minds. It prevented them from allowing each other the freedom to properly express their affection to each other.

Imar and Dalla had both been tense, holding back, doing the right thing, being proper—it was almost more than Imar could bear, and he knew it was difficult on Dalla as well. They had not been alone together for more than a few minutes since their flight from Daishon Ferry a thousand leagues to the north. Perhaps it was better they had not been alone—the temptation may have won out over Imar's moral code. It was one of those moments Imar did not want to let slip. It was like a pressure cooker with a stuck valve; the pot is near bursting, the valve is cracked open enough to let off some steam, but the pressure remains high and the flame is still hot.

Dalla put her hand on his chest and gently pushed him back. "So, does this mean you are accepting an emotional separation from your marriage?"

"Wow," said Imar. "That was like getting dumped on with a bucket of cold water."

"It's a reasonable question, Imar. I don't want to be drawn into a relationship just to have you back off with worries about your bad marriage. We are adults. I do not want to be teased like a teenager."

"Teased...teenager..." Imar stammered incredulously. He felt his ire rise and then forcefully put it in check. He realized that this could be one of those emotional outbursts common to his type of brain injury, which Dalla had warned him about. He calmed and then resignedly said, "I'm sorry. I know what I want, but I don't know what to do. Through all the hardships we have endured together I have been happy." He paused and added with a sideways grin, "Well, except for the time Sigurd threatened to give you to his men, I just wanted to kill them all, that time." Reassured by her smile, he plunged on. "Every minute I have spent with Anisha is pure misery, a trial in patience. I can't stand her, but she is my daughter's mother, and I gave my word—we took vows. It would be easier if she would just give me a divorce. She's adamant about the 'till death do us part,' part."

"Vows," Dalla murmured.

"Hmm? What was that?"

Dalla looked at him. "You said vows, right?"

"That's what people say when they get married."

"Yes, I know, but vows sometimes vary with marriages. You may have a legal loophole, depending on what vows you actually gave. You would have to see the marriage license and have someone recall your oath."

Imar sighed, feeling tired. "I need my memory."

The sound of menus being placed on the table brought Imar out of his brooding. A dark woman sporting silver streaks in her hair was setting the table. The woman had a rounded physique under her golden burnous. Dalla took out a small metal mirror and adjusted her mussed up hair. The woman gave them a patronizing smile. Hager entered the main room, chuckling as he took a seat.

"Duco had a fresh lamb slaughtered this very day," said the woman in a slightly accented common tongue. "It has been turning on the spit over a mesquite fire for hours. Will you be dining with us?"

"We will," answered Imar.

"Just talking about it is making my mouth water," rumbled Hager. "Could you bring us a pitcher of ale as well?"

"Most certainly sir, it will be but a moment." The woman went to greet three newcomers, two men and a woman all in desert garb, which had seated themselves on the opposite side of the tavern. She then departed to the kitchen and returned with the ale and a mixed bowl of dates and pecans.

Hager filled three mugs with ale and announced, "Vidar has made us an embarrassingly good profit. I am tempted to hang up my sword and become a merchant."

"I hate to tell you, Hager," replied Dalla, "that there are as many bands of raiders in the desert as there are pirates at sea, perhaps more."

"Oh I know," responded the burly man. "But if Vidar taught me his skill, I could hire enough swords to discourage any thieves." He popped a date in his mouth and chewed thoughtfully.

Imar grinned sardonically and said, "Do you think, old friend, that you could just sit and watch your hired men repel raiders while your sword sits idle in its sheath?"

Hager snorted a laugh, "I suppose not, but you know Imar, we're not getting any younger—though you still look pretty good for your age. What I mean is," his face grew serious, "with age the reflexes get slower and endurance wanes. It is a matter of time before a younger hand wielding a faster blade finds my flesh. I think I would like to find a wife I could grow old with." He glanced at Dalla and back to Imar. "I'm sorry, I didn't mean…"

"To rub salt into the wound," Imar finished for him, instantly reminded again of his situation. "It's okay, my friend. I know you meant no harm. Not a day passes without a prayer to any of the gods who will change Anisha's mind to give me a divorce. I've even prayed to this new nameless god. And I can't even remember if I was an atheist, or not."

Hager's sympathy softened his face with a small smile. "You prudently never spoke of religion, but I know you better than anyone." Imar's ears almost seemed to flick forward to rake in any revelation of his past hidden to him by his amnesia. "You confided to me that your belief was one that viewed the gods as a shared energy in all things alive and inanimate, even extending to the spirits of our ancestors. You once said that energy cannot be destroyed; only transferred."

Imar looked at Dalla to get her response to this, but she had missed it. Her attention was absorbed with watching the group across the room. She turned back to say something to Imar and Hager, but she was interrupted by Vidar, Aksel, and Egil, led by Duco. They all seemed to be talking at once, apparently in high spirits.

Hager looked to Vidar and asked, "The horses?"

"Our esteemed host gave the boy Aziz a coin to watch the horses and I gave him another to brush them down. It has been a good day for trade."

"Indeed, my friend," said Duco, placing a hand on Vidar's shoulder. "It is a good trade when both sides are smiling."

After two weeks on the trail, enduring monotonous meals of carrots and potatoes from their trade goods, with only the supplemental trout or grouse taken along the way, they feasted with gusto on the leg of lamb, dates, and copious amounts of chilled ale. All that remained of the meat was the bone sitting on the platter. Imar was not surprised that the vegetables remained untouched; being the same carrots and potatoes they had just traded to Duco. During their meal, other patrons entered and ordered meals and beverages. Duco's tavern was filling up.

Imar turned to say something to Dalla, but she was distracted, her mind elsewhere. He shrugged it off as nothing new and turned back to the men. "Hager, would you pass the beer?"

CHAPTER 14

Dalla's neck hairs prickled, her senses warned her to caution. The source of her concern was the group of three that had come in earlier before the place had filled up. The woman reminded her of the old world Amerindians of the southwestern United States. The two men with her had the typical look of the desert, which Dalla knew was a descendant mixture of the blended American races and the transplanted Arab and Persian refugees from the Middle East when Damascus became radioactive.

When other survivors fled to the far north or the southern Polar Regions to escape the chemical and biological warfare literally plaguing the Midwest and Southwestern states, the settled in expatriates, together with the remaining tribes of Native Americans, had dug underground warrens to escape the death and torment on the surface. The underground colonization had lasted for countless generations until life could again be sustained above ground. It surprised Dalla that after thousands of

169

years of racial blending this woman could still show the features of her Amerindian ancestors. Dalla drew her attention away from the woman and her mate. It was the fidgety man with them that concerned her the most.

Had it not been for Dalla's senses she may not have noticed the man's interest in them—namely in Imar. She felt the first warning pang when Hager was telling what he remembered of Imar's theological belief as it tied in with the science of energy transference. It was an astounding hypothesis for someone born and raised in such a primitive atmosphere. Normally she would have jumped feet first into a discussion of that sort, but the man stealing so many furtive glances their way could not be a coincidence.

Each time Dalla tried to get a word in Imar would be swallowed up in conversation with Hager or Vidar. If the man in the brown burnous was a spy, or even someone seeking a reward for Imar, the last thing she wanted was to alert him and scare him off to go get armed help. She ruled out spy—too much of an amateur. He had been glancing at them far too often for him to be a professional.

She was well aware of her attractiveness, but such was not the case this time. When Fidget thought no one was watching him, he just stared flatly at Imar, so she knew the man wasn't checking her out, nor did she think he swung the other way. It wasn't that kind of look. The other man and woman were more discreet, but they too took frequent opportunities for observation. Just as frequently they would huddle together as if speaking conspiratorially.

Dalla wondered if she was just being paranoid. Still, the furtive one wasn't looking at anyone else. The important thing now was to avoid being caught or allowing the key to be taken.

They had an urgent mission to help Aideen, which took precedence over their other urgent mission to keep the octagon key hidden. Now it was a double mission. The world would be so much safer once they destroyed the old world technology —no more fortress, no more weapons of mass destruction. In Dalla's world, before the cataclysm, there had been too many destructive technologies that could not be uninvented, but in this world, she could prevent its rediscovery if only she could get the key to the control center in the habitat under the ruins of the Octagon.

Dalla wanted to share the good technology. Medical science and clean energy would help the planet, but would there be time to extract the data? Even now the war was being waged in a battling exodus to old DC, or what they now called Oldeisie. Word was out and people wanted to seize the buried technology. There were too many delays; if they didn't hurry they would find an army dug in around the ruins when they got there. She had hoped to travel incognito and unimpeded, but the actions of the group across the room hindered those hopes.

Their own group was having such a good time. After the long journey through the Kandian wilderness, battles on land and evasions at sea and the rigors of the trail, a little break was well deserved. She hated to be one to rain on the campfire, but it was time to go again. When a moment finally presented itself, she touched Imar's arm again, leaned slightly toward him and spoke casually as if commenting on the sfouf dessert cakes that the serving woman set before them. "Try not to be obvious, but we have been recognized."

"Where?" he asked quietly. Trying not to move his head too sharply, Imar's eyes scanned the room. "How many?"

"Against the wall, third table from the bar," she whispered from behind her napkin.

Dalla saw Imar's eyes fix across the room. She followed his gaze, and sure enough, it was locked with the furtive one in the brown burnous. "I told you not to look," she hissed.

"Sorry," Imar apologized. "It's kind of like telling a kid not to eat the last cookie. When you tell somebody 'don't look,' that's the first thing they're going to do."

Fidget spoke animatedly to his companions while they stood and downed their ale.

Imar leaned toward Hager and spoke low, but Dalla heard him say, "We've been spotted. Tell Vidar we're leaving and have the boys get the horses. You and I need to stop that bunch over there." Hager looked to where Imar indicated. "But let's do it outside. I don't want to make a scene."

Hager nodded and scooted his chair back. The three watchful ones were out the door before Aksel and Egil were on their feet to go ready the horses. Imar moved quickly after the three, with Hager on his heels. Dalla stood and considered following, but Imar and Hager returned a moment later.

"They were fast, I'll give them that," said Hager.

A few patrons threw some half-interested glances their way but went back to minding their own business.

Imar stopped only for a second in the common room. He leaned close to Dalla and said, "We have to catch them before they bring back trouble."

"They rode off on camels," commented Hager, as

if it were the strangest thing.

Vidar was shaking Duco's hand, thanking him for the trade as they pulled him free of the tavern owner and into their hurried procession out the back door.

Within a minute, they were all mounted and moving at a trot. Imar took point with Hager at his side followed by Vidar and Dalla with Aksel and Egil riding rear guard.

Upon entering the street, Dalla spotted the other three about a hundred meters ahead in the dim blue glow of chemical streetlamps. They were making for the city center on trotting camels. Dalla's enhanced vision could clearly make out Fidget turning in his saddle. He spotted them, but she couldn't hear his voice over the thudding of hooves on the packed sandstone of the street. "Imar, they've seen us," she warned.

Dalla's warning had no sooner come when the trio kicked their camels into a run. There was no hesitation from the men, and Dalla was only a second behind. Like cats bolting after mice, they shook their reins and raced after the departing three.

Dalla's horse accelerated under her as she heard Imar's belated command, "After them!"

There was more traffic in the streets now that the sun had set. The scorching heat was gone, replaced by cooler air wafted in by a light breeze. It was one of those pleasant evenings Dalla would have enjoyed sitting on a lanai with Imar, sipping iced tea and looking at the stars, but instead, they were chasing camel riders through the streets of Juana Napur in order to prevent being arrested. It was another one of those times she asked herself, *Why am I doing this again?*

Dalla began chuckling at the thought. Vidar, riding at her side, looked at her curiously. She shook her head as if to say, *never mind—private joke.* She looked ahead up the straight thoroughfare to take her mind off subjects that, in her current mood, could drive her into hysterical laughter. The timing was most inappropriate for the seriousness of the situation and might be considered to be in bad taste.

As they drew near the city center they gained on their quarry. The growing traffic caused them to weave in and out of pedestrians, handcarts, riders, and wagons. Heat lamps perched on street poles were becoming more numerous, and most were set to the brighter orange or yellow setting.

They entered a large market area where vendors were setting up their wares. A farmer stopped his melon laden wagon perpendicular to the road in order to back up to a fruit stand, and the pursued trio had to turn sharply to avoid a collision. One member of their party fell off his camel with the maneuver, bouncing off the wagon to plop face down in the dirt. The other two looked back; one pulled up and returned to aid the fallen, the other rode on. Startled by the fast approaching horses, the fallen rider's mount fled through the marketplace. The other rider extended her hand to aid her comrade, but the man appeared injured and was having difficulty getting on the side-stepping camel. The farmer at once came to the man's aid, but upon seeing armed horsemen bearing down on the strangers, he quickly found other business to attend to.

Imar called out, "Wait, we want to talk."

Hager flanked him on his right, and Vidar pulled up and secured the harness of the woman's camel as Imar and Dalla dismounted.

The couple eyed their pursuers and their relief at seeing undrawn weapons was evident. The man and woman looked to each other. They wore matching off white burnouses. The man wore a kufiyah headscarf, and the woman's hijab was worn loose and thrown back like a neckerchief. The man was cradling his right arm and trying to keep his weight on his left leg. The woman dismounted, went to the man, and checked his injuries, often glancing at his eyes. Dalla would have done the same thing to assess pain and level of consciousness. She wondered if the woman had some healing skills. They both carried crescent-shaped knives the length of a man's foot but prudently kept their hands from the hilts in the face of greater numbers.

"Why did you run from us?" Vidar asked, climbing from his saddle without releasing the camel's harness.

"Armed men chasing us seemed like a good reason to us," said the woman earnestly.

"She has a point," said Hager.

Vidar looked back at the dromedary. "Hey, your camel is chewing. I didn't see it take anything. Where'd it get food?"

"He's chewing the cud, like a cow," replied the woman.

A belching sound from the camel was followed by Vidar swearing. "The flea bitten son of a whore just puked on me."

When Dalla looked, the tall man was wiping mush off his chest and out of his beard.

"Careful," said the woman. "They spit."

"Thanks," Vidar said dryly. He slacked the animal's reins and backed a few paces away.

Imar ignored his friend. "You seemed to have quite an interest in us at the tavern."

The woman made a furtive eye-flick to the lamppost and then tried to cover the action by pulling off her hijab to make a sling for the man's arm.

Dalla looked to where the woman's eyes had gone and noticed a paper tacked to the pole. Imar caught the action and nodded to Egil with a gesture to retrieve the flyer.

Dalla spoke to the couple. "Hi, I'm Dalla. I am a healer," she said in the formal ages-old ritual of requesting consent. "I can help if you will let me."

The man and woman looked at each other in silent question for a moment. The man turned to Dalla and nodded his consent. The healer stepped up to him, placed her hands on his shoulder, and closed her eyes. When she opened them the man seemed no longer tense, but calm and relaxed.

"What's your name?" Dalla's voice was low and smooth. She took his hand and cradled his elbow, forming his arm into an 'L' shape.

"Jamar," the man answered with only an instant of surprise followed by relief as Dalla rotated his forearm toward his body with a slight momentary downward tug on his elbow. The pop and consequent, "Ahhhh," from Jamar was a testimony to the replacement of his dislocated shoulder.

"Now let's look at your leg," Dalla said, stepping back to kneel while Jamar gingerly flexed and extended his arm a few times.

"It's my knee," he said, now anxious to have the healer tend his injuries.

Dalla lifted the man's off-white pant leg to palpate his knee for a few moments, then went to her saddlebags. She returned with a jar of unguent and a roll of stretchable cotton cloth and bound his knee after applying a pain relieving ointment. "It is just bruised. Ride more and walk less for the next week or two if you can."

While Dalla tended the man's injuries, Imar read the flyer from the lamppost. "This describes us all in some fair detail." He held the poster up for Dalla to see the sketch of his own face below the bold letters—REWARD.

"How much is the reward?" Hager asked.

"Five Kalusian gold sovereigns for me or my heirloom," said Imar, handing the bulletin to Hager. "They are also offering two gold pieces for any one of the rest of you."

"That's ridiculous," said Vidar. "It was ten gold pieces for you in Abezda. I bet some enterprising officer is planning on skimming the reward."

"It is still a fair chunk of change," said Hager. The flyer was now being passed around the company. "A person could live well on one gold coin for a while."

"Or finance a small business," said the woman.

Everyone looked at her.

Dalla tied the final knot on the leg wrapping and stood. "What's your name?"

"I am Kaya," she replied proudly. "I am descendent of the first desert people to roam this land." Her emphasis on 'first' was unmistakable. "There is an officer from Kalusia with twenty soldiers; he arrived two days ago and put up this reward. It is posted all over the city."

Dalla looked at Kaya very closely and asked, "Are you Hopi?"

Kaya's eyes went wide. "How could you know that?"

"I would have guessed that or Navajo," replied Dalla.

"I am part Hopi of the old blood. There are no full-bloods left, but the line runs strong in my family."

A crowd was forming across the street. An occasional finger pointed in their direction.

"I think we ought to get moving," said Hager, indicating the crowd.

A boy approached leading Jamar's camel. The desert man thanked him and slipped him a few coppers.

"Cheap, eh," the boy remarked. "A new camel would have cost you a lot more."

Jamar pressed his lips together and handed the boy two more coppers.

The boy grunted and walked off muttering, "I should've taken the beast to the thieves' guild. They would have given me silver."

"Wait," Imar said to Jamar and Kaya. The

grumbling boy stopped and turned expectantly, but when he saw that Imar was not addressing him he continued on his way. Imar continued, "What of your friend that left you, the one in the brown burnous?"

Kaya lowered her brows and replied, "Yasser is probably half-way back here with the Kalusian soldiers to collect the reward."

"That is true," added Jamar. "We had better get you away from here." He mounted his camel.

The others followed his example and stepped into their saddles.

"Weren't you planning on collecting the reward as well?" Imar asked.

"I cannot now," said Jamar.

"You healed him," said Kaya, looking at Dalla, and then at Imar. "You are now his friends. His friends are my friends. Come, we waste time."

She turned her camel and led them a short way back the way they had come before turning into an ally with Jamar behind her. Next was Imar, with Dalla guiding her horse behind him, and then Vidar following her. Hager rode rear guard with Aksel and Egil. A few watchful people gathered in the street, led by a man holding a wanted poster. They attempted to follow on foot, but Hager pointedly gripped his sword and offered a menacing scowl. That was enough for the mob to go back to being merchants. The route Kaya and Jamar chose took them down numerous unlit streets and alleyways.

"Do you think this is wise?" Aksel asked Hager after a few turns down dark side streets.

"Better than waiting for the soldiers," rumbled the stout veteran.

Aksel acquiesced with a rolling nod.

After a time, the apartments, stores, and offices gave way to houses with yards and private stables. Rock gardens and cacti were common. Dalla observed one large and opulent house sporting a garden filled with lush growth. She noticed it also had a well in the yard, and in a chair next to the well sat an armed guard.

"Water is precious and wells are few," explained Jamar when he noticed their curious looks. "Many holes are dug, but only one in fifty yield water. They either sell the water or sell the well and live in wealth for the rest of their lives."

"So that's why Duco charged us so much for the water," said Egil. "I thought Vidar had finally met his match at striking a deal."

Vidar turned in his saddle with a sour look. "It'll never happen. No one gets the better of me in a trade." Then more soberly he added, "Duco said that only a few sultans control the water and I believe him. There weren't many crops outside the city, so they have to import much of their food. That is most likely due to the water shortage."

"What is a sultan?" Aksel asked.

"It used be a title of nobility," replied Jamar. "Now anyone with wealth calls himself a sultan. Many of the nomadic war chiefs have taken to hanging feathers in their headscarves and claiming the title of sultan even though they live in cone tents and raid their cousins for their goat herds."

It was not long before the houses grew smaller and the streets became deserted. There were no more streetlamps and only an occasional heat lamp on the low blue setting could be seen glowing in a yard or on a porch. Now and then a window emitted some light, but the majority of houses they passed had drawn curtains. Dalla assessed that they were in a lower working class neighborhood. The streets and yards were clean and lacking the sense of lurking crime common to unlit city streets.

Kaya signaled them to stop in front of a small house. She went to the door and knocked. The door opened and a hushed conversation followed with the occupant poking his head out briefly to look at the waiting group. The shadows were too dark to make out the features of the one with whom she spoke. The door shut with a light snick. A moment later a tall broad-shouldered man with long straight black hair came out wearing a light linen pullover that hung to his knees. He walked beside Kaya using a staff as thick as his wrist, but his steps betrayed no indication of handicap. As he approached, Dalla could see that his face featured the same high cheek bones and reddish brown skin as Kaya's.

"This is my cousin, Ahote," Kaya introduced the man with solemn pride.

Ahote swept appraising eyes across the company, gave a single nod to Jamar, and said, "Come." He turned and walked down the way beside his house.

Jamar dismounted and limping beside Kaya they led their camels after Ahote.

Dalla let out a long breath. "I was so looking forward to a bath and soft bed at the Mozar Abibi."

Egil sniffed his underarm, grimaced, shrugged, and followed without comment.

With grunts and weary moans they climbed down and pulled their mounts along the pebbled path.

There was a large covered corral adjacent to a dozen open-air stalls, half of which were full. Ahote instructed them to use the corral to house their horses for the time being. Once the horses and camels were tended to they went with him to his house, each carrying a bedroll.

"I live alone now," their host said, "but my place is small and cluttered. All I can offer is some cramped floor space. You are wanted; the reward is very high and very tempting. I have accepted you as guests, so have no fears from me, but you cannot let yourselves be seen. Please stay inside or out back. My cousin and Jamar have vouched for you, and that is good enough for me. I won't turn you in, but you will have to pay for what water you use. I just put in a large store, so there is plenty."

Dalla cleared her throat and addressed him with serious intensity, "Is there enough for a bath?"

For the first time since meeting him, Ahote smiled. He made a gesture to his cousin.

Kaya led Dalla to a small room with a tub. "The valve on the left is the cold, but it's actually not much cooler than room temperature," Kaya said. "Be careful of the hot. It is heated by the sun, and it can scald you, even at night. The tank is insulated."

Dalla immediately began filling the tub, adjusting the temperature. "Oh, I have needed this for a long time," she breathed with emphatic anticipation. She sat on the edge of the tub and began removing her boots. "Will Yasser bring the soldiers here?"

"I don't think so," replied Kaya. "He and Ahote don't get along. My cousin has banned Yasser from his property and Yasser is afraid of Ahote. They have an old grudge that will not be easily assuaged. For the time being they are content with avoiding one another, but should Yasser intrude in Ahote's business, or worse, trespass on his property, I think your healer's skills would be hard pressed to save what little that would be left of Yasser. Still, you should not stay long. Yasser's greed will eventually overpower him." Kaya diverted her attention to a cabinet while the healer removed her travel-stained top and leather breaches. Dalla stepped in and slowly lowered herself into the warm water with exclamations of pleasure and relief that bordered on ecstasy. Kaya took a clean towel from the cabinet and hung it on the back of a wooden chair adjacent to the tub. "Yasser isn't really that bad once you get to know him. He just doesn't know when to mind his own business. His mouth has earned him more than one beating."

Kaya scrutinized Dalla's clothes where they were draped over the seat of the same chair she had hung the towel on. "Your western attire makes you stand out like a shadow cat in sunlight. You need desert clothes so you can blend in and not burn up under our fierce sun. I will send Jamar back to the market before it closes down for the night. He will need some money."

"Of course," Dalla agreed. "Have him take Vidar with him. If Ahote could loan him a robe he will not be easily recognized." Dalla liked these new acquaintances, but her trust only went so far.

Kaya looked as if she were about to object, but then nodded and left the healer to her bathing.

Vidar and Jamar returned before midnight with fresh supplies and a burnous for each of them. Imar and Ahote were lounging in chairs, each with a mug of ale.

"No sign of Yasser," Jamar said as they entered. They dumped the gear on a pile of cushions.

"No soldiers either," added Vidar. "It surprised me to see so many wanted posters put up in just two days."

Aksel was on watch having just relieved Egil and Hager was on his blanket snoring like a sawyer. Dalla was just laying out her bedding. She wore a knee length sleeping gown that had belonged to Ahote's late wife.

Ahote's living room had no floor space left once the bedrolls were laid out around the furniture. Jamar and Kaya bedded down as well, thinking it best to avoid their own abode should Yasser look for them there. They did not fear Yasser, but they didn't know to what lengths the soldiers would go to extract information. Too many people had seen Dalla treat Jamar's injuries as well as witness them all ride off together. It would not take Yasser long to figure out where they all had gone.

The men decided to wait until the following day to use Ahote's water and tub—they were all long overdue for baths. The plan was to depart Juana Napur the following night. They had to get out of the city and get to Juana Pohala.

Dalla settled down in her blanket feeling clean for the first time in a long time. She had had opportunities during their travels to bathe in clear ponds and cold mountain streams, which was exhilarating and met the needs of cleanliness, but was hardly as relaxing as a hot bath. She was so relaxed she opted to forego her routine meditation before drifting off to sleep. Dalla was in that state of slumber when dreams begin, while awareness of one's surroundings is still there when Aideen's voice sounded in her mind.

Dalla, can you hear me?

Dalla forced herself to rouse but did not move or open her eyes.

Dalla, please hear me. Aideen's mind-speech came stronger.

I hear you, Aideen. The healer was impressed with the girl's skill; her pupil was becoming adept at mind-speech. She often wondered at this, not knowing anyone with the talent that wasn't from the old world and genetically enhanced, until Aideen. Even Imar showed some small promise of talent. *Where are you?*

I am in the mountains.

Describe your surroundings.

There are tall evergreens and bald peaks cluttered with boulders. It was mid-day when I last saw a tree with golden leaves. Lord Townsend is taking me to Juana Pohala.

What is this? Ivan's powerful mind-voice jumped in.

Dalla was both surprised and relieved. *Father,* she exclaimed. *Forgive me, much has happened since Aideen was kidnapped. I meant to contact you at my first opportunity.*

Kidnapped! You should have contacted me immediately. The old wizard's tone was obviously angry. *So, Townsend expects to ransom the girl for the key.*

I may have made some friends. Aideen's thought words

were coming easier. *At least one, anyway, doesn't seem to like his boss much, or Khaled. There's at least half a dozen free-lance sell-swords contracted only as far as Juana Pohala. His lordship intends to bargain a new contract and hire more men to cross the Hamaudi Desert.*

Beware of thinking the names of your enemies, little one, Ivan chided, his thought-tones seemingly more impressed now than angry. *Your skill has improved considerably, but you must try to guard your mind around the assassin.*

Dalla could sense Aideen's pride at the compliment.

We cannot go to the inn for the rendezvous, Dalla interjected. *Kalusian soldiers have littered the streets of Juana Napur with wanted posters offering rewards in gold.*

If the wizard seemed angry before, he burned with rage now. *Damn that two tongued Gerald! I should have known better than to believe the word of a politician. The king said he would back off on his search for the key. The lying sack of…*

Father, we are tiring.

He caught himself, aware now of his own weariness. *Okay, if Townsend intends to ransom Aideen in Juana Pohala, then that is where we shall go. It will be even more dangerous for you there. Be careful and goodbye for now.*

For now goodbye.

There was a pause in the thought connection as Dalla and Ivan waited for Aideen until they realized that she had gone to sleep.

CHAPTER 15

Seal Bay's autumnal rains coated everything that was not covered and soaked anyone not huddled inside by a warm fire. The locals grumbled, cursing their own foolishness for not moving to a warmer, drier clime. The constant wetness and the ever pervasive booming of the surf forced against the rocky breakwater, sending sheets of salt spray skyward with each resounding crash, was an unignorable reminder that icy wind, sleet, and wet snow would be coming soon. However, the weather did not keep the people of Seal Bay from chores and duties that required attention. On the contrary, it encouraged motivation to pick up and stow items left out over the summer as well as stimulated the completion of unfinished projects. Besides the pre-winter cleanup, this particular season had an extraordinary number of people outside enduring the rainy weather in order to prepare for the coming invasion.

With each passing day, the number of sentries standing vigil against the impending Kandian invasion grew. Coastal patrols increased, lookouts along the bluffs were added, and construction to dilapidated sections of defensive walls that have long been in a state of disrepair resumed. Low areas and weak sections of the wall were spiked with steel bars, filled with concrete, and reinforced with sandbags. Empty stables became storage and billeting for soldiers. Markets were transformed into commissaries and armories.

Any available space that could accommodate a platoon was put to use for drilling soldiers with the new small arms weapons—rifles and pistols. The new spiral bore rifles were proving their accuracy over the smooth bore musket which was *new* only a month ago. Cannon practice was held along the wall of the city and aboard the warships at sea guarding the harbor. The new technology of firearms had produced a new industry and the impending war created a boom in production, putting literally thousands to work to fill the demand. Seal Bay economy soared in a way only a disaster can provide.

From the wall, watchers could not see much beyond the rectangular stone breakwater that calmed the surf a half a click from shore. It ran a full kilometer north and south of the marina. The five-kilometer breakwater had openings every thousand meters to allow maritime traffic, but loaded vessels greater than thirty-five meters drafted too deep and had to anchor offshore.

The nearly empty harbor faded in and out of view through the grey precipitation fog. Fishing boats normally resigned to remain tied up in bad weather either had departed south to avoid the conflict, or hired on as scouting vessels. However, any bark away from the home port would either sit out the fog or spend tedious time sounding their way into shore with a weighted line knotted for each fathom.

Occasional flashes, dimly visible through the fog, were followed by the report of the cannons fired by the ships at drill. Catapults and trebuchets were strategically placed behind the seaside wall and manned by overflow reserves from the artillery brigade. A few ballistae still had placements along the wall but the main defensive weapon was the new cannons. They glistened with beaded rain upon their shiny black surfaces.

Beside each cannon, covered with tarpaulins, were powder kegs and stacks of fused cannonballs filled with black powder. Most of these volatile items stood protected behind breastworks or mantlets to prevent detonation from fire arrows. Firepots heated in tin buckets filled with whale oil, tar, pitch, or anything flammable to cast on siege towers and scaling ladders were placed every few meters. Covered braziers stood ready for firing torches, linstocks, and arrows. Around these braziers hunkered soldiers warming their hands and backsides against the damp chill.

To one side of one of these clustered warming zones stood a scarred middle-aged gunnery sergeant, peering hard at the distant fog as if he could will his vision to bore into and burn away the mist. He had one hand resting on his sword hilt while the other grasped the haft of a short battle axe tucked in his belt. The sergeant gripped both with such force that once he realized what he was doing, he inspected the weapons for signs of finger imprints. His belt also sported two pistols. He liked the new weapons, but he had yet to develop the muscle memory to reach for them first.

Ramirez stood straight though his blocky frame seemed almost to lean toward the horizon, so intense was his concentration. Rain dripped off his round painted steel helm. He looked down to where his oiled cloak did not cover the front of his chainmail—rust. It did not take long in this wet weather. Each day his weapons and armor rusted and each night his loving wife scrubbed his gear with sand. She saw to it that all his battle harness was oiled and that grease was rubbed into his rain-cloak before he returned to duty each day. He reached into his belt pouch, withdrew one of her biscuits, and took a bite.

Ramirez heard a runner's rapid approach pounding towards him from the right. "Ho there boy," he hailed the runner, turning to intercept him. "What news? Any word from up north? How 'bout from the captain?"

The messenger stopped and leaned on his knees breathing like a bellows. Ramirez handed him a skin of watered wine. The boy took it, leaned back and squeezed a long stream in his mouth and handed back the skin.

"Thank you, Sergeant," said the messenger. "There is no news other than rain and fog up and down the coast."

"So what's new?" Ramirez replied sarcastically. "When will this blasted weather lift? The whole Kandian armada could be anchored a kilometer off shore and we would be none the wiser."

"Do you know Gustav?" asked the boy.

Ramirez lowered his brows and rubbed his stubbled chin. "You mean the old sergeant that works at the weather shack?"

"Yes Sergeant, that's the one," answered the messenger. "I guess he broke a lot of bones when he was younger."

"What's your point?"

"Well, he tried to retire, but the army won't let him because his arthritis never lies. He has no duties other than to predict the weather based on his level of pain. He gets full pay even when he walks around town hopping from pub to pub, so long as he checks in twice a day to report—drunk or sober." The boy shook his head. "Except, he hasn't gone to the pub in three days."

Ramirez eyed the boy closely in case he was being set up for some joke, but the messenger kept a straight face. "Aren't you the regular chatterbox?" He was tiring of the boy's gossip. "Okay, so Gustav has decided to be sober for the invasion. What's this got to do with the weather?"

The messenger boy furrowed his brows. "I was getting to that," he said impatiently. "Gustav wouldn't give up his drink if his dying mother begged it from her deathbed. He's been sending me out for spirits stronger than his usual beer. The man is so crippled up these past three days he can't walk, much less get out of bed to relieve himself. This past day and a half when the storm has been at its worst he's done nothing but moan and groan. That is until about an hour ago, but he still strained through the words."

The boy stood there waiting as if for dramatic effect. Ramirez felt his patience slipping. "Okay, so what did he say?"

"He said it will rain for the rest of the week, only the wind is supposed to pick up today."

Ramirez glared at the boy. He pictured in his mind what it'd feel like throwing the lad over the wall. Of course, he wouldn't do that, but it made him feel better thinking it. "All that oratory for just that? You missed your calling, kid. You should be in the theater."

The boy bowed with a flourish and turned to

leave.

Ramirez rubbed his shoulder and grunted his agreement with the forecast. He looked at the lad with a lifted brow. "What's your hurry?"

"Third platoon is starting a pool for when the first enemy boot steps ashore. I want to get in on it before I get too busy to bet. I say they won't be here till next Monday at noon."

"I'm in," said a soldier within earshot. He came over followed by a few of his fellows. They started handing the boy coins with the time and day they guessed the invasion would commence.

Word of wager spreads fast among warriors, thought Ramirez. He pulled out his purse and handed two silver coins to the lad. "Put me down for today at three hours past noon and another for seven in the morning."

Within seconds, men and women were migrating towards the messenger like fish to a feeding pond.

"Wait," the runner railed at them. He pulled a notepad and pencil from a pocket and began scribbling names, times, and their bet. "I'll be wantin' a copper for each wager," the boy announced. When they grumbled, he said, "I'm really too busy to do this, and soon I won't have any time at all, so if a copper's too much to add to the silver you're puttin' to chance, then go do it yourself."

Corporal Jensen removed her helmet, revealing auburn hair with wide woven scalp braids which extended from her nape and wrapped around her neck for both style and warmth. She elbowed her way to the front of the growing crowd. "You know we're all confined to our posts while we're on duty."

The lad smiled and held his head high. "Yes, I most certainly do."

Ramirez laughed. He handed the runner another silver coin with three coppers pressed against it, "Put me down for eleven o'clock today as well."

The lad took the coins and wrote down the sergeant's three bets. Jensen raised a brow and said, "That's only two hours away. Don't you think that's a little soon?"

"No," he replied grimly, "I do not. I have a feeling, a gut feeling. It's kind of like the itch you get between your shoulder blades just before an ambush."

She nodded and then proceeded to place another bet thirty minutes after the sergeant's time.

"Okay, you pack of degenerates," Ramirez sounded off in his best drill sergeant's voice. "Break it up and return to your posts. There could be a fleet of enemy ships out there floating in the fog."

To accentuate his comment, a blast of training fire sounded from a distant cannon. The warriors hurried to finish their wagers and returned to their posts.

Time ticked away till boredom got the better of many along the wall. Ramirez yawned. A dice game began a few paces away to the right where soldiers crowded under a tarp to escape the rain. A billowing breeze ballooned the canvas from time to time, causing it to shed water and flap noisily. The rain receded to a tolerable mist, and two soldiers to the left found space for sword practice. The occasional blast from a ship performing training drills rolled in through the mist. Soldiers counted seconds between the flash and bang to guess the distance. Then the simultaneous reports of a full broadside erupted from the fog.

Ramirez looked to the right and saw a few heads turn briefly, but no one seemed concerned. He then looked left and saw the same. "Jensen," he called out loudly to his corporal, his eyes back on the horizon. The wind rose suddenly out of the south—it whipped his short ponytail from where it protruded out of the back of his helm. The tarp over the dice game pulled free from one corner and flapped at the soldiers underneath like a great angry bird.

Jensen stood by him two seconds later and saluted fist to chest. "Aye, Sergeant," she said.

"Send runners down the line," he said as another series of cannonade echoed their report, followed by another right after that. This time, dim flashes flickered in the fog. "Warn them to be ready. Pass the word that *I* think this is it."

"Yes, Sergeant," she answered smartly.

"Send a message to the captain as well. Warn him of the increased gunfire at sea. I'm sure he heard it, but send a runner anyway."

Her breastplate rattled from another salute and she was gone. The wind worried the mist, allowing more flashes of fire to be seen from shore. The concert of cannons increased, and the smell of gunpowder seasoned the swirling air with increasing frequency. Ramirez ordered cannon loads checked and touch-holes cleaned and re-primed, trebuchets cocked, naphtha loads readied, catapults and ballistae cranked to full stretch, and braziers stirred. All archers had been issued fire arrows.

When the sergeant turned his gaze back to the sea he saw ghostly longboats emerging from the thinning fog. Rowers pulled up and down the waves, riding the final surf as they were pushed through the breakwater's ports and into the docks. Farther down the beach, more longboats were grounding on the strand. The sailors abandoned their boats to hobble up the beach, assisting their less ambulatory mates. Many wore bloodstained bandages—some were carried on litters. The gate opened and a team of medics ran out to their aid, escorted by a platoon of riflemen. As Ramirez watched the low-level fog lift away into a low ceiling of grey overcast, he caught his breath at what the unrestricted visibility revealed. Exclamations, curses, and cries of despair could be heard on along the wall.

Ramirez was one of those who had encouraged people to stay and fight. He was now glad some of his family had fled to the safety of the mountains. He had thought the city truly had a chance—until now. At the sight before him, he fervently wished he had seen his wife to safety as well. He felt thunderstruck as he gazed upon the vast armada filling the horizon into the endless distance, north, south, and west. To say 'thousands' was a gross understatement; there were tens of thousands of ships rolling to the rhythm of the sea's swells.

Within six kilometers of shore, the red flags of Kandia flapped above scarlet sails. A meager few hundred barks seemed to be granted leave to toy with the puny half circle of Alliance ships. Sedaran, Abezdan, and Kalusian ships battled bravely against impossible odds. Pagentia and Renauld chose neutrality, but several privateers from those countries could be seen dancing upon the waves, tacking in, striking fast, and darting out again with a flaming enemy left in its wake. Longboats from sinking ships began an exodus to the shore—most were alliance boats. The Kandian longboats fleeing sinking ships rowed to the safety of the vessels flying the red. Those few that were too far from help came to shore and were taken prisoner.

Out of the mass came the biggest ship anyone had ever seen. "The *Sea Dragon*, the *Sea Dragon*," they murmured down the line. That notorious *Sea Dragon* that people knew from tales told of the battle of Valekrie. She was sixty meters long and cruised slowly into the fray blasting ships out of the water from chase guns and broadsides. The biggest ship on the Western Sea was packing seventy guns, all big. Never since the forgotten past had the Ocean Paciphia bore a ship this vast and powerful. She tore into her foes until she anchored directly abeam the city. Then the *Sea Dragon* began her assault upon Seal Bay's wall.

Artillery from the wall commenced firing cannons. Trebuchets on the ground behind them slung boulders and baskets of stones. Catapults were useless until targets came closer. Ramirez kept his cannons hot and firing. The artillery aided the Alliance ships, but the *Sea Dragon* was too much for them. Even without that floating behemoth, the odds looked to Ramirez like ten to one.

With at least a hundred ships of the Alliance fleet in flames and foundering to the bottom, their only recourse was to flee in hopes of fighting another day. A large contingent of Kandian ships gave chase. Sergeant Ramirez hurried along the right flank of his platoon offering support and pointing out targets that came too close to the shore while Corporal Jensen did the same on the left. The noise of the cannons soon made his ears ring and his soldiers began asking him to repeat his orders with hands to their ears. He wondered if a person could go deaf from too much exposure to loud noise.

Ramirez saw the messenger boy running towards him. He was probably returning to the captain with bad news. Ramirez grabbed his shoulder and yelled to be heard. "We need more powder and ball. We also need something for our ears, cotton or cloth, anything will do. Bring us rags if you must."

The boy nodded and ran off. *Not so talkative now*, Ramirez thought as he watched the agile boy skip around working artillery teams and hurdle over a cannon rolling back from recoil. When the sergeant turned back to the battle he saw a dozen of his riflemen firing at the closest ships. Looking out over the water he could see the splashes of their volleys landing just beyond the breakwater. "You're wasting ammo, you fools, cease fire. There'll be plenty to shoot at soon enough."

He looked back at the *Sea Dragon* and saw seven or eight puffs of smoke erupt from the gun ports followed by the report in matching sequence, *boom-boom, boom-boom-boom, boom, boom-boom*, and then he heard the whistle and saw the black cannon ball coming right towards him. "Incoming!" he yelled. He hit the deck of the battlements when an explosion to his right rocked his world.

If Ramirez had had ringing ears before, he was deaf now. He climbed to his feet and looked to his right. Vertigo washed over him, so he leaned against the wall for support. Atop the twenty meters high wall, along the crenelated battlements, once notched for archers, now gave cannons a half-meter high wall to shoot over. The higher sections in between were chest high to a tall man. These sections were a meter thick and, combined with the wall they walked on, there was a total of three meters of solid stone. Before this moment, Sergeant Ramirez had thought the wall was impenetrable. A half a dozen meters to his right, the wall was gone—destroyed—obliterated.

Ramirez staggered dazedly to the edge. Powder smoke and rock dust settled, swirled, and slid off north on the wind. As the haze cleared his hearing began to restore, if only partially, but the ringing returned. Before him was a half-circle gap in the wall five meters deep and ten meters across. Another two meters would have taken out the wall all the way to the ground.

Pieces of rubble, anywhere from fist to carriage size, littered the ground as far back as thirty meters, taking out buildings with its collateral destruction. At first, Ramirez thought he gazed upon granite, but as he watched, patches of red soaked through the rain-speckled dust. He then realized the rubble was littered with bloody body parts. Arms, legs, heads, and torsos torn in bits were strewn across the broken stones. Bitter bile rose to the back of his throat, and in the next moment he emptied his stomach.

Ramirez turned around and to the south, beyond his platoon he saw another section of wall burst, causing stone blocks to disintegrate and cascade into the city. Other sections of the wall suffered a like fate. The gates in front of the docks were gone, now burning splinters scattered in a half-moon on the main boulevard. The marina suffered only minimal damage.

He limped back to his platoon. They were a sorry lot, dazed and confused from the concussion of the blast, but they were coming around. They appeared otherwise unhurt. "Listen up," he yelled. His voice sounded distant in his own ears. "Stuff your ears." He pulled up his chainmail shirt and with his dagger cut two small scraps of cloth from his tunic and crammed them in his ears. "You'll go deaf if you don't. They'll be landing troops soon." He pointed to the damaged wall. "That's where they'll come through, and other breaches like it, but the main landing force will go for the gates in front of the docks."

"Sergeant, look," Corporal Jensen faced the

enemy armada. "They've stopped firing." Her braid, no longer circling her neck, hung down over her right shoulder, and the rock dust that coated her began to darken as the rain turned it to a thin layer of mud.

As they watched Ramirez heard only sporadic cannon fire, and that came from the few placements along what little wall remained. There were a few good hits at sea, but most of the rounds splashed ineffectually in the water. The ships began deploying longboats.

"Let's be ready to give them a true Sedaran welcome when they come," said Ramirez. "Keep your guns quiet and your heads low, and maybe they'll think we've been silenced. Jensen, have your squads turn their cannons on our marina. Blow the damn thing up, all of it, but wait until it fills up with Kandians." Ramirez deployed two guns to the breached wall and had the rest point their muzzles at the waterline. Once all was set, he said, "Now we wait."

A thousand longboats filled with red-coated Kandian soldiers rowed towards the city. As the first wave neared the breakwater, the second wave assembled and came.

CHAPTER 16

The Sea Dragon sank several Alliance ships with its ten-kilo guns before it began belching fire upon the city with twenty-kilo exploding cannonballs. Sections of wall exploded into rubble while gun emplacements were blown sky-high. Behind the gates formations of riflemen with fixed bayonets, fidgeting, and pacing, stood ready to raid the beaches and docks when the first longboats landed. The blast that blew the gates swallowed the front ranks in fire and flaming splinters. Men and women were rendered to bits of flesh and bone shrapnel. The next twenty or so were lifted off their feet and thrown several meters back on top of their knocked down and rolling comrades.

King Gerald stood with his fellow kings atop the palace's west tower, watched the destruction of Seal Bay's defensive wall. Bertil's General Pavel had chosen the location as a tactical headquarters and his own General Jakez had approved. The palace sat upon a hill three kilometers from the seaward gates, and now that the clouds had lifted, the west tower penthouse sported a view of the entire seaside conflict.

"My gods," exclaimed Thorson. "That blast just killed forty men."

"Men and women," corrected Bertil quietly.

Gerald lowered the brass spyglass, his face reflecting the horror of the scene below them. Though Jakez had warned them of the possibilities of these new black powder weapons, he had not expected the devastation they had just witnessed in the last half hour. The bloody carnage of war was not new to him but never before had he seen arms and legs blasted from bodies and hurtled through the air with stone and bits of wood. "We need to pull back."

"Yes, your majesty," replied General Jakez without taking his eye from his scope. "Unfortunately, those soldiers on the wall will have to stay."

"What?" said Bertil incredulously. "There's no way they can stand against that." He pointed to the advancing longboats with an outstretched arm behind him as he faced the two generals. "Even if we brought up our reserves we're outnumbered at least ten to one."

"Your majesty," said General Pavel. Where Jakez was thick, Pavel was tall. The corded muscles on his bare forearms were reflected in the lean tightness of his face. "Sadly, those brave souls on the wall will have to be sacrificed. We need them there to give us time to retreat. General Jakez told us that Seal Bay would fall, but I don't think any of you were listening. We have planned an evacuation and a fighting retreat. It is set in place awaiting the order to begin."

Thorson turned and asked, "Won't they just

swarm over us?"

"Not if we burn the city," answered Jakez.

Bertil slumped as if he had just aged forty years. He looked tired, mentally drained. "I know. You both warned us, but I guess I just didn't want to believe it. I didn't think they could blow down our wall so easily, but must we burn our city?"

"It's not your city anymore," said Gerald. "It's Drayden's, or will be in a few hours. If you can't have it, burn it. Drayden needs this port to supply his advance to the east. The Kandians will have to fight the fires to salvage what they can. That should keep them busy while we fall back." He stepped closer to Bertil and placed a comforting hand on the portly king's shoulder. "Look at the bright side, my cousin king. When we take back your city, Drayden will have rebuilt it for you out of his pocket." He smiled, trying to ease the king's pain, but Bertil only nodded sadly.

"Okay," said Bertil. He straightened, and the grief in his face was replaced with anger. "If we must fight the Kandians all the way to Eastonia, so be it. Let us get there before him and use these weapons that Drayden desires so badly, on him." He turned to Pavel and said, "Start the evacuation and…" He paused as if he had to force the next words out. "Burn the city."

Generals Pavel and Jakez turned and began giving orders to the waiting officers and messengers. Runners departed one by one, their rapid footsteps down the spiral stairs barely heard over the sounds of battle nearby.

When Gerald looked back he saw a tear form in Bertil's eye, but the king turned and raised his monocular to watch the battle. Thorson had already resumed his vigil, and when Gerald looked through his spyglass he gasped. Much had happened during their few minutes of discussion.

For every ship blown to bits by city artillery, there were two more to disembark a shipload of attacking marines. Longboats in the bay became so thick they bumped into one another. When a cannon or trebuchet found a target, the sea turned red amid the wreckage, and survivors, if there were any, were hauled aboard the rowing flotilla. Overloaded enemy boats landed on the beach and ships began docking in the harbor until the piers were full.

Screaming Kandians ran to the damaged wall with scaling ladders under a hail of rifle balls and explosions. A Kandian phalanx formed up at the marina. It was surrounded and roofed with shields, and it marched like an armored bug towards the ungated entrance, now defended by reinforcements reforming into an Alliance phalanx equally shielded and bristling with spears and swords.

Arrows flew, some finding flesh but most catching shields or sand, while the rifles penetrated both shield and armor like knives through soft cheese. A company of Kandian riflemen lined up to shoot, but the rain fouled the flash pans and their weapons misfired. They were cut down in short order by the more advanced percussion cap rifles used by the defenders.

Gerald saw a platoon on the wall about two hundred meters north of where the gates had been. There was one trebuchet below them hurtling pieces of broken wall stones over their heads and into the bay, which was thick with longboat targets. The guns of the platoon began a cannonade on the marina with devastating effect. Other surviving emplacements along what remained of the wall turned their cannons on the enemy at the docks as well. Soon the marina was destroyed and the ships were in flames. Black smoke boiled in a column and curved under the grey sky to blow north on the wind.

"Who leads that platoon?" asked Gerald, indicating the soldiers trapped between two blasted sections of the wall. "They just blew up about thirty ships."

"That is Sergeant Juan Ramirez," replied Pavel. "His left flank is led by Corporal Rebecca Jensen. They are indeed valiant. Too bad…it is doubtful they will survive."

"A woman?" asked Thorson. The others ignored him.

Pavel cleared his throat. "My lord kings," he said. "It is time we go."

"Wait," said Gerald. "If those brave fighters will die so that we may live, let us, at least, give them the honor of witnessing their victories before they fall."

"A moment more, your Majesty," said Jakez, "but only a moment or their doom will be in vain. General Pavel is right, we need to go."

As they watched a horde began swarming into the breach north of Ramirez's cannons. As the hole filled with Kandians, the cannons fired into the swarm. Enemy infantry fell by the scores.

"Grapeshot," said Jakez with professional interest.

"Works well," agreed Pavel. "Until now we've only used it on targets."

"Why didn't he just use exploding cannon balls?" asked Gerald.

"Too close," answered Jakez. "The shrapnel from firing danger close could have killed or injured his own men."

"We originally planned to use it as a substitute when out of ammo," added Pavel.

Gerald watched as gun emplacements on the wall were being systematically overwhelmed. The battle at the gate raged with steel on shields while riflemen picked off soldiers in the enemy phalanx. The defense held and the Kandians had no replacements because the ships behind them were in flames, but other entry points had been penetrated. There was fighting in the streets. Ramirez drew his pistols and fired them both into enemies on the ladders. His men and women spent their rifles and with no time to reload began shoving ladders over with the empty weapons. Many drew sword or axe to defend the few comrades still able to man the cannons. The trebuchet behind them was in flames and the other cannon emplacements were overrun. One by one the artillery fell. It was down to edged weapons warfare for Ramirez and Jensen.

Ramirez filled his hands—sword in his right hand and an axe in his left. He hacked, whacked, stabbed and slashed. His last cannon was overwhelmed. Only a third of his platoon still stood, and they now fought only for survival. Blood spattered and slipping in gore, he worked his way to where Jensen was slicing ribbons in the attackers all around her. Like a crazed cat, her blade seemed to never dull nor fail to find a mark. Her feline growl rose into a battle cry that Gerald could hear shrieking above the din. The sergeant cut his way into her circle of adversaries, careful not to trip over the many slain. One of the Kandians, down and wounded, thrust a long dagger up at him. The blade pierced him mid-thigh. He ignored the pain and slashed off the offending hand;

arterial blood pulsed over both him and Jensen as he moved to fight back to back with her, the knife still protruding from his leg.

The bodies piled around them, nearly making a barricade. Gerald saw a sword enter Jensen, the bloody point protruded her back and was then yanked free. She fell, but not before she killed her killer with a slash to his neck. Ramirez parried a slash with his sword and buried his axe through helmet and skull, felling his foe but losing his axe. Gerald could see the man was tiring and probably weakening from blood loss.

Slash, parry, slash, slash, stab, thrust, riposte, step, and slash; the moves had no breaks, but they were indeed slowing. He felled two more, one with a throat slash, the other with a mid-thrust—then stopped, but only for a second. Gerald saw a half-meter of a bloody sword sticking out of the man's belly, but still he fought. Ramirez turned and slashed down, both wrenching the hilt from his killer's grasp behind him and making a fatal blow on the same man. His momentum carried him forward and he fell dying upon his dead adversary.

As Gerald watched he saw a fire arrow strike a powder keg and it exploded, effectively clearing the top of that part of the wall. In seconds, the broken sections of wall were filled with screaming Kandians.

As Jakez and Pavel literally dragged their kings to the stairs, Gerald saw a dozen plumes of smoke sprouting around the city with orange and yellow flames dancing below.

CHAPTER 17

King Drayden stood on the quarterdeck of his flagship, the Sea Dragon, glassing the destruction of the Seal Bay wall. A large contingent of his warships and longboats were docked at the enemy's piers, and his marines assembled in phalanxes to storm the breached defenses.

The Kandian king wore a simple circlet of gold over a black woolen hat. His straight brown hair, recently cut and absent of even a single strand of grey, was bound in a short tail, no more than four fingers in length.

"I see you took my advice," said the man next to him. His melodious deep voice was unmistakable.

Drayden brought down the glass and looked at the man who spoke. His ebony skin was as dark as strong coffee and his eyes were as green as his own. The king had never met anyone as black as this man. "You mean to just destroy the wall and not the city?" He smiled coldly. "Why would I destroy assets I plan to use or citizens whom I intend to tax?"

Two naval officers approached and saluted the king. The captain began to speak, but stopped and waited while the noise of the stern anchor chain rattled through the locks. When it ceased, and the men on the aft capstan drew up the slack and set the locking dogs. He began again. "Your Majesty," said Captain Torgny. "Fore and aft bridal anchors are set, port guns are primed and ready should you need them."

"All ships have ceased fire, your Majesty," added Fleet Admiral Orvar. "Except for those barks in pursuit of Alliance ships and others on perimeter patrol, the fleet are dropping anchors."

"Thank you, gentlemen," said the king. "That will be all."

The officers saluted again and moved away to give the king and his advisor some privacy.

A rapid series of explosions turned all heads towards the shore. Drayden saw his ships at the marina, one after another, burst into flames and flying debris. With that debris were sailors and soldiers thrown with the blasts. Several vessels began cutting free to make a run for it, but they too succumbed to the few cannons that remained on the wall. In minutes, every ship at the pier, and the marina itself was burning. Men and women caught fire and dove into the quenching water while others not so lucky collapsed on burning decks or flaming docks to be consumed.

"Perhaps you were premature, in sending those ships in so soon," said Sumas. "I told you it would be best to wait until you capture the city."

"You like telling me you told me so, don't you Sumas?"

"I live for it, your Majesty."

"I didn't think they would be so hard to overcome." Drayden raised his spyglass again. He was in time to see a company of riflemen cut down. "Why are our rifles misfiring in the rain, and theirs are still operational?"

Sumas unfolded his arms and cradled his chin in his palm. He tapped his cheek thoughtfully. "I will have to inspect a captured weapon to be sure, but I would suspect they have modified their weapons to percussion cap firing—more reliable. Their accuracy has improved as well, I suspect they have rifled the bores."

The king brought down the scope and leveled a look at Sumas. "You have obviously been withholding this technology, and now our enemies have it. Why?"

"They have good engineers and figured out a better design, or Ivan and Dalla have given them some hints."

Drayden was known for his stoicism, but his voice took on a steely edge. "No," he said. "Why are you withholding technology?"

"Too much too fast could destroy you."

The king was about to respond when General Khan came up the starboard steps to the quarter deck. "General," Drayden greeted. "I was just about to send for you. Let us dispatch an envoy to King Bertil to arrange the surrender of Seal Bay. We will listen to his terms though he's not exactly in a position to demand any."

"Your Majesty," replied Khan. "I'm sure King Bertil has evacuated Seal Bay." He gestured towards the city.

"Why would he do that? We only fired on the wall." He turned to look while he talked. "We spared the…" He stopped when he saw dozens of smoke plumes column up and bend north on the south wind.

Khan answered just as stoically as his king. "Seal Bay burns, your Majesty."

CHAPTER 18

Hawkins brought up the rear, absorbed in his mount's progress around some large rocks. Once he cleared the precarious section of terrain he caught sight of three things at the same time. The first was Ivan leaned back and taking a long pull on a wineskin while his horse picked its way down a rocky mountain path. The second was Aris, who was in the lead and happened to look back at that moment. The boy rolled his eyes, turned back, and mumbled something unintelligible to Hawkins at this distance. The third sight was the magnificent backdrop that neither of his companions seemed to notice.

They were descending into a canyon. On the opposite side, a waterfall cascaded off a cliff, sparkling white and silver as it fell a thousand meters into a vaporous mist where it reformed and collected into the head of a small blue ribbon river far below. The trail they followed took them diagonally down into a deep and forested ravine, which Hawkins could only assume would take them to that same river somewhere downstream. There were occasional open areas on the hillside allowing him to absorb the view, which soothed his eyes and brought him peace. He had not seen much of the sun in many days, so he constantly looked up to drink in the cloudless blue sky. He tried not to let the boy's sullen attitude sour his enjoyment of the day.

The first few days of their journey Aris had been a polite and capable guide. They had traveled southeast, staying in the mountains in order to arrive in the Plains of Hamaud far to the south of the Northern Caravan Route, which would not only be filled with soldiers of the Allied Kingdoms but would soon be engulfed in pitched battles with Kandian forces once Seal Bay fell. When they traveled beyond territory that Aris knew, he chose safe game trails, aptly circumnavigated gullies and mountains too steep to easily cross, and avoided sky lining them when possible.

Upon reaching the bottom of the ravine, the path grew wider and paralleled the river for a few kilometers until the way opened into a small valley. When shadows grew long and faded to evening dusk they filled their water skins and followed Aris away from the river to a sheltered campsite atop a small knoll. Aris shot three fool hens and in short order, they were lounging around a small campfire, each with a spitted grouse roasting over the coals.

"Why don't we just camp by one of these streams that feed into the river?" asked Hawkins. "We would have all the fresh water we could want without having to haul it."

"All animals come to water," replied the boy. "That includes predators. The sound of their approach would be masked by the noise of water rushing over rocks."

"Makes sense, I suppose," agreed Hawkins.

Ivan reclined against his saddle, drained the last swallow from his wineskin, and tossed it aside. "Quinlan trained him well. Have you noticed his choice of routes rarely dead ends at cliffs or in box canyons? The boy doesn't skyline us on ridgelines or lead us across open areas to be spotted by unwanted eyes."

"My grandpa calls them danger zones," Aris piped in. "He says you'll never see a cat cross one except at high speed unless it has cover."

Hawkins thought the praise boosted the boy's spirits. It certainly beat the former sullen attitude, sarcasm, and lack of patience with everyone and everything. If complimenting the boy made him this pleasant all the time he would sing praises to the lad from dawn to dusk. "Well, you're certainly a competent hunter. We appreciate you stretching our provisions." He turned to Ivan. "Will we have time to jerk some venison should the boy slay us a deer? Our stores are getting low and I'm getting rather low on funds."

Ivan fished another wineskin out of his saddle bag and smiled at it the way sailors long at sea would smile at an exotic dancer. "Sorry, we haven't the time. If you weren't such a pushover for all the pretty girls conning you out of drinks, you would have more money."

Hawkins furrowed his brows. "Every girl I bought drinks for ordered the most expensive thing in the house."

"Of course, they did. If you ever find one that doesn't, don't let her go." Ivan turned to Aris. "If you can bag a small deer before we reach Hamaud, we can dry some of it on our bedrolls as we ride. I'd rather avoid villages in case King Gerald has people looking for us. I would hate to lead them to Imar and his key. The less contact we have with people, the better."

The next day Aris was back to being himself again. Hawkins knew the boy was a good guide, but he was still a young teenager. The polite manners Aris had had when they left his home were short lived. After three days on the trail, he became sullen and impatient again. He began to scowl at suggestions and he answered advice with rolling eyes and muttered remarks riddled with sarcasm. He complained often. First it was only a little, and then it progressed to a regularity that could only be considered constant. The sailor thought the boy had straightened up after his previous night's good behavior, but Aris relapsed with a vengeance.

Ivan and Hawkins began passing the wineskin back and forth with frequent rapidity. Aris saw his role picking paths and providing game as sufficient contribution to their welfare. Gathering firewood, helping with the cooking, hauling water, setting up camp and tending the horses were, as far as he was concerned, beyond him. He even balked at cleaning the game he killed. The chores, which they all shared in doing, were met by the boy with whining and sarcasm. By the sixth day, he had to be forced into pulling his own weight by Ivan threatening to turn him into a toad. That was also when they ran out of wine, making the already grumpy Ivan, even more irritable.

"The little demon is driving me mad," growled the exasperated wizard as he squeezed the last few drops from the empty wineskin.

"Yes," replied Hawkins, "Aris does present himself as a good argument in favor of birth control."

"And the little ingrate wonders why I drink."

"You are not alone. My thirst has increased as well. I am not accustomed to this kind of stress and insubordination on the *Bedford Lee*. His insolence aboard a ship would be corrected with a cat o' nine tails." Hawkins' eyes sparkled, and a barely perceptible smile lifted one corner of his mouth. "I can braid one for you if you like."

"Don't tempt me," Ivan growled. He sat on a log and turned the bacon he was frying for their breakfast. He stood up. "Risk or not, we're stopping at the next village."

Aris heard this as he came into camp carrying four large skins of water that he had filled at a nearby spring. "Why's that?" he asked in a saucy tone. "Is it because you're out of wine?"

The boy's sarcasm grated on Hawkins, but Ivan's face flushed a deep red.

"You're damn right," retorted the wizard. He pressed his lips together and clamped his teeth. Hawkins watched the wizard take a deep breath and count to ten. Ivan took another breath and then continued with forced calm, "We will be down on the plains by this evening where avoiding people will not only be more difficult, but more important. Game is less plentiful as well; we will need more supplies."

The boy nodded. "It makes sense, I suppose," he said evenly. Hawkins thought Aris was becoming rational until he finished his sentence loudly and childishly, "If it's not just an excuse for you to get more alcohol."

Hawkins let out a weary breath. He saw Ivan's anger rekindle, so he spoke more to head off conflict than out of need. "We could all use a hot bath," he said. "It will be our last chance for a while I fear. We will be in the flatland by tomorrow I'll wager. Those lands are my province, and it will be my turn to step in as guide." Aris seemed interested at this revelation so Hawkins added, "I was not always a seaman. I grew up as the son of a caravan trader. I know the Hamaudi plains, and as we travel south into the desert, water will become scarce and very expensive. I will be your guide there."

"There is also a need for haste," Ivan grumbled. "I communed with my colleague last night. Imar's daughter has been kidnapped."

"What?" Hawkins was aghast. "Little Aideen kidnapped?"

Ivan nodded. "She is being held ransom for the octagon key. We need to hurry to Juana Pohala. That is where the swap will take place."

Aris dropped the water skins and said, "So what's she to me?" He stormed off, not waiting for an answer.

Fire flared in Ivan's eyes. He moved toward Aris' retreating back, but Hawkins put a hand on the wizard's shoulder. "Let him go," he said in a disappointed tone. "Besides, your bacon's burning."

The wizard pulled the pan from the fire. "It's ready. Have some while it's hot. You can call the boy if you want. He can have it cold for all I care." Ivan grabbed up his share and stalked off grumbling. At that moment, Hawkins thought Ivan and Aris were a lot alike.

CHAPTER 19

Aris' horse cropped the roadside grass as he waited for Ivan and Hawkins. Ivan came up the narrow path first and looked around as his mount went to the edge to eat. "Is this Smugglers Road?"

Hawkins came off the path at that moment. Aris headed off the question on the seaman's face by answering Ivan's. He nodded, and said, "It's called 'The Cutoff' now, and sometimes 'The Shortcut.' Smugglers still use it, but they try to discourage being so blatant with the name."

"I don't remember this shortcut," said Hawkins with furrowed brows.

"I'd be surprised if you had," said the wizard. "This road was probably not even a trail back then. It's hardly fit for wagons even now, or so I heard. When Bertil took the crown, like most kings, he raised the import and export taxes, so…"

217

"A few traders began bypassing the customs station at Sepur," Hawkins finished for him. "We always bribed the customs agents to lower our assessment. This road would have been handy. Where does it come out?"

"I've never been on it," said Ivan. He looked at Aris.

"I haven't been on it either," said the boy. "I was told it comes out in the mountains about eighty kilometers west of Sepur on the Northern Caravan Route. It then connects with the Western Route just shy of three hundred clicks south Sepur. We should come to a small town about two more clicks down the road. There is only one inn, but my grandpa said to drop his name when we get there."

"Oh," asked Hawkins, "will we get a discount?"

"No," answered Aris, shaking his head. "Grandpa said there'd be fat chance of that. There's only one inn in town and the price is extreme. Theft is high there. He said if you drop his name he'll give us a room with a good lock and a bathtub."

"That works for me," said the wizard. "Come on," he added, pulling his mount away from the horse mowed section of roadside grass. He nudged it to a trot down the road.

Aris looked at Hawkins who shrugged, and together they followed the wizard.

The town of Squires Landing was so small Aris thought they could put the entering and leaving signs on the same post. He had seen communities with more facilities to offer. There was an inn, a stable, and a store, but nothing more. Oskar the innkeeper owned all three. He was a bulky man with thinning ginger hair and a scar above his right eye that made his eyelid droop. His facial features looked as if he would sell you a room, serve you a meal, or slit your throat without any change in expression.

Aris felt Ivan nudge him when they stood in front of the bar facing the innkeeper. He glared at the wizard, but Ivan glared back, which sent a chill down the boy's spine. He knew he was on the edge of going too far with the old man again. He turned back to Oskar and tried to sound pleasant. "My grandfather said we could get safe lodging here." The innkeeper's face didn't change nor did he answer. "His name is Quinlan," added the boy.

Oskar grunted and Aris thought his left eyebrow may have lifted a fraction of a millimeter. The balding innkeeper kept his dead gaze on them as he reached under the counter and produced a key, which he tossed on the bar. "That'll be six silvers."

Hawkins gasped, and Ivan sputtered, "For only one room?"

"I charge by the head," replied the innkeeper. "If you want to stable your horses, it will cost you another three silvers. My boy will brush 'em down, and give 'em each a scoop of grain. You can leave 'em out front on the rail for the night if you wish, but I doubt they'd be there in the morning."

Hawkins stepped up and said, "How about we give you…"

Oskar interrupted by pointing at a sign high on the wall behind him. It read: ALL PRICES ARE FIRM – NO HAGGLING. Hawkins gave up. Ivan counted out the coins.

As promised the room had a lock and a tub. They kept the innkeeper's boy busy hauling buckets of hot water for each of their baths. The hot water was so relaxing that Aris fell asleep in the tub and dreamt of a girl he knew in Seal Bay. He sat with her on a bench overlooking the marina, but when he finally mustered the courage to give her a kiss he woke up. He was thankful Ivan and Hawkins had left to get supplies. He sat in the cooling water until he relaxed enough to not be embarrassed should they return.

The food was good and plentiful, and after a good night's sleep, Aris felt restored. When they had finished a hearty breakfast, they left the inn and rode towards the lowlands. They were three hours into their ride before the boy realized their occasional saddleback conversations had interested him, and that he was getting along with both of his companions. He found that he liked the old wizard and the seaman, at least, when they weren't annoying. For the first time in a long time, Aris was actually happy. No one was upset with him for speaking his mind, and his short comments weren't coming out with his usual sarcasm.

As they descended in elevation, Aris noticed that the air was dryer. The tall evergreens were becoming sparse, to be replaced with stunted and crooked digger pines and scrub brush, and what few deciduous trees remained seemed skeletal and bare but for the few dried leaves still clinging to bony branches. It was if those leaves were waiting for a breeze to free them from the twiggy grip. The terrain was rockier and there were fewer areas of red dirt. The deer were darker and had big ears like mules. The squirrels were as big as cats and grey instead of red. One time a flash of black caught the corner of his eye. In and out it leaped so fast he thought it may have been a shadow cat though the nocturnal creatures were almost never seen in the daytime.

The road was good, packed sand and clay with hardly any ruts, allowing them to make good time, but the flora and fauna were changing as rapidly as the terrain. Aris was beginning to feel exposed and apprehensive. It was as if they had been in the lush mountain forest that he knew so well one day, and then the next day finds them in rocky foothills riddled with rattlesnakes and jackrabbits. The few patches of dried up scrub oaks did little to beautify these barren brown hills. Even the golden grass was dry and lifeless, lacking any green whatsoever.

Aris was out of his element. He looked back for reassurance, but his companions seemed not to notice that they had just entered an alien land. Hawkins was working his way between some tall roadside boulders and Ivan was tilting the skin. It baffled the boy that the seaman seemed so at ease in such a place so void of water and it disgusted him that the wizard would start in on his wine before the sun stood straight up in the center of the sky. No one noticed him rolling his eyes.

Aris didn't realize that he rolled his eyes. Ever since moving to his grandfather's cabin a year ago his mother had been trying to break him of the habit, and for some reason, he hadn't done it as much as he had back when his father still came home from duty on weekends. That was before all leave had been suspended. He did the eye rolling even less when his grandfather showed up with a wagonload of books and supplies from town. His grandfather brooked no nonsense from anyone and said as much all the time. Aris smiled as he heard the gruff man's words in his head. *"I'll not take any sass off a grown man, so I sure as all the hells won't take it off a smart-assed teenager."*

Aris' musings drifted to the girl he had dreamt of the day before when he dozed in the tub. The thought took his uneasy mind off the foreign countryside, so he was not paying attention when he rode beside a large overhanging rock. The large oblong boulder was common to this dusty land of dry grass, pinnacled with stone protrusions and rocky monoliths. It stuck out from the hillside and jutted over a shelf of dirt that bordered the roadside for several meters. The shade was cool as he passed under the rock, drifting in pleasant daydreams.

The survival part of his mind assessed it to be a good spot to shelter from either the rain or sun, but that was only a very small part. The larger part of his mind saw a girl's lips that needed kissing. Consequently, he failed to notice the nest of snakes sleeping in the shade.

"Aris," Hawkins exclaimed from behind. "Look out! Snakes under the rock!"

At the same moment that Hawkins roused him, a startled snake set off its own warning with a sharp and very distinct rattle. Aris had never encountered a living rattlesnake before but had seen dried rattles and skins. In fact, he had a snake rattle, one he had purchased at the market in Seal Bay when he was Jimmer's age. He knew the sound and he knew that the rattle making it was attached to a live, angry, and very venomous snake. He pulled in on the reins to steady his startled, wide-eyed mount.

Aris looked to his right and saw a double coiled diamondback vigorously shaking its rattles, its upper body cocked. It hissed deadly anger in a way that made the boy's neck bristle with goosebumps. The wide open mouth displayed long venom dripping fangs that protruded from a v-shaped head. Fear froze the boy. His arms chilled and his body tensed.

The dry wispy shake of another rattle shook, and then a few more. Everywhere he looked the ground either circled or slithered. His horse whinnied and the coiled viper's hissing strike preceded the hot pain below his knee. A scream of surprise shot from his throat.

His horse bolted headlong down the hill, heedless of rocks and scrub brush. It leaped and bounded, picking up speed with his momentum. The snake, still latched onto Aris' leg, dangled out behind as the frantic horse plunged down the hill. Gravity won out over the speed. The horse stumbled and plowed into the ground as Aris was launched into the air, the snake trailing like the tail of a kite. A bush rushed up to meet him, breaking his fall with its thorny branches.

Aris lay on his side stunned amid the brambles, dimly aware of his companions shouting his name. The snake writhed in broken-backed agony atop a melon sized rock. A hundred points of pain pierced the boy's senses, causing him to groan miserably as he rolled over onto his back. He winced with the jab of the broken bush poking his spine. His horse walked over to him and nosed him on the side of his face and then wandered a few feet away to sample some grass. The minute it took for Ivan and Hawkins to reach him seemed an hour to the dazed boy. First one, and then the other broke through the brambles and leaned over him from each side.

The wizards face was scrunched with worry. "Can you wiggle your fingers and toes?" he asked. Urgent concern was evident in his voice.

Aris waggled his fingers and then knit his brows while he worked his toes inside his boots. He nodded.

"Good," Ivan responded. He reached down and Aris felt the wizard's fingers probing the back of his head, neck, and upper back. "Well, at least, you didn't break your neck. Just lay still. We need to check the rest of your bones, and see if you have any cuts besides the snakebite." Ivan looked at Hawkins and flicked his eyes to the boy's leg.

The seaman drew a knife and slit the boy's trousers from cuff to knee. He paused only a second to inspect the snakebite before removing his neck scarf and tying it above the wound.

Ivan quickly surveyed the boy for other breaks and bleeds. "Looks like just the bite," he said.

Together Hawkins and Ivan lifted Aris clear of the scrub brush and set him on a patch of ground clear of all but some dried grass and a few small pebbles.

Hawkins gave Aris a short direct look and said, "This will hurt." Without waiting for a reply, he sliced both bite holes, and the boy stiffened.

"Ouch," exclaimed Aris. "You could have warned me."

Hawkins ignored him, leaned in, and sucked blood and venom from the wound, spitting to the side with each draw. After a few repetitions, he stopped the sucking but continued to spit for another minute.

Ivan cleared his throat. "It is debatable whether or not that drew out any of the poison, but I think it would be best if we just rest here and try to keep your blood from flowing too fast." He pulled his wineskin from his belt and held the spout to the boy's lips. "Here, drink. It might not help, but it will relax you."

Aris took the skin and drank.

The wizard noticed Hawkins eyeing the wineskin, his hand reaching for it. "Oh, no you don't," he said, standing and going to his horse. Removing a water skin he tossed it to the seaman. "You can drink my wine, but I'll not have you washing your mouth with it. Use water."

Hawkins snatched the skin and began rinsing and gargling with the warm water. When he finished he saw Ivan looking at a copse of stunted trees a few kilometers to the south. "We're in a bad spot to camp," he said, joining the wizard. "There's, at least, some cover in those trees. There may be water as well."

"There is little we can do about the delay," Ivan said. "We'll move the boy there, set up camp, and let him rest." He looked at Aris with furrowed brows and said, "You're looking a little green around the gills."

"Uh, I don't feel so good," Aris replied. He was sweating and was jittery and he began to feel like he would hurl.

"Come on," said Hawkins. He bent down and putting Aris' arm around the back of his neck he helped the boy to his feet. "Let's get you on your horse, and into some shade."

CHAPTER 20

Aideen leaned back in the saddle as her horse descended the steep grade. Her soreness from the first few days of travel was gone and she was actually feeling good now that the weather had cleared. Riding and camping in the rain were not at the top of her list of favorites. Three days of precipitation had nearly driven her mad with misery, but the day before had been the worst because the wind had pelted her with stinging drops as they crossed over the crest of the Western Range. The wind had flapped her tent while the rain played a staccato rhythm on its roof late into the night with crescendos of lightning and thunder.

When Hazim roused Aideen with her usual breakfast of spiced oatmeal, the brightness through the open tent flap brought her outside immediately where she found the fresh clean smell of a dripping forest around her and a blue sky above. The air was pleasant if a bit humid as the puddles evaporated in the morning's warmth. When they set out it did not take long for the ground to dry. As the day aged on to afternoon the heat became stifling hot, causing little clouds of dust to rise from the horses' hoofs. It was as if the desert forced its arid air up the eastern side of the mountains to keep the moisture in exile to the west. However, it was obvious that some of the precipitation had penetrated over the top of the range, what with the size of the swollen creeks they had to cross.

Aideen could not think of a time in far northern Abezda when it had been as warm as it was now, and they were still high in the mountains. What she would have given for some cut-off breeches and a sleeveless top. She thought of asking Hana for a knife to hack away the skirts and sleeves of her dress, but she knew the prudish Lord Townsend would not approve.

The road wound back and forth like a red dirt snake down a long stretch of descending slope. The dust made her nose itch and she kept trying to scratch it, but the clay nose cast made it impossible to do so. Aideen satisfied herself with picking at the stitches in her lip.

Far below, the desert stretched off into the distance. Aideen thought she could see the curve of the earth on the heat shimmering horizon. Huge golden barked ponderosa pines spread out uncrowded along the eastern slope, their massive roots gripping rocks and barren soil like the talons of giant birds.

Aideen was becoming apprehensive. The tell-tale knot in her stomach that let her know Khaled was near had grown even though the assassin's proximity had not changed for most of the day. She wondered if it was a premonition of another danger. Khaled rode in the front, impatient with their slow progress as if the distant sun-blasted land that lay baking far below called to his desert blood. Aideen was in the middle of the procession with Hana riding just ahead of her and Townsend behind. The two sell-swords between them and the assassin were Jamal and the other female fighter Maha. The two riding security and bringing up the rear were Akil and Ghassan. Hazim was out of sight, scouting the back trail.

It had been a few days since Aideen had contacted Dalla with the mind-speech; not that she hadn't tried, but her attempts seemed to be met with a preoccupation on the healer's part. She had tried to call Ivan as well, but Aideen sensed that the wizard was also busy or, at least, distracted. Aideen was roused from her self-pity by the sound of pounding hooves.

"Ho," shouted Hazim as he maneuvered his horse down the narrow mountain road at a hazardous speed. The mercenary concentrated intently on the task at hand as he rounded switchbacks and skirted the fragile edge as small stones broke free and preceded him by the most direct route down the steep slope. Red dust boiled from each hoof into a cloud that resembled a big ghostly worm of red vapor that grew with its undulating advance behind rider and horse. Aideen twisted in her saddle to watch Townsend turn his horse up the hill to meet the urgent scout. She felt her neck hairs rise in chill warning as Khaled ascended past her on his black steed. She briefly thought that the mount should have red eyes, fangs, and clawed hooves in order to permit such a despicable person upon its back.

"My Lord," Hazim began before he pulled up to a full stop in front of Townsend. "Twenty mercs ride in haste less than five minutes behind us. They bear the banner of a white square-rigged bark over crossed swords on a black field."

Townsend's face flashed an instant of worry before he quickly covered it with confidence. "That would be the Murdoch Free Companies." He clenched his reins.

"Damn, I underestimated Akala's steward. He sent out patrols within minutes of the kidnapping, which is why we waited to depart. When they returned with no news, the road was clear or so I thought. I did not expect him to send another."

"A few of them are carrying longbows," added Hazim. "Murdoch mercs are reputed to be expert with the bow."

"Indeed, they are," Townsend agreed. "New recruits do little else but practice at the butts until they can consistently shoot half-meter groups at two hundred meters." To Khaled and Hazim he said, "They outnumber us and they have the advantage of higher ground. Get us off this road and find a defensible position."

"Wait," said Hazim. "A few of them carry some sort of weapon I have not seen before. It has a stock like a crossbow, but no bow arms and it is much longer."

"Muskets," exclaimed Townsend. "It is a very new weapon. I haven't time to brief you on firearms, nor the opportunity to buy any, just know they sound like thunder and can pierce shields and armor like butter." He paused briefly then impatiently added, "Now go."

Without nods or salutes, Khaled and Hazim flicked a glance at each other. Aideen saw much in that split second of meeting eyes. Before, she had thought they hated each other, but now it seemed more like a grudge that each of them carried. She had assumed that Khaled hated everyone and that people just returned their dislike and distrust based on the reputation of the Hamaudi Assassins. She thought that should a confrontation occur between these efficient killers it would probably end poorly for Hazim, and on the rare chance it didn't, then the assassin would kill his adversary later at his leisure by stealth or poison.

Aideen had let her own conflict with Khaled skew her understanding of him. Until now, in that half-second of the two men's resentful agreement to work together, she had seen Khaled as a hateful religious fanatic who was very good with his swords, but now she saw something else. Acceptance, she thought, or maybe compromise? Could there be a human beneath that black aura?

Khaled looked at her briefly before he and Hazim turned their mounts off the trail. Aideen noticed again how Hazim looked almost like an older version of Khaled, except that the older mercenary had bouts of kindness and occasional expressions of compassion, which the one-eyed assassin lacked completely. *Or did he?* The thought was fleeting and buried under her desire to escape. She wanted to wheel her horse and ride towards the pursuit, which was surely there to rescue her. Unfortunately, she was wedged in the middle of her captors who were now spread out all around her, staggered in two by two formations. She could easily race by the rider below her, but the hillside was so steep she suspected a stunt like that would probably get both her and her horse killed. Furthermore, downhill was the direction away from her rescuers. They continued in a treacherous side-hilling route diagonally down the slope.

Just before they rounded a hump in the hill that would hide them from the view from the road, the first men of the Murdoch Free Companies came down the path where Hazim's dust now floated low on the slope. Aideen's spirit soared with hope when she saw her family's flag flutter between the massive trunks. She knew that even if the Murdoch mercenaries had not seen them they would not fail to miss the lack of dust below where the tracks had turned off the trail. She thought she heard them maneuvering above them.

They came to a thick stand of bull pines that protruded between big horse-sized boulders where they dismounted to navigate the steep rocky terrain. A stream gushed between the rocks. The horses got a couple short swallows as they were hurriedly pulled past the water. Khaled glared impatiently back at them more than once.

Hazim kept them meandering behind boulders or between big trunks within the tree line as he followed the stream down the hill. "Stay undercover if you can," he said. "Their bowmen could pin us here while they flank us from each side. We need higher ground. Without it, we are dead." He turned to Khaled and said, "Find a place where we can stand against their numbers, perhaps across that ravine below and up that ridge. I'll lead them down along this stream. The trees will give us cover, but I fear they will attack any minute." As if to add meaning to Hazim's words an arrow whizzed over their heads and struck a tree down the hill. "A warning shot," he said. "Apparently they don't want us to go any farther."

Someone from above yelled, "Parlay." The word was drawn out and sounding like both request and threat. Aideen captors ignored it.

Khaled's eye went to the arrow and back to Hazim. The muscles below his patched orbit tightened slightly, but the assassin left the cover of the trees, leading his horse at a scramble diagonally down away from the creek. He positioned his horse above him on the slope as an equine shield. An arrow hit the ground in front of Khaled's horse. It was another warning. The next arrow was a heart-lung shot, the shaft sinking to the feathers behind the horse's shoulder, felling it instantly without a sound. The beast crumpled on collapsed legs and rolled to its side, gasping twice before it died. Three more shafts whizzed through the space where the assassin should have been, but he was gone. Aideen saw his feet just before the horse was killed, but he disappeared. The tree line that filled the ravine was a dozen meters beyond the dead horse, but she hadn't seen him cross the space. It was as if he had just vanished.

Aideen had heard that Hamaudi assassins were masters of illusion and deception and that Khaled had escaped confinement aboard the *Bedford Lee* by using this skill. It shocked her to actually see this trick, and it increased her fear of the assassin all the more. She had no time to ponder this phenomenon because Hazim was pushing their pace faster, weaving them in and out of the tall trunks, rarely exposing them for more than a second to the open field of fire from above.

The occasional thwack of a shaft sinking in the thick ochre bark urged them not to leave the cover of the great trees. The arrows came nowhere near their center where Hana hurried Aideen along, half running, half slipping, using all available cover as they raced for the thickly forested ravine that traversed their path below. Townsend's sell-swords had all prudently slung their shields across their backs and led their horses in a manner to provide live cover when those rare moments required them to step in the open.

Aideen knew the marksmanship of the Murdoch mercenaries well enough to know that none of their shots missed. Many of them had had years of experience with the bow. When a shaft hit a tree, it was because the tree was the target. Except for the vanishing assassin, had any of Townsend's sell-swords been targets they would have been dead or wounded. Her captors were being bracketed to slow the lead and hurry the rear in order to bunch them up for a concentrated attack. If not for the cover of the trees Aideen suspected that all of her captors would have been shot down without any danger to herself. The archers were that good. It was probably why they had not yet deployed the new, and unfamiliar, rifles with which they had not had time to train with to a comparable level of proficiency.

All of a sudden Aideen saw Hazim's horse rear up, screaming, its lead reins tearing from his grasp. The animal bounded forward two strides before it collapsed on the ground. Hazim dove behind a tree. Three shafts filled the air where he would have been had he not acted instantly. The horse's hooves dug at the dirt as it convulsed with blood frothing from its mouth and nostrils. A feathered shaft protruded from behind the stirrup at an angle to pierce the lung.

Another horse shrieked and Aideen looked behind her up the hill. Akil and Ghassan had passed an opening in the trunks that proved fatal for Ghassan's horse. Akil's mount was limping badly with an arrow in its leg, so he abandoned it. The two men grabbed their saddlebags and moved to cover, but they kept the standard three to five meter interval between them and the rest of the group.

A voice called out from a hundred meters up the hill. "We know you have the girl. Stop and hear me out."

Hazim was fifty meters ahead and nearly to the edge of the ravine. Aideen saw him look to Townsend, who was behind her and crowding closer. Hazim raised his brows in silent question. She looked back. Townsend was shaking his head and signaling to Hazim to keep moving.

After a few seconds, the voice called again. "I am Lieutenant Hawthorn of the Murdoch Free Companies. We will take Aideen Amirson. I give you my word; if you surrender none of you will be harmed. You are outnumbered and we have the advantage of high ground and ballistic weapons. If you don't surrender you will all die."

"Come any closer and we'll kill the girl," Townsend yelled back.

Aideen didn't like the sound of that. She let go of her horse's reins and ran away from Townsend to the safety of Hana.

"Foolish girl," hissed the woman warrior. She looked back, but Aideen's horse just followed along dragging its dangling reins. "We've lost three horses already. Here," she said, handing the reins of her own mount to the girl. "Don't get any funny ideas. If you charge out in the open you'll sprout enough arrows to look like a porcupine before they realize it is you." Hana stepped back, retrieved the reins of Aideen's horse and then returned to the girl's side. Hana took back her horse and stayed close to Aideen except when there was not enough room to do so and still retain cover from arrows.

"I don't think you will," replied Hawthorn loudly. "She is the only bargaining chip you have. You would not throw it away."

At that moment, an arrow killed Jamal's horse and another struck him between the shoulder blades and knocked him to the ground about five meters ahead of Hana. Aideen could see that the arrow had pierced his back slung shield. Maha went to him and pulled shield and arrow off of him. The broadhead had failed to penetrate the many rings riveted to his leather armor. The dark woman yanked out the arrow and handed Jamal his shield as she helped him to his feet. The shaft had knocked the wind out of him, so he was gasping as she guided him to the cover of her own mount.

"Okay," said Townsend. "How about if I start cutting off fingers for every minute that you don't pack up and go away."

"You do that and we will do the same to you until you die screaming," retorted Hawthorn. "How about this," he said loudly. "We just kill the girl, blame you, and we go home as rewarded heroes with your heads mounted on pikes."

Aideen really didn't like the sound of that. She sincerely hoped that Lieutenant Hawthorn was bluffing. Regardless, she wasn't going to run out in the open waving her arms.

To emphasize his threat, a buzzing sound like an angry bee zoomed overhead followed by a sharp impact on a tree causing exploding bark to fly outward from where the projectile struck. It was followed by a thunderous boom. It was the ball of a rifle traveling faster than sound. Three more rounds were fired, one grazing a trunk causing it to ping as it ricocheted. Following this was a hail of arrows. One shaft sunk in the rump of Aideen's horse and another struck Townsend's saddle. Aideen's wounded horse pulled free and ran limping out in the open where it was quickly shot down. Hana pulled her short bow and quiver of arrows from her saddle and slung them across her shoulders. She had no sooner pulled off the saddlebags when a shaft caught her horse's neck and another caught her high on the left shoulder from behind. Her horse ran off and it too was cut down.

"I'm not hurt," said Hana, flexing her arm.

The arrow had gone through the top edge of Hana's boiled leather armor. She snapped the feathered end off by brushing her back against a tree and then pulled the shaft out the front and cast it to the ground. Aideen saw a trace of blood on the shaft when she walked by the broken arrow, indicating the woman had been at least nicked if not badly injured. The armor piercing steel head was long and narrow like a needle, only thicker.

"Bodkins," Hana yelled to her comrades. "They are using bodkins now."

Aideen was concerned for Hazim and Hana. They had been decent to her if a bit gruff at times. She liked them, but they were presently in the employ of Lord Townsend. She had to escape, but now she was having doubts about this Lieutenant Hawthorn.

Only Townsend and Aideen were without protective armor, but the shafts were not aimed at either of them. At least, for now, the assault appeared to be a rescue. Nevertheless, Aideen thought the recent barrage came much too close. It could have killed her even if it was a bluff.

Maha's horse caught an arrow in the flank. The mare reared, but it calmed to her soothing words. She inspected the arrow and said, "It only slipped under the skin." She pulled the shaft from the subcutaneous tissue beneath the hide. The horse flinched and tried to rear. It was agitated but she kept it under control. She looked at the slender steel arrowhead, recognizing the armor piercing design. "You're right, Hana. They're using bodkins. Our mounts are no longer their target." She stuck the arrow in the ground without stopping. "It's still in good shape. Maybe you'll get a chance to give it back."

The only horses that remained were Townsend's and Maha's. "Leave the horse, my Lord," said Hana. She picked up the standing arrow as she walked past it. "It is only a burden now. We need to run if we are to live." Hana took Aideen's hand and ran down the hill past the other fighter and her horse, saying "You too Maha." Aideen looked behind her as she ran. Maha pulled her saddlebags free and followed them. His lordship had indeed abandoned his horse, and Akil and Ghassan were catching up.

Ahead, Hazim stopped short of a drop-off. He windmilled his arms to arrest his fall, recovered, and then waited for them to catch up. Townsend breathed heavily and his face was red. Aideen could hear a waterfall and see that Hazim stood on the edge of a rocky cliff.

"There's a gully below," Hazim said. "A small river runs at the bottom separating us from the rise on the other side. The water looks deep, but I doubt it spans a dozen meters. Come on, we have to find a way across and up the other side. Without higher ground we're doomed against their numbers. We will be in the open until we find a way down. Stay close. Maybe they won't shoot for fear of injuring the girl." Aideen was dubious, but she hoped Hazim was right. Her initial elation of imminent rescue had been considerably dulled by Hawthorn's threats.

They broke from the trees and ran along the cliff edge for about fifty meters when from above came the screaming charge of a dozen men on foot with shields raised and swords held high. Higher on the hill the rest of the mercenary platoon stood by their horses with bows ready. No more arrows flew and no one shot at them with rifles. Aideen hoped it was to prevent hurting her, but she was still hesitant to break free and run to the ones that had made the threat to kill her a few minutes ago.

Aideen, even as young as she was, could see no hope for her captors. She would have been pleased with the situation had Hawthorn not made what she hoped was a bluff. The probable loss of Hazim and Hana saddened her—she liked them and had hoped to ask her father to hire them once their contract with Townsend was finished. Her best course of action in the next few minutes would be to stay out of the way while the Murdoch mercenaries overwhelmed her sell-sword captors. Aideen had not seen Khaled since he had mysteriously disappeared. She wished that the maimed assassin was here now to be hacked down by her family's soldiers. *If only I could see that one's head spitted upon a pike.* Her line of thinking gave her pause. She could not remember ever being so bloodthirsty. Recent events had changed her and she was not sure if it was for the better.

Aideen heard Jamal state the obvious about being outnumbered. She could not help but add in a pleasant voice, "And they have archers."

Hana scowled at her, but sheathed her sword and strung her bow. She took aim, fired, hit a shield, and did it again twice more with the same inconsequential results.

As the twelve mercenaries closed the distance, Hazim yelled, "Shield wall!" Townsend's half dozen sell-swords raised their wall of shields. It was a hopeless position to be in—disadvantaged by lower elevation, the steepness of the slope and a drop off at their heels.

A shout came from farther along the precipice; Khaled stood twenty meters away waving his arms for them to follow. They broke and ran towards the black robed assassin who then darted down a narrow trail. The charging mercenaries curved their route to follow.

Aideen struggled as Hana dragged her down the escape path past Akil and Ghassan who guarded the retreat at the top of the trail. They followed after Hana and the girl but turned on the defensive at the base of the short descent. The tree-lined slope leveled before the last fifteen meters of clearing to the river. At the sound of steel on shield Hana swung about, releasing Aideen, and in a half second fired a shaft into the first man's thigh. He tumbled, causing the second man to trip over him. The two desert men slowed the advance with their shields braced against the onslaught while Hana fired arrows at any opening she could find, but they were being forced back into the small clearing beside the river.

Hazim was helping Townsend into the river, with Jamal and Maha splashing their way into the water ahead of them. Aideen did not see Khaled, but she was aware of the danger warning lump in her belly. Everyone was engaged in battle or flight. No one was paying attention to Aideen, so she ran.

The two-man shield wall was being forced step by step back towards the river under the downhill push of Murdoch mercenaries pushing in a line, squishing and crowding the men in front. Akil and Ghassan braced their bronze shields against the advancing wooden shield wall, their feet sliding over dirt and tree roots. The desert men stabbed over and under the shields while Hana fired arrows into the fray. She killed one man with an arrow to the eye and wounded two more with hits to the legs. A few mercs tried to flank around the trees, but Hana's bow quickly discouraged such maneuvers. Ghassan's sword found an enemy's crotch, but he paid for the score with a slash to his left shoulder. He was having trouble holding up his shield. Akil was bleeding from a cut below the knee.

The narrow trail down the embankment was clustered with enough trees to prevent flanking, but the ground leveled and opened out into a small gently sloped clearing next to the river. To each side of the clearing were tall evergreens and thick brush that still retained half of their red and yellow leaves. In a few more steps the attackers would be in the clearing and able to flank them. They would have to back up to the river to minimize that. If they could hold a few minutes to give their comrades a chance to form up on the other side they might be able to retreat into the river.

Hana glanced behind her for Aideen. The girl was

gone. She swore like a Sedaran fishwife. In that glance, she saw Hazim and Maha drag the exhausted Townsend out of the water on the other side of the narrow river. Jamal was climbing up the meter high bank to a level spot between two massive trees. Aideen wasn't with them either, but Hana judged the spot to be defensible enough for the few of them to hold off a company.

Townsend staggered to his feet and yelled across the river to Hana, "Find the girl. We need her."

Hazim was livid, but Hana could not hear what he barked at Townsend. The old mercenary waded in up to his knees and yelled, "Jump in. Make a break for it."

"Here," Hana yelled. She threw her bow across the narrow river to Hazim. "Cover us." She pulled off her quiver and tossed it over as well. There were only seven or eight arrows left. She unslung her shield, drew her hand-and-a-half Pagentian saber from over her shoulder and rammed the buckler into the widening line to Akil's right. They were now pushed up to the water's edge and defending their flanks.

The attackers had four in their shield wall and another four in a line behind them resting and trading off every half minute or so. Hana thought she could see four bodies on the ground, but one was trying to get up and reinforcements were gathering at the top of the bluff. An axe hooked the top of her shield and yanked it down. She barely had time to raise her sword in an overhead block to keep her head from being split. With a down and up jerk, she slammed her shield into a man's jaw, breaking his teeth. She yanked back and swung her sword around into his neck. Blood sprayed her as her foe fell, but a fresh adversary took his place. She shoved her shield forwards, slashing and stabbing with ebbing energy.

Hana wiped the blood from her eyes with her sword arm sleeve when from her right a burly woman came screaming with morningstar held high. It was a berserker's charge. Hana hooked her blade under the crazy woman's shield and let her run onto her sword. Dropping her shield she stooped, took the berserker on her shoulder, twisted, and using the momentum threw her over into the river as she yanked her blade from the berzerker's guts. Hana picked up her shield and resumed the fight. Fighting rested soldiers was taking its toll on the three. They all had wounds.

"We need to jump," Akil yelled, but his words ended in a shriek of pain as the point of a blade slipped in and out of his thigh.

Akil fell, and then Hana and Ghassan were being pushed into the river while stabbing and slashing at their flanks. Then out of the trees to the left, Khaled came with his whirling scimitars. He went through their enemies like a reaper harvesting lives. He hacked his way through the middle of their two lines leaving hands, heads, and severed legs in his wake. In a few seconds, the assassin disabled them all, leaving the ground littered with bodies. In as many seconds the fight was over. The reinforcements coming down the embankment decided to withdraw and regroup on the hill.

Hana guessed that four or five lay dead, including the one caught on a snag and bobbing in the current. Of the wounded, most would not survive. To Khaled, she said, "The Murdoch Mercs have lost more than half their number, thanks to you, assassin."

Khaled looked at her with his one eye. In place of the bandage he now sported a strip of black cloth tied at an angle to cover his empty orbit. Over this, he wore his usual black shemagh head scarf. For the first time that

Hana could remember, Khaled looked unsure of himself as if he didn't know how to respond to a compliment. He squatted next to a man with a severed arm and cleaned his scimitars on the dying man's clothes. After sheathing his weapons, he took the man's money pouch and jewelry.

Hana went to Akil who was now fading in and out of consciousness. "Come on Akil," she said to him urgently. "We've got to cross the river." She looked around for Ghassan and found him pilfering a couple coin purses. She too would have liked to claim some booty, but she feared the time lost would be detrimental to Akil's life. She needed to get him to safety and bind his wounds. Ghassan had just lifted a dagger and slid it into an empty sheath on his belt when Hana said, "Ghassan, help me with Akil."

Ghassan looked to the fallen and muttered, "Poor lot this is anyway." He stood and went to her. "I will take his sword, shield and saddle bags." He gathered the gear and entered the water.

Hana couldn't argue with the logic. They needed the gear and Akil would be easier to manage in the water without the extra weight. She turned to the assassin who knelt beside a different man. He was struggling with the wounded man's ring. The injured merc was pale from blood loss, but he screamed when Khaled drove the point of his dagger into the base of his finger, wedging and working the inside of the knuckle till the finger popped free. The soldier grabbed Khaled's sleeve with his good hand, but the assassin's slapped it away. Hana called to him, "Khaled, come help me with this man. He is sorely wounded."

Khaled removed the ring and tossed the finger aside. "Kill him, and he won't need help." He rose and went to his next victim.

"You waste your breath, shield maiden," came the words from a dripping Hazim.

Hana had not seen him swim back across the river as she struggled with Akil. As Hazim helped her with the wounded man she asked him, "Have you seen the girl?"

Hazim grunted. "No. We'll worry about that later. For now, let's form up in case they attack again. At least now we can tell them she escaped."

"If they believe us," Hana replied.

CHAPTER 21

Aideen found thick brush about twenty meters along the base of the embankment and dropped into it. She got down low on her belly and looked to see if anyone had spotted her. She couldn't see much between the thicket of branches and yellowed leaves, but everyone seemed to be busy fighting or fleeing. It was time for her to flee too.

While remaining on her belly, Aideen turned around and crawled away from the battle. The clash of steel on steel and wood, the yelling, and the screams of the wounded and dying were terrible. She had heard it before at the battle of Valekrie. It was there that she had watched her father fight in the shield wall. Aideen had heard stories about the shield wall. Battles usually began with each side casting insults and oaths. Her father told her they did it to cover their fear. Some fighters drank spirits before a fight while others threw up. There had been no time for such preludes at Valekrie or here, only the bloody brutality of close and vicious in-your-face combat. Along with the screams and moans, Aideen could smell the blood and the opened bowels wafting to her hiding place.

Khaled was not in the battle, but Aideen knew he was near. A chill shiver swept over her as she thought about him. She stopped, listened, and heard Lord Townsend shouting orders to find her. Looking around the girl could see little, but she estimated she had not gone far. Aideen crawled faster. Hazim and Hana's voices came to her, but she could not make out their words over the crackle of the dried leaves. A branch caught and tore her dress. She was thankful for the leather trews Hazim had given her, without which she was sure her legs would be a mess.

Aideen could see some large boulders ahead and hear rushing water. She ascertained it was the stream they had followed earlier, now falling over the cliff. The ground rose slightly, causing her to quicken her pace to the cover beyond when she heard the battle cries behind her rise to a fevered pitch. She turned and through a small opening in the leaves she saw Khaled cutting down the last of the attackers. The clamor of battle ceased, followed by the moans of the dying. Motionless, she watched as the assassin squatted next to his last victim, but she could not make out what he was doing.

She dared not move for fear of rustling the bushes from where she hid. Her heart pounded and her desire to breathe was powerful, but she rationed herself shallow drafts in order to remain still and quiet. She had to get to the Murdoch mercenaries. They had come to rescue her, probably sent by her grandmother's steward, Dorfin, or perhaps by her mother. Aideen still had her reservations about Lieutenant Hawthorn, but she decided to worry about that later.

Khaled knelt beside another wounded soldier. He

pulled out his dagger and did something that made the man scream. He threw something aside and then spoke to someone she couldn't see. Then he froze, slowly raised his head, cocked it, and looked with his one eye in the direction where Aideen lay. *My thoughts!* Her thoughts, she realized, were formed into words the way she projected the mind-speech. The assassin was sensing her soliloquy. She clamped down on her mind, wondering if he actually perceived her words or if he just sensed her the way she did him.

Aideen made her mind blank by meditating on a candle flame conjured in her mind. She focused on the flame, detaching herself from her body while a very small part of her watched the black robed man. He still stared in her direction.

It was like there were two Aideens; one sat in an unseen bubble in the lotus position meditating on a motionless candle flame, while the other lay on her belly under a shrub with yellowed leaves. This latter Aideen barely breathed and her heart thumped only once every two seconds, a soft, slow, barely perceptible thump…thump…thump. She was hardly aware of the dried leaf that broke loose and floated down, settling in her hair. The seconds ticked away as she watched him looking in her direction. Her only friends among her enemies were dragging one of their own out of the river on the other side, leaving the assassin on the same side of the river with her, and much too close for her comfort. The distraction drew the assassin's attention away. Aideen relaxed and returned to her body. She let out a breath of relief and her pulse returned to normal.

Noises of scuffing feet and muted voices came from the hillside above them. The Murdoch mercenaries were mustering, Aideen assumed, to either make another charge or to come take away their dead. Khaled stood and looked up at the five men standing at the edge of the gully, all with blades bared. He drew one of his scimitars but said nothing.

One of the men spoke. It was Hawthorn. "Give us the girl," he said. "You're outnumbered."

Aideen, now calm and calculating, her panic gone, commenced to low-crawl out of the bush, using the distraction to depart. She planned to go upstream and circle around to the safety of her rescuers. She realized that she could make out the voices now and wondered if it was because there was less background noise or if it had something to do with her recent meditation and brief astral detachment. Dalla once told her that enhanced hearing complimented sensory awareness.

Khaled swept his scimitar slowly to indicate his vanquished foes. "Oh, not so much as before," he replied to Hawthorn's bravado. "You are only eight or nine now. I will send you all to the nameless one should you care to dance."

Aideen was far enough now that their words were fading and becoming drowned out by the waterfall. She stepped lightly as she moved in a low crouch, now hidden from view by large rocks. Curiosity got the better of her. She poked her head around a boulder and strained her ears.

"How 'bout we just kill you now," said the mercenary to Khaled. "We have the advantage of numbers and high ground. It would be smarter to hand over the child."

Khaled drew his other scimitar but stopped when he saw Hawthorn raise his free hand and signal. Two bowmen stepped briskly out from behind the commander and fired. Khaled darted left, barely fast enough to spare his life. One arrow nicked his shoulder and the other grazed his side. Two more archers stepped up and launched shafts at his back as he ran downstream, using the trees as cover. The assassin had vanished again.

The mercenary leader turned to the man next to him and said, "Find them, but don't get too close to that one. He is too dangerous. We will take them at first light."

The man next to Hawthorn nodded. Aideen almost stepped out of hiding to run to her rescuers, but Hawthorn's earlier threat stopped her and she was unsure how far the assassin had fled. She pulled back and walked briskly towards the waterfall. She decided she would try to sneak up on their camp and spy on them. Perhaps she could listen and learn something in hopes of hearing their true intentions. If her rescuers were true, she would urge them to escort her with all possible speed to her mother at her grandmother's estate in Port Augustus. If they meant to kill her and blame it on Townsend and his sell-swords, she would find her own way back and report them to Dorfin. Right now, more than anything, she wished she was with her father.

Aideen came to the falls realizing the day had waned. The water seemed grey in the dull evening light as it fell from the rocky cliff above and poured into the dark pool. From here the water fell over meter high step of granite and joined yet another creek to form the head of the small river she had followed.

She checked her back trail for the thousandth time and listened for possible pursuit, but the falls masked all sound. She couldn't dally here knowing her former captors could sneak up on her with stomping feet and rattling harness without her the wiser. But she was tired.

Stretching out on her belly she scooped up several handfuls of water till her thirst was sated. Then she assessed her torn dress. It was far from practical, so she tore away the skirt and the sleeves, ripped off a strip for a headband and hid the remains under a rock. She walked around the pool to where the creek gushed between large stones and into the river. Hopping from rock to rock she crossed the span with relatively dry boots. Still tired, she trudged on.

Aideen considered her situation. She needed to circle up and out of the gully to reach the safety of her family's soldiers. It was getting dark and she didn't want to spend the night alone without food, fire, or friends. If she got to the mercs before they made another costly attack on Townsend's sell-swords she could save lives and get away. It was not that she thought the Murdoch mercs incapable of overpowering the lesser numbers of his lordship's hirelings; it was the danger of engaging the deadly assassin.

Even with one eye, Khaled was a force to be feared. She had just witnessed his murderous efficiency slaying several soldiers in as many seconds. Aideen wanted no part of him, nor did she want her rescuers reducing their numbers further with vain attempts to save her, especially when she was no longer a prisoner. She had to get to them and assure herself of their intentions. Failing that, she would find her own way back to Port Augustus. Aideen swore she would hound her mother until she agreed to send a company of troops to go help her father.

Aideen picked up the pace because the night was fast approaching, and with it, her fear of the dark. This time, the dark did indeed hold a lurking evil—Khaled. Her escape had gone far beyond where she had wanted to change course. The cliff was beginning to lean into a slope although it was still too steep to scale. Goosebumps prickled her arms, making her wish that she had not been so hasty to cut off her sleeves. She knew she would soon miss her cloak as well.

Aideen's ambling pace suddenly slammed to a stop when just a short way ahead of her a large cat roared a challenge. The sound echoed briefly in the narrow canyon. Eyes wide and heart thumping with adrenaline, her nasal passages and bronchi opened to allow great gulps of air to feed her body's need. She pressed herself against a tree and strained her ears. Tingling fear washed over her and she wanted to cry. It was getting dark.

Another growl ripped the twilight. She did not know if it was a mountain lion or a shadow cat, but the thought of either terrified her. Aideen forced herself to calm down by recalling her lessons on wild felines. Shadow cats are black, desert dwellers, fifty to a hundred kilos, and have seven claws on each forepaw. Cougars are tawny and fierce. Both are big.

Aideen waited in the still forest and realized she was holding her breath. All birds and squirrels ceased chirp and chatter. They had probably fled elsewhere as she intended to do now. Bolting for the rise, scrambling in the poor light, she climbed hand over hand, pulling herself up by roots and rocks, some of which pulled free and tumbled down to the darkness. Low growling moans accented with an occasional hiss gave the girl some hope that the cats weren't interested in her. This girl wasn't sticking around to test that theory. She could just make out the edge only a meter above her when the cacophony of combating cats erupted below into what the girl considered the mother of all catfights. She hurried her ascent without care of the loose and dangerous purchase. Dirt, rocks, and roots flew as she climbed. The sound of giants ripping great sheets of steel could not have rivaled the screeching of the large cats in combat.

Aideen pulled herself over the edge and ran up the mountain slope until exhaustion overwhelmed her. It did not take her long before she realized that she was on the road that they had been traveling on earlier. She could no longer hear the cats, but was almost too tired to be wary. After a few moments catching her breath, she turned north and, hopefully, in the direction of her rescuer's camp. Unfortunately, her enemies were out there too. She was scared, but determined, so she clamped her jaws, widened her eyes and ears, and spread her awareness the way Dalla had taught her. It was not long before she crossed the same creek she and Townsend's sell-swords had crossed earlier that day.

An orange glow lit tree branches a short distance ahead. Aideen moved cautiously with stealth from tree to tree until she saw the flames of a low campfire. Knowing there would be sentries picketed, she looked for positions that would be covered by such lookouts. Her perceptions located a guard to her left, so she moved in that direction. As she neared the camp she could see about six sleeping forms not far from the campfire and one soldier sitting up tending some meat roasting on a spit. No one was talking, so she abandoned her earlier plans of listening first to learn something. She was cold, scared, and wanted to warm herself by the fire. She wanted to feel safe.

Aideen had no idea how long her ordeal had taken, but it was quite dark and the sliver of a waxing moon was beginning to peek above the trees. She suspected that it was later than she thought and that the Murdoch mercenaries were planning a predawn raid on her former captors. Not wanting to alert the sentry she moved very quietly in his direction until she could make out his outline in the dim silvery light.

Foreboding crept beside her fear—goose bumps bristled on her neck. He was sitting with his head resting on drawn up knees. She hoped he was only dozing, but Aideen knew better than to wake a sleeping warrior, at least within striking distance, so she took up a stick of suitable length and tapped the man's shoulder—no response. She tapped again—nothing. The third time she prodded him harder, harder in fact than she had intended.

Aideen was on the verge of a soft apology when the man fell back on the ground displaying his blood covered leather armor and a wide gash on his throat that severed all but his spine. The cartilaginous rings of the cut ends of his trachea glistened in the moonlight. The grizzly sight made her stomach clench. The smell of blood and bile was strong. Now that she thought about it, she had smelled it before he fell over, but not as strongly. Perhaps the odor had been blocked by her mind hoping it not to be true. Then her mind raced.

Aideen's panic returned with a vengeance. It was no easy task to control it. Dropping to her belly, she looked all around, knowing there should have been one more picket outside of the firelight. Through her perception, she felt rather than saw Khaled's dark aura in the direction that the other sentry should have been. Had she been quicker the assassin would have caught her. As she watched, the man still up tending his meal grabbed at the knife handle that suddenly sprouted from his throat. He struggled and tried to gurgle a warning, but he fell over a moment after he pulled out the blade. Bright arterial blood squirted sizzling into the flames, each pulse weaker than the last.

Aideen's fear froze her as the assassin entered the camp. His grin, to her, was a baring of teeth—a showing of fangs. He was a hell-spawn, a demon, a diner of death, an insane monster with only murder to drive him. Soundless footsteps carried the assassin to the sleeping soldiers; the silver arcs of his low-slung swords enveloped his shadow. The assassin whisked off one head and then another with systematic efficiency. A mercenary woman woke as Khaled hacked into the man next to her. The woman yelled as she thrust a dagger at his leg. The assassin danced back, kicking the knife away, and then skipped forwards, sliding his sword into her belly.

The shout roused the last two men. Aideen saw the head of the first man fly away as he rose from bed. The second man gained his feet. His hands filled with the haft of a double-bladed battle axe. The man towered over the assassin, and the huge axe looked big enough to split a horse. Khaled's swords caught the weapon's haft just below the heavy head. Parallel scimitars deflected the great axe. The sheer weight carried the massive weapon on and sunk it fifty centimeters into the dirt, wedging, the girl suspected, into a root.

The big man tugged twice and abandoned the stuck axe. He leaped back and kicked dirt up at his enemy's eye, buying him time to draw his dirk and retrieve a dead comrade's sword. Khaled thrusted with one sword, slashed with the other. The merc parried the thrust, and barely dodged the slash and then returned one. The assassin dropped as the man slashed for his throat, but the merc's blade only brushed Khaled's head scarf. From a knee the assassin chopped down into the man's thigh. The merc screamed as he crumpled.

The man's agony wrenched Aideen's heart as she watched him growl and struggle to his knees. With effort he got one foot up and leaned against his good thigh, breathing in heavy gasps. Khaled, still on a knee, waited with swords crossed before him. The merc steadied, sucking air through gritted teeth as he got his pain under control. He then met the assassin's gaze and raised his weapons defiantly. "Do it."

Khaled's scimitars whispered apart. The scissored shing finished with thunk-snick and the man's head rolled off the back of his neck. Blood squirted as the body fell over. Khaled stood. All else were dead, except for a scared little girl watching from outside the firelight.

The assassin wiped his blades on the garments of the dead, and then he kneeled and bowed his head. Words of prayer drifted to the girl. Khaled was thanking the nameless god for the lives given him to slay.

Aideen wanted to vomit, but she dared not. She didn't understand thanking a god for death. People thanked gods for life and love, a successful hunt or a good harvest, but not death. She saw no favors being done for the victims. The killer gained little; it wasn't self-defense and the pickings were poor for robbery. It was as if he gained some sort of euphoric sustenance from murder. The glassy-eyed fanaticism he displayed that afternoon when he had joined the battle was back. Thinking back, she recalled seeing it back in Valekrie when he had attacked her father.

His mind was sick, she sensed it now and it disgusted her, but she also wondered if Khaled could be healed. What events in his life could have made him seek so many murders? Her fear suddenly immobilized her. She couldn't breathe but in shallow puffs.

Khaled got up, and after pilfering what wealth he could, walked out of the camp's firelight. He became one with the night. He had not vanished, she felt that in her stomach, but all she could see was the dull red of his aura.

Aideen heard Khaled's movements around the horses. A whinny, a snort, and a hoof thumping the ground drifted to her with the odor of manure. After a few moments, the shadowy line of horses moved down the hill, fading into the night. The knot in her gut faded as well.

CHAPTER 22

Aideen lay still for a while—for how long she couldn't say. She was tired, hungry, and scared. She wanted to run, but she could not will herself to do so. Her growling stomach told her she needed food before she could flee. Fear urged her to bolt, but it was fear that kept her rooted in place. *Does Khaled know I'm here? Does he suspect? Is he lurking in the shadows waiting for me to come out? Leading the horses away could have been a ruse.* She remembered how he had looked right at her when she was hiding during the fight by the river. She tried to guard the way she structured her thoughts, but she wasn't sure if that was how he sensed her if he even did, and then she noticed the knot in her gut was completely gone.

The stomach cramp that warned Aideen of danger was perplexing. Whether it was a signal for Khaled or any danger she couldn't be sure, but right now it was telling her she was safe. She decided to trust her feelings, and her fear began to fade, if only a little.

Without a glance at the corpse she had lain beside for so long, she stood and stretched out her cramped muscles. She strode to the cooling cook fire, averting her eyes as best she could from the dead soldiers scattered about the camp. The meat that had been spitted over the flames earlier was a clump of charred flesh, nearly indistinguishable from the burnt remnants of wood now bereft of flames. The orange glow of coals was all that remained of the fire.

Taking a few sticks from beside the fire pit and placing them on the coals, she blew the fire to life. She then rummaged through a canvas bag finding hardtack, jerky, and oats. With a pot and some water, Aideen prepared some oatmeal and ate her fill. She then stuffed the dried meat and old biscuits in a smaller bag. Hardening her resolve, she went to the dead soldiers searching for weapons. All of the swords were much too heavy for her, so she settled for a long dagger. It was awkward and made her wish for her lightweight katana. There were plenty of bows to choose from, but they were all half again taller than her and far too stiff for her to string, much less draw.

Aideen went to a pile of things next to the dead woman. She was bigger than Aideen, but quite a bit smaller than her comrades. Her bow, though still a longbow, was smaller than the others. Aideen found she could string, and draw the weapon. After taking a practice shot, she added the bow and a bundle of arrows to her pile of booty. She also found a small dagger with a ten-centimeter blade. The girl pulled off her boot, tied the knife and sheath to her ankle, replaced her boot, and rolled down her trouser cuffs.

She looked down at what was left of her dress, now no more than a sleeveless top. She was thankful for the boots and trousers Hazim had given her, but the Medimian cloth had to go. Pulling off the garment, she donned a maroon shirt salvaged from the women's gear. It was a little large, but using a belt to gather it at her waist, she let the tails fall over her thighs. It would suffice far better than the dress. From the same pack, she took a cloak made of dark grey wool. It was a little long, so she cut a strip off the bottom and used the scrap to replace the headband torn from her dress earlier. Her next duty was to procure a horse.

Aideen hoped that one of the mounts still held a deer carcass—the source of meat that roasted to ash earlier—but all she found at the picket was horse droppings and a discarded nosebag. "Khaled took every last one of them," she exclaimed, barely above a whisper.

She had thought he only sought to replace the mounts lost earlier that day. Then it dawned on her. *He did it so I would be stuck on foot*, she thought. Shrugging at her misfortune, she slipped her arms through the straps of her bag of victuals and pulled on the oversized cloak. With her back encumbered she chose to fasten the quiver of arrows to her belt, and using the bow as a walking stick she strode out of the camp towards the road.

It did not take long before Aideen's self-confidence started to slip as night once again closed around her. She stopped while still in sight of the dwindling campfire, and strung her bow. Her options were simple: follow the road back across the mountains to Port Augustus and seek the aid of the first travelers she came upon, or else go sniveling back to Lord Townsend, as he probably suspected a young girl alone in the woods would do. *Yes, that is exactly what he would think*, she thought, *that I would come in tired, hungry, and scared like a whining whelp wanting forgiveness and something to eat.* The thought of it made her angry. *I will do no such thing!*

With an arrow nocked she went on, her way lit

with the light of the Milkmaid's Swath and the moon only a week shy of full. When her feet found the road, she wearily ascended the winding route. Aideen was both physically and emotionally exhausted. The wounds and deathblows she had seen dealt that day, and the assassin's heinous work that night, had kept replaying in her mind as she trudged up the steep grade. When considering her own confrontation with Khaled, it was a wonder she had ever survived.

Aideen wanted distance behind her. She was tired but too scared to sleep for fear of the unknown lurking in the dark unseen, and she was still too close to her former captors to take comfort in stopping.

The night was quiet, but for the occasional owl hoot. Thoughts of the assassin alternated with wild cats and caused her to swing around with drawn bow at the slightest sounds, real or imagined. The worry of pursuit was not the only fear keeping her from lying down to rest; she feared the nightmares of the bloody battle playing over and over in her wide awake mind. She started to cry.

When the grey light of dawn allowed her to see where she trod her fatigue made her stumble more frequently. Leaving the road, she followed a game trail for about a kilometer. She came to a dead tree killed by fire and felled by nature long before she was born. The trunk lay draped diagonally up the slope, its silvered sides stubbled with branches broken by time and rot, and seasoned with bits of moss on the north side of each stub.

The hollowed stump's charred crown stood nearly three meters high, like a squat monolith of nature, while allowing ample room for the girl to curl up inside once she squeezed through the blackened triangular opening between two roots. She wanted only to rest awhile, promising to keep vigilant, but sleep overtook her the moment her head touched the food bag she had rolled into a pillow.

Aideen woke to the sound of scrabbling. She opened her eyes, feeling disoriented for a few moments as she lay on her side looking out the opening on the side of the stump. Blinking grittiness from not near enough sleep, but not yet raising her head, she heard the scrabbling again and saw the cloth of her pillow-pack move as something very small wriggled inside the sack. The motion went towards a tiny hole in the cloth that Aideen was sure had not been there before. A second later a little mouse backed out of its fresh-chewed hole dragging a piece of broken biscuit behind it. The little creature was, in Aideen's opinion, quite cute as it stopped to chew a bit of its prize. A grin began to form on her face as she watched the mouse's cheeks fill to little round balls. Her breathing caught the rodent's attention. Little beady black eyes met hers for a brief second before the tiny thief bounded off, propelling itself on its hind legs while it clutched the stolen booty in its fore claws.

Aideen raised herself on one elbow and looked up through the hollow stump to blue sky fringed with the branches of the surrounding pines. She wanted to go back to sleep, but she dared not dally since Lord Townsend was sure to have his sell-swords searching for her by now. She rubbed the crust from her eyes and lightly stroked the ends of the sutures in her lip. The swelling was nearly gone, making her wonder if she still had a black eye.

She inspected her bag of victuals, glad for the absence of mouse droppings; she ardently hoped the rodent had abstained from urinating on her food as well. Aideen sniffed a biscuit and then gingerly took a small bite. Upon ascertaining her breakfast was free of mouse pee she wolfed down the biscuit and nearly inhaled a second. She stuck a piece of jerky between her molars, gathered her things and crawled out of the stump.

The day was already too warm for her cloak, so she stuffed it in the sack and proceeded straight up the hill, opting now to avoid the road. She had not gone far before her thirst made her tongue stick to the roof of her mouth. Berating herself for not salvaging a canteen, she veered northwest towards a thick clump of firs. Upon crossing the forested ridge, she descended into a small vale in which was centered a quiet pond. Remembering her father's warnings about drinking standing water, she resisted the urge to run right in to lap up the pond water. Instead, she skirted the basin until her circuitous course brought her to a babbling brook that tumbled over small rounded pebbles as it rushed into the pond.

Aideen drank her fill, rested, ate, and drank some more. Her belly sloshed as she resumed her course, still avoiding the road. She occasionally veered over within sight of the road so as not to wander too far away, wanting to be close enough to hear travelers so that she could ask for aid and sanctuary. Positive that her enemies were tracking her, she did her best to stay close to cover in case there was a need to hide in a hurry.

Hardtack and jerky for breakfast and lunch were all very fine when one was roughing it, but Aideen desperately wanted something a little more substantial. She had seen deer and rabbits as well as a few grouse that would have provided easy meals for a skilled huntress such as herself. However, she was not hungry enough to eat raw meat, and a cook-fire would be like hanging a sign for the kidnappers to come get her.

The sun was low in the sky when the coolness of the higher altitude caused Aideen to don the woolen cloak. She was just preparing to find a suitable hiding place to spend the night when she heard horses. Running towards a copse of small spruce trees that formed a circle, she worked her way into the center of small poles, glad that the branches hung low to the ground. Her position was close enough to a curve in the road to provide an adequate view of the party coming towards her. Two men garbed as typical sell-swords rode in front of a familiar-looking carriage. Another four horsemen rode behind it.

As the party rounded the corner Aideen gaped when she recognized the passenger of the carriage. It was her mother. Relief washed over her as she scrambled out of the thicket snapping branches and calling, "Mother, Mother, wait, I'm here." She ran to the carriage, arms waving in the air, but two guards moved to bar her way.

"Stop, you idiots," Anisha snapped from the door window. "That's my daughter. Let her pass." She climbed out of the carriage and embraced her daughter as the girl slammed into her.

"Oh, Mother," Aideen sobbed. "I was so scared. Lord Townsend did it. He's the one that took me—kidnapped me. He and that assassin," she cried. Words, broken and jumbled, spilled out of her of all the terrible things that had befallen her over the past several days—her failed fight with Khaled, her drugged dreams thinking her mother was there, her waking bound and blindfolded on a horse. When she got to the failed rescue by their family's soldiers, she started to sob. "Khaled slayed them," Aideen felt her mother tense each time she said the assassin's name. Her voice became a whimper as she said, "He slayed them all. I saw it…after I escaped."

"Shush, shush," Aideen's mother soothed as she held the girl, gently rocking side to side. "It's okay, you're safe now. Come, tell me about it as we ride," she said, helping her daughter into the carriage. Anisha gave the guards a curt nod as she closed the door. As they proceeded down the road Aideen told her tale, aware of the driver's frequent application of the brakes, as they slowly wended their way down the mountain. She stopped mid-sentence on one of the few uphill rises in the road. "Mother, what are you doing here? Aren't we going the wrong way?"

"The ransom note, dear," Aideen's mother replied softly. "The note instructed Dorfin and me to find your father and have him bring the octagon key to Juana Pohala to trade for you. Dorfin sent out a flock of pigeons in hopes of getting the ransom demands to not only your father but to your grandmother as well. I could not sit by while you were held hostage. I left Port Augustus a day after Dorfin sent out another platoon to find you."

"The platoon," replied Aideen. "They're all dead. I saw it." Her words became frantic again. "They're the ones I just told you about. They're the ones the assassin killed. We have to turn around; we're heading right towards Lord Townsend."

"It's much closer to Juana Pohala. We'll need to resupply before going back over the mountains. Not only that, it would be best to let your father know you're okay."

"He knows. I told Dalla with the mind-speech. They're on their way to Juana Pohala, but the assassin," exclaimed Aideen. "I saw him kill half the platoon by himself. We have to flee!"

"Now, now," soothed Anisha. "I'm sure you are exaggerating. These men escorting us are all very capable soldiers. We will be fine. Besides, wouldn't you like to help your father?"

"Well, of course, I would, but…"

"Here," Anisha interrupted. She reached for a basket on the floor. "Have some dinner."

Aideen wanted to argue more, but her hunger overpowered her distress. She ate five pieces of cold chicken and a large hunk of bread and washed it down with some tea that her mother had in an insulated jug. Accumulated fatigue, a full belly, and the rolling of the wagon put her to sleep within minutes of her meal.

CHAPTER 23

Aideen awoke disoriented a few moments before she realized she was in her mother's carriage. She was alone. It was dark and the vehicle was still. Cautiously she leaned over to look out the carriage window. An orange campfire glow lit the face of a man a few meters off. He stood as if on guard. She heard voices from the other side, so she slid silently across the seat to look out the opposite side. Another soldier stood there as well. Beyond the sentry and a little forward and to the right of the carriage horses was a campfire where two people stood. Aideen's surprise nearly came out as an inhaled gasp when she recognized her mother and Lord Townsend standing there in what appeared to be a serious conversation.

The sight of his lordship chilled the girl. A thousand questions popped into her mind. Maybe he didn't know she was in the carriage, and her mother was making up some story to let them on their way. *That's it*, she thought. *That has to be it. Mother is pretending she doesn't know about Lord Townsend's treachery. She posted the guards so his lordship's sell-swords wouldn't approach the wagon and find me out.*

Aideen slunk lower and looked around. A little ways behind the carriage was another campfire, around which stood a number of familiar faces. Hana, Jamal, and Maha stood while Ghassan sat with his arm in a sling. Hazim crouched by a supine form she assumed was Akil. She slid to the floor and sat cross-legged. Part of her feared recapture but another part was relieved the sell swords still lived—mostly Hana and Hazim. Khaled was nearby, according to the lump in her stomach, but she did not see him. She considered her surroundings.

Even in the darkness, Aideen could tell they were out of the mountains. The ground seemed sandier and there were no trees in sight. The air was cool and dry, but not uncomfortable. Then she wrinkled her brow as an image flashed back to her from her survey. It was the armband.

Uniforms on professional soldiers were rare. To minimize confusion in battle mercenaries and conscripts would don a colored armband, sometimes bearing the sigil of the company or lord they served. Aideen's father's company often wore brown tabards with a tan hawk within an octagon, but armbands were just as common when tabards were impractical or unavailable. Her grandparents' soldiers wore black armbands with a white ship above crossed swords. She had seen many of those same armbands in the camp of dead soldiers, but that was not the armband worn by her mother's escort.

Aideen crept cautiously up on her knees to peek outside again. Thereupon the sentry's arm was Lord Townsend's white boar on a field of blue. *Why would Mother's escort be in Lord Townsend's employ?* She heard arguing and her eye flicked over to where her mother and

Townsend were becoming louder, but she could not make out their words. Aideen sat up on the padded seat where she had slept and looked for her bow and arrows—they were gone. The long dagger was gone as well. She could feel the overlooked boot knife still against her ankle, but there was little she could do. She was surrounded on all sides. Escape was futile.

She didn't want to face it, but it was there, blatantly obvious—her own mother had betrayed her.

When her mother returned to the carriage and found her unhappy daughter avoiding eye contact and answering her comments with silence, Anisha tried to explain. "My dear," she said, as the wagon lurched forward. "I never meant for any harm to befall you." She reached up and twisted the striker in the chemical heat lamp, raising the brightness through the low blue setting to the medium orange intensity. "It's just the only way we could help your father."

The carriage rolled along on the first flat road Aideen had seen in days. Townsend and two horsemen led them while the rest of the sell-swords were obliged to eat the wagon's dust in the rear. Judging by the distance of Juana Pohala's glittering lights, Aideen guessed they would be in the city within the hour. She still wasn't talking to her mother. Aideen only scowled and adamantly ignored her.

Aideen glared at her mother and raised one brow at the last comment, but kept her lips sealed tightly together.

"You see," Anisha hesitated as she scrutinized the girl. Aideen then saw her mother's face tighten into annoyance before she continued. "That healer has corrupted him. She has talked him into destroying all that amazing technology from the old world. We live in barbarous times, Aideen. The knowledge and the weapons buried in the fortress can bring order to this chaos of constant war and death. Your father is the perfect man to lead us—I tried to tell him that more than once. With the octagon key and Lord Townsend's help, we can put your father on the throne over the whole continent. He could establish peace and stop all this fighting and bloodshed between Kandia and the Alliance."

Aideen pointedly looked away.

"I am so sorry you got hurt. I never wanted that assassin involved, but Lord Townsend insisted." Anisha's voice lowered to a conspiratorial tone. "Khaled is dangerous and not to be trusted." A moment passed and then her mother smiled at her and continued conversationally as if they were visiting over tea and biscuits. "I was overjoyed when you cut out his eye. It was a very brave thing to do, and no one deserved it more, but you could have been killed." Reverting again to serious tones, her mother warned, "You must be very careful around that one."

Aideen forced herself not to smile at the compliment. Her mother quieted for a while. After that, when Anisha attempted conversation, Aideen completely ignored everything her mother said. *Why listen when it could all be lies?* she thought. As they drew closer to the city she realized that the lump in her belly was gone. Did that mean Khaled was gone or did it mean she was safe? She did not know, but one thing was certain—she did not feel very safe.

Aideen brooded as the carriage passed the first few buildings of the city. Her curiosity tugged at her as she stared into space, pouting her disapproval. It was more a silent argument than the act of ignoring her mother. She wasn't sure of what she wanted to project, but her mother's betrayal boiled inside her like a pot of water left too long over a fire.

When the buildings grew taller Aideen found herself edging closer to the side and leaning towards the window for a better view. She noticed that the dust had ceased and the wagon wheels hummed as they rolled across smooth paving; unlike the cobblestone rumble in Port Augustus or the granite flagstone thump and grind back home in Border City, this surface was flat, seamless, and comparatively quiet.

The road they were on ran straight as an arrow between structures higher than anything Aideen had seen before, but what caught her attention was the backdrop to downtown Juana Pohala. Out of the desert sands stood tall rectangular skeletons of the old world's past glory. They rose into the night sky like dark shadows that refused to be buried by time.

When the carriage pulled to a stop Aideen leaped out into an east facing courtyard to gaze at the ancient relics. About a kilometer from where she stood, the road stopped at a fence, and the desert began. At the forefront of the half-buried blackened steel frames stood the shell of a cracked dome structure that reflected a dull gold sheen in the lights of both moon and city. Atop this dome sprouted a damaged pinnacle which thrust skyward like a broken spear still defiant to centuries of erosion.

No life stirred above ground beyond the fence, or in those condemned ruins, but Aideen sensed many presences below the desert floor in the very direction she gazed. It surprised her how easy and naturally her sensory perception came to her without first clearing her mind in meditation. Her intense scrutiny was disturbed by a hand on her shoulder.

"We're here," her mother said.

Aideen turned and blinked at her and then at the opulent hotel standing before them. Red adobe architecture, the like of which she had never seen before, rose in carved and curving tops around her. Desert plants and cacti ornamented every corner and blue heat lamps lit every walkway. She looked to the carriage where servants in the hotel's livery scurried around the carriage to assist with the baggage. One of the attendants slipped under the weight of a heavy trunk. He grunted in pain as he saved it from dropping to the street.

"Careful, you fool," Anisha snapped, her face twisted in anger. "If you drop that trunk I'll see that you are whipped for your carelessness."

"Your pardon, my lady," the servant groaned as he and another assistant struggled with the baggage. "Upon my word, no harm will come to your things."

Anisha sniffed with haughty disdain. "See that it doesn't," she replied coldly. She turned back to Aideen and said, "You are a sight, my dear. Perhaps the concierge will mistake you for a servant. I'm sure no one will recognize you once we get you cleaned up and dressed like a proper young lady."

Aideen resumed her fuming pout but said nothing. Lord Townsend hailed them from across the courtyard. When her mother led her to his lordship Aideen tried to assume a stoic expression, but Townsend's smirk betrayed her failure at keeping anger out of her face.

"I have rented the penthouse suites," his lordship

announced. "I procured ground floor lodging for the sell-swords, but we will have guards on the top floors at all times." Townsend pointedly looked at Aideen with this last statement. "Be sure to inform your healer friend where we are. This hotel is called the Mozar Hamaud."

His lordship nodded to the two sell-swords standing behind the girl and then turned and strode towards the lift. Her mother took a step and then stopped when Aideen remained rooted where she stood. The girl looked behind her knowing escape was impossible, but longing for it anyway. Her mother's baggage train passed on her right under the labor of eight hotel staff.

"Come, dear," her mother said in that annoying voice that always set her teeth on edge. "Wouldn't you like a nice hot bath? It will make you feel so much better, not to mention a soft feather bed."

Reluctantly and without choice, Aideen let her mother lead her into the depths of opulent luxury.

CHAPTER 24

Akala stood on the quarterdeck, the wind fluttering her white bloused linen sleeves between her black gauntlets and matching leather vest. She now sported a brace of three pistols across the front. Wishing for a second gun on the last mission, she had decided to pack as many pistols as she could comfortably carry. Prudence and practicality were only a couple of Akala's strong points. She watched the crew as the *Elbienus Raptor* cruised low along the coastline, bucking a stiff south wind. The propeller spun smoothly under cruise power, sails were furled for streamlining, and all sources of drag had been taken down, including clotheslined laundry, flags of color, and any non-essential rigging not needed for immediate sail deployment. Even so, their headway was slow against the building gale.

Spirits were high amongst the crew. Pistols were primed, rifles were readied, and razor sharp blades were whetted one last time. Akala could feel their excitement from where she stood on the quarterdeck. It reminded her of her and Travin's buccaneer days when they were tacking towards a prize—only this was different. Back then it had been ship against ship, each relying on the skill and efficiency of the crew as well as the experience and cunning of the captains with only sails and rudder to manipulate maneuvers.

Now they sailed the skies in an airship. They needn't tack an arduous zigzagging course against wind and current because they had powered flight that could push headlong into the wind. They could hide in the clouds if they chose or skim above the surface as they did at present. The technology was moving fast.

Akala knew the crew's confidence came not only from what was quite probably the modern world's first air assault. They had the element of surprise, and they had guns. It would be a simple grab-and-go job. Things could always go wrong, but the risks had been substantially minimalized, thanks to technology.

Only a few months ago the *Coastal Raider* had brought flintlock firearms from the battle of Valekrie, and in a few weeks, Akala's engineers had modified the open flash pan priming mechanism, virtually useless in the rain, to a faster and more versatile cap and ball system. She wondered how long they would have the advantage before someone built something better.

Akala leaned on the quarterdeck's port rail, looking forward past the prow, her thousand meter stare focused on nothing while taking in sights, sounds, and smells. White waves rolled in lines upon the shore, casting silver spray from their crests. She heard the waves beat the beaches with each resounding crash. Her nose knew the tang of ozone in the salty air, and she noticed the absence of seaweed stench, no longer baking in the humid heat along the jungle's verge. She could feel the soothing green of the forest only a kilometer away and the descending yellow sun warmed her right cheek as it began its change to sunset red.

Amidst the cacophony of sounds driven by the wind, Akala's thoughts took her to places she would rather not ponder—politics. She tried a philosophical approach, but when considering their advantages with having guns she could not keep cynicism from her thoughts.

She wondered how long the weight of gun technology would be tipped in their favor. Edged weapons once had a similar unbalance, at least until swords became plentiful. However, an armed farmer was no match for a skilled fighter. This, all too often, left the choice of good or ill deeds to fall upon the stronger and the skilled—the survival of the fittest.

A skilled fighter could easily overpower an untrained adversary, yet even skill had its limitations over brawn. There were many exceptions of course. When skill matched strength the circle of chance grew wider, giving the attribute of luck or cunning to the victor.

Akala had bested numerous foes twice her weight and strength, but she had had time to train and practice her sword art as a matter of self-preservation. She was, after all, in a profession that required such expertise. She had spent years developing her craft as well as honing her reflexes to become one with her weapon, but good as she was with the rapier, she knew an amateur could take her down with an arrow, bolt, or ball shot from a gun.

A bow took strength to draw and skill to hit a target, a crossbow a bit less. A rifle or handgun at close range still required some skill, but strength was not an issue. Armed with only her sword, she could be defeated by anyone out of her reach who was packing a pistol, lest she was quicker with her own gun.

Akala considered the advantages to the average person; the farmers, tradesmen, and even the simple maids walking home alone. The gun was the true equalizer. No more would the weaker be subject to the brutality of the strong, so long as they were packing. With more armed commoners there would be less robbery and rape. It's not to say that good will always triumph, but guns would give honest people a fighting chance, at least until the lords and rulers made laws against firearms, which of course wouldn't apply to the enforcers of those rulers or the lords themselves.

Such laws, banning edged weapons, were implemented in Port Augustus with the intention to provide law and order, to protect the citizens, but it had a reverse effect. Instead of disarming the citizenry, only a portion of the populace complied with a law that had proved difficult to enforce. Criminals continued to carry weapons, and farmers and traders, needing defense outside the city, compiled by leaving weapons too large to conceal in their baggage or stowed away in their conveyances. With the higher probability of hidden weapons in unguarded personal effects, thievery increased as did the supply and demand of black market arms.

The violent crime in Port Augustus had soared to new heights once citizens were prohibited from carrying blades longer than ten centimeters. Even the spikes on bucklers were restricted. Criminals had a field day knowing their targets were likely unarmed. When crime climbed out of control, the ruling officials were urged by the populace to drop the weapons ban, but many of the lords, fearing an uprising by armed citizens, pressured the officials to keep the blade law as it was.

A concession was made allowing weighted canes and walking staffs for personal defense, but the law was only obeyed by law abiding citizens, and lawful citizens are not dangerous except to the criminal that would harm them. Disarming the people proved difficult and only partially successful, but disarming criminals proved futile. Weapons bans insured the advantage to the criminals and weakened the defense of those who obeyed the law.

Akala pushed these depressing thoughts from her head and sought to lift her spirits with the beauty of the reddening sky.

The burnt orange sun was a few hand breadths above the western sea. Heat and distance distorted the fiery orb with each centimeter it sank into the sea. Blurry streaks of deep crimson paralleled the horizon, magnifying the magma-like brilliance as it passed each layer as if it were a stage of change in the descent towards the coming night.

A few fishing boats and one three-masted merchantman were silhouetted against the tropical sunset. Their prows rose and fell in rhythm with the white-capped waves casting spray to the wind with each dip of their dancing bows as they crabbed their way into Port Equanos. Akala imagined the awe on the faces of those sailors watching in wonder as the flying ship made way directly into the wind.

"We're almost there, Lady," said Beros as he turned the tiller and eased back on the elevator.

Akala gripped the rail as the ship banked and ascended a few meters. In only seconds, they were cruising over rooftops on course to a point just leeward of Egan's office.

Now totally focused on the mission, Akala nodded without taking her eyes off her objective, a small wooden building one street back from the main waterfront way. There were adjacent buildings, probably also offices, and living quarters behind the structures facing the street. Most of the living quarters, out of view of the street, were indeed in a sorry state of disrepair. An outstretched arm from a crewman perched in the ratlines pointed at a mansion amid the ramshackle poverty. The sight drew the attention of all hands on deck.

"That's our objective," Akala called to the away teams assembled in the waist. "We'll secure the office first."

"Ready for landing," shouted Beros as he dialed back on the power. He began bleeding off lift gasses for the descent.

"Get a pair of eye on that house," Akala said to Beros. "I'm here for Egan and the money he cost us."

"Lady," Beros began. "Why don't you have Coulig or Gavin lead this away party?"

Akala turned her head sharply, her high tied ponytail tossed in the wind. Her left hand rested casually on the basket hilt of her rapier, and her fierce smile was accented by her piercing predatory eyes. "What, and miss all the fun?"

The astonishment on Beros' face made Akala laugh. "Fear not, Captain, I'll be fine. Besides, you and I are the only ones that have actually seen that greasy swine."

"Jax's drawing was pretty good."

Akala turned away with a wave and said, "Sorry, I

gotta go."

She danced down the larboard steps to where the away teams waited for her in the waist. She appraised the dozen men and women assembled there. Their spirits were high, and she could almost smell the adrenaline as they paced. It was as if they all contained coiled springs just awaiting the signal to release.

"Okay," Akala announced to her team. "We're after Jade Egan. You all saw the sketch."

"Yeah," said Brin. "Looks like a shaved pig."

Laughter rolled around the group. "It's actually a good likeness," Akala agreed with a crooked grin. "But, by proof of a letter written by Travin's hand, Egan has taken our money for our honest business, and now he denies it." She let that sink in and was pleased with the angry comments rolling through the assemblage. "Any spoils you see are up for grabs."

Cheers spread from the away team to the rest of the watch. Akala didn't mention the lives of the Avenger's crewman or that they were probably lost or enslaved. They were there to capture Egan, and she wanted to keep it at that. If the crew got too primed with anger it could turn into a bloodbath that she would rather avoid.

The ship lurched, tightening grips on handrails, as the captain swung the *Raptor* to line up with the street and then descended just low enough to prevent a collision. The pontoons barely cleared the flattop roofs on each side of the narrow street and the hull hovered only four meters off the cobbles when Beros reversed the drive long enough to bring the vessel to a full stop. He reengaged the forward gear to keep the prop idling in order to hold the ship in place against the stiff south wind. Grapples were cast and set fore and aft to assist with keeping the stationary position.

"One more thing," Akala said to the away team. "Try not to kill anyone if you can avoid it. Shoot to wound if you can." She looked at the grim faces around her, all previous mirth now gone. They were serious and she approved—it was time to go to work. "Okay, let's go."

On the starboard side Coulig, Jax, and Brin swung over the rail and slid down lines at the same time that Gavin, Jon, and another crewman repelled off the portside. Akala led another five across the airfoil, to the outrigger and onto the roof of Egan's office. She ran to the backside of the building and was both surprised and delighted to find a ladder leaning against the eves.

A diminutive man holding a tar bucket and trowel stared up at the armed assemblage gathering at the top of his ladder. With a shriek, he dropped both bucket and tools and ran screaming the alarm towards the mansion, which stood fifty meters down a flagstone path.

Akala swung around, grabbing the ladder rails, locked her ankles on each side and slid to the ground without touching any rungs. She hit the ground with a grunt but didn't stumble. As she darted out of the way for the next man sliding down, she reminded herself that she wasn't as young as she used to be and resisted the urge to rub her lower back.

A lithe woman with copper braids and dressed comparable to Akala leaped off the roof with a cutlass in one hand and a pistol in another. She landed like a cat, making it look easy as she rebounded and stood ready. *Bitch*, thought Akala and then chided herself for her momentary jealousy. She quickly replaced her envy with admiration. The young woman reminded her of herself some twenty to thirty years ago. "Enola," said Akala, remembering the petty officer's name. "Stand guard here and shout if there's trouble."

Enola gave a stoic nod.

Akala drew her sword and one of her pistols. "You," she said to a skinny, pockmarked airman with a red bandana, "with me."

Without waiting, Akala went through the back door, pleased that it wasn't locked. She heard Enola ordering a defensive half-circle around the back door. The room Akala entered was dark, but the light from the open door revealed it to be empty of people and full of barrels, crates, boxes, bottles, jars, and junk. There were all sorts of items of trade on shelves and scattered in disarray on the floor. In the center stood a square table, which had some scattered cards in the middle surrounded by a few clay cups, and an empty bottle. Akala wrinkled her nose at the stale alcoholic odor of old rum. Voices from the front drew her in that direction. Down the hall, she met Jax and Brin standing outside a private office. She knew they had come through Egan's front office and was confident it had been cleared.

At her questioning look, Brin said, "He's not here, Akala. Egan slipped out as soon as he heard a flying ship was approaching. He didn't sound the alarm, though."

Brin was one of the few, after repeated requests, that called her by her name without formality. The others were trying, but old habits die hard. "No, a handyman has roused the guard by now I think."

"I heard somebody yelling," agreed Jax.

"That was him," Akala confirmed.

Akala went in and found Gavin and Coulig standing before a middle-aged woman sitting unafraid behind a desk as if she were dispatching the help rather than being interrogated. Several strands of silver mixed evenly in her shoulder length black hair, giving her hazel eyes an eerie but confident look. They all turned as Akala entered.

"Her name is Talia," said Coulig. "She says Egan scurried off to the house."

Akala addressed Talia directly. "How many men does he have? Are they soldiers? Will he lock himself up in his house or will he bolt?"

The woman smiled coldly. "Oh, he'll bolt, but not before he gathers as much of his gold as he can carry," She smirked. "You have plenty of time. He has about eight brawlers on duty. None are true fighting men." Talia opened a drawer and was rewarded with the simultaneous cocking of three pistols aimed at her. "Easy," she soothed with a half grin. "It's just a dispatch from your steward." She drew the paper out slowly and handed it over the desk.

Akala uncocked her pistol, holstered it, and rested the tip of her sword on the wooden floor. "It's okay, gentlemen." She took the paper from Talia and read while Gavin and Coulig gently let down the hammers of their firearms. Akala gasped, "Aideen!" She read it again.

"What is it?" asked Gavin, his deep voice exuding concern.

"Someone has kidnapped Aideen. They want the octagon key. Anisha is on her way to Juana Pohala. Dorfin sent out a hundred birds in hopes of getting word to Imar, so he may be on his way by now." Akala deigned to say nothing of the link between Dalla and her granddaughter, and she was glad Coulig and Gavin also kept their mouths shut. To Talia, she asked, "When did this come in?"

"Yesterday," replied Talia. With the slightest of smiles, she added dryly, "The morning after your last visit."

"What are we going to do?" Coulig asked. "Do we go back, or do we go on?"

Akala thought for a minute. Time seemed to press on her as she pondered her choices. Gavin fidgeted and looked at her, but she ignored him, looking at Talia instead. Akala raised one brow and demanded, "Why are you so helpful?"

"I was wondering when you were going to get around to asking," Talia replied smoothly. "You wouldn't have come back but for two reasons. You're not finished asking about your husband or you intend to get even. Which is it?"

"Both," Akala snapped. "We're wasting time." Anger fueled her irritability. That someone would kidnap her granddaughter was bad, but she was half a world away on the trail of her missing husband. Her frustration was growing. She feared not finding Travin even though she was getting closer, but now she feared to lose little Aideen. She wanted to scream, but she clenched her teeth and willed herself back under control until she was sure she appeared confident again.

At that moment, Jon appeared in the doorway. He looked unsure of who he should address, so he spoke with eyes darting back and forth between the owner and the mate. "There's a crowd forming outside. I think they're just curious, but some of them are armed. Ziggy is keeping them back with the help of the watch topside."

Akala was about to respond when Gavin said, "Good. Go help Ziggy. We'll be along shortly."

With a knuckle to brow, Jon was gone. Akala turned to Coulig and Gavin. "Take the team to the house and get Egan. Have Enola leave one of her squad to watch the back door." She turned to the pockmarked kid and said, "Go with them."

Coulig smacked fist to chest and went out the back with Jax and Brin in tow.

"What about you, Lady?" Gavin asked, eyeing Talia suspiciously.

"I'll be along shortly." Akala lifted her sword and took a chair, placing the slender blade casually across her left arm. She leaned back.

Gavin nodded and moved out to catch up with the away team. Akala turned and looked at Talia expectantly, "Well?"

The two women stared at each other like two cats appraising each other's strengths and weaknesses. Akala guessed that under different circumstances they could probably be friends.

A minute passed before Talia spoke. "This is an opportunity," she began. "Oh, I have other reasons for helping you. Let's just say I've been in your shoes before, and there's no great love lost with Egan out of the picture. Were you just planning to carve information out of him, or are you taking him with you?"

"I thought his services as a guide could be best put to use."

"Good," Talia replied with a nod. "If you could

arrange his absence for a while I will tell you where your husband and his crew are."

Akala sat up gripping her sword tightly, but keeping the point away to the side. The distinct sound of pistol shots rang out from outside, drawing their attention briefly. Akala saw the curiosity on Talia's face change to deducted realization of their new firearms. She thought the woman would question her on the weapons, but she stuck to the subject at hand.

"Oh, don't kill the little grease ball," Talia continued. "I need him to return in a month or two." She pursed her lips with scrunched brows and tapped a finger thoughtfully on the side of her chin. "Well, no more than a year. Any longer than that and his assets could go into probate. That would be rather inconvenient."

Akala's eyes narrowed. "And the *Avenger*?"

"Gone," replied Talia flatly. "I'm sorry," she added in a softer tone. "Egan's slave raiders sank your husband's ship, and two-thirds of the crew died fighting. Captain Travin Murdoch is alive, as are a dozen of his crewmen." She paused and said, "Do we have a deal?"

Akala stared at Talia for a few seconds and said, "We do."

Akala stepped out the back door and slung the rolled leather map case across her back. One of her pistol holsters was now empty; her powder horn and a pouch of ball ammo were gone as well. The pockmarked airman was there. His disappointment at being left out of the action was obvious.

"So, you drew the unlucky straw," Akala consoled.

"Worry not, young man. There'll be other chances for action. When you get older you'll yearn for the action while being glad for its absence."

"Yes, Lady Akala," replied the airman somewhat glumly.

"Go to the front and help Jon and Ziggy with crowd control."

The young seaman turned airman knuckled his brow and departed through the building.

Akala strode towards the house and noticed six wounded men lying on the lawn near the front door. They all had empty sword sheaths, but no visible weapons. Four had leg wounds and two cradled arms and sported bloody shoulders. Akala walked between the moaning men and had no sooner placed a foot upon the first step when the front door opened to Coulig coming out with Egan in tow.

The rotund shipping agent was gagged and had his hands bound in front of him and tied to a lead rope. Coulig gave the hempen line an occasional yank. Next in line came two of Egan's henchmen, now unarmed and bearing heavy bags that jingled. Jax and Brin walked behind them carrying smaller bags in one hand and pistols in the other. The rest of the away team was similarly burdened.

"It really wasn't much of a fight," Coulig greeted Akala. "Selective wounding is easier and more efficient with guns," he said, indicating the disabled guards. "Had we been using swords, I think most of them would be worse off."

"Oh, I approve," Akala agreed. "Just remember, you won't always have the time or luxury for wounding shots."

"I know," said Coulig. "If they had had guns we would've been forced to shoot to kill."

Egan made some noises through his gag, which Akala ignored. "I know where Travin is," she said to Coulig and Gavin. The revelation silenced Egan.

"What about Aideen?" asked Gavin.

Akala's face grew hard. "We'll get Travin and the *Avenger*'s crew first, and then we make all possible speed for Juana Pohala, in the Desert of Hamaud."

CHAPTER 25

The morning smelled fresh. Imar wondered if he actually detected a little dew in the air. The sun was just beginning to spread its golden brilliance across the desert, causing long shadows to cast from cacti, which looked like robbery victims reaching for the sky. The waxing gibbous moon paled with the growing day as it slowly slid behind the Western Range. The beauty of the morning was dampened only by the cloud of dust dogging their trail. Imar hoped it was only a caravan, but his lightly burdened party should have outdistanced it by now.

Imar and Hager rode in the lead. The party still burdened the same mounts that had brought them over the mountains. Camels were better suited to the arid conditions but slower than horses. Ahote had advised them to delay switching to dromedaries until they were ready to go east into the heart of Hamaud. Because the higher temperatures there the desert would probably kill their horses. Imar didn't see how it could get any hotter than what each day had brought so far.

With the exception of a whole day's delay holed up in their tent, pitched in a cave to escape a sandstorm, their week of riding through the night and resting in the day had been uneventful. Imar was thankful for the nearly full moon to light their nocturnal travel. He would have ridden day and night had the heat not stopped them. He considered his party lucky to find caves or rock overhangs to rest from the midday's furnace, but just as often they had to suffer the heat of the day in only the shade of their tent.

Each time they ran low on water they came upon a well or an oasis, and they had yet to stop at either and not be approached by a band of burnous clad riders claiming ownership of the water and demanding tribute. Imar let Vidar handle the negotiations. He did not complain of the exorbitant cost, having other things more important on his mind—Aideen.

Each band of desert riders had, at least, one black robed Hamaudi assassin with them. Imar studied them each time, watching their moves and mannerisms, learning everything he could against the day he would kill Khaled. It was a constant reminder to practice the sword, which he now did twice a day with Hager, Vidar, Aksel, and Egil. Because of the constant practice, they were all in peak shape and at the top of their skill, but Imar's ability, already considered uncanny, became almost supernatural.

The brief hint of morning dew evaporated in the rising temperature, warning Imar that the next few hours should be devoted to finding shelter. He was anxious to get to Juana Pohala, but the discomfort, as well as the danger, of pressing on through the afternoon heat could hurt the horses, if not his friends and himself. His eyes roved the horizon in search of a suitable camp.

"It doesn't seem like Townsend is trying very hard to be incognito," said Hager. His eyes also roamed, but Imar couldn't tell if his vigilance was for hazards or shelter.

Imar never knew when his friend would get talkative. The moments were rare, but he had learned over the past few months to pay attention when he did.

"No, he's not," Imar agreed. "Dalla says the Mozar Hamaud is a hotel for only the wealthiest patrons. He seems to be taking a high profile approach. Why shouldn't he? There is no law in Hamaud to stop him."

"And you're just going to walk right in?" Hager's usual stoicism slipped. "Dalla's mind-speech with Aideen indicated that Townsend has, at least, a dozen professional fighters, and he's hiring more. That was over a week ago. He could have fifty sell-swords for all we know. And your daughter is being held on the top floor of a five-story building." He absently patted his mount's neck. "Imar, you're not thinking clearly. Townsend is choosing the ground, and he has the advantage of elevation and numbers. You go in like he's instructed and he'll kill you. He'll kill all of us and get the key. What about Aideen?"

"Anisha is with her now; she won't let anything happen to her."

Hager spit. "You can't be serious. By all accounts, Anisha is just as responsible for the kidnapping as Townsend. She betrayed you Imar, and she betrayed her own daughter. Don't forget Aideen's wounds are because of this."

The muscles around Imar's eyes tightened and his jaw clenched. "That was Khaled's doing."

"Yeah," Hager responded vehemently, "with

Anisha's help. Imar, you can't trust her."

Galloping hooves made the men turn. Aksel and Egil passed on each side of Dalla and Vidar, who were riding abreast of each other roughly five meters behind Imar and Hager. The party had stretched out to minimize the dust. Imar's face revealed his softening mood when he looked at Dalla. Even through the folds of her sky blue burnous he could make out her shapely figure. Only her eyes were revealed through the wrappings of her headscarf and veil, but those eyes looked drawn. She had been mentioning the need of a bath for days now, ever since leaving Juana Napur, but as Imar had learned after months of traveling with her, that was nothing new. She always wanted a bath.

"Captain," Aksel called out, as he and Egil reined up beside him. "Look," he said, indicating the distant dust cloud behind them. "They're closer today."

Dalla and Vidar caught up with them. "If we stop, they'll catch up," Vidar commented.

"They'll catch us if we don't ride hard," added Hager.

"Let them," Imar said grimly. "I tire of this pursuit. If we walk our horses, theirs will be tired when they catch us. We can find out who they are and then outrun them if we choose."

When the riders came within a kilometer, Imar signaled his friends to a halt. "Mounted wall," he ordered. "Close formation and string bows. Dalla, behind me."

They positioned their horses three meters apart to face the oncoming riders. Imar was in the middle with

Hager to his right, Vidar on his left, and Aksel and Egil on either end. Their bows were long and could not be put to full potential while mounted, but Imar had trained his warriors to use them effectively while on horseback and with frightening accuracy on foot.

When Imar began to make out the cut of the Kalusian uniforms his memory tugged at him with such vengeance he felt as if a knife had stabbed his temples. The flash of pain lasted only a second, but his bond with Dalla caused her to cry out behind him. He looked back, but she had recovered as fast as he had. Her face was exposed now, the thin cloth draped down over her left shoulder.

The soldiers were coated with dust, and as they slowed the cloud of dust rolling from their mounts hooves dissipated with decreasing momentum. They rode four abreast, five deep, with their leader and a standard bearer in front.

"Aksel, Egil," Imar called out. "Warning shots on my order."

The young men nocked and drew. When the platoon was within fifty meters, Imar said, "Loose!"

The arrows fired from each end of the line crossed flight just before sinking in the sand in front of the leader. His horse snorted as he simultaneously reined in and signaled a halt with an upraised fist.

"That's far enough," Imar called out confidently. He was relieved to see no bows in the platoon; at least, none were strung or visible. To the leader, he said, "You alone may approach."

The commander spoke to his men before he and the standard bearer walked their horses forward.

"Vidar," Imar said calmly.

In half a second Vidar drew and shot. The twang and thwack of the shaft striking the flagpole stopped the two horsemen instantly. Oohs of admiration rolled through the formation. The standard bearer looked relieved when his commander ordered him to stay behind before proceeding forward.

"I am Captain Rutger," the commander introduced himself when he stopped a few meters in front of Imar. "We are searching for Captain Imar Amirson."

"I am Imar. I think I know what you want." Rutger nodded without surprise and Imar added, "You can't have it."

Rutger sighed as if he expected as much. "I have my orders."

"Captain, my daughter has been kidnapped and the ransom is the octagon key."

Rutger's eyes widened and his face showed compassion for a moment before he said, "I am sorry, but…"

"Captain," Imar interrupted. "Even if my daughter was safe I would still not hand over the key. It is too dangerous an artifact to hand over to anyone, especially an ambitious monarch, much less a kidnapper. However, I may have to use the key to get my daughter back." He paused a moment, considering his words. "We are on the same side, I don't wish to hurt you or your men, but I will for the sake of my daughter and the sake of mankind."

"You're vastly outnumbered," Rutger countered.

"Vidar," Imar said. In an instant, Vidar let fly another shaft. The arrow stuck a few centimeters below the last one, driving the point home and causing a chorus of exclamations in the platoon. The platoon's sigil now sported two shafts from its pole. Imar calmly queried, "How many men will you lose before we draw our swords?"

Rutger let the question hang a few seconds before he said, "What if we help you rescue your daughter?"

Imar felt a surge of hope at this suggestion. Just as fast, his expectation deflated. "I would love to have your help, Captain, but I still won't give you the key."

"Look," Rutger began, "I have to do something. As you said, we're on the same side. How old is your daughter?"

"Aideen is eleven years old."

"I have a daughter too. She's nine. I can't begin to imagine your distress, but I know I'd let nothing stand in my way to save her. Let me help you. Once she is safe we can worry about the key then. If you have to give it to the kidnappers, then I will delight in taking it from them. If you have the key when this is done...well," Rutger looked pained, "you have my word; your daughter won't be harmed."

Imar didn't know what to think. The aid of twenty soldiers was too good to be true, but what would happen later? Fighting together created bonds between warriors. If they had to go into battle with Townsend's sell-swords, these soldiers would be like comrades—brothers in arms. Would these warriors become battle brethren only to become enemies after the action? Could he kill this man offering to help him save his daughter?

Imar looked to his friends. They watched him. The boys, barely seventeen, looked eager. Vidar seemed unsure as if he were calculating investment returns. When Imar looked at Hager those indistinguishable flashes of memory danced like wraiths in his mind. He clamped down on the distraction. Though Hager remained impassive, Imar perceived the nod in his eyes. Before he even looked at Dalla, Imar felt the comforting flood of her empathy. When he looked in her eyes, the love he felt there gave him strength. He wanted to go to her and take her in his arms but now was not the time. With difficulty, Imar broke his gaze with Dalla. It was like tearing off a piece of his heart. He was still not used to the emptiness he felt after doing so.

Imar twisted back around to face Rutger, and said, "Thank you, Captain. I will gratefully accept your help."

"Excellent," Rutger replied. "We have a fortified camp outside Juana Pohala." Imar appeared confused a moment when Rutger added, "There are numerous tribal tent camps around the city. For the most part, the war chiefs observe the agreed upon truce inside the major trade cities, but anything outside is fair game." He smiled, but his expression was serious. "You are welcome to stay at the Kalusian camp."

Imar considered Rutger's words before carefully replying, "Thank you for your invitation, Captain, but our alliance is new and trust can only be earned with time and deeds. Though you seem to be a man of your word, it would not do to temp any of your overzealous men. We will find lodging in the city, and stay in contact through messengers."

"As you wish, Captain," Rutger replied as if he had expected that answer. "I trust you will not be offended if we escort you to Juana Pohala."

Imar answered with the adage, "All roads are free in Hamaud. It's the water that is costly."

CHAPTER 26

Aris swayed in the saddle. He felt like vomiting again, but he hadn't eaten, so he knew it would be painful. He thought he should be feeling better by now. Ivan said it had been more than a week since he was bitten by the snake. He had only foggy, agony filled memories of the first few days after the bite. He had lost track of time; only fragments of severe sweats and severe thrashing filled his memory and those were alternated with shivering chills which were unassuageable by layers of blankets even when Hawkins and the wizard were complaining of the heat.

When it was time to go, Aris felt nowhere near ready for travel. He remembered Ivan's apologetic face when he and Hawkins lifted him onto his horse and tied him to the saddle.

"I'm sorry, lad," the wizard had said, the sense of urgency evident in his voice. "I would delay longer if I could, but our friend's daughter...no," he corrected, "our *friend* has been kidnapped. Her name is Aideen, and she is only eleven years old. We started out to help her father. Now he needs our help more than ever."

Aris swooned and felt as if he was going to fall out of the saddle, but the seaman's lashings kept him secured. Ivan's brown eyes locked on his for a moment, then the wizard added, "You're important too, so we will go as easily as we can and take as many breaks as we dare, but we cannot tarry."

The boy was touched. Those words revealed a soft side to the crusty old wizard that, before then, Aris hadn't thought existed. It made him regret some of his previous harsh words. He knew he could be difficult at times. It just happened, he didn't really mean it, but by the time he thought he should apologize, the moments seemed awkward or inappropriate. When he thought back to the things that had annoyed him, they seemed silly and trivial—hardly worth his ire at the time.

The subsequent days on the road were an uneventful and monotonous experience of hot and dusty travel on a straight road through flat land that gradually and occasionally, with increasing frequency, displayed barren hills, mesas layered with red and tan sandstone, and arroyos lacking even a trickle of water.

Aris had no appetite and his leg still hurt, but the pain was dulled thanks to the vile concoction of poppy tea the wizard boiled in a pot for him each day. When he first tasted the nasty stuff he spit it out in a spray. It took some convincing, but Ivan assured him he would feel better if he drank it, which was only partially true. The foul brew did indeed ease his pain and help him sleep, but it didn't stay down at first. His nausea gradually grew less, but he had to force himself to eat. He got to where he looked forward to his medicinal tea, but the wizard was giving him smaller servings with decreasing frequency. This had angered him.

Aris had demanded more of the boiled poppies just the day before, and when Ivan gave him something else, he tossed it out. "This isn't what I asked for," the boy said hotly.

"No," the wizard replied calmly, "that was lobelia. It is good for pain and better tasting. I thought you'd like it."

Aris went to the gear, forgetting to limp, and began rummaging through the bags, looking for the dried poppies. "It doesn't work. I want the good stuff," he retorted vehemently.

"Yes, I'm sure you do," Ivan agreed dryly. "The opium in the poppies is an excellent pain medicine, but very habit forming. If you'll recall, you hated it at first, but now you want it all the time. You want more and your pain is less. The low dosages I am giving you are sufficient to control your discomfort even though you no longer feel the effects like you did at first."

Aris upended a sack of supplies on a blanket, finding everything but what he wanted. He glared at the wizard. "Where is it?"

Ivan pulled a small cloth bag from inside his robes and shook it. "Right here," he answered. "This is all that's left. Do you want to finish it now, and wish you had it during the long ride into Juana Pohala tomorrow when you'll need it most? Trust me. I've been slacking you off a little at a time for a reason."

Aris stood poised considering the wizard's words. He stared at the pouch where Ivan lounged against a saddle, wondering if he could snatch it out of the man's fingers. Slowly, he relaxed. He was being ridicules and he knew it—his liking for the medicine was making him act like a fool. He sat down. "I'm sorry. You are right, of course." Aris' eyes followed Ivan's movement as he stuffed the pouch in an inside pocket. "May I have some more tea?"

Ivan smiled at him. "Certainly. Help yourself, young man."

Aris just noticed Hawkins sitting with his back to him. All he could see of what he was sewing with some heavy thread was a strip of leather.

The morning was indistinguishable from the dark of night, but for the clean smell of the cool air and the position of the full moon. Aris woke wishing he could sleep more, yet thankful his restless night had come to an end. His bedding was a mess, currently cast off from either the warm night or his bout of the sweats, he was not sure which.

Ivan and Hawkins were huddled over a small fire of dung chips and broken up tumbleweed. They had donned the airy cloth robes of the desert. An outfit lay bundled with a pair of sandals at the foot of Aris' bedding. Through the smell of skillet cakes and coffee, Aris detected the bitter odor of poppy tea. His craving pulled at him. When he got up and moved several paces away to relieve himself, the cramped muscles in his bitten leg caused his limp to be genuine. Goose bumps rose on his bare legs, standing there as he was in his small clothes. He hobbled back to his bedding, donned his new attire, and took a seat by the fire. He wasn't really hungry, a sure sign he wasn't over the effects of the snake venom, but he forced himself to eat one of the hotcakes. After a few bites, he felt only the slightest trace of an appetite return.

Aris thought about his behavior from the night

before. At least, he had apologized for his childishness. His stomach clenched each time Hawkins or the wizard took a sip of coffee. He was far from ready for that, but his eyes strayed to the boiling poppies and tracked them as Ivan removed the pot from the fire to cool. Aris stared as the wizard skimmed the white foam off the top. He wanted to just reach over and drink right from the pan, knowing he would burn his lips. When Ivan finally poured the dark brown liquid into a flask his anger began to flare, but the wizard saved enough to fill a small cup and handed it to him before he had a chance to object.

It was all Aris could do not to snatch up the cup. "Thank you," he breathed, gently accepting the cup and forcing himself not to chug it. The warm liquid was pleasantly repulsive. He felt relief and restoration when the first twinge of nausea signaled him it was working. It wasn't enough for any euphoric effect, but it would do. He knew asking for more would be a waste of time.

"Here," said Hawkins, handing him a rolled band of leather. "I doubt you remember eating your snake. Oh, by the way, it was excellent."

Aris unrolled the offering to reveal a snakeskin belt reinforced with tanned deerskin underneath. The buckle was fashioned from the head of the viper, but the fangs were replaced with brass pins that locked into a double row of holes for fastening.

"I...I...thank you," stammered the boy, for once lost for words.

Hawkins grinned. "Don't forget this," said the seaman, holding up the snake's rattle. The leather thong tied to it gyrated when he shook it, causing the dead viper's alarm to silence a chorus of crickets.

The sound chilled Aris, but he took his new necklace and put it on, letting it hang on the outside of his garments.

"We will have to find shelter to sit out the heat this afternoon," said Hawkins, "but I think we can make it to Juana Pohala sometime tonight."

"Come on then," grumbled the wizard. "We're burning daylight."

Aris and Hawkins looked up at the sky. Daylight was still hours away.

CHAPTER 27

Akala had all the information she needed without dragging Egan along, but a deal was a deal, even though the landlubber was more trouble than he was worth. She almost regretted her treatment of him, but his duplicitous behavior, most especially at her husband's expense, had angered her to a level she had previously thought herself incapable of.

Their egress from Egan's estate was fairly simple for the crew but not so much for Egan. Most of the away team simply climbed up the ladder at the rear of his offices, strode across the roof to the outriggers, and over the airfoils to the deck of the ship. Egan, on the other hand, was too out of shape to climb up the ladder, even to the encouragement of a prodding cutlass. Akala wasn't so sure it wasn't an act of resistance to being taken against his will.

Nevertheless, Akala had Coulig, Jax and Brin haul Egan to the street where a line was lowered from an amidships boom to which he was securely fastened and hoisted only a few feet into the air. She was, at least, kind enough to order his gag removed before she ascended the rope ladder with the remaining members of the away team. The ship lifted off to the awe of the crowd and the screams of Jade Egan. The *Elbienus Raptor* climbed a hundred meters, nearly vertical with the propeller laboring against the gale, and then turned 180 degrees to the north, catching the stiff south wind while unfurling her sails. Each canvas caught the wind with a snap, causing the airship to accelerate into the darkening sky.

When Egan's incoherent screams became yelling pleas to bring him aboard, Akala waited. When his voice became hoarse, she waited some more until he finally became quiet. After a quarter hour of silence, she had the dangling shipping agent hoisted up and held in place horizontally, out from the rail, a meter forward of the airfoil's leading edge. The sound of the surf could be heard below, but the white caps and sea foam were barely visible in the scant moonlight filtering through the gathering clouds.

Blue heat lamps were hung all around the waist and quarterdeck, which gave the main deck an eerie aspect. The brighter orange or yellow settings interfered with the pilot and crew's night vision, so extra lamps were hung and set to low blue for the shipping agent's interrogation.

Egan's hands were still tied in front and the line holding him suspended in open air was wrapped several times around his middle, preventing him from bending, but positioned at a point of balance that held him prone. The wind pushing the ship caused him to rotate at a steady, if not stately, pace.

"Mister Egan," Akala addressed the shivering shipping agent. She stopped, perplexed, and turning to the mate said with unusual formality, "Mister Gavin, he's spinning."

"Yes, Lady Akala," Gavin agreed with equal ceremony. "He is."

"He looks like he's going to vomit," Jax observed. "That's the same green-around-the-gills look that Brin gets when he's seasick."

Brin elbowed Jax in the ribs.

"We might want to step back in case he spews," Coulig advised.

"Would one of you gentlemen please do something to stop his rotation?" Akala asked.

Gavin reached out one long arm and caught a foot, but Egan's shoe slipped off, as did the mate's grip and the shoe fell into the darkness below. "Oops, sorry about that," the tall man apologized in his deep voice. He reached again, this time securing the agent's stockinged foot. Now that they were under sail with the engine shut down, the relative wind came from abaft, so the first mate was careful to point Egan forward and downwind.

Akala sidestepped to bring herself even with Egan's head, and said, "There, that's much better. Now, Mister Egan, I hope you're not going to continue this mummer's farce about not knowing where my husband is."

"La...La...Lady Akala," Egan stammered in a raspy voice. "P...Please bring m...me aboard. Surely we c...can talk about this on d...deck."

"Answers first," Akala replied.

"I...I assure you, I know n...nothing about..."

Akala turned and nodded to Watkins, who was standing beside the boom's capstan. He flipped the latch and let the winch spin freely for two seconds before engaging the brake. Egan's shriek silenced when the cable jerked to a stop. His whimpers could be heard, if only barely, over the wind.

Gavin, Coulig, Jax, and Brin leaned over the rail.

"Well?" Akala asked. "Is he still conscious?"

"Oh, he's conscious all right," answered Coulig, "but I can't tell if he's squirming or if it's the wind swinging him back and forth.

"He does not look very happy," added Gavin. "I think he is weeping."

With lips pressed tightly together, Akala exhaled heavily through her nose. She squeezed in between Coulig and Gavin and peered over the rail to see that Egan's sways were accented with each gust of wind. He spun a quarter turn one way and then a half turn the other way from where he swung two meters below the scuppers. She called out without turning around, "Hoist him up, Mister Watkins."

"Aye, aye," Watkins replied as he began cranking on the windlass. The shipping agent slowly rose into view to the steady 'click, click, click,' of the winch ratchets.

Once Egan was again secured beside the gunwale, Akala said, "No more lies, Egan." Her voice became hard and deadly. "My desire to keep you alive is growing less by the minute. I want a glass of wine and my bed shortly after that, so if you don't start cooperating I'll just kill you outright and be done with it." She turned to Gavin and said, "Have Captain Beros plot a course for the Bovillan Peninsula."

"Aye, Lady," Gavin responded, knuckling his brow and striding aft to the pilot station.

Akala was satisfied with Egan's astonishment. "You see, Egan, you could be useful, but I don't really need you. I know where my husband is and how he got there." She paused a moment to let that sink in. "There are a few details about the mining camp that you could help us with. Such as the exact layout of the settlement, fortifications, and the type and number of armed resistance we could be facing, etcetera, etcetera, but first, I need some honest answers from you." She stepped back to where the boom line holding Egan was low enough to reach. Pulling a dagger from her boot top, and setting its edge against the line, she said, "It's confession time. Yes or no. You took gold from Captain Travin and set him and his crew up for an ambush by your slavers."

Egan's eyes were wide and fixed on Akala's blade. When he hesitated, she touched the hempen line with the razor sharp edge. One strand popped, causing a jerk to run its course along the line. "Yes," he said rapidly, his voice frantic. "Yes, I did."

The crew within hearing distance began to murmur.

"Your slavers murdered all but a dozen of Travin's crewmen, and sank the *Avenger*."

"Yes."

The murmuring grew louder.

"You betrayed our goodwill by taking our money meant for cargo and then selling my husband and his surviving men into slavery."

Egan delayed only a second, but Akala did not. Another strand popped, causing the two severed strands to rapidly unwind a meter up the line. This made a humming sound for a couple seconds and caused the remaining strand to stretch enough for Egan to drop a third of a meter.

"Yes!" shrieked Egan. "But it was..."

"That you instigated," Akala countered.

The nearby crew members witnessing the event began to grumble angrily and loudly. Insults, threats, and a few shouts of 'Kill him!' erupted.

"The gold we took from your house," Akala continued, "is reimbursement, plus interest, for the thirty Kalusian gold sovereigns you stole from Travin. Do you agree?"

"But you took…"

Akala pressed her blade against the last strand.

In less than a second, Egan spouted, "Yes, by all the gods, yes. Please don't cut the line."

"You still owe us a ship, and you will generously compensate the families of the crewmen your slavers murdered."

"Yes," Egan answered, obvious defeat in his voice.

"Okay, bring him aboard," Akala ordered, her disappointment evident. She reluctantly removed her blade from the last strand of line supporting Egan's life. She again reminded herself of her deal with Talia.

Watkins swung the boom, bringing the dejected shipping agent in over the rail, and plopped him on the deck. Akala slid her blade back into its boot sheath and wrinkled her nose at Egan's odor. It was the second time she had seen him lose his continence with fear. "Cut him loose. Give him clean clothes and some water to wash with. He can billet in the gear locker in the fo'c'sle." She faced Egan where he lay on the deck. "I trust you'll behave while you're with us, or do we need to lock you up?"

Egan looked around at the angry faces glowering at him. Akala guessed at what he was thinking. She turned to the crew and loudly said, "This man shall not be harmed." There was more grumbling, so she added, "Anyone who mistreats Mister Egan shall answer to me."

Egan looked at her but still would not meet her eyes. He spoke sheepishly. "You'll have no trouble from me."

"Good." Akala turned aft and strode to her stateroom.

The *Elbienus Raptor* slid on smooth air as she sped before a stiff nor'wester. The cool, high altitude air was pleasant, but it required warmer wear in the early hours before the severe equatorial sun lifted above the eastern horizon. The crescent moon had begun waxing towards first quarter just days after the airship had departed Port Equanos. They originally planned to go east over the high peaks of the Anderan Mountains, but a persistent cluster of clouds preventing visual navigation forced them to take the low route around the northern end of the range. They had been lucky those first couple of days when the south wind pushed them north. When they turned to tack an easterly course along the north shores of the Anderanian continent, the wind had changed and howled out of the east, making them furl sails and run the propeller against the wind with very slow progress.

After three days of a snail's pace progress, the wind finally abated, but the overworked energy converter began to overheat and had to be shut down. Power reserves dwindled rapidly and then squeaking noises began to issue from the output shaft. Soon the propeller drive engine also had to be shut down.

The power derived from light, heat, and rapid decomposition of organic material could not be transferred into fuel for the engine nor could lighter-than-air gas be produced for lift. The airship started to lose altitude, and they had to land for repairs. The *Elbienus Raptor* was grounded on an uninhabited strand of beach for another three days.

Akala chaffed at the delay, until Beros said, "The *Raptor* is still a ship. Why don't we just sail? You know, the old-fashioned way."

"You mean with canvas to the wind upon the sea?"

"Of course, the ship is light but seaworthy. She won't take a hard thrashing, but so long as the weather's fair we can make some headway while the converter is under repair."

Akala laughed. She felt like an idiot, mentally kicking herself for not thinking of it first. "Of course, let's do it," she agreed.

With the converter down and lift gas production ceased, the big oblong balloon had begun to sag, so they deflated it entirely and let it lay flat in its cradle, and then shoved off the strand with set sails. The *Elbienus Raptor* wasn't as smooth on a rolling sea as a deep keeled rig, and the empty balloon made her top-heavy and a bit unstable, but the outriggers kept her from tipping. By the time they rounded the continental corner and headed southeast into the archipelago, the thickening half-moon lit their nightly navigation.

It was on a clear night when the converter overhaul was completed. The blue heat lamps around the deck seemed to enhance the silvery moonlight reflecting off the calm seas.

"We're ready to fly, Cap'n," the chief engineer reported.

"Excellent," replied Beros. "Fire it up, Chief and start filling the bag."

"Aye, aye," the engineer responded, knuckling his brow before departing down the main deck hatch to the engine room.

"How long will it take to be airborne again?" Akala asked.

Beros was about to respond when a bell rang eight times, signaling the change of the watch. He answered as crewmen came out of the hatches and went to their duty stations to relieve their counterparts. "It's midnight now. I'd give it four or five hours."

Akala nodded. A high-pitched whine sounded for a second followed by a low hum and then Akala heard gas running through the lines. "I'm going to get a little shuteye then."

"Me too," said Beros. "It's Gavin's watch now."

As if on cue, the tall first mate came out on deck, and Akala said her good nights to both men and went to her cabin. Her head had no sooner hit the pillow and she was sound asleep.

Akala roused herself and came groggily out on the main deck, where she was rewarded with two bells, indicating she had slept nearly five hours. The balloon looked like an oversized game ball in its cradle.

She watched the big oblong bag fill and take shape until it created sufficient lift to raise the hull enough to bounce off the tops of the gentle swells. The ship skipped along like an albatross taking off from a rolling sea. Then it was as if the keel gave the sea one last kiss and the *Elbienus Raptor* rose gracefully into the air. Akala then made her way up to the quarterdeck.

The soft lunar luminescence faded as the three-quarter moon set behind the starboard stern, making way for the blue dawn as the sky slowly turned orange in the east. Gavin was at the pilot controls when Akala took a standing position to his right. They watched the magnificent sunrise.

"I don't recall ever seeing you up this early, Akala," commented the mate.

Akala couldn't help but notice that Gavin finally abandoned his usual formality. "I wanted to see the liftoff," she replied. "Besides, I'm getting anxious and I couldn't sleep. We're getting closer to the mines and I want to be up on deck when we arrive."

"Ah," Gavin said with a sigh. "My relief is here, just when the day was getting nice."

Akala followed Gavin's gaze to where the ship's captain was just exiting his cabin. Beros ascended the portside steps to the quarterdeck. He cradled a steaming mug of coffee in both hands and took a sip upon reaching the pilot station. "Good morning," he greeted cheerfully.

Akala and Gavin both responded in kind.

"It is good to be aloft again," said the captain.

"It is," Akala agreed, "as long as it stays smooth. You know how much I hate turbulence."

"What's the word mate?" Beros asked as he leaned against the control stand. Gavin made to move, but the captain shook his head and waved him to stay. "A moment longer, please," he said as he turned to take in the brightening morning. "I'm hoping the weather holds though I wouldn't mind a little rain to quench the heat."

"I couldn't agree more, Captain," replied Gavin. "But for the pain in my joints, I fear we're in for a blow. We haven't seen a sail in a while either. At least, none with a lamp through the night's running, nor has the watch spotted a canvas since we lifted off. They all probably ran for coves knowing a storm is brewing."

Akala worked her shoulder. "My joints do ache. That usually means rain, but not necessarily a big storm."

Beros gulped his quickly cooling coffee and set the mug in the cup holder. He then took up his position at the pilot station, sliding into the seat as Gavin vacated it. The first mate stood to the side as the captain checked his gauges and made fine tuning adjustments to the trim. "You should go raid the galley and get some rest," he said to his first mate. "I'll want battle drills this afternoon. I don't want the crew getting rusty."

"Aye, sir," said Gavin. The tall mate strode down the few steps to the waist. A few seconds later he was ducking into the fo'c'sle.

A moment after Gavin went in Coulig came out with Egan in tow. They went up the starboard steps to the forecastle and then to the prow. Egan was dressed in sailor's slops. Akala thought the barefoot agent looked rather comical fit out in cutoff trousers and loose work shirt. Coulig explained something to him that Akala could not hear across the length of the ship. He handed the little fat man something and then barked at him with a gesture. Egan reached up and began rubbing at the figurehead. Coulig walked aft and joined Akala and Beros on the quarterdeck.

"What was that all about?" asked Beros.

Coulig grinned. "Oh, just a little humility to keep teeth in the poor sap's head," he replied.

Beros raised the brow above his good eye and Akala looked at the stocky veteran expectantly.

"The crew is not very happy with him," began Coulig. "I've seen several murderous looks directed at him and even heard some serious threats. It's been getting worse because all the hands have duties and he has none. When they're doing chores, it rankles them that Egan can stroll around the deck taking in the sights. Some of their pranks at his expense were getting somewhat serious, so I set him to scrubbing the figurehead with a toothbrush. It's menial and degrading, but they can't say he's loafing."

"That's brilliant, Coulig," Akala said.

"You probably saved the penguin's life," Beros agreed. "When he's done with the figurehead, let's put him on washing dishes and dumping chamber pots."

An hour after the coloring on the clouds faded into grey overcast, the Bovillan Peninsula came into view. It was still a long way off but Beros began a slow descent.

"We got here faster than I would've thought," said Akala. "According to the charts, it's well over two thousand kilometers from the northern tip of the Anderan continent."

"Well, we have been pushing pretty hard for a few days, and we've had a tailwind ever since we set sail in the middle of our overhaul," Beros opined.

"I had better rouse the watch for some weapons practice," said Coulig. "Gavin can relieve me when he gets up." He strode to the waist bellowing orders like a drill instructor.

"So how are we going to do this?" Beros asked. He interrupted his own inquiry by calling down to his amidships man, Watkins. "Furl the sails and then call down the top men. The engine has rested long enough, it's time for some speed."

"Aye, aye, Captain," Watkins answered with a salute.

"I'm not sure," Akala said to answer his question. "We've got all the information out of Egan that we can use, and the maps Talia gave us indicate that the mining area is only about two kilometers back from the shoreline. Why not go in guns blazing? The mine is basically a big rock quarry dug into the side of a mountain. They can't know about us unless Talia sent an extremely fast pigeon, but it's against her best interest to betray us. They don't know we're coming; they don't have guns, and we have the first and only airship ever built. It'll be a complete surprise."

"How 'bout we divert to Argen Island first?" suggested Beros. "We should get there this afternoon. The water crossing to the Bovillan shore is only about forty or fifty clicks if Talia's charts are accurate. We could plan and prep this afternoon and head out an hour before sun up. We can have Travin and his crew back before breakfast."

"I like it. Go ahead and divert."

CHAPTER 28

The *Elbienus Raptor* skimmed a meter above the placid ocean after leaving Argen Island. A slate overcast was creeping in from the south, swallowing stars as it advanced. The early morning air was calm, and slight steamy swirls of mist twisted off the flat sea. Akala gripped the portside rail of the pilot station, calming her accelerated mind. Her innards spun with exhilaration, fear, anticipation, and dread, but mostly she felt the hollow emptiness of longing. She had tried meditating earlier, and that was as impossible as sleep. Was she too late? The nagging fear that had plagued her for months would soon be answered, but what if he wasn't there? What if they had moved Travin somewhere else? What if he was dead? Akala knew her strong-willed husband wouldn't survive long under the lash and yoke of slavery.

They had made their preparations the day before. All firearms were loaded and distributed to the crew with the extras positioned around the deck. The sixty-millimeter swivel gun was mounted on the bow and primed with shot. One enterprising crewman had modified the exploding rounds, meant for the swivel gun, into time fused hand grenades.

At the battle council, the squad leaders and officers had agreed that they would face stiffer and more professional opposition than they had with retrieving Egan. Resistance would have to be met with shoot-to-kill tactics. These slavers were seasoned fighting men, ruthless killers who would fight viciously for their gold. Nor would they willingly part with their live property—the slaves who mined that gold, farmed their food, and did all the work under the encouragement of the whip.

Just as the sun was cracking the eastern horizon, they encountered fog. Akala swore under her breath as Beros cut the engine and climbed to one hundred meters—they hadn't planned for fog. The disengaged propeller decelerated down to very slow revolutions until it came to a stop in the calm air.

Beros turned to his right and said in a low voice, "Gavin, deploy sails, and ready the men, but do it quietly. We didn't plan for this mist, but we're surely going to use it. I want no noise until the shooting starts."

Instead of a knuckle to the brow, Gavin gave the battle salute of fist to chest and went forward to issue whispered orders. His first stop was Watkins, who in turn used hand signals to order the top men to unfurl the sails. The limp canvas hung in the calm air. The airship drifted almost to a stop.

As the morning sun poked the top of its face into a narrow band of clear sky in the distant east, it chased cool dew filled air across the earth's surface, causing the lightest of breaths to push against the slack sails. The white canvas turned golden in the morning light just as the sheets lifted, if only slightly.

The *Elbienus Raptor* drifted into the thick fog at a slow crawl. The light turned grey and the moisture chilled the bare skin of Akala's hands and face. A lookout in the bow signaled the captain. Beros ordered the spanker sail swung to port as he turned the tiller.

The airship nearly pivoted in place as it swung hard to larboard and paralleled the shore. The spanker was reset, and the sounds of small waves lapping against the shore could be heard, but only seen when looking directly down through the mist. Waves a hand's breadth high appeared from ahead out of the gloom, lapped gently on the pebbled shore below, and disappeared into the grey void behind as the ship floated through the ghostly gloom.

All hands on deck were busy, as tacking to a perpendicular wind in an unpowered airship took vigilant attention and quick reflexes to stay on course. They made slow progress navigating blindly along the shore, but after several minutes, a dozen heads cocked at distant sounds. It was muffled and indistinguishable at first, but in time Akala could hear voices accented by an occasional shout. Then the crack of a whip snapped somewhere in the void, followed by a cry of pain. The mining settlement was waking the laborers—rousting the slaves.

Beros ordered the braziers lit for fire arrows and fuses. Lines with buckets were cast over the rails and hauled up to douse the decks with seawater. Suddenly top men and the lookout in the bow began waving their arms and pointing ahead. That was when the vilest of gods' awful stenches assailed Akala's senses. She clamped her mouth shut, pulled her scarf over her nose, and took short small breaths. A ship hove into view, tied to a wooden quay. The smelly old bark had to be a slaver; no other vessel could smell that bad. It rode high in the water.

"Grenades," shouted Beros, discarding the noise discipline.

All free hands on the main deck, eager to blow something up, ran to the braziers, lit fuses, and then cast their grenades over the port rail as Beros steered to starboard directly over the vacant slave ship. More than a dozen grenades fell down on the docked vessel, bouncing on the forecastle, main deck, into the open hold, and onto the poop deck.

The *Raptor* slid beyond the doomed ship as the explosions began. Beros ordered the sails furled, and engaged the propeller. With little forward visibility, he kept the speed slow, but Akala still feared they would crash into the mountain. She could no longer see the ship behind them, but the fog flashed orange in concert to the staccato booming of explosions. She realized that since the ship may have been empty, they would have more enemies to fight at the encampment. Visibility was still poor, but the mist had thinned enough to see men and structures fifty meters from the airship.

Crossbow bolts began striking the hull. Beros ordered the top men down, but as one man ran to the mast along a yardarm, he caught a bolt in the back and fell to the deck. Riflemen along the rails began picking off armed targets and the swivel gun rocked the ship with each blast. Beros made s-turns across the compound, and based on Egan's report and sketch of the compound, they wreaked hell on any buildings they were sure did not hold slaves. There was one very nice house, which they shot with the small cannon and then blew apart with half-a-dozen grenades.

The fog was lifting. Beros brought the ship down

to seven meters over a clear area where men with whips and clubs were herding chained men inside thatch-roofed huts. Akala assumed the buildings were barracks. Four crossbowmen on the ground fired at the ship, wounding a rifleman, but a volley of musket fire from the foredeck cut them all down. Reversing the prop briefly as a brake, Beros brought the airship to a halt and then kicked the drive into idle. Akala walked briskly to the waist to join the away teams. Twenty men and women slid down port and starboard lines. Once on the ground, Akala waved Beros away and the *Elbienus Raptor* moved off to wreak havoc from aloft.

Akala went with Coulig, Jax, Brin, and a crewman named Hans. They immediately engaged four slavers, using their swords in order to conserve their pistols. The slavers were dispatched efficiently, but Hans was injured with a deep wound to the thigh. Jax and Brin helped him to the safety of Gavin's squad where Jon and Ziggy applied hammers and chisels to chains tethering a string of slaves. The eight chained men were half naked and thin, but muscular from hard labor. None of them were from the *Avenger*.

Akala addressed the men. "You are slaves no longer. We seek Travin Murdoch and his crew. Do you know where they are?"

Jon and Ziggy freed the last men in the string from his fetters and then set to work on another set of slaves.

Three of the men extended pointing arms towards the slave barracks at the end of the line of buildings. One of them said, "They're over there. Come, I'll show you."

"Akala," Coulig called, "we've got company."

An assembly of thirty men dressed like ill-kempt sailors was coming towards them carrying an assortment of axes, maces, and cutlasses. Two men carried crossbows. Slavers were joining them from different parts of the compound. Their numbers were growing rapidly. Coulig, Jax, and Brin advanced, forming a shield wall of three. They were the only ones that had brought shields.

One big brute of a man stepped forward. He wore a wide-brimmed hat but appeared to have short cropped hair. His black beard was thick and bushy. He said, "You're outnumbered. We could easily kill you, and we should for destroying our ship, but if you throw down your weapons we will let you work off the debt."

Akala stepped up behind Coulig and asked, "Are you, Del Pero?"

The away team had formed up on each side of the meager shield wall. The clank of hammer and chisel cutting rivets and links continued with an occasional rattle of chain. To a man, each prisoner freed retrieved the clubs and knives from dead or wounded slavers.

"I am," said the big man. His face was angry. "Decide quickly, better slavery then death, eh?"

Akala drew one of her pistols, cocked it, extended it between Coulig and Brin over their shields, and fired. The shot blew out a donut-like smoke ring. Del Pero, having seen what rifles could do from the airship's attack, knew to dodge out of the way. The ball struck and fell a man standing behind him. The crossbowmen fired, but the shields caught the bolts. One of the bolts extended ten centimeters through the wood, making a gash along the edge of Brin's hand. He broke the bolt's head off with the hilt guard of his short sword.

"Get them!" Del Pero yelled.

The enemy charged. Akala drew another gun and joined it to a dozen rounds of pistol fire. The slavers' frontline fell, and the men behind them tripped over the fallen as they crowded forward. Coulig turned to Akala and said, "Go, take some men and find Travin." Then at the top of his lungs, he yelled, "Charge!" The away team, along with a few former slaves now armed with fallen weapons, attacked. The battle was joined.

Akala grabbed the man that had offered to lead her to Travin earlier. She took Jon and Ziggy with her as well. There was one other crewman with hammer and chisel in hand, and to him, she said, "Find slaves wherever you can and free them. Urge them to join the fight." The crewman nodded and ran to the nearest barracks.

The slight breeze that had brought them inland began to pick up and blow away the fog, but Akala barely noticed it or the reddening of the sky as she ran to the end structure. Stepping inside and out of the lighted doorway, she stopped to give her eyes time to adjust. There were four standing figures tethered to a line of recumbent figures that she could barely make out in the windowless hut. She heard her name murmured and then a chain dragged on a wooden floor.

Steel scraped on flint behind her and then Jon said, "This ought to help." He came up beside her; the yellow glow of a candle in his hand brightened the dim hut.

"Oh, may all the gods have mercy," said Ziggy. Akala envied his younger eyes.

The freed slave that had guided them to the hut said, "This is all that's left of the *Avenger's* crew. They suffered the lash and club more than most."

Jon lit a second candle off the first and handed one to Ziggy. They walked forward and Akala's eyes adjusted with the help of the meager candlelight. She could see that the men still prone were belly down and that their bare backs were laced with red stripes intermingled with darkened scabs. It was easy to ascertain that they had been recently whipped while still healing from old lash wounds. Crude herb poultices had been applied to the lacerations, giving the fresh wounds a greenish red appearance where the blood had seeped through.

One of the standing men addressed her. "Lady Akala. We all thought we'd never see you again. Well, except the captain of course; he knew you'd come. They whipped him the worst because he's the captain. He refused to 'show a good example.'" The man spoke the last phrase with obvious contempt.

"They weren't stingy with their cudgels either," said another. "That dirty swine Del Pero threatened to dismember him if we didn't work harder. These men lying here tried to escape and this is the treatment they got." The speaker stretched as far as his shackles would let him but he couldn't reach the man lying down on the end pallet. "They really put it to him yesterday."

Akala knew her husband the moment she laid eyes on the unconscious man at the end. She ran to him, collapsing to her knees at his side. "Travin...Travin...It's me, Akala."

His wounds were ghastly. She wanted to hug him, but she didn't want to hurt him. His head was facing the other way. She stroked his dirty, tangled hair and he groaned. "Oh, Travin," she said again, and he began to stir. She was hardly aware of the hammer and chisel striking chains behind her, or the shouts and cries of battle, the ringing of steel, and the cries of the wounded.

Travin turned his head towards her and opened his eyes, but they appeared to be unfocused. She could see the pain in his visage.

"Oh my dear, my love," she cried, tears running freely down her face and dripping off her chin. She wiped them with the back of her sleeve, but they continued to flow, and she had to keep wiping at them.

"My dearest, is that really you?" Travin asked weakly.

His eyes cleared as he pulled himself out of his lethargy, which Akala suspected was a mixture of both unconsciousness and sleep.

"We're getting you all out of here," Akala said, control returning to her voice. "Can you walk?"

"I…I don't know," replied Travin.

"We had to carry him in last night," said one of the crewmen.

Travin's leg shackles fell away. His chains were the last to be cut loose. Akala turned to Jon and Ziggy and said, "Take two men and go free the other slaves. Find more hammers and chisels—keys if you can find any—free anyone wearing a chain, and ask them to help us disarm and capture the slavers."

The other men lying prone were able to get up and stand with the aid of their crewmates. In a minute, Akala was left alone with Travin.

"Help me sit up," Travin said.

With many grunts and groans, Akala helped him up. She urged him to wait for a litter, but he declined and she knew better than to argue with her stubborn husband. It took a few minutes, but with her aid he got to his feet. They embraced, Akala careful not to touch his back, and then they kissed. The kiss was long and passionate followed by others of moderate length and then finishing with a series of pecks, more hugs, and more kisses.

"Gods, I've missed you. How did you get here?" he asked, his voice strained.

"Airship," she replied.

"It works?" His face shifted from surprise to pleasure. "That's outstanding. What did you name her?"

"The *Elbienus Raptor.*"

"After LB?"

She nodded. "Beros is captain, and the crew from the *Coastal Raider* now crews the *Raptor.*"

"Good choice," Travin complimented her.

They slowly made their way to the door and outside. His shuffling steps were limping and painful. When they stepped outside the fog was completely gone, revealing a red morning sky as if it were reflecting the bloody battle below. Above were clouds scattered in layers of ashen slabs. The sun graced the morning with a brilliant sunrise in all its crimson glory. It painted the cloud bottoms red and lit the mountainsides, whose bases still lay in the last lingering shadow of night. Only the distant horizon was clear of clouds—like a blue cornea abeam a solar iris, bordering the earth from the sky.

The fighting was winding down. At first, the away

team had been hard pressed and terribly outnumbered, their survival due in the beginning to the confusion of that initial volley of pistol fire. That action had almost balanced the scales, but as more slavers joined the melee, the away team began falling back. Then the *Raptor* came about and riflemen from the airship began picking off slavers.

Jon, Ziggy, and another crewman worked as fast as they could to cut shackle rivets. Some men and women, once freed, went to fight, while others found tools to free their fellows. Soon it was the slavers who were vastly outnumbered.

The away teams had used up their pistols, and with no time to reload they continued to fight with axe and cutlass. Soon all but the bravest and most stupid of the slavers broke and ran. The battle was won.

A few of the slavers threw down their weapons and surrendered, but the former slaves offered no quarter and killed them where they stood. Only the away team took prisoners, but most of the airmen rested hands on knees, breathing hard to catch their breath.

Travin looked with amazement at the airship as it circled, firing at the few targets still offering a fight. He then looked curiously at the three pistols fastened to Akala's vest and was about to ask her about them, but she spoke first.

"My dear, detailed explanations will have to wait." She stopped, drew one of her spent pistols, loaded it, primed it with a fresh cap, and handed it to her husband. Repeating the process to her second spent pistol, she said, "Just cock the hammer like this, point it at your enemy, and squeeze the trigger."

Before she had a chance to let down the hammer

a slaver came at them from between two buildings with a dagger held low. Akala shot him in the chest. The impact knocked him backward, laying him out flat. "You see how easy it is? You shoot a scrawny little slaver with one of these, and he'll do a somersault." Akala grinned. "Now you try it."

Two half naked men in rags wielding clubs chased a slaver on a route that would pass the couple in a few seconds.

"There, my love," Akala offered. "Try a running target."

Travin cocked the pistol and aimed low, leading the target a little, and fired. The ball caught the slaver's leg, causing him to fall and flip in an ungainly cartwheel. The ex-slaves finished their former tormentor in short order with their cudgels.

Travin grinned broadly. "You're right, my sweets, they really do somersault, don't they." He handed her the gun. "Would you reload my pistol, please? I'd like to try another shot."

"I'll reload it," Akala said, taking the weapon, "but it appears your comrades have cleaned up the yard, so to speak."

Travin seemed truly saddened by this revelation. He raised an eyebrow but winced with the effort. "I see," he said with a sigh.

Now that they were outside in better light, Akala noticed a cut near his hairline and one eye blackened and swollen.

They worked their way slowly to the battle site. The fight was over. About a dozen remaining slavers ran into the woods. They were pursued by freed slaves wanting vengeance. Beros landed the ship, and crewmen began setting out a gangway.

Coulig limped up to Travin and Akala, blood trickling from a gash below his knee, and said, "Good to see you, Captain. You've looked better, but at least, you're alive."

"I think a bath and some clean clothes will make a significant improvement," Travin replied.

"And a trim job," Akala added. "Your hair and beard look like a nest for squirrels."

A few meters away, Gavin wiped his cutlass on the shirt of a fallen enemy, sheathed it, and then joined them. "We lost four men," he reported regretfully. "Two more are badly wounded, and nearly all of us will need a few stitches."

Akala noticed the growing wet patch that darkened Gavin's scarlet shirt around the slice on his side. "You better get that tended to."

"A scratch," Gavin evaded. "We probably wouldn't have won this battle if not for the guns and air support."

"How many casualties were there among the freed slaves?" asked Travin.

"I would guess about eight or nine, and at least twice that of the enemy," replied the mate.

"The freed slaves are doing the mop up," added Coulig. "They're not taking prisoners."

"Good," said Travin. "The world doesn't need

slavers."

"We don't have room to get everyone out of here, and we blew up that cesspit of a ship," Gavin interjected. "Even with our losses we're going to be heavy with the *Avenger's* crew."

"Oh, I think we can afford to buy another ship, or possibly two or three," said the man that had helped Akala earlier. He had his arm around the waist of a woman wearing ragged clothes. "I'm Hector," he introduced, "and this is my wife, Cleo." She nodded.

"We are grateful to you for freeing us," said Cleo, "but there is plenty of gold here and even more in the quarry. If you could send us a ship, we can pay for it in advance. Of course, anyone wanting to leave will be welcome to do so, but a lot of us will stay as free miners."

"I see no reason to leave," said Hector. "It is not a bad place now that the riff raff has been cleaned up. Mining will be pleasurable without working under a whip."

They laughed and Travin said, "That's true. I saw a vein of gold as big as my wrist. You should have enough here for everyone to have a comfortable start."

They turned to the sound of cursing. Jax and Brin held a bound man struggling between them who was spewing some of the most colorful language Akala had ever heard. It was Del Pero. His hat was gone, revealing a bald pate with a half-circle of close-cropped black hair around the sides and back. He was forcing Jax and Brin in their direction when he saw Egan looking over the ship's rail at him. Apparently Beros had let him out of the gear locker after the battle.

"Why you treacherous little snake," Del Pero spat. "You brought them here. You dare to betray me? I'm going to twist off your head and pull out your heart, you spineless little maggot."

Even though Del Pero's hands were tied behind his back and he was held between two strong men, Egan looked genuinely scared. Akala wondered if he'd peed his pants again.

The commotion got the attention of a group of freed female slaves whom Enola was leading from a barracks. There were at least a dozen of them. When they saw Del Pero they swarmed him with screaming curses. Jax and Brin could do nothing but get out of the way. In a second the big overseer was on the ground suffering their kicks and stomps. The snap and wet crunch of breaking bones were unmistakable. Akala was sure he was dead while they continued to rain blows upon him. When they finally stepped back, Del Pero's corpse was a broken and bloody mess.

Travin grunted. "Pity," he said. "They beat me to it. Well," he added weakly, "maybe I can give Egan some payback."

Akala, remembering Egan's young slave girls, looked up at the shipping agent's shocked face. "Take a good look, Egan," she said to him. "This is what happens the first chance a woman gets to repay enslavement and degradation."

For the first time, Egan looked her in the eyes.

All of a sudden Travin slumped against Akala. She almost fell with him, but Coulig caught his other arm.

"He's weak," said Coulig. "We need to get him aboard the ship."

"Yes," Akala agreed. "We need to get out of here

as well and make all possible speed for Juana Pohala. Aideen needs us."

As Akala and Coulig assisted Travin to the gangway, Travin inquired, "Aideen...our granddaughter Aideen? Why are we going to Juana Pohala?"

"I'll explain it to you when we are under way," Akala replied. "I have a lot to tell you, and I do mean a lot."

CHAPTER 29

Aideen lounged in quiet comfort and contemplation. There were no chairs in the suite of rooms assigned to her, but the low couch and the many huge pillows were more than adequate for her needs. She wore a salmon colored dress with far too many frills for her taste. A linen shirt with leather breaches and vest would have been more to her liking, but neither Lord Townsend nor her mother would permit it. *Some exercise would be nice*, she thought, but his lordship had denied her request to go downstairs and spar with Hana and Hazim, and he still refused to return her blade, as if she would think to use it against trained mercenaries twice her size. *Well, I did damage Khaled's eye, but that was self-defense.* She rewarded herself a small smile at the thought.

The view out her eastern windows was both spectacular and spooky. Aideen had always thought of the desert as a flat plain of colorless sand, so when she first laid eyes on the multiple shades of red and tan layered sandstone rising in mesas and indefinable shapes, she had to force herself to stop gazing at it.

Contrasting with the desert's multi-shaded beauty was the twisted skeletal remains of the old-world civilization, now little more than blackened, time-worn frames of beams and girders sticking crookedly out of the sand. The heights of these ruins dwarfed all other buildings in Juana Pohala, including the great hotel in which Aideen was now imprisoned.

She had heard of various ancient city remains but had never seen one before in the west or in the north. Her tutors had told her that ancient civilization had overbuilt and the excessive weight on the continental shelf had caused the west coast to fall into the sea. She, of course, did not believe such nonsense, but it seemed to be a common story told to children.

At the forefront of Juana Pohala's ruins was the dome. It alone had lasted the ages with some semblance of strength. The curving roof of gold plated clay had resisted the ravages of time, but Aideen saw no one go near the relics of humanity's past. Her curiosity pushed her to investigate while her senses warned her to beware. She sensed human presence—more entities than she cared to count—underneath those old twisted structures, but no one went in or came out and she began to wonder if what she sensed was real, imagined, or spirits of the ancient dead.

Aideen asked a servant of the hotel staff about the ruins. The girl that brought her meals told her that the structures were dangerous. Sometimes only a beam would fall, other times a towering frame would collapse with a crash that would startle the whole city, causing dogs to bark and puffed-tailed cats to run for cover. These occurrences were not frequent, but enough injuries had occurred over the years to warrant warnings to children to avoid the site. It was then that the serving girl looked around as if checking that they were alone, and with an honest face said in a whisper, "Them ruins is haunted." Then she turned to the east, facing the ruins, and made some strange hand gestures with one hand while covering her face with the other hand, bowing her head slightly, and mumbling something inaudible. The girl left, leaving Aideen to wonder at the strange customs and superstitions of foreigners.

The hum of the evaporator that cooled Aideen's rooms provided quiet white noise for her meditations. She had no sooner entered a state of calm when Dalla's mind-voice came to her. *Aideen, are you there?*

I am, Aideen responded confidently. *Are you here yet? In Juana Pohala I mean.*

We are, replied the healer. *We were nearly captured by a Kalusian patrol, but your father made a truce with them to help us. However, he asked me to warn you not to trust them. They want the key as badly as Townsend does.*

Sound advice, Ivan's mind-speech stepped in. *Trust no one in government. We're here as well.*

We? inquired Dalla and Aideen together.

Hawkins is with me, he knows the desert, and a boy named Aris. The boy was snake bit and I'm not much of a healer, so we were delayed. Where is the exchange to be?

Townsend's messenger said we are to meet under the dome in the ruins of the old city.

I just want to get out of here and back with my father, Aideen's thought projected powerfully.

Soon, Dalla soothed.

Aideen could sense that Dalla was impressed with her skill.

You are getting quite strong, young lady, Ivan added. *I will see you both in a few hours. Goodbye for now.*

For now goodbye, answered girl and healer together.

The link ended. Aideen got up and paced, her mind racing with excitement. Her father was here—he would save the day. When Aideen heard a light thump on the window, she absently ignored it, thinking another bird had bumped into the glass. The second time she heard it the tap was tripled—not the bumping of a bird.

She turned to the glass but saw nothing. Then she approached the pane and her eyes widened when she saw Hana hanging from the ledge by her fingertips. She quickly slid the window open.

"About time you let me in," Hana hissed as she reached in and pulled herself inside, collapsing on the floor. "I could have fallen had I hung there much longer." The warrior woman had a coil of hempen rope slung across her shoulder. She got to her feet and began looking around, for what, the girl knew not.

Through her shocked surprise at having just seen the mercenary climb five stories to her well-appointed prison, Aideen finally found words. "Hana, what are you doing here?"

"Don't be foolish, girl," Hana snapped. "What does it look like?" The woman went to the couch, pulled the rope off and flipped the couch over with a thump. "We're getting you out of here." She looped the line around the divan, tied it and dragged it to the window.

"We?"

"Hazim and I."

"What about your contract?"

"It's done, and we didn't re-up. Neither did Jamal, Maha or Akil, but Akil is still in the hospital." Hana frowned. "Enough questions; get down the line." She pulled a small pair of leather gloves from her belt, tossed them to the girl and went to the door, presumably to bolt it.

Aideen caught the gloves and donned them just as the door began to open and a male voice from without inquired, "What are you doing in there, jumping on the furniture?" The mailed warrior's face registered surprise at Hana's presence. Without hesitation, Hana stiff-armed him in the chest, slammed the door, and rammed the bolt home.

"Go!" Hana yelled as she braced her shoulder against the door.

The doorframe cracked as the thudding weight of the heavier soldier impacted the door. He slammed against it repeatedly, yelling to his comrades for aid. Aideen looked down and saw Hazim waving at her to hurry. The scariest part was climbing over the ledge and trusting to the rope. The sofa slid a dozen more centimeters before it stopped against the wall, causing the girl's stomach to lurch. Her heart skipped a beat, and goose bumps prickled to her elbows before she realized she wasn't falling. She moved down the line, below the elevation of the window, as the pounding continued. Her progress was slow, her muscles tense, but her confidence grew.

When Aideen had descended more than a meter below the window sill, she heard the splintering burst of the door. Hazim began calling to her to slide. She then heard the distinctive sound of a swordfight above her. The girl fought the urge to climb back up when she heard a metallic meat cutting sound, like a blade parting chainmail and flesh. It was followed by a moan and a thump. Aideen looked up to see Hana scrambling out the window.

"Slide girl, slide," Hana urged, "they're coming up the stairs, and they'll cut the rope if you don't hurry."

Aideen slid. She passed cracks in the adobe and flew past two windows, but she couldn't tell if the rooms were occupied. Even through the gloves, her hands burned from the friction. The moment she hit the ground Hazim pulled her aside just in time for Hana to land beside her. The woman hit the ground running. Aideen and Hazim followed right behind her. Shouts of alarm continued inside the hotel.

A two-meter high clay wall surrounded the establishment, effectively fencing them in. They rounded the corner and ran towards a table and two chairs that looked out of place sitting against the wall. On the table rested a wooden crate. In four bounds Hana stood on the wall, turned and extended her hands. Two of Townsend's guards ran at them shouting for them to stop, with five more behind those two.

Aideen leaped to the chair, table, and crate when Hana caught her hand and hauled her up on the wall. To the girl's amazement, there was a ladder propped against the outside of the wall. She belatedly guessed that these props had been preset by her friends before her jailbreak.

"Down you go," said the shield maiden before she jumped to the ground.

Aideen saw Hazim slash one guard down, riposte

the other's thrust, and follow through with his own thrust to finish the fight. In a few seconds he was up on the wall, bloody sword in hand. Aideen slid down the ladder's rails—she'd always wanted to do that. Hazim sheathed his saber and jumped down next to her, throwing down the ladder as soon as his boots struck the dirt. As they ran, Aideen heard their pursuit climbing up the table on the other side.

They ran along the wall, turned down an alley, up a street crowded with an open-air market, and then into another ally. Noise erupted in the marketplace behind them as the guards followed. The alley dead-ended in a wall, upon which was heaped piles of stinking refuse from an adjacent restaurant. Hazim tried a door, but it would not open. A startled dog of indeterminate breed shot out from underneath a crate and ran out into the street just as the opening filled with five of Townsend's sell-swords. Together Hana and Hazim drew their back-slung Pagentian sabers and stepped in front of Aideen.

"Give us the girl," said the leader. He had a crooked nose that looked as if it had been broken more than once.

The sell-sword next to him said, "You can't win against five of us." Below his headscarf Aideen could see that he had no ears. Probably cut off for some crime against a war chief or sultan, as was common in the desert, or so she had heard.

The five sell-swords advanced, blades bared, into the ally. There was only room for them to go two-by-two, but before they closed half the distance, the fifth man in the rear screamed and fell.

"Four," said Maha. Her and Jamal now stood blocking the alley exit.

"The odds look pretty even to me," Jamal said lightly, but his face was deadly serious.

The two sell-swords nearest the street turned and attacked Jamal and Maha. Crooked-nose and Earless charged Hana and Hazim. Aideen watched intently as blows were given and blocked. They were all very skilled fighters, but one of the sell-swords that turned to fight Jamal tripped over the fallen fifth man. Jamal quickly dispatched the stumbling soldier. A second later the man fighting Maha was impaled with his and her scimitars. The couple stepped forward and cut Earless down as Hazim blocked a double-gripped overhand slash from Crooked-nose, whose face paled as Hana's blade slid diagonally through his belly. He fell without a word.

"Thanks," said Hazim.

The four mercenaries cleaned their swords on the clothes of their enemies.

Hana straightened and faced Jamal and Maha. "Have you changed your minds?"

Jamal nodded, but Maha said, "My mind was made all along. I just needed more time to talk sense into Jamal."

Hazim pulled a cloth sack from his belt and handed it to Aideen. "A boy's burnouse," he explained. "Hana and Maha will help you tie the headscarf. Be sure to keep your face covered. Now change quickly. Townsend has, at least, forty swords and he is hiring more as we speak. They are probably looking for you right now."

The men went to the alley entrance to stand guard and give the girl some privacy as Hana and Maha helped her with the desert attire. Luckily no one was curious enough to investigate the sounds of the swordfight.

"Thank you," Aideen said sincerely. "But...why are you helping me?"

"You're a pain in the butt," said Hana with mocking gruffness, "but we kind of like you." She pulled the girl's scarf up and said, "To cover your face, just tuck the cloth in here, above your ear." Hana pulled the blue and white material free, letting it hang on the left side.

Aideen smiled. "My father is in the city somewhere. Will you help me find him?"

"Of course, we will," replied Maha as she buried the pink dress in the refuse. "We're all out of work and need to ask him for a job."

Aideen's smile spread nearly to her ears. "Well, I will certainly put in a good word for you."

CHAPTER 30

Anisha paid the rickshaw driver a few coppers. The young man looked at the coins with such exaggerated contempt, she thought he would cast them into the street and demand gold. The two sell-swords escorting her were, at first, less than pleased with having to keep up with the fleet-footed taxi, but they were now grinning at each other as if at some private joke at her expense. Their payment would come later.

There wasn't time for this nonsense. Anisha had to see Imar as quickly as possible. Drawing a Kalusian silver from her purse, Anisha placed the coin on the driver's palm next to the three coppers. The young man raised a brow and held rock-still as if he were posing for an artist painting his portrait. Two more silvers hardly clinked into his hand as the man smiled his thanks and shuffled away down the busy street.

Anisha gave the two sell-swords her best dagger-stare, effectively wiping the grins off their foolish faces.

She turned and entered the moderate upscale hotel. The Mozar Wahalia was a very nice place for a well-to-do middle-class commoner, but Anisha could not help but sniff her disdain at the lack of a doorman or a fountain or any of the other sumptuous displays of wealth evident at the Mozar Hamaud. She swept past the front desk, ignoring the gracious greeting of the concierge. Knowing her husband, Anisha went directly to the common room. She was not disappointed.

"Anisha," Imar greeted, as he, Hager, and another man she did not know stood. "What are you doing here?"

Hager bent and flipped over a sketch of something they had been looking at. He looked at Anisha suspiciously, and then gathered up the sheaves and stowed them in a leather satchel. His eyes then began sizing up her two escorts.

"Imar," said Anisha. "We need to talk." She scanned for the healer, relieved that the uncanny woman was absent.

Imar introduced the tall, dark, and very handsome stranger that seemed vaguely familiar to her. "Anisha, this is Captain Rutger."

Rutger stepped around the table and offered his hand. "Lady Anisha," he greeted with a modest bow. He kissed the back of her fingers, and then properly stepped back. His dark brown hair was very short, and his pencil thin mustache led into a closely trimmed goatee tinted auburn from the sun. He was nearly a head taller than Imar but thinner. "I saw you at King Gerald's ball a few weeks ago. I was most disappointed we were not introduced then, but I had to leave early on royal business."

Anisha suddenly recalled seeing him before. When

she had first spotted Captain Rutger at the ball, her mouthwatering desire for a new nocturnal conquest had been dashed when he had abruptly left the dance. He had to be of good social stock and wealth to be worthy of an invitation to the king's ball. Putting her amorous thoughts aside but moving the good looking captain to the top of her list, she moved to do what she came here to do, but Imar was faster.

"Shall we speak in private, Anisha?" Imar asked, gesturing to a pair of empty chairs on the far side of the large common room. They excused themselves and moved to the indicated seats. "How is Aideen?" Imar inquired coldly. "How are her wounds?"

"The stitches in her lip have been removed," Anisha replied calmly. "She has only a slight scar now, hardly noticeable. All the other bruises are gone."

Imar's face remained impassive. "Aideen's been doing that mind-speaking thing with Dalla, so we know about your involvement with Townsend."

"Imar," Anisha began, trying her best to sound sincere, but Imar cut her off.

"Don't," he said harshly. "She's your own daughter, a part of you, a part of us both, and you let her be taken and hurt by that assassin."

"Wait," pleaded Anisha. "I had nothing to do with that," she lied. "You must believe me. I didn't even know Lord Townsend was behind the kidnapping until I found Aideen in the mountains on my way to Juana Pohala." She studied Imar's eyes while saddening her own, unable to determine if he believed her. "The ransom note said to come here with the octagon key. I came with gold in case something happened to you, and…" Anisha buried her face in her handkerchief and sobbed, using the move to hide poking herself in the eyes. She had even gone to the trouble of rubbing her fingertips on an onion before departing her suite of rooms at the Mozar Hamaud.

Anisha sat up and feigned pulling herself together. "Like you said," she sniffed. "Aideen is my daughter. I had to come." She changed her voice from distraught to solemn and earnest. "She actually found *me* after she escaped, but when my carriage overtook Lord Townsend and his sell-swords, what was I to do?"

"You could have resisted or, at least, tried to flee."

"Come on Imar, do you really think we could've gotten away? I admit that I agree with his lordship that the key should be used, but with you in charge of the power, not Lord Townsend. I had to play along and pretend to join him or I would have become a prisoner too, without any way to help Aideen." Anisha's left eye hurt horribly and the induced tears blurred her vision. She hoped her fingernail hadn't scratched her cornea. Her right eye could barely make out Imar's face. He seemed to be considering her words.

"I truly didn't think you would intentionally hurt her," Imar grudgingly admitted.

Anisha bit the inside of her cheek to hide her elation. She had him hooked. *Now to play him*, she thought, *before reeling him in*. "His lordship wants to bump up the swap."

Imar looked up sharply. "Good," he exclaimed, "the sooner, the better."

"He wants to bump it up because our daughter has escaped."

"Escaped? When? Where is she?"

Anisha held up a hand. "Let me finish. She escaped with the aid of some of Townsend's former sell-swords. They brought her over the mountains but refused to reenlist when they got here." Anisha smiled. "She apparently made some friends. His lordship wants to dupe you into giving him the key when he no longer has Aideen." She turned to one of her sell-sword escorts. "You," she snapped, "bring me the sword."

The guard came over and handed Aideen's katana to Anisha, saying "Here you are my la…"

"Shut up and leave us," Anisha cut him off rudely. The guard scowled but went away. Anisha handed the small sword to Imar. "This is supposed to be a token of proof." She gave him a moment to look at their daughter's sword. "Wait till you see what she did to Khaled with that thing."

"I heard," Imar replied. He drew the blade from the wooden scabbard, inspected it, and then slammed it home. "I'm glad she saved me some. I have my own appointment with that one." Imar sighed. "Does Aideen know where to find me?"

"I don't see how, but she is resourceful. She does know where the meeting was supposed to be. She may try to find you there at noon."

"We'll have to go there then. If she goes to the dome and Townsend's sell-swords are there…" He let the sentence hang.

Anisha hoped his use of 'we' included her. *Now, time to reel him in*, she thought. "Imar," she began, placing her hand on his. "I know we've had some disagreements, and I'm sorry for saying some things I didn't really mean, but," she paused, forcing a tear down her cheek. She took a breath, let it out emphatically, took another, and said, "Imar, I would like you to consider us, our marriage, and Aideen. Let us try to work things out, at least for Aideen's sake. We need to reconcile our differences for her sake."

Imar looked stunned. She had him right where she wanted him. If Townsend didn't recover from losing his only bargaining chip, his lordship would be useless to her. However, if he and his assassin overcame this setback she could always say she had gone to Imar to aid his lordship in recovering the key. Either way, she would follow the victor and to her would go the spoils.

A noise drew Anisha's attention to the stairwell. The healer stood on the bottom step, looking as beautiful as ever in her robin egg blue desert garb, but her face spoke volumes. Anisha did not know how long Dalla had been standing there, but her shocked expression said she had heard at least the last part.

Anisha gave her victory smile to the healer as she took her hand from Imar's and stood.

Imar also stood and saw Dalla. "My…" he stopped, and said, "Dalla, how long have you been there?"

"Long enough," replied Dalla without emotion. She turned and went gracefully back up the stairs.

CHAPTER 31

"Whew, it's hot." Aideen let her breath out in a soft whoosh. "We've been standing here for an hour. Isn't there somewhere else we can get water? This heat is killing me."

"The other wells have lines just as long as this one, and it's only been twenty minutes," replied Hana. "There is only this man and boy with their two camels ahead of us. Would you give up your place to stand in a longer line?"

"No," Aideen sighed exasperatedly.

The boy was about Aideen's height. She watched as he poured water from the well's bucket into one of the four large clay jars fastened to the camel's back. The other camel, also festooned with jars, stood chewing its cud as if there were nothing else it would rather do. The man overseeing the boy's work talked nonstop to anyone in the crowded line that would listen, though most of the people did their best to ignore him, so he directed his oratory at anyone who had the misfortune to catch his eye. He ranted about western politics, the war in Sedar, and the battles in Northern Hamaud. His blather covered salt, silk, and spice prices. Then he lowered his voice to whisper conspiratorially about the rumors of the Hamaudi Assassins raiding a village for slaves and initiates and to call it a purging of nonbelievers that refused to convert to the nameless god.

Worried looks in the crowd caught the man's attention and he too rubbernecked his gaze of the square. He then covered his gossip by loudly complaining about the weather and shifting his subject back to the beginning of everything he had already said. When the boy topped off the last jar on the first camel he spilled some water.

"Careful, you fool," the man admonished, leading the camel with the empty jars to the well and pulling the burdened beast away, "you just spilled a day's pay into the dirt. I should make you scoop it up and strain out the water." Without waiting for a reply, the man began babbling again, but Aideen could not be sure if he was taking up where he left off or starting some new subject.

The boy turned to Aideen, rolled his eyes, and then winked. She grinned weakly under the veil of her shemagh headscarf, but the smile was reflected in her eyes. Even though the thin cloth allowed air to pass through it, she felt smothered by the baking heat. Her tongue stuck to the roof of her mouth, and the man's incessant chatter pierced her dehydrated brain with a stabbing headache. She whooshed out another breath of exclamation about the obvious heat. "I am so thirsty. If only we would have been a minute faster, we'd be done by now. This is taking forever."

"Oh, may the nameless one help us all," Jamal

muttered his agreement. He paced back and forth looking none too happy with the delay.

Aideen couldn't take it anymore. She yanked down her face scarf and darted forward, but a firm hand caught her shoulder and squeezed hard. "Ouch," she squeaked, slumping under Hana's grip.

The boy looked in her direction at her high pitched squeak, but the man continued rattling on about the price of salt in Nacuscus, oblivious to the interruption.

"Don't," Hana whispered harshly. "Never touch another's water without permission." Hana's eyes darted to the boy, and she added, "Cover your face."

Aideen followed Hana's gaze. The boy's eyes had widened slightly when he looked on the girl's face, but his attention was suddenly diverted by a company of soldiers marching up the street. The girl saw Lord Townsend at the head of the column on a horse. Another in the garb of a sell-sword rode beside him. She quickly turned her back and pulled the loose cloth over her face. Hana, Hazim, Maha, and Jamal, now garbed for desert travel, also covered their faces and tried to blend in with the crowd.

A knot began to form in Aideen's stomach. She scanned the soldiers and the locals, but she did not see the assassin anywhere. He was near, she knew it. In a few minutes, the procession had passed. The boy had gone back to work filling water jars, but he looked her way from time to time.

Aideen tried to thank him for his silence with her eyes. Townsend had people looking for her, so she knew word of a runaway girl was out, with a tempting reward offered for her whereabouts.

When the company had passed, Hazim stared

after them rubbing his chin. "Hmm," he said. "Looks like he's got about seventy swords, maybe eighty."

"Yeah," Jamal agreed. "He's early too. It's still an hour and a half before noon."

"Oh my gods," Aideen exclaimed. "You mean it's going to get hotter?"

Maha knelt beside the girl. "There is only one god, little one," she chided. "This is not hot. You should be here in the peak of summer when you can cook meat on a flat rock. No, what Jamal is saying is that Lord Townsend must have arranged an earlier meeting with your father. If so, then he plans to trick him into thinking you are still his prisoner. If your father's force is smaller Townsend can just take this heirloom he holds."

Aideen scrunched her brows. "So if his lordship is going now to meet my father…" Her eyes rounded. "We have to go to the dome now," she added excitedly, her thirst forgotten.

"Not without water," Hazim stated matter-of-factly. He moved to the well as the boy led the sloshing camels away behind the chattering man.

While Hazim worked the hand winch on the well Maha asked Aideen, "Why don't you try that thing you do to talk to your father's ur, eh…"

"Friend?" Aideen interjected helpfully.

"Yes," Maha confirmed. "His healer friend. Can you do it? You know. That mind thing?"

Aideen had nearly forgotten in all the excitement. "I'll try," she said.

"Have some water first," said Hana. She took one of the water skins that Hazim and Jamal had filled from the stone rim of the well and handed it to the girl.

Aideen lifted her veil, guzzled half the skin, and handed it back to Hana. "Thanks."

"If you refill that," said the well-guard, pointing at the half skin, "you'll pay for a whole."

Hana counted out the silver for the water and handed it to the guard. "When you go home I hope your mother runs out from under the porch and bites you."

The well-watcher ignored the remark, either because he didn't get it or because he was accustomed to insults. He looked disappointedly at the exact change. "What, no tip?"

"Here's your tip," said Hana. "A silent tongue yields a silver purse." She turned to the group and said, "Let's go over there."

They went to a corner of the square and Aideen closed her eyes and focused on Dalla. *Can you hear me?* She thought. *Dalla, are you there?* She listened with her mind. Dalla didn't respond, but Aideen sensed her presence through their link. She could tell that the healer was troubled by something and could not focus her thoughts for mind-speech. *Dalla*, she shouted with her mind. It wasn't so much a shout as a gathered force of will cast with her mind.

Aideen sensed the healer's flinch, but all she could hear in her mind was weeping. Dalla's grief was overwhelming. The girl wished she could run to her and console her with hugs. Then something seeped through. Aideen saw, or rather sensed, the image of a woman that looked like Dalla, but wasn't. The image wavered, then strengthened, and some of Dalla's distress seemed to soothe. A name, *Dalia*, came to the girl. She tucked it away for later and called again, *Dalla, please*. There was a tendril of recognition, but her friend was still unable to answer. *Dalla, if you can hear me I am going to the dome. I don't know where you are, and I don't know what else to do. To the dome, go to the dome*, she repeated. *Goodbye for now*.

Aideen broke the link and opened her eyes. Four sets of eyes looked at her expectantly. "I'm sorry," she said. "Something is wrong with Dalla." The girl chose not to tell them about her friend's crying. "I think she heard me though."

"What did you tell her?" asked Maha.

"I told her that I was going to the dome."

"Did you not see the eighty soldiers marching to the dome?" Jamal asked rhetorically. "Perhaps you did not," he added sarcastically. "You were rather busy at the time complaining about the morning heat, and your thirst." His voice became stern. "You said your father has five men, including him, that can fight. That makes nine of us to sixty professional soldiers."

"A Kalusian cavalry patrol is helping him," Aideen retorted.

"Oh, that makes me feel so much better," Jamal fumed. "It is still four to one odds against us."

"You don't have to come," the girl said loudly. "I have to find my dad." Aideen stormed off and stopped after a dozen paces. She came back, an embarrassed look on her face, and said, "I'm a little turned around in this city. Could one of you please give me directions?"

Maha stepped forward and softly said, "No one is

abandoning you, little one. Jamal just gets a little excited sometimes." She glared daggers at Jamal who got a pained expression on his face. Maha turned back to the girl and said, "We are going with you, but we will go cautiously and look for advantages that will favor us should it come to fighting."

"We waste time stepping like sore-footed cats around the child." Hana strode in the direction the sell-swords had taken, and called over her shoulder, "Are you coming or not?"

CHAPTER 32

Dalla could not believe her ears. That bitch, she thought to herself, after all she's done, had the nerve to smooth-talk Imar into reconciliation, and the fool fell for it! It was written all over his face. Dalla could even feel his confused emotions, and sense his thoughts considering the pact for his daughter's sake. Each time she thought of Anisha, her blood boiled for a fight, but Dalla was not a violent person—quite the opposite actually. She was angry, but her feelings were hurt, so she cried into her pillow instead. Her enhancements weren't engineered to overcome grief as easily as the others of her kind. She had never felt so empty in her life, not even when Sumas had broken her heart back when she was still a teenager. That was infatuation, this was love, and it hurt badly, so she cried, and cried some more.

After the things Anisha had told Imar about restricting their relationship until he worked out his divorce, and now she was acting like a jilted lover. The thought of him going back to her was ripping her insides to shreds. Dalla didn't think she could handle a sexless relationship much longer, but now even that was threatened. Her frustration at bottling up her passion and desire these past few months was driving her to madness so much that she often thought it would be better to end their tentative union altogether, yet the thought of that made her blood run cold. She couldn't do that anyway without vacating his presence, and the mission—the fate of their very world—took precedence over her relationship with Imar. As much as she had previously argued the contrary, being near him was better than not at all, and now Anisha wanted back into his life. She cried some more.

Dalla was different from her genetically enhanced colleagues. The others, her parents included, had been conceived in a glass tube, whereas she had been born naturally. She had unique abilities and high intelligence like the others; except that they were crèche babies and she had parents. This gave her a feeling of belonging, and it taught her love and caring from a young age, but that was family love. This love she felt for Imar was the kind that draws two people together and bonds them. Though she had prepared herself long ago for the troublesome burdens of helping others, she had never prepared herself for true love.

When Dalla was distraught, as she was now, she would conjure an image of her mother, and that would console her and help her cope with difficulties her father could not understand from a male point of view. She floundered in an emotional flood of her own grief so deep that she ignored Aideen's call tugging weakly at the back of her mind. She rolled over on her bed facing up and closed her leaky eyes, trying to meditate, but she could not focus.

Dalla knew she should try to contact Aideen, but

that just had to wait right now. Thinking of the girl's escape made her think of the bearer of that news—the girl's mother, Anisha. Mental blocks snapped into place the instant Anisha came to mind. Unfortunately, her angered defense also blocked Aideen's projected mind-speech.

Thinking of Anisha brought another flood of tears, tossing all of her focus to the four winds. Dalla thought of her own mother—she needed her mom. An image took shape, whether formed from an old pixel-graph or a real spiritual specter, Dalla didn't know, nor did she take the time to consider the metaphysical philosophy of ghosts with her agnostic mind. She just accepted the possibilities of an afterlife, spirits, alternate dimensions, and even a god or gods as a connection of the universal oneness of all things, but only as possibilities, since she knew that what her mind conjured was probably her own doing. She looked at her mother's blurred features as if she had opened her eyes underwater, but as the vision cleared she felt her tension ease, and her grief, though not gone, became controllable. Her sobs quieted.

As Dalla relaxed and her vision faded, she heard Aideen's mind-voice in her head.

To the dome, go to the dome, Aideen repeated. *Goodbye for now.*

Wait, Dalla projected, but it was too late, the link was broken. She tried to focus and call the child back, but Aideen was too distracted now to sense her call. She had to tell Imar.

Standing, she looked at herself in the mirror. Her eyes were red, her face tear streaked, and her hair looked like a site for mouse wars. With no time to lose, she covered the blonde nest with her blue headscarf, letting the end hang on the left so her face was uncovered. She went down to the common room, found it empty, and then to the front desk.

A young lady wearing a beige hijab looked up from a scroll she was reading and said, "May I help you?" Her brows rose and her countenance expressed concern when she looked at Dalla's face.

"Yes," Dalla answered. "The men that were here a few minutes ago, do you know where they went?"

"The tall man with the braids, the one that haggles for every coin, the one who arrived with the boys? Don't tell them I called them boys. My son gets his hackles up whenever I make that error. Anyway, they all left together with the captain's soldiers. You just missed them."

"What about the woman that was here?"

The lady's eyes blazed and her nostrils flared with irritation. "The rude one?" she asked.

"That's her," Dalla agreed.

"She dismissed her escort and went with the handsome man giving orders." The woman scrunched her brows. "I thought he was with you."

Dalla didn't deign to comment, but said, "I must go."

The horse drawn taxi stopped near the stone fence separating the city proper from the ruins. It was waist high, but there were numerous walk-through openings. Rutger's Kalusian cavalry was positioned on the southwest corner of the dome facing twice their number of Townsend's sell-sword infantry who were in phalanx formation on the northwest corner.

Dalla didn't see her friends, so she assumed they were under the dome as planned. She paid the driver and stepped down from the open carriage. "Keep the extra."

The driver's eyes lit up when he counted the coins. "Thank you very much. Would you like me to wait?" He gazed curiously at the assembled soldiers. "By the looks of things, it could get quite interesting here. Blood feuds are common outside the city, but that looks serious. Let me take you somewhere safe."

"That won't be necessary," Dalla replied. "My friends are inside."

"Inside the dome?" he asked nervously. His native accent was thick around each articulated word. "That is dangerous. None of these ruins are safe. Pieces fall all the time and…" With wide eyes, he looked at the ancient sunbaked beams and girders, then at Dalla. His voice dropped to a whisper as he earnestly added, "They are haunted." Facing the ruins again, he covered half his face with one hand, bowed his head, and with the other hand made what looked to Dalla like the sign of the cross with fingers split between middle and ring finger. The gesture looked like a combination of old world Christian, Jewish, and Islamic hand signs joined into one, but the driver did it with a fluidity that bespoke much practice. It only took a second, and when he finished he shook the reins and said, "May the nameless one protect you."

Dalla's mind calculated a dozen theories of evolution that would explain what she had just seen until a shout from one of the soldiers brought her back to the matter at hand. That was the problem with an intelligent mind, curiosity bred distraction. The shout had not been for her, she realized. The insults common to pre-battle tradition were beginning.

Walking toward the dome, Dalla was careful to arc her route behind the Kalusian soldiers. Both sides banged weapons on shields from time to time, but they had not worked themselves into a testosterone building frenzy yet. No one stopped her; they were too intent on their adversaries. When she stepped past the encircling pillars and through one of the many oval openings in the dome, the cooler air and soothing shade refreshed her.

"Dalla," Imar said as he came to her.

A few meters off Dalla saw Anisha doing her best to look down her nose and gloat. On the opposite side of the dome, Townsend stood with six sell-swords. She did not see the assassin or feel his presence, but she suspected he was here—somewhere.

She was not very happy with Imar at the moment, but when he took both her hands and bathed her in his gaze with his soft brown eyes, her resolve slid away. She tried to sound distant, but instead her words came out pleading. "Why didn't you wait for me?"

He squeezed her hands gently, and for a moment she thought he was going to embrace her, but he stopped himself and said, "You seemed…upset. I thought you needed a moment alone." He paused only a moment. "I knew you would come." His voice was like cool water to parched ears. "Thank you for coming." Then without a care of who was watching he bent down and kissed her lightly on the lips. All her cares were lifted in that brief second, but the world would not wait. Aideen was here, somewhere. A company of sell-swords stood poised to take the key, and Imar had effectively confused her to bewildering distraction, while power seeking Anisha, the cause of all this trouble, stood there like a smiling cat that still had feathers in its whiskers.

Another familiar voice roused her from her reverie. "My dear," Ivan said gently. "I hate to interrupt, but there's a boy here that needs your attention."

"Father," Dalla said with only half the tone of a question. She had known for most of the day that Ivan was near, but he surprised her none the less. She blamed Anisha again. *For what,* Dalla asked herself, *wanting her husband back?* But she knew that was a lie. Anisha wanted power, even if it cost Imar and Aideen their lives.

She looked past her father and saw Hawkins standing behind him. He nodded, and said, "It's good to see you again, Dalla."

Dalla returned his nod and saw a boy of early teens sitting against one of the many pillars that rose into the dark dome's interior to support the upper balconies. His pallor was yellowish, and she immediately sensed his body fighting more than one demon. "Aris?" she asked. "You said he was snake bit. He looks like he's having some withdrawals." The healer in Dalla took to the task like an arrow in flight. She had a target now, someone she could help. Anisha was forgotten. All other thoughts were shoved aside and her peripheral sight blurred around her tunnel vision on the sick boy.

"Yes," Ivan replied. "I gave him poppy tea for the pain, probably longer than I should have, but we had to travel, and I don't have your healing talent. I have been weaning him off the poppies, but we ran out yesterday." He paused. "You can help him," he said simply.

"I can," the healer agreed. She started moving toward Aris.

"We need him," her father added.

"I know," she replied. Kneeling down in front of the boy she said, "I'm Dalla. May I help you feel better?"

"Please," he answered tiredly. "I really feel like crap."

Dalla put her hand on his clammy brow. "Close your eyes. I'm going to join minds with you." Under her touch, he went from cold to hot, and sweat beaded his skin. She immediately felt the poison which had not yet purged from his body. Her awareness also picked up on his craving for dopamines. His body was laboring with the need to produce more. Endocrine and nervous systems struggled for balance. She put her other hand on his wrist, closed her eyes, and went in.

The speed with which she traveled up the synaptic pathways was exhilarating as usual. It was like being shot through a microscopic observatory tube, zooming by spherical and disc-shaped cells interspersed with lightning strikes in all directions, many of which passed her in both directions. In a nanosecond, she had entered the hypothalamus.

This mind-meld took special care. When Dalla healed with a melding of minds, it created a bond between the healer and patient. She doubted that to be the cause of Imar and her falling for each other, but she was not about to take chances. Things were confusing enough without having a teenage boy doting after her while she had feelings for a married man.

Dalla put up barriers as she guided Aris' subconscious. Within the hypothalamus, where body temperature is regulated and dopamines are released, she adjusted hormonal levels for heat. Usually this maneuver would be to reduce a fever, but instead, she did the opposite. This brought on tachycardia. The boy's heart raced rapid and weak.

Counting by sensory feel, the healer found the tenth nerve. Leaving a part of their awareness to regulate his temperature, she led them down the left vagus nerve to the heart as if riding on the neurotransmitter, acetylcholine. His heart slowed and grew stronger with each beat. Careful not to let any signals travel farther down the vagus nerve to the boy's bowels, the healer ascended back to the hypothalamus. Meanwhile, it was getting very hot.

On the outside, Aris was soaked with sweat. Dalla could feel the last vestiges of the poison leaking out his sweat glands. She then lowered his temperature to a normal level. There was one more thing to do. The healer made another small tweak in the hypothalamus in order to release some dopamines—these neurotransmitters helped with the pain in the earlier stages of the poison, but without the opium poppies to stimulate more, the body craved the higher levels of endorphins. With a subconscious suggestion to slowly return the level to normal over the next few weeks, the healer pulled free of the meld.

Dalla and Aris opened their eyes at the same time. His forehead and wrist felt normal under her touch and his sweat had nearly dried in the warm desert air. Dalla removed her hands. "You'll need lots of water," she said. "How do you feel?"

Aris made a few slight eye movements then said, "I'm thirsty, oh so very thirsty, but I feel good. I'm tired, and a little jittery, but that gnawing feeling inside me is gone.

Ivan and Hawkins knelt beside Dalla. Hawkins handed Aris a canteen, and the boy drank it empty. "You do look a lot better," said Hawkins.

"Are you up for a little action, boy?" asked Ivan.

"I'm not a boy," Aris retorted. His habitual scowl returned for only a second. He stood, stretched, and looking like he had never been sick, asked, "What do you have in mind?"

Once Ivan explained his instructions Aris began examining his surroundings. Dalla decided to perform her own survey. The inside of the dome was dark, but not so dark that someone without her or Ivan's enhanced vision could not see. Light burst through a few cracks and holes, mostly low around the bottom portals, causing the dust filled, slanting beams to illuminate the dim interior. There were oval openings around the circular base though most were blocked with debris. A few of these arched apertures were clear of rubble, including the one on the north side behind where Townsend was now. The upper portions had tall, narrow, rectangular windows, the glass long ago broken out by earthquakes.

On the east side of the dome, a row of pillars supported a balcony, but it had the appearance of either being thrust up into the dome or perhaps that the dome had crashed down on the lower levels of the building through the numerous earthquakes from continental shifting. There appeared to be rooms on the upper floor a short distance from the rail. The north end of the ground floor supported a few cubicles as well, but many of the walls had long since collapsed and the rubble of decay was strewn heaviest in that area.

When the boy finished his assessment he dropped to a knee and scooped some dirt into a pile, and with his knife made another smaller pile by scraping a piece of broken plaster with his knife. Dalla watched curiously as

Aris poured water on each pile and stirred the mud with his finger. A light hand on her shoulder interrupted Dalla's study of the boy's labors. It was Imar. Ivan, Hager, and Hawkins stood with him. Rutger and Vidar were walking to the center to speak with Townsend. Vidar had Aksel and Egil flanking him, and Rutger was followed by two of his own men. Anisha stood to the side like a spectator at a pit fight.

"Come, we haven't much time," Imar said. "If Aideen is here we have to find her."

"You would think she'd come running once she saw you," Hawkins said to Imar.

"Maybe," Imar agreed uncertainly. "Unless she was afraid of being caught by Townsend's men, or…"

"Or by Khaled," Dalla finished for him.

Imar nodded grimly. "Yes, I feel…" he trailed off, scanning the shadows, then turned back to the group. "I don't know what I feel, but I know he wouldn't miss this."

"I too feel like we're being watched," added Hager. The stout warrior also scanned his surroundings. "My back itches between my shoulder blades."

"Let us go cautiously," Ivan warned sagely.

The wizard led them to the wide stairway leading down. Dalla heard Townsend's complaints when Imar went with the party going below. Rutger returned his bluster, and Vidar began negotiating a trade as if he were bidding on a caravan of potatoes. The healer knew they were just stalling, and she hoped his lordship wouldn't attack since he had a clear advantage of numbers.

Just as Dalla started down the stairs she looked

back and saw Townsend flick a glance at Anisha and then towards their departing party. The gesture was slight, and Townsend covered it with complaints, but his message got through. Anisha turned and ran to the group with her skirt plucked up to prevent tripping.

When Anisha caught up she said, "Wait for me."

"Oh, may the gods truly help us," Hager groaned from the head of the line.

Aksel rolled his eyes and Egil looked down, muttering and shaking his head. Anisha descended the stairway and took her place beside Imar. Ivan grumbled under his breath and resumed the lead. No one spoke as they descended the lower levels of the dome.

CHAPTER 33

When they arrived at the ruins, they were a kilometer north of the dome. Aideen appraised the assembled soldiers south of their position. "Infantry phalanx," she commented approvingly. "Light horse will have a hard time against that."

"That's Townsend's phalanx, little one," said Maha. "Whose side are you on?"

"Ours, of course," replied the girl. "I was just admiring their commander's choice. Had they formed a line without pikes, the light cavalry would easily mop up at five to one."

Maha lowered one brow. "You know an awful lot about tactics for a little girl."

Aideen puffed up and smiled.

Hazim raised his spy-glass and scanned the two

forces outside the dome. "I only see about half of Townsend's troops," he observed. Aideen suspected the old veteran was nervous because his desert accent had become stronger and his phrases were slower as if he struggled to articulate each word. "There is a platoon of Kalusian cavalry. They are outnumbered, but the given advantage of mounted warriors should even the odds."

"The other sell-swords are either hiding and held in reserve or they've been dispatched to find the girl," added Maha. "I wonder if Townsend expects her to come here."

"I have a name," Aideen complained. She was ignored.

"I would expect the latter," said Jamal. "I know an underground way into the dome, but it would behoove us to assume that they do too. Follow me."

Ignoring local taboos, Jamal had previously explored the ruins, so he and Maha took the lead while Aideen trotted behind Hazim and Hana.

They stayed low, darting from rubble to scrap piles, and so on until they were out of sight of the soldiers and sell-swords. Hana backtracked briefly in case they had been spotted, but she reported no pursuit. They had not gone far when they came to a depression from which sprouted the corner of a granite building at the bottom. Their feet slid in the loose sand as they side-stepped down the decline. At the bottom, Aideen could see that the ancient doorway had been recently dug out and that a fair amount of foot traffic had passed through the opening.

Jamal stopped them before going in. "I lived in Juana Pohala for a few years. That is how I know about this. This whole area is a buried ancient city. Much is rotten and very dangerous. Try to step on stone and avoid wood even if it is petrified, and be wary." He paused as if forming the right words. "They say these ruins are haunted. I have heard voices down there, but unless spirits leave footprints, I do not believe spirits speak to the living."

"Nevertheless," added Hazim. "Your voices could belong to either friend or foe. We would do well to treat anyone we encounter as enemies until proven otherwise."

Jamal nodded. "There is a good chance that we could run into some of Townsend's warriors down there," he warned. "I am sure there are other ways in, nor am I the only explorer to walk the underground ways."

Hana peered into the dark hallway. She drew one of her daggers and said, "It's too confined for swords. Lead on."

About three meters beyond the entrance, while still within good lighting from the doorway, Jamal went into a room on the left. He returned a moment later with a heat lamp, which he handed to Aideen. "I think it best if you hold the light in case we have to fight. Do you know how to light it?"

Aideen rolled her eyes and said, "Pa-lease." She deftly twisted the striker and cranked the brightness up to the full yellow setting.

Jamal looked away. "That is too bright. It will ruin our night vision. Set it on low."

Aideen adjusted the chemical flow till the light glowed a soft blue. "Does anyone have an extra knife they can loan me?" They all stared at her. "I don't intend to fight if I can avoid it, but it would make me feel a lot better."

Hazim opened his robe, drew one of the six throwing knives sheathed horizontally on his chest and handed it to her. "I know what you mean. I feel naked without steel."

Twenty minutes later they were three levels lower. Twice they had to backtrack due to cave-ins. One time Hazim's foot fell through the floor, sinking to his thigh, but Hana gave him an arm and within a second they were again navigating ancient ways. Aideen was impressed that neither of them spoke, as if the incident was nothing more than a small inconvenience.

They entered a large area that may have been for dining at one time. The tables and chairs were made of a smooth synthetic material. Aideen could not remember what Dalla had called it, but the healer had said that it was used for all sorts of things in her day and that it would last a million years after humans became extinct. Crossing the hall, they went towards a door on the far side. Halfway across the big room, Jamal held up his fist for them to stop.

Voices from without came to them, indistinguishable at first, but then some clarity was mixed in with the muffled discourse; they heard the words, 'girl,' 'gold,' 'fight,' 'hassle,' and 'cheap bastard,' but they were unable to put any of it into understandable context. Jamal signaled, and they moved quietly against the nearest wall. Aideen extinguished the lamp, hoping the strangers would pass by.

A blue light filled the doorway a moment before a five-man squad entered, oblivious to Aideen and her friends. As they were passing through the dining hall, nearly abeam the girl's party, one of the men spotted them and cried out. "Ho there, contact right! That's them!"

As one, Aideen's friends drew their swords and advanced on the five as she fumbled for the striker on the heat lamp. The startled squad clumsily drew their weapons and counterattacked. Their lantern hit the floor and went out. In the moment of total darkness, Aideen heard the sound of a blade on flesh followed by a moan just as she got her lamp lit. The blue light revealed a man falling before Hazim, his sword arcing around another's defense thus defeating a second enemy. Hana's adversary went down next and together Jamal and Maha dispatched their foes. The battle was over in seconds.

"Nice little fight," said Jamal.

"This bunch was not very skilled," Maha commented. "Perhaps Townsend kept his best up top near to hand."

"Don't count on it," replied Hana. "Let's go before the noise of that 'nice little fight' draws more unwanted company."

Sheathing swords and drawing daggers, they resumed their journey in the narrow hallway. They had not gone far when they saw a blue light from the corner of an adjoining corridor. The sell-swords must have seen Aideen's light as well because they came running head on. There was barely room for two abreast yet the attackers wielded scimitars. The first one came at Jamal with an overhead slash while the next charged Maha with his sword thrust out before him.

Maha batted the blade with her bracer to the right and plunged her dagger into his belly with her left. The man's sword stuck in ancient plaster as Maha's stab-slammed him against the wall. At the same time, Jamal darted in under the overhand slash and, catching the man's collar while planting a foot to his crotch, he dropped on his back using his assailant's momentum and launched his enemy up, over, and behind him. The man did a somersault and landed on his back, grunting as the wind was knocked out of him. Hana dispatched him with her dagger plunged up under his chin and into his brain.

The third man's throat sprouted one of Hazim's throwing knives, and the fourth doubled over in pain from Jamal's kick to the groin. While the fourth tried to fall back Maha finished him. The fifth man stood stunned holding a heat lamp in one hand and a saber with the other. Jamal retrieved his dropped dagger, got to his feet and slowly advanced on him with Maha by his side, her bloody fist gripping her dripping blade. The man prudently turned and ran.

Maha squatted by one of the bodies and cleaned her knife and hands.

"Ah," commented Jamal. "The man chose discretion over death."

"Maha," Aideen exclaimed, "You're bleeding."

"Eh?" replied the woman.

The girl approached with the light and pointed. "Your arm, it's cut."

Maha looked at her wound. "Oh, I feel it now."

Aideen tore a strip of cloth from her burnous and bound the wound.

"It's just a scratch, but thanks, little one," Maha said. She inspected the girl's work and added, "Good field dressing."

Aideen dimpled.

They continued warily, prepared for the reinforcements to come from the man that got away. It surprised the girl when no attack came after a few minutes. They came to another large room, but this one had no chairs. A broad stone stairway had survived the centuries, but the chamber was littered with the rotted debris of eons. It looked as if an upper floor had crashed down from above sometime in the last millennium. One wall had old cracked and faded paintings leaning against it. A soft white light preceded voices coming down the stairs.

"Back in the hall," Hazim whispered urgently.

Aideen turned off the lamp as they ducked into the shadows. She had first thought she'd heard more than one voice, but now she wasn't so sure. As it grew louder she could distinguish the words.

"… may or may not have withstood the continental shifting, but much of the old city of Denver lies under centuries of sedimentary rock layers and sandstone. The descendants of old world refugees who survived the chemical and biological warfare did so by tunneling deep underground. They eventually moved up to the surface, but many remained below. Without printing presses, books had to be rewritten by hand. This caused stories to change and religions to blend, but when…"

Aideen knew that voice. With pleasure she yelled, "Ivan," and ran out into the chamber.

Hana reached out to stop the girl, but Aideen was too fast. Halfway down the stairs was a half-dozen of her friends and family. Ivan was in the front with a glowing white ball of light the size of a man's fist floating a half-meter above his head. His shocked expression shifted to delight when he heard her voice and saw her run towards them. Her father brushed past the wizard, bounding down the stairs taking two at a time. She met him as he reached the bottom. He swung her into the air and nearly crushed her in a hug, spinning her in circles before finally setting her down.

Imar drew Aideen's wooden sheathed katana from his belt and handed it to her. "I hear you took Khaled's eye out with this. You know, there are times when it's better to run than fight, but we'll talk on that later. I am so very happy to see you."

"Thank you," she replied, sliding the sword in her belt. Next she was hugging Dalla, and then she saw her mother. Her jubilation vanished. "Mother…" Words of warning stopped on the tip of her tongue. Her father and everyone else was looking past her.

Aideen turned around and saw their object of interest. "Those are my friends," exclaimed the girl. "They helped me escape Lord Townsend and," her voice grew serious as her brows lowered, "my mother." She faced her mother then, and with a voice dripping venom, asked, "What are you doing here?"

"My dear," Anisha replied smoothly, "you know I never meant for any harm to come to you. That's why I came to your father."

"Dad, don't trust her, she and Townsend…"

"Shush," Imar soothed. "Let's talk about it later. Why don't you introduce your friends?"

Aideen absently rubbed the scar on her lip and gave her mother one last scowl, before introducing her friends.

Hazim cleared his throat, as if hesitant to speak, then said, "The truth is, Captain, we were working for Townsend. We were bound by our contract until we got to Juana Pohala. None of us signed on to kidnap children, so we drew our pay when we got here and then went our own way."

"Yeah," added Hana. "We just took Aideen with us when we left."

Maha was eyeing Anisha suspiciously when Jamal elbowed her in the ribs. "Ow," Maha barked, reflexively backhanding Jamal on the shoulder.

Jamal nodded towards Imar and said to Maha, "Ask him."

"You ask him."

"No, you said you would."

"Oh, may the nameless one help us all," Maha exclaimed exasperatedly, shaking her head while looking up at the ceiling. She turned to Imar and said, "Please excuse my mate. He is a little shy until he gets to know you." She cracked a crooked grin at Jamal and barked a good natured harrumph at him before turning back to Imar. "We are now out of work mercenaries, and we were wondering if you would hire us on." Maha raised her brows and held up her hands palms out. "Oh, needing jobs was not our only motivation for helping your daughter; she kind of grows on you," she soft punched the child on the shoulder, "for a spoiled little brat."

"Hey," Aideen responded with smiling eyes.

Imar replied, "Of course you can join us. We can work out a contract later once we get out of this mess. You definitely have a reward coming, but right now there's a Kalusian cavalry platoon helping us until I get Aideen back, and after that they'll want to take something of mine."

"That would be the talisman Townsend spoke of?" asked Maha.

Imar nodded. "Townsend has about forty swords up topside and we have to go back up and face him and then somehow evade Rutger's platoon."

"Why can't we go out the way we came in?" asked Aideen.

"Because Vidar, Aksel, and Egil are up there stalling Lord Townsend," her father answered.

"Aris is up there as well," added Ivan.

"Townsend has more than forty men, Captain," Hazim interjected. "We saw, at least, seventy in the square earlier on their way here. There may be more. We dispatched nine on the way here. One got away, and he could be bringing reinforcements as we speak."

Hager began scanning the doorways. "I've got that itch again, Imar."

Dalla went to Imar and touched his arm. Her eyes looked distant. "Imar, I sense ten, no, eleven men coming this way."

Hawkins drew his cutlass and Hager's hand gripped his sword hilt. Aideen spread her awareness. She located the enemy quickly. "They will come through there," said the girl, pointing at the doorway across and diagonal to the stairs.

"I wish we had shields," Hager commented.

"Okay," said Imar. "Everyone pair up and spread out. Dalla, Anisha, Aideen; stand there behind us, up the stairs. The banister will prevent them from flanking us."

Aideen whisked her light sword from its wooden sheath.

"Oh, no you don't, young lady," Imar said firmly. "You stand right there and defend your mother and Dalla if we fall, but you are not to engage."

The girl was crestfallen. "But Da-ad, I can help."

"Enough talk," her father barked.

Aideen knew better than to push it any further.

Imar and Hager paired up to the left of Hazim and Hana, and to the right of Maha and Jamal. The three pairs of fighters formed a wedge and filled the width of the stairway. They were positioned about six or seven steps the stairwell for the strategic advantage of elevation. Ivan stood a few steps higher in the center and bore a concentrated gaze above the doorway that Aideen had said the enemy would come through. Hawkins stood by the wizard with his cutlass at the ready. The girl noticed that, unlike the others, the seaman wore no armor.

The wizard's light floated up a meter and centered over the stairway above him. It then grew to the size of a melon and became much brighter. Aideen could feel the power building in both Ivan and Dalla.

The sell-sword who had run for help earlier came through the doorway first. His blue heat lamp appeared dim in the brilliance of Ivan's light. He stopped and the men behind him crowded into that end of the chamber. They squinted in the bright light, all with swords bared. When the last man passed under the doorway the lintel burst down and then the ceiling of the outer hall collapsed, effectively blocking the doorway. A cloud of dust rolled into the chamber.

"Father," said Dalla. "You were supposed to do that *before* they got here."

"Sorry," Ivan apologized. "I'm a little out of practice." He straightened his back and then added, "But I'm warming up."

The leader stepped up to the front and sized up the men and women with weapons out, ready for attack. He wore chainmail, unlike his fellows who had opted for studded or ringed leather armor. They all wore steel helms, which did not seem too uncomfortable below ground where it was cooler, but topside in the afternoon heat a metal brain-bucket would roast the head like a small oven. Aideen suspected this squad of sell-swords was from somewhere with a cooler clime. The leader was broad and bulky, even more so than Hager, and he had black, pig-like eyes that chilled the girl when he stared at her. He then looked at Imar and addressed him directly, "I am Bashir. We have orders to capture the girl or the key."

"No," Imar said simply.

"You are Captain Imar Amirson," Bashir stated. "You have a reputation. I heard of you, even before I took this job. Some say none but a Hamaudi Assassin can beat you with a sword, but how many will fall if we fight? You know anything can happen in combat. What if you lose?"

Imar huffed a half-laugh. Aideen couldn't see his face, but she could picture her father's crooked grin. "You know we can hold off a hundred with this position."

"Yes," Bashir replied, "but there are another hundred men three floors up that will hear the battle, and then they will have the advantage of higher ground."

"You have only forty up there," Hazim corrected, "and they are outside. They won't hear a thing."

"Townsend might," Bashir countered. "A squad could take you from above and I'm sure he has at least that many with him."

Imar was silent. He turned and looked at his daughter. She could see he was considering a surrender of the octagon key. His eyes then went to the healer and his face softened. Aideen could see her reading his mood.

"Imar, you can't," Dalla whispered as loud as she dared. "No matter what, you can't give up the key."

"Think of the ladies," Bashir continued with oozing confidence.

Aideen saw the muscles around her father's eyes tighten before he turned back to face his foe. She felt the warmth of anger kindle in him, but it was building in all her friends as well. With her second sight, she even saw a tinge of aural red in all but her mother. The girl didn't think Bashir noticed his error, however, because his next line of reasoning did more to pick a fight than to stop one.

"You know what will happen to the women if we fight," Bashir said smoothly. "I can't guarantee the child's safety either."

Aideen gasped, and she heard Dalla gasp beside her. She had opened her awareness, thus exposing herself to the empathic waves around her, which now hit her with the force of a towering ocean wave. Dalla placed her hand on the girl's shoulder, but Aideen wasn't sure who she meant to steady. Her second sight saw the red aural flash of anger burst from her friends' emotions.

Hager stepped down two steps and said something vulgar. Aideen blushed. She was not entirely ignorant of such things. She had once overheard Ninole tell the housekeeper that a maneuver like that was actually possible for some men.

Bashir's face flushed. "Mica, Rashid, now," he barked.

A crossbowman at each end of the enemy formation stepped out and fired. Aideen felt Ivan flick a kinetic force in front of her father and Hager at almost the same instant. The two men flinched too slowly to avoid the projectiles, but the bolts glanced off an invisible shield an arm's length in front of them and stuck in the ceiling. Bashir roared as he and his troops charged. Imar blocked an overhand strike and followed with quick back and forth side slashes, effectively opening the leader's middle. The stone steps were made slippery by Bashir's blood and entrails, and his corpse was the first in the building barricade of bodies.

No one had shields, so the forceful pushing and close in fighting so common to the shield wall was replaced with the open combat of one-on-one swordfights, only the paired fighters worked in effective unison against single targets when possible. A riposte from Hazim allowed Hana to thrust at his foe. Before she recovered Hazim took off a slashing arm meant for her.

Aideen's friends held their ground. She guessed that had it not been for the confines of the stairs things may not have gone so well for her family and friends. Hager dispatched his adversary and took on another, and then Hazim felled his foe. He barely had time for a breath before he was battling the next.

The man and woman with the crossbows were

cranking back their cables for another shot when Aideen felt the power in Dalla's mind surge. The weapons burst into flames causing the crossbowmen to fall back with shrieks and singed brows. In seconds, the crossbows were clumps of ash.

From one of the open doorways, five more of Townsend's sell-swords entered the chamber and joined the fight. Two more bodies lay at Imar's feet and Aideen's friends either disabled or killed each of their own adversaries, but she could see that they had all taken cuts and they were tiring. Another squad came in, and then another after that. The chamber was crowded with enemies and more kept arriving. The enemy front line was now striking only a few blows and then stepping back as the second rank moved to the front. This trading off maneuver allowed a constant flow of rested fighters and caused them to have fewer casualties. They would soon overpower Aideen's fatigued friends.

"Back the line," Imar called, accentuating each word with a slash, parry, and riposte.

Aideen was impressed with the way her father and Hager fought in concert side by side as they backed up the stairs. It was almost as if they knew what the other would do, which allowed them to fight within the circle of each other's sword reach without fear of striking the other. Even though the tactical withdrawal was a defensive maneuver Imar and Hager were disabling the majority of their attackers.

Jamal and Maha had the bond of being mates, so they had a rhythm in their style as well. Aideen thought they were married, but she wasn't sure. Regardless, their moves were so smooth and efficient that the girl was reminded of Medimian dancers, but with carnage to their enemies.

Hazim and Hana were still getting to know one another, yet they each had exquisite skill and fluidity which enhanced their professionalism in working together. In the heat of mortal combat, Aideen made a mental note to play matchmaker with the two. They looked good together and would make a great couple, even if Hazim was probably fifteen years Hana's senior. She shuddered and chastised herself for such thoughts at a time like this.

Hawkins, unarmored and unpaired, stayed behind the line lashing with his cutlass those few times an enemy slipped through, but for the most part, he stayed near the wizard, who seemed preoccupied with gathering his will. As skilled as they all were, her father and friends were slowing. Aideen knew they would not last long.

Ivan's muttering grew louder and he began to sway. He seemed unaware that the battling line was backing up and nearly upon him. Aideen wanted to go tug on his arm, but Dalla pulled her up the stairs with her mother.

Just as Hager nearly backed into Ivan, Dalla yelled, "Imar, Hager, open the line."

As one, both men made a two-stroke move and stepped back to each side of the wizard. Ivan thrust his arms forward, fingers splayed, and the front three ranks of sell-swords flew backwards into their fellows as if an invisible log had slammed into them. None of the sell-swords kept their feet, and many appeared to be unconscious while others groaned with sluggish movements. The shock of the sight stunned her friends, but their inaction lasted only a second.

"Go," Imar said between his gasps for air. He turned and started up the steps. "Go," he repeated, "before they rouse."

The fighters were too winded to run, but they climbed at a steady pace, puffing with the effort. Ivan moved slowly as if each step caused him pain. Dalla went to him and took an arm. Aideen sheathed her sword and ran lightly up the stairs. Hawkins was in the lead, but she easily overtook and passed him. She was dimly aware of her mother and Dalla calling to her to slow down, to wait. She rounded a landing and kept on running up to the next floor. It was dark, but she found that she could see well enough, so she continued on.

Hawkins' footsteps sped up behind her. Aideen assumed he would catch up with her. "Wait," he gasped.

Aideen stopped at the next level. She wasn't even breathing hard. "I think we're almost to the top. Light is coming down the stairwell, but it's faint." She rekindled the lantern and adjusted it slightly past the low blue setting, but not quite to the medium orange. The greenish light chased back the shadows of what was once a wide hall so filled with rubble the girl doubted anyone could approach from either direction undetected, but she scanned for danger anyway.

The tell-tale knot in her belly grew, which reminded her of Khaled. Her sensory sweep located her friends and family, the incapacitated sell-swords below, and, at least, sixty people above on the surface, but she could not locate the assassin. She assumed he was shielding.

Hawkins slowed as he caught up. He stopped and leaned on his knees, breathing heavily. "Don't," he gasped between breaths, "get separated...huh...from us...huh...like that." He took a few more heavy breaths, and said, "Townsend is up there, and he has about forty soldiers. You can't let him take you again."

"Oh, all right," Aideen replied dramatically. She looked at him critically. "You're all red, and you're sweating a lot. You need to drink some water." She pulled her canteen bag from her belt and held it out to him. "Here, drink."

Hawkins took the offering, straightened, and drank half the volume. "Thanks," he said, handing back the skin.

The others caught up to Hawkins and Aideen. Dalla was helping Ivan by supporting him with his left arm over her shoulders. He looked pale, and his eyes seemed unfocused.

"What's the matter with him?" Aideen asked.

"He overtaxed himself," replied the healer. "Throwing eighteen men like that used as much telekinetic energy as if he had done it the normal way, only he used his mind and did it all at once. He's exhausted. I'm surprised he can walk." Dalla set Ivan down and leaned him against the wall. "He'll be okay, he just needs rest."

"We all need to rest," Imar said, leaning on the pommel of his claymore.

"I do not think we will have much time before they regroup and follow us," said Hazim, articulately.

"You're right," agreed Hager. "They'll come, but they'll come cautiously. Most of them are no match for us." He grinned at Hazim. "You're all very skilled. I'm glad you joined us." Hager turned to Imar. "The gods smiled on us today, old friend."

Imar nodded, "We're lucky to have them."

"There is only one god and he is nameless," Maha

said automatically.

Hager looked at her suspiciously and was about to respond, but Aideen cut him off. "Followers of the nameless god are no different than anyone else, Hager," she said. "Most worshipers I've met in these parts aren't like the mushroom eating lunatics we know back in Border City."

Imar looked at her curiously. "It sounds like you have learned a few things."

"Lessons will have to wait," Jamal said with his head cocked for better hearing. "Listen."

They all took a breath and held it to listen. Aideen noticed that everyone seemed somewhat restored. All but Ivan; he was still lethargic. Booted feet on stone echoed up the stairwell. It was faint and revealed a cautious, measured pace.

Dalla went to Ivan and said, "Come, Father, we have to go."

Hazim aided her in helping the wizard to his feet. "Let me take him."

"No," Dalla declined. "Your sword may be needed again I fear, but thank you."

Imar started up the steps, stopped, turned, and said. "I'm on point. Hager, take slack, but keep it close."

Aideen remembered her father teaching her about the slack position supporting the leading point man in looking for traps and enemies. He had told her that the enemy will often engage the first contact when ambushed. Hager moved to what would be a little rear of his friend's right once they started up the steps. Imar faced the seaman and his daughter. "Hawkins and Aideen, behind us, but keep back about three meters and close to the center."

Aideen swelled with pride at being given a combat position, but she had a sneaky hunch that her father was patronizing her since the immediate threat was coming from the rear, or so she thought. She drew her light katana and tried not to grin.

"Hazim and Hana on rear guard," Imar continued. He turned to Jamal and Maha. "I need you two on floating flank near Dalla, Ivan, and Anisha. Be ready for either front or rear contact."

They started up the stairs.

CHAPTER 34

The light grew brighter as they ascended the stairs. Aideen turned off the heat lamp and set it down by the handrail. She mimicked Hager's positioning to her father by placing herself two steps below Hawkins and another two meters to the seaman's right. As Imar and Hager cleared the top of the stairs, she heard Vidar's greeting. A moment later she rose to the dome's floor and saw the relief on the tall man's face. His sword was out and Aksel and Egil flanked him as if they were guarding the stairway. Each of the young men flashed a quick smile at her and then resumed their serious vigil with swords in hands. Two uniformed Kalusians stood with them.

"I'm glad you're well, Aideen," Vidar greeted her. He looked questioningly at the new additions as the party entered the area atop the stairs. Aideen noticed that everyone stayed in battle ready positions. When Hana and Hazim reached the top they turned and faced down the stairway, on guard.

"They're with us," Imar explained. "Introductions will have to wait. They helped Aideen escape. What happened here?"

"We heard battle sounds," Vidar replied. "Townsend tried to send a few of his sell-swords to 'investigate.' We didn't let them. I told him we would wait. He didn't seem too concerned, but he did look a bit surprised when you arrived."

Aideen looked to where Townsend stood. Two of his soldiers were binding arm wounds on another two men. His lordship was pacing and looking their way.

"I thought he would attack," said the Kalusian officer. "In fact, he threatened it. I told him he'd be the first to die if he did. He backed off, but he's confident having twice our numbers."

"Thanks, Rutger," Imar said to the officer, "but we encountered another forty or so downstairs. We thinned their numbers a bit, but…" Imar looked at Townsend and then back to Vidar and said, "About thirty able sell-swords are going to be coming up those stairs in another minute. I'd rather not be caught between two forces."

Imar ordered his group to a damaged doorway guarded by two men in Kalusian army uniforms. Aideen could see several horses tethered outside beyond the broken portal. The group moved in a patrol formation and then spread out in a line defending their exit. Dalla sat the exhausted wizard down on a square block and gave him some water. He drank halfheartedly, but he was still listless.

"We should just leave him and go," Anisha said waspishly. "His mind is gone." She paced agitatedly. "We have the key, don't we? Let's just go."

Hawkins looked at the girl's mother with a face that had sipped sour milk. He refrained from speaking to her, instead saying to Aideen, "Stay here and watch over your mother, Dalla, and Ivan." The derogatory inflection on 'mother,' was not lost on the girl. Hawkins joined the line on the end. He looked around, and with knit brows asked, "Where's Aris?" No one answered him. Aideen looked around for the boy and thought of searching with a sensory sweep, but there were too many distractions as each side formed into defensive positions.

"Not so fast, my Lord Imar," Townsend called out from across the dome. "We still have the business of the octagon key to settle."

The sound of many booted feet echoed in the dome.

Aideen's father looked at her for a moment with a concerned expression on his face. He then looked at Dalla with as much concern, but when he looked at Anisha, his visage lost its compassion and if anything seemed exasperated. Imar's gaze may have lasted all of a second. He turned back and faced Townsend, but instead of addressing his lordship, Imar spoke softly to his friends. As he spoke, wary sell-swords came up the stairs and moved to a formation behind Lord Townsend. Some assisted wounded comrades. One of the sell-sword leaders directed half the new arrivals outside to join the phalanx.

"We should try to flee," said Imar.

"I couldn't agree more," agreed Hager.

"They'll try to swarm us," Vidar countered.

"If I attack his phalanx with my horsemen,"

offered Rutger, "it may give you enough time to get away."

"You would do that?" asked Imar. "What about the octagon key?"

Rutger grinned. "I'll break off the attack once you get your daughter and your..." he paused a moment glancing at Dalla and Anisha. "Just get your family out of here. Once I get my men clear, I will come for your key."

Townsend called out to Imar again. "What's it to be, my Lord? Do we fight or will you give me the key in trade for your safety?"

Imar ignored his lordship again. He turned to Rutger, and they clasped forearms. Aideen saw her father nod slightly, and then the Kalusian officer exited the dome, taking his soldiers with him. Imar then spoke low, "Close the line, but do it slowly. Be ready to run for the horses when Rutger attacks. We'll go south, but stay together."

Aideen counted Townsend's line. He had roughly fifteen men and a few women warriors in a line that sliced across the far third of the dome. Some of them had shields. What she could see of the enemy phalanx outside was wrapped in shields. She looked to the right, to the passage between the pillars, which led to the stairs they had just come up. It was no good going that way, she realized. Townsend's soldiers would hunt them down until they were cornered and overwhelm them with numbers as they were about to do here. Her father was right; they had to make a break for it.

Acute pain flared in Aideen's belly, nearly doubling her over. Recovering and pushing it back, she scanned the dome for the assassin. He was here, but she saw no sign of him.

"The boy, the boy," Ivan muttered. He grinned, but he still seemed oblivious to his surroundings. "He drives me to drink, but damn, the little smartass is a good hunter." The wizard looked at his daughter with owl's eyes and then spoke as if enjoying pleasant conversation over lunch, "Oh, there you are, my dear. Would you be so kind as to fetch me some wine?"

"Come, Father," Dalla replied. "We have to go." She tugged on the wizard's arm to help him rise.

"Oh, no," replied the confused wizard. "Not without the boy."

"Father, he's gone. He already left."

Dazed and confused, Ivan asked, "Left?" He began shuffling towards the broken doorway and stopped. His eyes began to focus and his voice grew stronger and more confident. "I'm staying for the show."

Dalla was getting impatient with Ivan, and Anisha's muttered snide remarks were adding to the healer's frustration. Her friends were closing the gaps in their line, and Townsend ordered his sell-swords forward. Rutger's shouted order to attack came from outside. That was when Aideen saw the familiar red and black aural colors in the center of the dome's floor.

The yells of battle outside had barely begun when Aideen's father shouted, "Now!"

"Wait!" Aideen shrieked. She ran to her father's side and pointed. "Look, it's Khaled."

All eyes turned to where the girl pointed. Lord Townsend had just ordered his troops forward but stopped them as the black-robed assassin materialized in the center of the dome. He glanced once through one of the arched doorways at his engaged sell-swords and then back to his assassin. "I thought you had left us, Khaled. I'm pleased you have rejoined us. This time, kill only Lord Imar. Your rates for murder are breaking my bank. My men will handle the others." Townsend then addressed Imar. "It is not too late, my Lord. You can still hand over the key for safe passage."

Aideen was barely aware of the battle outside. Her peripheral vision saw horsemen using attack and retreat tactics, but her focus was on the one-eyed assassin. His good eye burned black hatred at her father. "No," he hissed. "The weapons master is mine. No charge."

Townsend smiled. "Well then, your generosity is overwhelming. Just bring me the key when you are done."

Aideen felt the wave of her father's anger roll out of him. Her right hand gripped the wooden hilt of her katana and her left hand rested on her father's sword hand. It burned with spiritual heat even though his skin was cool to the touch. She could sense the berserker's rage building in him as he worked to contain it with clear thinking, allowing the adrenaline to give him speed and strength.

Softly, but insistently, Imar said, "Go back and protect Dalla and your mother, and Ivan too. He is coming around, but he is still vulnerable and not quite with us if you know what I mean."

"Father, I have seen him fight. He is very, very good." She didn't want to dull her father's confidence by saying Khaled was faster or more skilled. She had always thought her father was the best swordsman in the world until she saw the assassin slay the Murdoch mercenaries as easily as if he had been scything wheat.

"I know," Imar replied. "I fought him before, but

I still have a few tricks." He paused. "If I fall, stay with Dalla if you can." He bent down and kissed her on the forehead. "I love you."

"I love you too, Dad."

"One more thing," Imar added. "Tell Dalla I love her with all my heart, but try to do it when your mother isn't around." Imar straightened and strode to the center of the dome.

Khaled drew his two scimitars. His lip curled as he spoke. "You let your daughter dress like a man and you taught her to wield weapons not meant for women." He spat to the side. "It is a sin against the nameless god. I will kill her when I finish with you."

Aideen saw her father's jaw tighten as he fought for control. She also heard women soldiers on both sides mutter angrily. Both Hana and Maha stepped forward, but Hazim stopped Hana, and Jamal stayed Maha's advance if not her tongue.

Loudly and indignantly, Maha called, "The masters of Kashan Castle lied to you, assassin. The nameless one sees us as equal, different only to share life together as men and women should. It is you who has sinned against the nameless one."

Mutterings of agreement echoed from both sides of the dome.

"Enough talk," Khaled snapped.

Imar held his claymore low and loosely in his right hand. He drew his short sword with his left. Aideen expected the usual one to three stroke attack and defend maneuvers common to one-on-one combat, which allowed opponents to test their adversary's mettle, probe their strengths, and find their weaknesses, so she was totally taken off guard when her father and Khaled went at each other with blinding speed in a cacophony of ringing steel, their blurring blades whirring and whistling with constant motion, seeking each other's defenses in their quest for flesh.

They circled each other, slashing and stabbing followed by parry and riposte without break or pause. The two warring sides of the audience held their breaths with lowered blades as they gradually formed a circle around the two men. Aideen, absorbed in the fight, was barely aware of the ceasing of hostilities outside. She tore her gaze from her father and Khaled for only an instant, but it was enough to tell her the combatants outside had stopped fighting to crowd the dome's portals to watch the sword fight between weapons master and assassin.

Some of the horsemen had dismounted, but the majority remained in their saddles to watch the fight. They were arranged along the southwest side of the dome while Townsend's sell-sword infantry filled the northwest openings to view the expert combat.

The eternal minute of nonstop swordplay finally ceased, almost as if on cue. The two men stepped back from each other, breathing heavily but never breaking eye contact. Aideen worried for her father. She thought he was getting old, even though his fortieth birthday was still two years away. Khaled was, at least, a dozen years younger.

As quickly as they had stopped, the fight was on again. Their movements were slower now and easier to follow since much of their initial steam was played out with neither scoring blood nor victory. Khaled came at Imar with double overhand slashes followed by horizontal slashes from each side. Aideen thought her father would block the overhands with both swords, but was glad he didn't as such a move would have been his last. The long claymore stopped both descending sabers and his faster and shorter short sword was ahead of the assassin's follow-up, stopping the side slashes with a quick left-right parry while bringing the claymore down.

Had the long blade connected, Khaled's arm would have left his body, but the assassin darted to his right, thrusting with one curved blade as the other arced up. Imar slid back to avoid thrust and slash, but the tip of his longsword cut Khaled's forearm, scoring first blood. Aideen knew her father probably felt the wind of the up slashing scimitar as it whooshed through the empty air he had just vacated, but the thrust should have pinked his belly. As they continued trading blows the girl saw the cut in her father's burnous without a scarlet stain, so she suspected he wore his boiled leather vest underneath.

The fight went on much longer than Aideen thought possible. Her father was tiring faster than the younger Khaled, but her father had already endured heavy fighting that day, and very recently as well. The two men broke apart again to catch their breath. The assassin looked confident. His breathing slowed sooner than Imar's.

Imar then sheathed his short sword. Aideen was curious, wondering if his fatigue was causing him to switch to a two-handed grip on the claymore. She saw the assassin smile, and it chilled her, but instead of grasping the long sword's hilt with his left hand, Imar reached under his robes and drew out a pistol. The assassin's smile vanished.

Aideen recognized the pistol. It was not the new type her grandmother's engineers had designed for the war effort in Sedar, but the more obsolete flintlock type they had taken from Jarl Bamsen's warehouse in Valekrie. She guessed that he must have kept one for himself.

Imar raised the pistol, cocked it, but before he could fire, Khaled darted to the side. Imar anticipated the move and followed the assassin's evasion by leading his target slightly when he squeezed the trigger. The hammer fell with a loud click. Aideen heard the sizzle of the primer as a small puff of smoke rose from the flash pan, but the gun did not discharge—it misfired.

Aideen's scowl mirrored her father's as he tossed the useless pistol aside and redrew his short sword. Khaled's toothy grin returned as the two combatants rejoined their battle. They were slowing as time wore on beyond the length of any common combat, but Khaled's younger reflexes met Imar's stronger strokes with determined, if waning, vigor.

Imar's slashes were becoming clumsy and he was now almost entirely on the defensive. He made a thrusting high slash with the claymore, but the assassin bent to his left, easily avoiding the sluggish move, and then returned a double slash from Imar's right. Then Aideen realized her father's fatigue had been a feint. Khaled's overconfidence blinded him to the older man's ruse, so he didn't see the short sword's point coming at his leading arm. The assassin's double side slash ran his right forearm onto Imar's blade. The point caught under the bone and came out the other side. Imar leaped back with a renewed agility and yanked out the sword with an added rip. The assassin's loss of grip on the leading sword fouled the following blade and both scimitars fell to the floor as Khaled screamed in pain.

He grabbed his arm and squeezed, trying in vain to slow the arterial bleed, but the wound was too big and bright red blood soaked into the dusty floor. Imar sheathed his short sword for the second time and took a two-handed grip on his claymore. Aideen could tell by the way her father wound up for the swing that he meant to remove the assassin's head. Khaled was bent forward gripping his arm and moaning, seemingly oblivious to his impending doom, but that too was a feint. The assassin let go of his arm and executed a forwards roll ending with a kick to Imar's stomach.

The wind rushed from Imar's lungs as he landed on his back. The claymore broke free from his grasp, sliding two meters beyond his reach. Aideen started to run towards the assassin, her katana held high, but her feet nearly flew out from under her when Hana grabbed her by the collar and yanked her back.

"Oh, no you don't," Hana hissed at the girl. "The snake is wounded but it still has venom."

Ivan started shouting incoherently, "Like shooting ducks in a pond."

The girl wondered if the old man would ever recover. She pushed the thought aside. She had to help her father, but Hana's grip was too strong. Her father got to his feet at the same time as Khaled. The assassin drew a baton from over his shoulder and attacked Imar before his short sword cleared the sheath. The blow took Imar on the side of the head and he crumpled like a sack of rocks.

Aideen struggled, but now Hazim held her too. Khaled discarded his baton and tore off his shemagh headscarf, binding his arm with it as he walked to his dropped scimitars. He staggered as if dizzy from blood loss. Aideen detected some movement to her right, but ignored it. Her father was out cold and in extreme danger. Khaled picked up one of his swords and went to the unconscious Imar.

"Noooooo!" Aideen screamed, and Dalla echoed her from behind.

The healer had sworn not to kill or harm anyone, but Aideen felt Dalla gather her pyrokinetic will. The girl knew her mentor was still too weak from the earlier battle. Khaled's right arm dripped blood through the makeshift bandage and his sword hung loosely in his left hand as he stood over Aideen's father. Hager let out a battle cry and ran forward, casting aside the honorable rules of single combat, but one of Townsend's crossbowmen put a bolt in his thigh, felling the stout Northman.

"Like a rat in a barrel," Ivan shouted insanely.

Aideen did not think that this was the time for bad-taste comments. She wished Dalla would quiet the delirious wizard. The girl watched in horror as Khaled raised his scimitar to slay her father. She had no bow to save him this time, but then the assassin flinched, and she saw a feathered shaft protruding from Khaled's armpit. The scimitar clattered to the floor. The assassin turned to his left to face the sniper and then fell to the floor. Aideen followed his gaze. She didn't see it at first until it moved.

On the upper portions of one of the pillars was the shape of a person so well camouflaged, Aideen couldn't see him unless he moved. The person slung his bow over a shoulder and then a knife appeared in his hand, contrasting with his dirt and plaster coloring. He cut a rope matched the bas relief on the pillar. The boy dropped a meter and a half to the floor and walked over to the wizard, who now seemed normal if exhausted.

"Well," said Lord Townsend, "so much for my assassin. I'll just have to get another." He turned to the captain of his sell-swords. "Order the attack, and bring me Imar Amirson or his body."

Aideen heard no more from his lordship because his sell-swords attacked in a screaming charge.

Hana and Hazim let go of the girl and went with the rest of Imar's friends to form a defensive circle around him. Hager got up and ran limping to meet the charge, the crossbow bolt still protruding from his thigh.

Aideen ran to her unconscious father. Nearby, a piece of old plaster fell from the ceiling. A moment later Dalla was beside the girl, checking Imar's pupils. The clamor of steel on steel startled the girl as the onslaught of Townsend's sell-swords met the blades of her friends. Outside the battle rejoined, but it was no longer an organized cavalry striking the well-ordered phalanx of professional soldiers. The restart of the attack while both sides were out of formation to watch the swordfight caused the battle to be rejoined in total chaos.

Without the shield wall, there was no phalanx. Horsemen waded through the enemy cutting left and right, felling foes with wild abandon, but without the teamwork of their brethren or the freedom to move quickly without obstacles, many of the mounted were pulled from the saddle and swallowed under a swarm of swords. Most of the cavalrymen who had dismounted had no time to mount again and found themselves trading blows toe to toe. Over the raucous noise of yelling men and screaming horses, Aideen heard Rutgers shouting commands in an attempt to organize his troops. Aideen turned her attention back to her father. Another piece of debris fell. She assumed all the activity was shaking things loose.

"Can you help him?" she pleaded to Dalla.

"I'll try," replied Dalla. She put one hand on Imar's head, took up his hand with the other and began to meld.

Aideen was disturbed by a movement to her left and realized her mother was beside her searching her father's pockets. "Mother," said the girl, both aghast and angry. "What are you doing?"

Anisha's hair was as wild as the gleam in her eyes. "It's got to be here," she said frantically. "He would have it on him."

Dalla's meld broke, and her gaze flared at Anisha, but she directed her words to Aideen. "There's too much noise. I can't meld with this much distraction," growled the healer. "We have to get him out of here."

Anisha looked up with dinner plate eyes. "Could he have hidden it?"

Aideen knew exactly what her insane mother was seeking. The way Anisha pilfered her unconscious father without a thought to whether he lived or died angered the girl beyond rage. Aideen's jaw clenched as she fought for control to speak. "Khaled's got the octagon key, Mother." Her snide tone was obvious, but her mother didn't seem to notice.

Anisha snapped her head in the direction of the fallen assassin, now beyond the nearest battle line. She leaned over to look between Hager and Vidar, fixated on the black robed form lying beyond their combatants.

"Don't you remember?" Aideen continued. "The assassin took it from father after he clubbed him down. You know," she urged, "before he picked up his sword and got shot."

Ivan and the camouflaged boy crowded in. "We haven't much time," said the wizard. Aideen thought he sounded weak, but he appeared to have all his faculties. "Aris," Ivan said to the boy, "take his legs." Ivan looped one of Imar's arms over a shoulder and Dalla did the same with the other arm. Together, they lifted Imar.

Anisha kept looking at the fallen assassin and back at Imar and her daughter. She grabbed Aideen's shoulders and shouted, "I don't remember." She shook the girl. "Is it true? Is it true?"

"Let's go," Ivan shouted.

"There," yelled Hawkins. He had a brief respite from fighting and pointed to the nearest opening in the dome. "That's our shortest way out. Be careful, there's a lot of rubble there."

"Tactical withdrawal," shouted Hager.

Hana and Hazim were nearest the exit, and they applied new fury to the fight, gaining ground in that direction. The circle began to move.

"Yes, Mother, I saw Khaled take the key," Aideen lied with an earnest face. They began shuffling with the moving fighters, stepping over broken stone and ancient plaster. "We're leaving, Mother." The girl shook her shoulders free with a jerk. "Are you coming with us?"

Anisha shifted her gaze back and forth, from assassin to daughter, then stopped and stared at the girl as if trying to read her mind. She screwed up her face as if judging her daughter's honesty, but her eyes were wild like a cornered animal caught before the hunter's bow. She looked towards the assassin again, now getting farther away. What sense and sanity keeping her within the safety of the circle of fighters drained from her face as they moved farther from her ultimate goal. With an animalistic scream, she bounded after Khaled's body. Aideen moved her blade out of the way as her mother tore past, bumping Egil's shoulder as she left the protective ring.

"No, don't!" shouted Dalla, reaching out for Anisha with her free hand, but the woman was too fast.

Anisha almost made it, ducking under a stroke meant for Egil, but then a slash from another sell-sword caught her side. She fell, then crawled, dragging herself to the assassin's corpse. Her side was soaked red and she left a bloody trail on the dirty floor.

Dalla let go her charge to aid the fallen woman, but Ivan, nearly collapsing with the added weight, stopped her with a word. "No," he shouted. "You'll save no one if you're dead. Now help me with Imar."

Dalla nodded, looking back with regret only once, and then assisted Ivan again. Once she settled Imar's arm over her shoulder she looked at Aideen with a sad and very disapproving face.

They were nearly outside and combating bodies blocked her view, but as the girl stepped over a stone block, the sight path to her mother opened for a moment. Anisha was lying next to the lifeless assassin, holding her wound with one scarlet stained hand while weakly frisking the dead Khaled with the other. Then her hand went still, and her head went limp on the assassin's chest. Anisha shivered once and moved no more.

Aideen, normally full of compassion for all her friends and family, felt as if the natural love for her mother had been dulled. The empathy she was so attuned to was locked in a box and stowed away in the basement of her heart. She forced herself into a coldness she had never experienced before. *This is not the time for tears*, she thought, but strangely, she felt no urge to cry. *Emotions must wait. It's time to fight and flee.*

Aideen walked with her sword in hand beside her supine father as he was carried unconsciously through the raging battle. She glanced once more at Dalla. The healer's face as shiny with tears as she and Ivan struggled with their burden. The mud plastered boy was holding his own as he walked face-forward with her father's feet held under each arm. His face flicked to nearly each battle clash but he never strayed from his job.

Hazim and Hana were now in the lead cutting their way through the chaos. Hawkins was to their left, and Maha and Jamal on their right. Behind her, walking backwards as they fought, were Hager and Vidar with Aksel and Egil flanking them. She just now became aware that all of her fighting friends were bleeding from multiple wounds. They would become weak from blood loss and they were already tired from their earlier combat and fighting egress.

Aideen knew better than to take on a full grown adversary, but as she now put her mind on the fight, she realized her skill, if not her strength, surpassed those her friends encountered, and her friends were all expert. That was probably why none had fallen—yet.

Aideen began stabbing here and slashing there. Soon she was moving around the inside of the moving ring adding her blade where it seemed most needed without staying long enough to become a target. Her light katana flashed bright silver in the hot desert sun with the first strike, then crimson as she danced on shuffling feet.

"Thanks," said Aksel.

"Nice slash," commented Maha.

When the girl parried a low thrust meant for Vidar, Hager advised her to avoid blocking to save her edge unless she could do it with the spine of the blade. They began moving faster, working their way to the south side of the dome towards the horses when suddenly a huge shadow shaded the battle. Aideen looked up to see a ship hanging by cables from a big oblong, tube-like bag.

It took the girl a couple seconds to realize it was her grandmother's new airship. She had seen it before. With no time to question what her grandmother was doing there, Aideen yelled, "Make for the ship. That's my grandma's airship."

Aideen saw sailors in the prow throwing apple sized, black balls into the crowd north of her position. The following explosions explained what they were. A few sell-swords flew through the air with the blast. Crewmen with rifles began picking off enemies near them. The confusion caused by this new threat to Townsend's sell-swords relieved nearly all the pressure off Aideen and her friends. Townsend's soldiers sought to flee the rifle fire, regroup, and seek cover inside the dome. His lordship's voice could be heard between musket fire, now that the battle sounds had slowed.

"Stop them!" shouted Townsend. "Don't let them take that man away."

No new charge came. A dozen bodies littered the ground outside the dome, and another twenty lay wounded and groaning. Rutger rallied his remaining nine horsemen and regrouped fifty meters to the south, where they stopped and watched the airship. Aideen wondered if he would still try to get her father's octagon key. The ship hovered three meters above the ground and rope ladders were cast from the amidships rail.

"Come on," a woman's voice called from the waist.

"Grandma," Aideen shouted with delight when she recognized the woman's voice and saw her signaling. "Grandpa," she added when she saw the man next to her grandmother leaning heavily on the rail.

Now unhindered, they went quickly to the ship. Upon seeing Imar unconscious and carried, Beros lowered the ship to the ground. The gangway was set out for easier loading. Aksel and Egil sheathed their swords and relieved Ivan and Dalla to carry Imar up the ramp. Two crewmen came down and relieved Aris. When they started up the gangway with Aideen's father Lord Townsend stepped outside looking frantic.

Townsend yelled at his troops, who were watching from the safety of the dome. "Triple pay and a thousand gold crowns for the octagon key."

There was some arguing from inside for a few seconds, but before Imar was brought to the top of the ramp nine screaming sell-swords charged out in a wedge formation with shields held high. At least, twenty rifles boomed from the ship. Aideen could not help but flinch at the noise, but she did not take her eyes from the charge as holes appeared in the shields and the sell-swords fell to the dirt. A few more had started to follow, but turned and ran back inside when they saw their comrades fall.

Akala gave Aideen a rib cracking hug. "Where's your mother? Dorfin sent a bird message that she was coming here." Akala's face had a thousand more questions on it when she saw Aideen's expression vanish.

"She's inside," answered the girl coldly. "I think she's dead."

Akala paled. "What happened?"

Aideen paused, trying to think of a brief way to answer while wondering just what to say. She didn't want to tell her grandmother that she had lied to her mother which led to her death. Akala's face went through a variety of curious expressions, the last being impatience, when Aideen said, "I, ah…"

Her words were interrupted by a loud crash, followed by another and then a few more. Dust spilled out the broken doorways and ancient windows. A few of Townsend's people ran outside just as a large section of the dome's roof began forming wide cracks across the golden convex surface. The airship began to rise.

"Hang on," Beros called out from the pilot station. "I'm taking us up."

The bottom of the gangway dragged to vertical as the ship rose. Two crewmen went to the rail and fastened a boom line to the hanging ramp while a third worked a windlass to hoist the gangway aboard. Beros arrested the ascent level with the dome's pinnacle. The ship listed heavily with so many people leaning on the starboard rail. Aideen felt a vibration under her feet and heard whooshing air carried to the outrigger. The ship soon righted to a level hovering position as the triangular piece of the dome broke loose, collapsing within.

Old studs and pieces of steel, mixed with plaster and bits of broken granite, flew out at ground level in all directions, followed by a wave of dust. Debris shot under the *Elbienus Raptor* where the ship had just been sitting. The noise was tremendous, but when the crescendo of the crash had passed, a cracking and creaking followed.

Aideen gripped the rail with one hand while holding her grandmother's waist with the other, comforted by the older woman's one-armed embrace across her shoulders. They watched as another piece of the dome crept down, and then with a screeching sound of tearing steel and grinding rock, the rest of the roof crashed within. Dust billowed up and around the airship and then slowly settled back to earth leaving a powdered grey coating behind.

"Wow," said a voice to Aideen's right. "That was awesome." It was the camouflaged boy who had shot Khaled, the one Ivan called Aris. Now that he wasn't blending in with granite and old plaster, he looked like a kid that had rolled in grey mud and let it dry. Some of his makeshift makeup was smeared as if he had wiped his dirty sweaty brow with a dirtier arm. The boy winked at her, causing a few flecks of dried mud to fall from his eyelid, and then strode to the bow.

Beros climbed a little higher to hover above the dust. A light wind from the west pushed them over the collapsed building. The captain swung the bow to point west and held their position. He righted the balance as some crewmen and passengers went to the port rail.

When the dust settled, the pinnacled golden dome lay like a broken golden egg upon a pile of granite. Aideen pulled free from her grandmother and went to the mainmast where her father lay, still unconscious. Dalla knelt beside him, eyes closed, hands on brow and wrist.

Aideen knelt across from the healer and took up her father's hand. She closed her eyes and prayed. She wasn't religious, nor did she come from a pious family, so she wasn't sure who she should pray to. Just to be sure, she went down a list calling to all the gods she remembered hearing about, asking them to spare her father. She even sent a prayer to the nameless god, but she didn't know what to call that one or what gender to use, so she settled on 'Nameless' for a moniker and called it good. She then asked for forgiveness, feeling the first pangs of guilt for the lie which had led to her mother's death.

CHAPTER 35

Imar's life flashed before him. The indistinguishable shadow shapes that had evaded his grasp for so long now took substance as the fog of forgotten memories lifted away and played like a thousand plays performing in simultaneous cue. He reveled with relief remembering—just remembering—the pure and simple fact that he could once again recall his own life. All those experiences that made him who he was were there again like a long lost and forgotten friend returned home, only the missing friend was himself. All those months of emptiness having to count on secondhand accounts, which only gave vague images like when one gets directions to a place they've never been, only he knew he'd been there. It was like looking in a mirror in the darkness and seeing only darkness until, after a long time, a light suddenly comes on.

As he floated below the surface of waking between dreaming and roused reality, Imar visited a thousand clear memories, once worn like an old hat now returned as if never gone, but kindling enlightenment nevertheless.

He remembered looking up at his mother at an age when he spent more time on hands and knees than on wobbly legs. She was stacking small pieces of wood in the cook stove. When the stove was sufficiently stuffed she concentrated on the pile, and then Imar felt rather than heard a whoosh as the wood whisked into full flame, bypassing the flint and kindle stage completely. He watched this phenomenon through a child's eyes and found it both normal and an interesting curiosity. He became aware.

Another time Imar was playing with wooden alphabet blocks, stacking them into what adults would call a pile, but what a child could easily identify as a castle. Ever so gently, he reached over to set the last block when his knee bumped the edge, causing the castle to crumble into a heap. He drew his hand in anger but stopped, remembering another way. His face flushed warm and then cooled as he gathered heat from the air and furnishings around him, focusing the energy on the offending toys the way a magnifying glass narrows a sunbeam to start a fire. The little wooden block burst into flames.

Pride swelled within him. He beamed at his mother but did not understand her frantic expression when she raced over to him. He felt a surge in his mind as she focused her will. The front door slammed open, and the flaming blocks flew like pitch fired pots outside, beyond the porch, as if launched from miniature catapults. She had touched neither blocks nor door, but Imar felt the shift of energy in his awareness. Now he knew both pyrokinesis and telekinesis.

Sitting down next to him his mother took his

hands in hers, closed her eyes, slowed her breathing, and then she spoke to him, but not aloud. *My dear Imar*, her thought-words came to him. Her voice was in his mind. *You have my talent, and I'm so very proud of you.* He swelled with pleasure, and felt warmth and adoration wash over him, but her expression exuded concern.

Imar had yet to learn more than a few words, opting for signs and expressions to communicate his desires, but now he was learning mind-speech. It was so much easier. He smiled at her, and thought-said, *Did you see, Mom? Did you see?*

Yes, she replied gravely, and he felt the weight of her next words before she spoke them in his mind. *These talents*, she paused, then began again more bluntly. *You are much too young to use these abilities. That fire could have hurt us. I am going to block your new skills, for now. I will lift the block when you are older.*

He felt a pinch in his mind and he tried to protest, but his thoughts didn't project nor did his mother respond. He looked across the room to his leather ball, tried to roll it with his mind, but could not. When he could not gather heat energy he knew his new talents were gone.

These memories explained a lot to the present and dreaming Imar. Had he not lost his memory he would have known why his daughter was so adept at mind-speech and sensory perception. His mother was enhanced, like Dalla, Ivan, and Sumas.

CHAPTER 36

Imar was aware. He realized it the moment he woke. Aware, with no barrier holding back his talent, not anymore. In that instant before he opened his eyes he could see with his mind's eye all existence within his sphere of being. As the second-hand moves between two ticks of the clock he could feel the light knee breeches and sleeveless shirt he wore and sense the dry air waft over his face, arms, and bare feet. He felt the sway of the hammock he laid upon and saw his daughter sitting in a chair beside him with his dream's-eye vision. He saw them in a stateroom cabin, and as if from a bird's view, he could see the airship held aloft by a bag of gas as it circled the collapsed ruins of the dome. Even stranger, he was aware of how and why it defied gravity and he understood the physics of the flying ship's propulsion.

On the crew deck, he saw Hager upon a table, propped on elbows and pillows, with the bloody head of a broken crossbow bolt beside him as Dalla applied needle and thread to his wound. Hazim stood bare-chested beside them, with a sutured slash a hand's breadth long across one pectoral. Vidar, also shirtless, stood on the other side, a bloody bandage on his upper arm.

Imar located his other friends in different parts of the airship. Coulig and Jax were amidships looking over the port rail while Brin sat upon the deck, pale and moaning. Beros sat at what passed for a tiller on the quarterdeck and to the larboard were Travin and Akala scanning the ground below.

Imar saw all these things in less time than it took to draw half a small breath before he opened his eyes on Aideen. When his physical sight flooded his senses his second sight paled, but he knew it waited in the deep recesses of his mind.

Aideen met his gaze with her soft brown eyes. Her raven hair was tied back in a warrior's queue. She wore a maroon top with rolled up sleeves, and her burnous and headscarf were draped over the back of her chair.

"You're awake," she said, her relief evident.

Imar struggled to sit up but a headache erupted within his skull. It felt as if someone had kicked him in the side of the head. He eased back down onto his pillow. Some of the pain evaporated as soon as his head held still upon the pillow, but the throbbing continued. He felt a little nauseated but smiled weakly. "You're safe," he said.

She nodded and then wrinkled her brows. "How do you feel?"

"I'm fine. I just have a headache," he replied with forced strength, trying to downplay the pain. He scanned his surroundings and confirmed that his brief touch with his second sight had not lied.

Aideen looked at him curiously and grinned. "We're on an airship," she blurted enthusiastically. "Grandma and Grandpa arrived and picked us up in their flying ship, the *Elbienus Raptor*." In an instant, her jubilation turned serious. "You almost died." She stepped closer and arrested the gentle sway of the hammock. "The assassin would have slain you if not for Aris' arrow. After that, everyone started fighting. If not for the arrival of the airship, I don't think we would have gotten away."

Imar was about to inquire into who Aris was but held his tongue when he felt his daughter's hands tighten on his own. He saw something in her eyes. Her face was still a child's but he could see that his little girl had aged beyond her eleven years.

A tear trickled down Aideen's face. She knuckled it away, but another came and another after that. "Aris killed Khaled." Her voice cracked and rose an octave, "and I killed Mother." She buried her face in her father's chest and sobbed.

Imar wrapped his arms around his daughter and held her while her sobs wracked against him. A dozen questions stood ready on the tip of his tongue, but he waited while she wailed her grief into his cotton shirt. He gently patted her back. "There, there," he soothed. "There, there."

Aideen's convulsions stilled and in time she straightened and wiped her reddened eyes with the corners of her collar. The moderate light lit the cabin, but it felt like needles in Imar's eyes nonetheless.

Noticing his squint, she asked, "Does the light hurt your eyes?"

"Yes," he replied, raising a shielding hand to his

brow.

She went to the stern windows, closed the drapes, then pulled a curtain over a small glass porthole, which was ajar and adjacent to her father's hammock. The air wafting through the small opening blew back the cloth slightly, causing flickers of light to dance across the dim interior. Imar immediately felt the ease on his burning brain cells.

"Oh, I nearly forgot," said the girl. "I'm supposed to check your pupils. Dalla taught me," she added.

Taking a heat lamp from a hook, lighting it, and closing the shutter to a narrow beam, she peered into each of her father's eyes while shining the bright yellow light into each eye one at a time. The pain lanced through his brain, but he had seen Dalla do this diagnostic procedure before, so he belayed his complaints.

"Good," she nodded professionally, extinguishing the lamp and returning it to the hook. "Your pupils are equal and reactive to light." She moved to a tray on a table, took up a small vial and handed it to her father. "You can have some pain medicine now."

Imar removed the stopper and tossed down the bitter fluid. His face soured. "Did we lose anyone in the battle?"

"No, but I think a number of Kalusian horsemen fell and most of Lord Townsend's sell-swords that weren't killed in battle probably died when the dome came crashing down." She paused, looking askance to the ceiling, one arm across her belly supporting the elbow of the other as she rested her chin in her hand. "Strange," she said, drawing the word out long and thoughtfully.

"What is it?"

413

"Well," she began, "Ivan, Dalla, and Aris carried you while everyone else formed a circle around you as we fought our way through the melee. Hawkins and I were also inside the circle, helping where we could, but everyone wearing armor was wounded."

"That's normal. Armor makes you braver, but it slows you down. I think that as guns become more common," remembering his own pistol misfiring, he added, "and more reliable, we'll see a decrease in body armor, at least until technology makes it bulletproof. How are the wounded?"

"No one was critical. Hager caught a crossbow bolt in the leg. The ship's surgeon wanted to cut off his leg, but Hager threatened to chop off his hands if he dared."

Imar chuckled. The medicine was taking the edge off his pain. "I could picture Hager doing that. How is he?"

"Grouchy as ever," replied the girl. "Dalla said she'll have him up and walking before the sun sets. I should be helping her, but she wanted me to stay here with you in case you woke up. She's been sewing up slashes all afternoon."

"How long have I been out?"

"A few hours," replied the girl. "Dalla did a mind-meld on you. She said you would be okay, and that you might have regained your memory."

"I did," Imar affirmed. Aideen's eyes widened. Imar held up a hand to ward off her inquiries. "You first," he said. "What happened? The last thing I remember was wounding the assassin. Tell me everything."

Aideen pulled up her chair, took a seat, and told her father all that had happened, from the fight with Khaled to his waking up within the last few minutes.

Imar listened to her story without interruption. She told him of Khaled's fall by the boy that came to Juana Pohala with Ivan and Hawkins. Aideen grew somber when she recounted her mother's part in searching him for the octagon key and her lie which caused Anisha to run into the chaos of the battle to find the artifact. She also told him the brief version of her grandmother's quest in finding and rescuing her grandfather.

"We're circling while an away team looks for survivors," Aideen said glumly. "Grandpa's injuries are too fresh for him to go ground-side and Grandma is afraid of finding mother…" she paused, "dead."

They sat in silence a few minutes. Imar felt sorrow for his daughter as well as for Travin and Akala. He even felt some grief for Anisha, but he could not help feeling relief at the news of her death. Part of him was almost ecstatic to be free of her, but he had never wanted her to die. The relieved part of him wanted to smile, but he felt guilty for thinking so and forced it back.

Aideen looked at him disapprovingly. Imar had forgotten his daughter's empathic sensitivity, and by her look assumed her skill had grown in their time apart. He was glad that his momentary elation at her mother's demise had redirected some of Aideen's self-condemnation to his own chastisement. However, he was also aware of his daughter's rapidly changing moods, so he did his best to cover his feelings as well as ease her pain.

Putting on a sad face, Imar assumed a consoling tone and said, "It's really not your fault." When she did not respond, he added, "Your mother was obsessed with power, you know that. When she didn't find the key on me she would have gone to the next likely person no matter what you said to her, and that was Khaled. No, your mother's greed killed her, not you."

Aideen looked up at him and he felt her grief ease, if only slightly. Then her face changed to curiosity, and a moment after that her brows knit. "Where is the octagon key?"

Imar raised one brow and smiled. "Guess."

She breathed in and bore into him with a penetrating gaze. He felt himself sinking into those soft brown pools as she probed his mind and studied his face. Seconds ticked by and when he was just about to tell her where it was, she exclaimed, "Your boot!"

He grinned. "Good job." He sat up gingerly, expecting a renewed attack of pain, but found his headache had dulled down to a tolerable ache. "Now, see if you can find it."

Aideen reached over and picked up his boots, then weighing one in each hand while looking off into space as if listening, she tossed the left boot aside with a thud. She reached inside the right boot to probe the interior and shook it, but there was no rattle. Then she stared at her father again, delving deep into his eyes. Imar felt almost feverish an instant before she broke the gaze. She began tugging and twisting at the heel of the boot. It wouldn't budge.

With a determined look on her face, she drew a small dagger from an ankle sheath and stuck the point into the top of the boot heel and pried. The piece came off slowly, the nails resisting till freed, and within was the grey octagon disc neatly fit inside the hollowed heel. She dropped the boot, upended the heel, and the octagon key plopped into her hand.

The girl's smile was in her eyes, if not on her lips. Imar thought it was a look of triumph, but then his daughter's face turned serious as she said, "This little disc sure has caused a lot of grief, hasn't it?" Imar could not have agreed more.

CHAPTER 37

Imar stepped out on deck led by Aideen's insistent hand. They strolled around the ship, his daughter chattering like a tour guide, fully aware that her experience with the airship exceeded his own by only a few hours, which he knew had been spent watching over him in a stateroom. His friends greeted him warmly, glad to learn his memory had returned. He nodded and waved at other familiar faces, acquaintances who now had a history beyond the few months of his amnesia. When they came to Beros at the pilot station he shook forearms with the captain in warrior fashion.

"It's good to see you, old friend," Imar greeted.

Beros eyed him carefully, and said, "You remember."

Unsure if it was a question, Imar nodded and replied, "Everything."

Imar looked over to where Akala and Travin stood at the quarterdeck's port rail. Travin wore a light, gauzy shirt but Imar could see through the loose weave that his entire torso was bandaged. His former employer was quite a bit thinner than he had remembered.

Akala dabbed at her eyes with her sleeve, quietly said something to her husband, and then they both turned around with gaunt faces and approached the pilot station.

"It has been a long time." Travin embraced him and added, "A long time indeed."

Imar returned the embrace, careful not to put pressure on the bandages. "It's good to see you again, sir." Turning to Akala, he added, "It's good to see you both." Releasing Travin, he hugged Akala and noticed her tears had returned. When he released her she wiped at her eyes again.

To Beros, Travin said, "Go ahead and call in the away teams, Captain. Short of excavating the whole wreckage, if they haven't found her by now…"

Akala leaned against Travin's shoulder and murmured, "The ruins are Anisha's tomb." She stifled a sob, then forced strength into her voice. "We were told that Lord Townsend and the assassin, Khaled, met their end there as well." Akala raised her tear streaked face, amazing Imar with her fortitude. She was in total control again. She turned to Beros and said, "It's time, Captain."

"Watkins," Beros called to the amidships man. "Prepare for landing, and signal Gavin to bring 'em in."

"Aye, aye, Cap'n," Watkins replied, knuckling his brow.

Imar was reminded of his days at sea when the

crewman sounded a whistle with a note sequence normally used for calling in longboats. He looked up to a topman standing on a yardarm just below the oblong balloon. The man waved a *Blue Peter*, which was a white square on a field of blue.

Travin cleared his throat. "Akala told me about your heirloom." He forced a smile. "Well, at least, the short version." He paused. "I've been out of touch for a while."

"Aideen told me," Imar replied. "I…"

Travin interrupted with an upraised hand. "We can talk about that later." He paused again, then made a sweeping gesture with his free hand, while the other held his wife's waist as much for support as for comfort. "This airship is really quite amazing, isn't it?" Without waiting for a reply he continued, "It's powered by the technology we extracted from that 'thing' that we found all those years ago. If it would have been finished sooner…"

"A lot of unpleasantness could have been avoided," Akala finished for her husband. "I would have helped you on your quest, but I had to find Travin."

"But we're all here together now," said a familiar voice.

Imar turned and saw Ivan coming up the starboard steps, followed by Hawkins, and a boy whom Aideen had pointed out earlier as Aris.

"I've called a meeting," Ivan announced. "As soon as the teams are onboard we'll get started."

Imar extracted himself from his daughter's grip and, ignoring everyone else, walked up to Aris.

The boy stopped, watching Imar's approach, unsure and a little defensive. He took an involuntary step back.

Imar instantly caught a wave of emotion off of Aris. Being unused to his newfound perceptions, it gave him a start for half an instant before he read and registered the visual clues which warned him of his own over exuberance. He only wanted to express his gratitude for saving his life and removing the threat to his daughter's life. Imar halted before the boy. "I…" He looked into the boy's pupils and extended his arm.

Aris was caught for a moment as he returned the stare, and then visibly relaxed and grasped Imar's forearm.

"Thank you," Imar breathed.

Aris' eyes scanned the many faces, suddenly aware that everyone was looking at him. "You're welcome," he said. His face flushed and then he began to fidget.

Imar heard his daughter bite off a muffled giggle.

"Okay," said Ivan. "Everyone hold on, Captain Beros is landing the ship."

Everyone took hold of a rail. The touchdown was so soft Imar was still holding on when crewman manned a boom and swung the gangway into place. The away teams boarded and Beros lifted off again as the gangway swung into its stowing bracket. The ship rose and leveled about a hundred meters off the ground. He set his controls then turned on his bench and said, "Where to now?"

The ship moved slowly to the northeast, drifting with a slight rotation, meandering at a rate that could be easily outpaced by a porcupine with a purpose.

Coulig, Jax, and Brin followed Gavin while Jon came up the larboard steps. Imar had seen them board with the away teams. Gavin went to the rails of the quarterdeck, folding down benches. "There," announced the mate. "We might as well be comfortable."

"I agree," said Ivan before taking a drink from his ever-present wineskin before sitting down.

"I wish I would have known those were benches," said Akala. "I would have used them long ago." She and Travin took seats next to Ivan in the center with their backs to the taffrail.

"I just learned of them myself," Gavin responded, looking slightly embarrassed.

Imar's back was to the stairs when he felt her presence. He didn't hear her approach or notice anyone look in her direction, but he knew she was there. He turned around. His breath caught as if seeing her for the first time, much like when they first met those many months before when he came to her feverish and near death. She wore simple knee-length sailor slops and a matching short sleeve pullover top. The bloody white apron had not spared her clothes from peripheral spatter. A white bandana covered her head and a leather lace bound the balance of her tawny tresses into a crude ponytail. Imar thought she'd never looked more beautiful.

Her gaze swallowed him into the blue sea of her irises and everyone but she and he disappeared. *I love you*, he thought.

Her smile was small, controlled, and it melted his heart. *I love you too.*

Imar flinched. He heard it in his mind as clearly as if she had spoken aloud. *I can hear you.*

I know. You hear me in your mind.

I hear you both, Aideen's thought added.

"Excuse us." Vidar's voice broke the mind-speech.

Imar's tunnel vision zoomed out to take in Vidar skipping up the steps with Hager behind him. Dalla moved aside to let them by, coming closer to Imar in the process. He felt high-speed butterflies spinning inside his chest, but maintained a serious attitude of decorum. In light of his late wife's demise, as well as being in the presence of family and close friends, anything less would have been in bad taste.

Hazim and Hana came next. They weren't holding hands but they walked close, stood close, and sat down together. Imar thought they might be closer than just battle buddies. Before he finished the thought, the married couple, Jamal and Maha arrived, taking the bench beside Hana and Hazim.

Aksel and Egil came next, going straight to Ivan. Aksel handed him a bulging wineskin, affecting a broad grin from the wizard.

"Thank you," said the wizard. He set the empty bota aside and after a sip from the new one, he addressed the company. "We have all come a long way." He looked around at the faces focused on him. His gaze lingered longer on Imar than on the others. He continued, "Thanks to Akala's tenacity and the crew of the *Elbienus Raptor*, Travin has been returned to us and thanks also to the technology of flight they were able to arrive in time for Aideen's rescue."

"I already escaped," Aideen piped in.

There were a few chuckles, then Maha said, "Yes, little one, we took you from the jaws of captivity into the fire of battle, but we survived that battle because of this airship and her brave crew." She stood and nodded to Beros, Akala, and Travin. "Thank you," she said with a gesture of fingertips to lips and forehead.

Ivan continued before further side-tracking began. "Imar's quest to Oldeisie had to be put on hold for his daughter's sake, but time is running out. Technology is moving fast. Sumas has shown the Kandians how to make rifles similar to those of the alliance. We should expect improvements. King Drayden's army will be camped outside the Octagon by spring." He paused.

Imar was surprised at the lack of comments. Everyone seemed to be quietly contemplating the wizard's words.

"You all are here for different reasons, but you know what is at stake," Ivan continued. "There is a naval war in the Western Sea, and it is extending to much of the Pacific. Pardon me," he corrected, "You know it as the Ocean of Paciphia. Seal Bay has been put to the torch and fighting is all over Sedar, northern Kalusia, and in the plains of Hamaud."

Muttering mumbled through the seated assembly. Imar looked over to Hazim who was listening to Hana, Maha, and Jamal's insistent whispers. Imar liked these new additions to his company, even if they were former captors of his daughter, but they were sell-swords and held no allegiance but to their current contract, which had been met and now stood open to negotiation. They had the freedom to go where they would. The fighting and profit would be good in Northern Hamaud, but he hoped they would stay on with his small company of fighters.

Ivan loudly cleared his throat. "Ahem." He began in the first instance of silence. "Imar's course is clear, he must go on to the Octagon, but the rest of us are free to choose. It's time for each of us to decide." With one more dramatic pause Ivan added, "I think, now that Aideen is safe, we all want to know the answer to Captain Beros' question; where to next?"

Imar sat quietly as discussions between small groups ensued. His eye caught Dalla's briefly and then roamed the assemblage.

After a minute, Vidar stood from where he had been speaking with Hager and said, "We're always with you, Captain. You know that." Hager nodded slowly as Vidar sat, his face grim. Aksel and Egil's heads bobbed in wide-eyed acceptance.

"We're with you as well, as is our ship and crew," said Travin. "At least for a little while," he added. "We need to go home and help the Alliance."

"Yes, for a while," agreed Akala. "There is much afoot in the world. Our businesses will need our tending. I'm sure our partner, Dorfin, is overwhelmed. We will fly you to the Octagon in Oldeisie. Travin and I are curious to see this old world structure, but we can't dally. However, the speed of flight will allow us to go home and return in a matter of only a couple weeks should our services be needed."

The desert folk whispered quietly to themselves until Hazim stilled them with a raised hand. He stood and stoically faced Imar. "The wars in the north are tempting. There is profit in war, but there is also death. We are not new to this, but we know nothing of this Octagon that you speak of. We too are curious. If you will have us, we would like to renew our contract with you to Oldeisie and to the completion of your goal."

"I was hoping you would say that," Imar answered. To Ivan and Beros, he said, "That answers your question. We're all going to Oldeisie.

About the Author

When Brian K. Kerley isn't writing he's flying airplanes in the Alaskan Bush, teaching kids or teaching flight or helping his wife with their small business. He lives in the frontier community of Tok, Alaska with his wife, grandson, and cat.